TAMARIND SKY

We gratefully acknowledge the support of the Canada Council for the Arts and the Ontario Arts Council for our publishing program. We also acknowledge the financial support of the Government of Canada.

Cover design: Val Fullard

Tamarind Sky is a work of fiction. All the characters portrayed in this book are fictitious and any resemblance to persons living or dead is purely coincidental.

Library and Archives Canada Cataloguing in Publication

Title: Tamarind sky : a novel / Thelma Wheatley.
Names: Wheatley, Thelma, author.
Series: Inanna poetry & fiction series.
Description: Series statement: Inanna poetry & fiction series
Identifiers: Canadiana (print) 20200203541 | Canadiana (ebook) 20200203614 | ISBN 9781771337335 (softcover) | ISBN 9781771337342 (epub) | ISBN 9781771337359 (Kindle) | ISBN 9781771337366 (pdf)
Classification: LCC PS8645.H41 T36 2020 | DDC C813/.6—dc23

Printed and bound in Canada

Inanna Publications and Education Inc.
210 Founders College, York University
4700 Keele Street, Toronto, Ontario, Canada M3J 1P3
Telephone: (416) 736-5356 Fax: (416) 736-5765
Email: inanna.publications@inanna.ca   Website: www.inanna.ca

TAMARIND SKY

THELMA WHEATLEY

a novel

inanna poetry & fiction series

INANNA PUBLICATIONS AND EDUCATION INC.
TORONTO, CANADA

For Angus
and
Thomas Orchard
Periya Dorai
Madeniya Tea Estate,
Kegalla, Ceylon

ALSO BY THELMA WHEATLEY

NON-FICTION:

"And Neither Have I Wings to Fly:" Labelled and Locked Up in Canada's Oldest Institution

My Sad Is All Gone: A Family's Triumph Over Violent Autism

*Our heart is the place where we have to look
for our deepest experiences.*
—Anagarika Govinda

PART ONE

TORONTO, 1967…

1.

THERE'S SOMETHING ABOUT FATHER-IN-LAW I'm not sure of. The faded old British Union Jack flutters again on the roof of the bungalow, the imperious red, white, and blue stripes tattered and worn, a remnant of the Empire. I'm sure he took it down when we went away. My new father-in-law peers through the kitchen window as we turn in to the driveway. "They're here, Mildred pet. They've come!" Exclamations of delight as Aidan and I step inside. We've been married one day.

"Welcome back, son, and ... er ... Selena." Father-in-law offers me a perfunctory peck on the cheek.

"*Aiyo!*" Mother-in-law hugs us warmly, her dark face glowing. "Married in Wales one day and next day here in Toronto. You must be suffering jet-lag."

I think, she's my mother-in-law now, we are bonded by family.

"Hail to the newlyweds," drawls Scottie, Aidan's younger brother. "Daddy raised the flag in your honour."

Scott's fiancée, Darleene, who is sitting next to him at the table, smiles hugely. "Congratulations! Wow! How did the wedding go yesterday?"

She's slim but solid, attractive with big, bright Canadian teeth and large grey eyes, like topazes. "It's our turn next," she gushes. She and Scottie are getting married next weekend at St. Raphael of All Angels Catholic Church, Mother and Father-in-law's parish in Willowdale. She and Scott were high-school sweethearts, and now they're attending York University together. They're awfully young to be getting married.

"Well, that's love," cries Felix. "Ah, youth!"

Scott has won a big scholarship—it's enough to put them through school and get them a cheap apartment in the married quarters of the college. He's in environmental studies and already guaranteed a good government job when he graduates. My in-laws, Jack and Mildred Gilmor, have done well in Canada.

"We've brought photos of Wales and a film of the wedding to show you," says Aidan with a cheerful smile. I feel a secret wave of gratitude towards him—of course he's keeping the truth of our wedding to himself, what a debacle it was.... But that was yesterday, already the past.

"Two weddings in the family in one month, spanning two countries and an ocean," marvels Felix. "It must be wedding season."

Felix is Father-in-law's first cousin, another Gilmor. He rises from his seat and shakes Aidan's hand in a pleasing, old-fashioned way. "Congratulations, old chap. Selena, you're as beautiful as ever, a veritable blushing bride—ah, that golden-blonde hair of yours, those sky-blue eyes!"

He's very tall, over six feet, and thin, with a long curved nose and slanting eyes. After two weeks in Wales, surrounded by white people in a small village on the outskirts of Cardiff, the brownness of my new Sinhalese relatives is a shock. Of course, I know I'll soon not notice, and it won't matter, which is the very thing Mother fears: that eventually I *won't even notice*. Felix, for instance, has very dark skin, bluish-black, that's different from the others. "Oh, that's his Tamil blood on his grandmother's side," Aidan had said casually when we first met. Tamil *blood*? What was that? I guessed, of course, but the words sounded so furtive. (What would Mother make of it?) I hadn't been sure then what race a Tamil exactly was. (Dravidian, one of the oldest in the world.) One did not ask, of course. There are some things one just does not touch upon.

Mother-in-law has laid out a feast in celebration. The table is loaded with bowls of rice, chicken curries, *brinjal, dhal* with spinach, and dried salt fish mixed with shredded Maldive fish that makes it piquant. Not to mention the *maloom*, chutneys, and pickles. There's a distinct foul odour that I try to ignore. "That's Bombay duck. I've cooked it especially for Jack, but I think you may like the taste too, Selena," says Mother-in-law. "I got it from Dalah's Indian Mart on Yonge Street."

"It all looks wonderful. Thank you so much."

"Hmph." Father-in-law heaves himself into a chair and opens a beer.

Mother-in-law puts down a pot of freshly brewed tea. "Ah, Uva tea from the Burundi district—I'd know that aroma anywhere," says Felix, sniffing. In Ceylon, Felix was something called a tea-taster, working for a leading proprietor, Carson and Cumberbatch; he sipped little cups of tea all day, delineating its grade and essence. The managers of the Colombo Tea Auction used his judgements to set their prices. "Very *pukkah*. My God, years ago now, another lifetime...."

He'd been a bit of a ladies' man, too, according to Aidan. He had had several broken engagements to beautiful Eurasian and Tamil girls, but never married any of them. Aidan had been too young to understand the implications at the time. (And what might such a liaison have meant in old colonial Ceylon, one wonders?) I look at Felix with interest. He's part of Father-in-law's elusive life as a tea planter, a life that has been subtly closed to me. For I'm coming to understand that I would likely not have married Aidan Gilmor, nor would Darleene be engaged to Scott, if we, two *memsahibs*, had been in Ceylon at such a time in its colonial history.

"Fiona said to go ahead and start eating without her—she's running late at the office," says Mother-in-law. Fiona is Aidan's older sister.

Darleene is already munching on tasty mini-samosas that Mother-in-law has made herself. "You must teach me how to make these," she cries.

"It is very easy."

Summer breezes flow through the open window, bearing intoxicating sweetness from the flowers on the trellis. A blue jay screeches from the top of the spruce. This part of Willowdale, though modest, is entrenched in trees and cottage gardens.

The kitchen is small and cramped, hot but for an old insert fan over the stove. A stove, a fridge, and a large table take up all the space. The bungalow is also small. It is familiar to me by now—just three small bedrooms, an old-fashioned washroom with a pull chain, a living-room, and a kitchen. Yet once, in the forties, a Canadian family raised four children in this place. The house has a white frame with a pretty green roof and trim, and a side porch half collapsing under the weight of honeysuckle and clematis vines. The beautiful garden is its saving grace. It consists of an enormous double lot filled with apple trees, flowering currant bushes, and Father-in-law's vegetable patch and flowerbeds. A towering cedar hedge dominates one side; it was constructed as a barricade against the neighbour, Mr. Babbit, after some dispute long forgotten. A grand old weeping willow droops in the front yard, its long flowing branches covering a small trailer permanently parked underneath. The tree sweeps the driveway, regularly dropping an array of branches and sap over Father-in-law's Buick—"that bloody willow."

The bungalow is one of hundreds of similar modest homes in Willowdale. Known fondly as "veterans' houses," many of them were built by the Canadian government for returning soldiers after the Second World War, mostly in this seemingly pleasant, middle-class neighbourhood north of Toronto.

"Beer, Aidan?"

"Thanks, Daddy."

"More gin, Felix, old chap?"

"Thank you. Gordon's London Dry is still my drink. And generous with the tonic, please, Jack. Have to think of my stomach."

I surreptitiously observe Father-in-law as I eat. His fair English-like features are clear-cut and chiselled next to Aidan's dark, powerful face with deep-set eyes. Aidan obviously takes after Mother-in-law's Sinhalese side of the family in Ceylon, I note thoughtfully. He is dark skinned, with a strong, stocky build like Mother-in-law. It's something I hadn't really taken in during the first throes of romance when we met here in Willowdale six months ago. Now I can't seem to keep myself from scrutinizing these members of my new family, my new in-laws. Each one is subject to my hidden, dark scrutiny. But what is it I'm trying to clarify? I'd tried to explain to Mother before the wedding that Aidan was half British and half Sinhalese, and that the family was from Ceylon, the island at the foot of the Indian subcontinent where all the tea comes from. "He calls himself Eurasian," I'd added cautiously.

"Huh. Heinz fifty-seven varieties, you mean!" Mother had tossed her fair, greying curls in scorn. They frame a lean, patrician face that she is proud of.

"What was in your *head,* Selena?" she'd hissed. We were closeted in the bedroom for a talk while Dad took Aidan out to see Cardiff Castle, obviously a pre-arranged move. What she meant was, how could I get involved with a "coloured" man, and then bring him home to Cardiff to be wed in the village church, in front of all the neighbours! Too late, I realized my mistake. I'd not really noticed—or cared about—Aidan's complexion during our torrid romance in Toronto. I'd only noticed how attractive he was. At that moment, I looked at him through Mother's horrified eyes, at his dark-brown skin I'd barely registered.

I look cautiously at my new mother-in-law with her heavy Kandyan build and her dark swarthy skin, much darker than Aidan's, if Mother but knew. Mother-in-law had been rejected for immigration to Australia under the colour bar in the 1950s. "Too dark," the authorities had pronounced her passport photo. But fair-skinned Jack Gilmor, Aidan's father, and Scott, Aidan's light-skinned younger brother, had been accepted. They had "passed." "Bloody hell," my future father-in-law had reputedly snarled, knocking back a whisky. "What's *White*? You tell me, bloody British!" They'd opted then to come to Canada. (This is one anecdote that must be kept from Mother.)

Scott is the fairest of the three Gilmor siblings, with light olive skin like an Italian. Handsome and slim, with thick, straight black hair and deep smouldering eyes, he could be a Hindu Bollywood star. He is Mother and Father-in-law's obvious favourite.

There's a sudden commotion. We all turn. Fiona, Aidan's older sister, jerks open the metal storm door that smashes shut behind her. The glass panes rattle in the steel frame.

"What for trying to break the bloody door off its hinges, Fiona, pet?" says Father-in-law. Fiona irritates him. Her arrival always seems like an event.

"Enough, Daddy! Hi there, Aidan, Selena, welcome back from Wales. How did the wedding go? It was yesterday, wasn't it? You must be exhausted." She glances around the table. "Everyone's here I see."

Before we can answer, Fiona plonks down numerous packages of food on the counter, with crabs' claws sticking out. "Enough for a siege," remarks Felix.

"Here, Ma, cassava for Daddy—I know he likes it. And some crabs from the fish market that I got on sale. Also fresh dinner rolls since I know you always buy day-old."

"What for bringing such things, Fiona? We have food plenty enough."

"Ughh, peasant food from Ceylon! *Pitu, dhal, maloom!* Ma! You're not serving Selena those smelly Ceylonese curries for her wedding celebration?" shrieks Fiona.

"Oh, but I *like* rice and curry," I say quickly, seeing the hurt look on Mother-in-law's face. She has a circular griddle on which she makes hoppers, which are like Western pancakes, puffed up.

"Me too," says Darleene loyally. She's tucking in to the hoppers as fast as Mother-in-law can turn them out. Soon, she and I will both be known as "Mrs. Gilmor"—three Mrs. Gilmors in the family.

Fiona is vivid and somehow admirable, having inherited a strain in the family genes that I haven't yet encountered. Her round, painted, crimson lips remind one of a rose; her fine Sinhalese oval features are like porcelain. Her eyes flash, and her voice crackles imperatively. I can tell that she's a fighter. Scottie told me once that the girls at the Kandy Convent boarding-school in Ceylon apparently used to call her "Mrs. Hitler."

"Mrs. Hitler," he drawls now, teasing.

"Enough, Scottie!" she flashes. "What would you know? You were in diapers."

"Ach!" she turns to me. "I will cook you good German food when you come to my place, Selena. Black Forest ham, nice German strudel. Come in a few weeks to dinner once Scottie and Darleene's wedding is over. The Germans know how to cook."

Fiona is married to a German immigrant, Deiter Mueller, whose parents apparently ran a delicatessen in Stutgart. Fiona still tries to emulate them, in cuisine at least. Mother-in-law maintains equanimity. "Ugh," goes Father-in-law.

"We used to have hoppers for breakfast at Holy Innocents, remember?" says Felix.

Holy Innocents Catholic College for Boys was the boarding school in Kandy that Aidan, Scott, Father-in-law, Felix, and another cousin, Colin, had attended long ago. Scottie had only attended for six months before the family emigrated.

"Not that Scott ate any Ceylonese food," Aidan mocks. "Daddy had to pay a fortune for special Western food for you, Scott."

"Yes! English cereal—*cornflakes!*" screams Fiona. "Can you imagine? In the tropics! And hot dogs!"

Scott smirks.

"He still eats kids' cereals and hot dogs," says Darleene.

"Well, I just didn't like the smell of curries as a kid," pouts Scott. He still doesn't. He's the "Canadian" in the family that my mother and father-in-law are so proud of, even though the role seems to involve rejecting their food. But he obligingly helps himself to a little rice and chicken. I make up for his reticence by serving myself extra hoppers and *pitu* and a great helping of chicken curry.

"See! Selena likes my food."

"She's just being polite, Ma. So, Darleene, your big day is coming up next at St. Raphael's. You've invited everyone from our side, Ma?"

"*Aiyo*. Yes, yes. Colin is coming."

"*Colin!*"

At once everyone is excited at the prospect of the three Ceylon cousins getting together again after so many years. Father-in-law had apparently sponsored Colin and Felix to come to Canada in 1958, after some riot. "And damn lucky we were to get out, too," says Felix. They refer to that year as "the '58." I'm silent. My position as the English daughter-in-law pre-empts any query from me about the British Colonial Empire, about their past....

"Bloody hell," says Father-in-law, knocking back a whisky, "damn British...."

"*Aiyo*, now then, pet...." Mother-in-law gives a warning glance towards me.

"Lally is invited, too," needles Scott, knowing all about Fiona's childhood rivalry with Lally.

"WHA-A-T? *Lally's* coming to the wedding?"

"Well, of course she is," says Mother-in-law sharply. "She grew up with you all on the estate, like a sister." Lally is Mother-in-law's youngest sister, part of the Gilmor children's childhood.

"That means her husband Jan must be coming too. And their five kids," protests Fiona. Lally and Fiona had both rushed into marriage as young women in 1957, as soon as they arrived in Toronto. Now, ten years later, Fiona is getting a divorce. ("Deiter wouldn't let me out of the house.")

"I said it would never work, marrying a German," observes Felix. "They don't use *hausfrau* for nothing."

"Hell, I was only nineteen. I didn't know what I was doing. I was crazy in love...."

I feel a secret little crunch in the pit of my stomach, a combination of pleasure and quick desire for Aidan, as I'm suddenly reminded of our secret love-making before we married. I'd thought Aidan was the most unusual man, full of social fervour for the underdog; that was part of his attraction.

Fiona tosses her head and returns to the subject of Lally and Jan. "I can't believe you're letting Jan come, Ma, especially since he will be meeting Darleene's family. Remember how he turned up in those ridiculous lederhosen for his wedding to Lally?"

Fiona won't let it go. She imitates Jan's knobbly knees, exposed by the ridiculous German lederhosen, and his heavy feet clomping down the aisle of St. Patrick's Church in Toronto. *Clomp clomp*, the farmer down the aisle. "All he needed was a pitch-fork," screams Fiona, and everyone has to laugh.

"Now, that is not nice, Fiona. Jan is a very good husband to Lally. He works very hard. He has three jobs."

"And that hair of Lally's," pursues Fiona, ignoring Ma and chuckling with amusement. "I hope Lally's cut it by now. Swinging like a rope to her waist, looking every bit like a Sinhalese villager at her wedding. She should have it cut shoulder-length like mine; she's in Canada now."

"Well, Lally always liked it to her waist in Ceylon. It was the custom, remember?" says Mother-in-law smoothly.

"Ach! Don't *talk t*o me about that savage place. They're chopping each other up over there!"

There's a shocked silence. So, it must be true, though only Fiona would dare say so.

"Ughh...." Trembling, Father-in-law takes a shot of Scotch.

Felix lights a cigarette and leans back, enjoying the commotion and his cousin Jack's obvious discomfort.

Fiona gathers up her purse. "What for leaving already, Fiona, pet?" cries Father-in-law. "You haven't eaten."

"I have to get back; the kids will be home from school. Old Mrs. Myers next door is looking after them. Deiter has taken off. He's moved out and is living in Ajax somewhere."

"Good God."

"This is what comes of not going to Sunday mass, Fiona. If you would only hear Father Matthew..." says Mother-in-law plaintively.

"Oh, fuck Father Matthew." Fiona tosses her head.

"*What?* You dare speak like that before your father, in his house?" Father-in-law staggers to his feet, whisky in hand, eyes bulging.

Felix lets out a short bark of a laugh.

"Oh, get over it, Daddy. Forget I said it. I'm *under stress.* Don't you realize? I'm *filing for divorce!*" Slam. Fiona flings open the kitchen door and it nearly rattles off its hinges again. She revs up her little Honda Civic outside under the willow and shoots down the driveway. Then she explodes up Violet Avenue like a firecracker, going something like a hundred kilometres per hour and taking half the willow branches with her.

"She was a little beauty as a child in Ceylon," says Felix.

Father-in-law buries his face in his hands. "What have I done, Mildred pet, coming to this country? Poor Babsey ... poor poor Babsey." He starts to sob at the sound of Fiona's childhood nickname. He repeats this ritual every time she steps out of line, calling up each infraction. His own daughter, going the way of the devil.

"Happy wedding celebration." Darleene winks at me slyly.

Aidan brings out the photographs of our wedding in Cardiff and passes them around. It's clear he's trying to change the subject and ease the tension left by Fiona. Father-in-law sets up a screen in the living room and puts together an old Russian projector with many a "Bloody hell" and "damn blasted thing!" Eventually he gets it to work with Aidan's help. The projector whirs, and the members of my new family sit on sofas and chairs gazing at a fuzzy, exciting rendering of our wedding: Aidan and I bobbing down the aisle of the church, Mother's big tulip hat looming in a sudden close-up. "What's that?" Mother-in-law is puzzled.

"My mother's hat."

Presently the camera shifts abruptly to a view of Montague Avenue and Mother's Tudor house with ivy-covered walls and the laburnum tree. Fernside, as she calls it, captivates them.

"Wow! That's a gorgeous place your parents have, Selena," cries Scott.

Aidan smirks modestly. "Yes, it's a Tudor with real oak beams."

"Is that a name plate hanging over the doorway?" Darleene peers. "Does your house have a *name*, Selena?"

"Yeah…. It says Fernside," I say, somewhat reluctantly. I can see what impression the photo is giving. But a photo can create its own reality; it's not necessarily true. Nanny Harcourt, on Mother's side of the family, is certainly well off and owns several properties in Cardiff. She gave Mother a generous gift a number of years ago that enabled Mother and Dad to buy Fernside and move up in the world. We'd lived in a rented house on a council estate for years before that, what Canadians refer to so deprecatingly as "government housing"—something Aidan, in his innocence, hadn't quite grasped.

"It's like a mansion!" Scott actually looks envious. He's used to being the best among the siblings.

"It's not so big."

"What are those walls around it?"

"Oh, well, lots of houses in Britain have walls instead of fences," I say.

Father-in-law, Mother-in-law, and Felix look hard at Fernside and Montague Avenue as the camera zooms in on houses with red-tile roofs, high laurel hedges, and rhododendrons. "Real upper class," Father-in-law says. He nods, giving Aidan an appreciative glance, as though he's done well with his English bride. But I tighten imperceptibly, for the wedding had, in fact, involved certain painful realizations about Mother and Aidan that would surely hurt and confuse my new in-laws. (Amongst other things, Mother had called him a flat-footed coolie thudding down the aisle of St. David's Anglican Church.)

My new family coo delightedly at the shot of the bridal party coming out of St. David's as the camera suddenly swerves, inexplicably, to another change of scene.

"Very *pukkah*," Felix agrees. "And how lovely Selena looks! The glowing happy bride! And her handsome groom," he adds quickly.

"Hey, your mother's so tall and good-looking, Selena. She looks nice," observes Scottie.

"Fine roses Mr. Harcourt has," says Father-in-law, as the camera swings abruptly again, without warning, to Dad's flowerbeds edging the front lawn of Fernside.

"Oh, the English love their roses," says Felix.

Mother-in-law is looking closely at Fernside and its mock-Tudor architecture. "You know, Selena, the English planters in Ceylon had houses just like this in Nuwara Eliya, upcountry—you remember, Felix? You used to go to the races there."

"Little England," says Felix, half closing his eyes. "The Governor's Cup every April, parties galore at the Hill Club.... Oh, that takes me back years."

Another glimpse of their colonial world, which has been kept hidden from me. I repeat, *Nuwara Eliya*, the rolling Sinhalese syllables slipping elusively over the tongue, seductive.

There's no denying that on Mother's side, Nanny Harcourt is well off, and it is due to her that Mother and Dad are now up in the middle class in the best part of our village. But the Gilmors can't be expected to know that. I feel obligated to reveal the true circumstances. "You know, we're just 'Jones.'

Harcourt is Mother's name," I mumble earnestly. "We're just ordinary working-class people really...."

Now the little homemade movie shifts in tenor, to a less attractive view of my "other" grandmother, Nangi Jones, on the Welsh side of the family. I explain that *nangi* is the Welsh word for grandmother. There Nangi stands in a worn pinafore outside a small row house, set against a vista of collieries and smoke-stacks under glowering mountains. She is from the "poor" side of the family, the coal miners.

But Father and Mother-in-law gloss over poor Nangi, convinced as they are of my Englishness, ignoring my confusing, stunted Welsh relations. They identify me with Uncle Clive on Mother's side, whom I know they deeply admire as quintessentially English.

Clive Harrow ("Clive of India," Mother calls him behind his back) is from Kent, English to the core. Last summer, he and Aunt Clarice emigrated from a small dull market town in England to Canada. They'd ended up in Willowdale as well, in a nice frame house on Violet Avenue, right opposite the Gilmors. She and Uncle Clive had been here only six months when Aunt Clarice was killed by a bus, just before her first Canadian Christmas. I came down at once from my teaching job up north to help out.

Throughout the crisis, Uncle Clive maintained the reserved manner of the English, keeping a stiff upper lip, the very epitome of the kind of attitude that Father and Mother-in-law so admire and identify with British Colonial Ceylon. They'd been particularly impressed by his composure at the funeral. Not one tear. "Fine chap, Clive Harrow. Poor fellow, losing his wife like that."

But when he'd had Aunt Clarice's ashes "thrown to the four winds" by the Anglican priest, and destroyed every photo of Clarice—"for little Robin's sake, best she be forgotten"— they'd reconsidered somewhat. Surely the English carrying things too far.

But one night during my stay, I caught a brief glimpse into another place in Uncle Clive's heart. I was sleeping in one room with Jenny, while Robin, the little boy, was sleeping with Uncle Clive in the double bed in the next room. At night, he'd whispered privately to Uncle Clive about his mother and her death. I could hear the silvery child-words through the thin partition: Robin whispered that he knew where Mommy had gone, that she'd turned into a butterfly and was flying around in heaven. At six, he still had a child's implicit belief in angels. Later, that night, I heard uncle's deep harsh sobs into his pillow.

But all that is over; Aunt Clarice's short life and death is already in the past, buried deep inside. Uncle Clive has apparently sold the house and made a good profit. He's gone out west, to British Columbia, Mother-in-law informs me. He is to marry a Canadian widow he met at swinging singles in Willowdale. She has two little boys. I am all right with that. I have a vague memory of a willowy blonde whom Uncle Clive was smitten with, and it seemed the tactful thing for me to move on and give them space. "There's a letter for you from him," says Mother-in-law. "I kept it for you."

While my new relatives exclaim and coo over the wedding video in the living room, I follow her into the double bedroom, which is like a sanctuary. It's like entering church—you try not to breathe. Sacred pictures hang on the walls—the Virgin Mary, Jesus, Michelangelo's *Last Supper*—for my in-laws are Catholic. There's another photo of the Buddhist Kandy Temple on the wall, but it's different from the one in the living room, which is bright and exotic. This one shows a row of young monks—Mother-in-law calls them *bhikkhus*—with saffron robes and shorn heads, gliding across the lawn beside Kandy Lake. The photo is pale, the temple indistinct and wreathed in mist, with shadowy hills looming vaguely behind. Perhaps this photo is a tribute to Mother-in-law's Buddhist mother, Aidan's grandmother. I've yet to discover how Mother-in-law became a Catholic. A flagpole flying the Union Jack stands in the foreground; it is colonial Ceylon.

"Here," says Mother-in-law, handing me the letter.

I open it. Uncle Clive has enclosed a cheque for a hundred dollars as a wedding gift, and he wishes Aidan and me a long, happy marriage. I can't help tightening, for I recall how Uncle Clive had not been too accepting of Aidan when we'd started dating. Mumbling, he'd implied that I should move out and find a place of my own, "considering the circumstances." He'd told me that he liked Aidan, but he "didn't want to be answerable" to my parents, especially Mother. He'd half smiled wryly as he said this. He'd obviously seen Aidan as a problem, but didn't identify exactly what. "Oh, he's a nice boy, certainly, Selena...." He had been evasive in that way the English have of not facing you, not looking at you directly. His eyes had shifted sideways, a habit of his. But I'd been so taken with Aidan I hadn't cared. Besides, I had found a small bedsitter in an old Victorian in downtown Toronto, near the university. I'd be free and private to make real love with Aidan. I couldn't wait until the wedding. After I'd left his house, Uncle Clive had maintained a certain distance that was confusing. Now he's moved to British Columbia, gone without a trace. Clarice's ashes must have dissolved in the cosmos by now.

So strange, what can take place in one moment in time. The bus driver had tried to swerve. Aunt Clarice, in the last frantic second of her life, in a flash of premonition, had pushed Robin out of the way and taken the brunt of force herself. The driver was rightfully exonerated of blame. "He wept at the inquest," Mother-in-law says, looking anxiously at my face as if for clues, but there are none.

Just then, the phone rings, a shattering blast from the kitchen. "Ceylon calling!"

"Selena! Come, come!"

The phone is an unwieldy, black, old-fashioned rotary phone, resting on the kitchen table next to a bowl of curry.

"Ceylon?"

"Aiyo, that will be my father Titus—Aidan's grandfather—calling from Normandy," gasps Mother-in-law, giving me a proud glance.

Scott picks up first. "Yes.... YES.... He's here."

"Daddy, it's Titus Delaney. Grandpa."

Father-in-law's father-in-law. "Good God!"

"He's calling especially for you, Selena and Aidan."

Titus Delaney still lives on the old Normandy Cocoa Estate in Ceylon, where he's manager. Upcountry. Somewhere. Somewhere in that vast olden world of tea estates, coconut and rubber plantations, waving palms, cadjan thatched huts, clouds of bats at dusk, and Buddhas that I try to envision. Father-in-law trembles. "My God. Titus!"

"TITUS...?"

Bellows and crackles come down the line to where we sit at the kitchen table. An old, scratchy, dictatorial voice, a voice from their past, whines across thousands of miles.

"WHAT? WHAT? YES.... YES.... WHAT?" bellows Father-in-law. He puts the receiver close to his ear. "Aidan is married.... YES. Selena Harcourt ... SELENA HARCOURT.... No, Jones, I think.... Hell.... English. ENGLISH GIRL.... Yes, English accent... ENGLISH ACCENT.... Lovely manners, VERY CLASSY FAMILY.... WHO? FIONA? JUST MISSED HER. GONE. YES, SELENA IS HERE. AND AIDAN."

"Ughh—"

Father-in-law passes me the phone. "Speak."

"He wishes to talk to you, Selena," says Mother-in-law proudly. I can't let them down. I'm the new bride in the family. They all watch expectantly.

I look back into the anxious faces of my new family, whom I love, and to whom I now belong.

"Hello."

"Speak *up*, Selena. SHOUT! He's upcountry, for God's sake."

"HELLO."

"YES, YES, THIS IS SELENA, AIDAN'S WIFE," I yell.

A scratchy cackle responds. I imagine old Titus cranking the handle of an ancient telephone on the wall of his estate bungalow, winding it up perhaps.

"WONDERFUL," I keep yelling. "PLEASED TO MEET YOU TOO. THANK YOU...."

Meet him? And what am I thanking him for?

More scratchy whistles. Titus Delaney's old voice is thin and cranky, but delighted. This is Aidan's grandfather, the man he is so fond of, whose voice is fading forever on his cocoa estate, across thousands of miles and likely swathes of jungle.

"HI GRANDPA," yells Aidan; it's his turn. "YES. THANK YOU. WISH YOU WERE HERE TOO. ER—WONDERFUL TIME IN WALES. YES. THAT'S ENGLAND—NO, BRITAIN."

"Monsoon heavy this year? MONSOON? Good yield of cocoa pods? WHAT? Sorry, Grandpa. CAN'T HEAR ... CAN'T HEAR YOU...."

Truncated whistles and hisses resume down the line. "He's gone."

"Bloody hell. They should fix that damn upcountry line!"

Nevertheless, Father-in-law is excited. He knocks back a whisky, his eyes bulging. Mother-in-law becomes strangely remote. Her father, her childhood.... How much longer will Titus last?

"Voice from the past, old chap." Felix looks resigned.

"You know, I barely remember him," says Scott.

2.

I'D BEEN SO CERTAIN MOTHER would be enamoured of Aidan's sultry dark looks and intelligence. I was sure I could count on her—after all she was a placement officer for overseas students in the sociology department at the university. Part of her job was to find digs for the African students in particular. She approached various landladies around Cardiff, trying not to rely on Tiger Bay, which was an immigrant area to the south side near the docks, where Jamaicans and Caribbean immigrants had tended to gravitate due to its low rents. Many of them have been there for generations, since the nineteenth century. Mother was concerned that an educated student on scholarship from Nigeria or Kenya might feel stereotyped, which was always a problem. We'd often been shocked and even had a laugh at other people's racism, especially the time one landlady had cried to Mother, "Oh, Mrs. Jones, I ain't racist, honest, but I don't want those darkies in my 'ouse. They smells awful, aye."

But something seemed to take over Mother, now that she was to be Aidan's mother-in-law. "He's ... *coloured*!" she'd cried. "You never told us." It hadn't occurred to me. It was from Dad I'd anticipated uneasiness; I had even warned Aidan that he'd likely see him as a "foreigner." ("Well, at least he's not a Black, mun," I'd overheard him say to Mother in relief when we arrived.) Dad was less educated than Mother, I'd explained. But it was Dad who had been supportive, as had my older sister.

Betsy had liked Aidan and said he was a "gentleman." ("Tell Mum to go to blazes. I did.") Dad had given Aidan a chance; he had talked to him man-to-man and taken him out to see Cardiff Castle. "Your father's a very intelligent man, Selena, you just don't see it," Aidan had said. *What else did I not see?*

"...And he can't pronounce his v's and w's!"

Mother had looked at me wildly, accusingly. It was true. Aidan did sometimes say "vunderful" for "wonderful," but it hadn't bothered me before. To me, it was like French-Canadians having trouble with the letter *h*; they often pronounced my surname as 'Arcourt-Jones instead of Harcourt-Jones. Now I began to cringe every time Aidan murmured, "Thank you wery much, Mrs. Harcourt-Jones." He was so polite, so deferential; I knew it was for my sake.

"But he's so intelligent, Mum, he really is! And kind."

There were blue circles under Mother's eyes; she was losing sleep over this.

I saw her anguish. I was the daughter she had taken the most pride in. My older sister had gone down in the world, in Mother's opinion, by marrying Evan the postman instead of the doctor Mother had had in mind, so I suppose her hopes had been pinned on me. Mother always imagined I'd marry a fine Englishman, tall and fair, or a good Welsh boy, and live in a nice big house in Cardiff.

Her lip quivered. Too late, I saw my mistake.

"But..."

"You'll face all kinds of prejudice married to a coloured," she continued. "And there's children to consider—have you thought of that? They'll face backlash too. *Coloured. Mixed. Half-caste.*" A kind of horror crossed poor Mother's face.

"Oh, not in Canada, Mum," I said quickly. "Not even in Wales," I added gamely. "What about Shirley Bassey?"

"Shirley *Bassey*?"

Bassey was the famous "coloured" Welsh singer from Tiger Bay itself. Wales was terribly proud of her. Our Shirley ...

one of our own, one of us. It was a mixed message, since as kids we were warned to stay away from Tiger Bay and "those people." But Shirley Bassey was the first Welsh girl to make a single; all the girls in grammar school knew "As I Love You" and "Banana Boat Song." Most of all, Shirley Bassey sang the theme song in the James Bond movie *Goldfinger*. I hadn't thought much about her parentage until that conversation with my mother. I pointed out that her father was Black from Nigeria and her mother was a white Englishwoman, which made Shirley, with her full head of thick black curls and light brown skin, "mixed," like Aidan.

Mother had stared. "You just don't *get* it, Selena."

"Aidan's from a good family, Mum," I'd tried to reassure her. "His father, Mr. Gilmor, was manager of a big tea plantation in Ceylon, with a large estate bungalow, servants, everything."

Mother's mouth had twisted in a painful grimace. Ceylon was in the past, once part of the glory of the British Empire. Now it was independent and rumoured to become Sri Lanka, a Sinhalese name they'd thought up from somewhere.

"His parents had an *ayah*, a gardener, and a *dhobi*." I tried to stress Aidan's superior background.

"A what?"

"A washer woman or man who comes to the house to do your laundry for you."

"Yes, in the river, whacking it on rocks. I've seen pictures too. In *National Geographic*," Mother had scoffed. "Well, if you believe all that balderdash!"

I'd realized in that moment how much it meant to me, the truth of my new in-laws' experience in old colonial Ceylon. I so wanted to believe in the tea estate bungalow at Madeniya that Aidan had described, with its sweeping lawns and tamarind tree out front, full of parrots swinging in the branches. I sensed a world of status that my own father had been denied; he'd grown up in a tiny row house in the South Wales coal field. Jack Gilmor had obviously been well paid by the British proprietors and the tea company.

"I know all that! D'you think me a ninny? And how the British mixed with the women over there. Don't forget *that* while you're at it. Where did he get the name Gilmor from?" Mother's lips had twisted into a sneer.

I'd felt suddenly anxious. I hadn't wanted to know whatever it was Mother was implying. I'd imagined loose, illicit relationships between the white British colonial masters and "coloured" Sinhalese women—was that what Mother meant?

I could hear the echo of pain in my father-in-law's voice as he'd knocked back a whisky in the kitchen in the Willowdale bungalow, half drunk. "Damn British. What's *white*? You tell me!"

3.

AIDAN'S BRONZE BURNISHED FACE glows from the sun as he comes in. He's gotten quite dark over the summer, but when he removes his watch strap I can see a pale strip of skin against his sunburnt arm. "See?" he grins. His lips are soft and full as we kiss.

He looks fresh in the light clothes he wore to summer school today: a fine lawn short-sleeved shirt with an open neck that reveals a dark V, light cotton slacks, and loafers. He's slim, with small sloping shoulders and a big head. He smells pleasantly of Old Spice cologne.

Aidan drops his books on the table and looks around appreciatively at our new house, sparsely furnished for now. It's an old white-frame two-storey built before the war, with bottle-green dormers and verandah, in the east end of Toronto. Morton Road is a quiet, ordinary street in a quiet, ordinary neighbourhood close to Lake Ontario and the Beaches, with its boardwalk and big old ivy-covered homes. Our little pocket is more modest: rows of small identical bungalows around Kingston Road, neat and orderly with net-curtained windows and prim plots of grass. There are moments I'm surprised I've ended up here after my zany old bedsitter downtown.

Aidan had given careful thought to where we could live; we hadn't been able to afford a house in Willowdale. He searched through the demographic studies at the Toronto Planning Board and found that immigrants tended to congregate in downtown

Toronto at first, before trying to move north up Yonge Street towards Willowdale—like the Italians. The Jews gravitated up Bathurst Street; the Ukrainians, Poles, and Germans settled in the west end; and the English settled in the east. Toronto was not unlike Cardiff's Tiger Bay, I supposed. He was certainly knowledgeable about it all. Central north Toronto had its own status; it meant blue-blood Ontario, old money.

"I thought you'd like it here in the Beaches, being British," he'd said shyly. "I thought you'd be more comfortable here among your own people." He said this knowing that he himself might not fit in there. I was touched and felt a sudden quiet gush of love.

There's a fish-and-chip shop on the corner; a British-style pub, The Cock and Hen, on Kingston Road; a small seedy local cinema that shows ancient films in black and white; and an Anglican church: Little England. No one seems to speak to anyone much on Morton Road—well, that certainly is English. We could be any excited young Canadian couple in their first home. (I push back a vague fear how people on the street might feel about us, about me.) We've certainly gone up in the world in Father-in-law's eyes, anyway; he's phoned everyone in Ceylon and the relatives in Australia about the house.

Aidan sniffs the air. "Mmm. Something smells good." He smiles.

"It's chicken curry and *dhal,* the way your mother showed me." I smile in return.

It's my first attempt. I sprinkled in cumin seeds, coriander, and a generous amount of powder and turmeric that I bought at Dalah's East Indian Mart in Willowdale—you can't get these things at the corner stores here. *Fresh from India, Ceylon, Indonesia, Malaya, West Indies, Bahamas....* The half-hour drive to Willowdale up the Don Valley Parkway was worth it. I'd enjoyed picking out the unknown spices, eager to show Mother and Father-in-law that I was open to Ceylonese cuisine, to them as my new family. They'd insisted on accompanying us to ensure we bought quality ingredients. "Some of these spices you wouldn't put in dog food, Selena," warned Mother-in-law. "No knowing what nasty ingredients they contain." Felix had also come along. He wanted to buy something called *rambutan*, which looked like a weird prickly pink ball and stank. "But very delicious inside, Selena, very succulent." My new life, I reminded myself.

"Ma! You're not taking Selena to that stinky old Asian den full of cockroaches?" Fiona had screamed. "Eat that rice, Selena, and you swallow Asian bugs and eggs that will hatch in your intestines. You'll be crawling with maggots."

"Such silliness, Fiona. We're living to tell the tale, aren't we," objected Mother-in-law.

Mother-in-law does not drive. It seems she'd always had a chauffeur in Ceylon in the old days. One of the servants was always there to take her shopping at some village called Nawalapitya. It was not the "done thing," apparently, for a woman of her status to drive herself, a fascinating little revelation. Now that the family is in Canada, Father-in-law has to take over the job. "Now I'm the bloody chauffeur," he growled.

The wooden shelves at Dalah's were full of bags of various types of rice: Basmati rice from Assam in big burlap bags, white rice, brown rice, and a reddish rough-textured kind labeled *from Ceylon*.

"Oh, look, Ceylon rice!" But when I moved the bag, cockroaches scuttled away. Fiona had been right.

"A*iyo*! Country rice the villagers eat. You don't want to be buying that."

"Make you shit five times a day," tittered Felix. Aidan snorted; he loved Felix.

A few hippies were also shuffling up the aisles, fingering the spices. They were drawn to the shelf with incense and brass Hindu gods and goddesses on display, especially a god called Ganesh with an elephant's trunk for a nose. The youths wore *kurta* tops and bead necklaces, and the girls were in peasant skirts with loose tops. Some of them had studs pierced through their noses. "Bloody fools," muttered Father-in-law. "Look like bloody Tamil coolies." Perhaps he thought he'd left this behind in Ceylon.

"That is how it is, pet, with the young people today," soothed Mother-in-law.

Now the aroma of Basmati rice fills the kitchen, just like at Mother-in-law's. Aidan and I sit facing each other in our kitchen at the small formica table we got from the thrift store. Our kitchen is spacious and airy, twice the size of hers. A window looks out over a small back garden and a tall privet hedge—now they are *our* garden and hedge.

"So how was summer school today?"

Aidan is taking the teachers' technical summer course to qualify for his first drafting job that starts in a few weeks at Brockhurst Technical School in Toronto. I help him with his essays. This latest one is on early settler architecture in Upper Canada. "Don't make it too good this time, Selena," he says anxiously. "The prof commented in front of the class on my exceptionally good vocabulary in the last one." He winces wryly, but I admire him for his assiduity. He's also going to take night-school courses towards his undergraduate degree in sociology. One of his courses is called "Insanity and Mental Aberrations"—something I'm not sure I'd want Mother to know about.

The sun flows into the room, reminding me of other sensuous afternoons in the old bedsitter downtown where I lived before we got married. But Aidan is carried away talking about the upcoming general election and Pierre Elliott Trudeau, a rising star in the Liberal party with ideals for a multicultural society. "That's us, Selena!" says Aidan excitedly. Trudeau's been all over the world, even Ceylon. Apparently he said that the Ceylonese people are the friendliest in the world, a claim that gained Aidan's approval. As a staunch follower of the socialist New Democratic Party, or the NDP, Aidan is torn between Tommy Douglas, its leader, and this new Trudeau. Women and girls are swooning over him as if he's a rock star. It's Trudeaumania. The staid and decent Methodist Tommy Douglas just can't compete.

Trudeau, a small dainty man—he wears a red rose in his lapel—is cocky and outrageous, something that Aidan admires. Take *that* for the British Empire, and *that* and *that*, with knobs on! I never paid much attention to politics as a girl back home, but Aidan's passion is catching. Isn't that what attracted me to him in the first place? And his dark looks, thickly lashed eyes and full lips. Excitedly I'd accepted his solitaire diamond ring.

I was swept along. It was all part of the so-called Summer of Love, 1967, when thousands of hippies swarmed the lawns of the Ontario Legislature at Queen's Park at a Love-In, flaunting semi-nude bodies in front of the statue of Macdonald. Of course, the media were there full force with huge cameras; CBC and ITV were taking in the scene: hippies lying about on the grass with their long streaming hair and faded jeans, smoking pot—or "weed" as they call marijuana—and having sex. It was overwhelming. What did it all mean? MAKE LOVE NOT WAR! PEACE! FUCK THE ESTABLISHMENT!

That was us. I realized with shock that Aidan and I were too old to be hippies, even though we were still young, we were just not young enough. We'd missed it by five or six years—incredible. I felt a stab of envy, resentment; it wasn't fair. Desperately I tore holes in my new jeans and threw away my lipstick, to Aidan's amusement. "Cripes, Selena," he said. But who wanted to be a twenty-four-year-old *square*?

The hippies didn't give a damn about convention; and we had to. That particular day I was wearing a mini-skirt and my hair was puffed up and back-combed in a bouffant, the current style, as we walked around the park. I could sense the hippies' mocking amusement as I stumbled past them over the grass in my silly stilettoes, the spiked heels digging into the turf. They were bare-footed, or wore clumsy ugly sandals. One girl was breastfeeding, her breasts exposed uncaringly. She was surrounded by girls, other babies, and toddlers crawling about. There seemed to be no husbands or young men around—maybe more evidence of free love, a term that confounded me in a way I couldn't quite identify. It was as if hippie girls were giving away something that we had kept close guard over through the fifties without question. It was rumoured that it didn't matter to the girls who the fathers were. Apparently everyone, even the men, was responsible for everyone's baby in a commune. A girl could have all the partners she wanted thanks to Free Love. "Thanks to The Pill," Aidan quipped. "The miraculous little hormones in a capsule invented by scientists in some laboratory so that hippies could screw whoever and whenever they want," he added drily. I got the point, but wasn't there something exhilarating about tossing off all your clothes and stomping about crazily before the Ontario legislature?

A disgrace to our fair city.... A disgusting display of immorality.... On and on went the letters to the editor in the Toronto newspapers over the next week. *Put them in reform school!*

"Ma and Daddy had an arranged marriage in Ceylon," Aidan had said, somewhat primly. (Mother would associate this with the foreign customs the sociology department was discouraging in those countries.) Their families had known each other forever, Aidan continued. They'd played doubles at the same upcountry tennis club; Mother-in-law had been approved. "Here it's hit or miss. No one knows who they're marrying, really, in the West." But does anyone really know another person? I wondered. (Perhaps my in-laws approved of me because they'd known Aunt Clarice and Uncle Clive and their social status. They were English ... that was enough.)

Then someone wrote an irate letter to the editor of the *Toronto Star* complaining about an Italian woman breastfeeding her baby on the subway "in full view." Italian women from nowhere rose up in spitting revolt. "*Madonna mia!* Italian men look away. What's wrong with Canadians?" More outrage:

"This is not Sicily! You're in a civilized country now." This was more in reference to Italian women in the fifties balancing bags of vegetables on their heads as they walked up Yonge Street in Willowdale, shocking the Anglo-Saxons. Aidan remembered it, amused.

"The poor immigrants," he said. They also kept chickens and pigeons (for pigeon pie) in their back yards, further alarming the neighbours. "When the Italians moved into certain streets in Willowdale, the Canadians moved out. It was the chickens and pigeons they couldn't take," Aidan said, chuckling at the memory. Then the municipality passed a law against it.

"Well, Dad had a chicken run once at the bottom of our garden, after the war," I said. "Otherwise it would have been more powdered eggs for us." I didn't think *I* would have moved out.

"Ma breastfed me until I was three," Aidan said calmly. "What's all the fuss about?" I tried not to show how much this truly shocked me. A three-year-old toddler running about with a mouth full of teeth still at the breast? I was glad Mother was not there to hear it. Of course, these were just the sort of crazy rules the hippies liked to break.

They believed in the power of *ohm*, a sacred Sanskrit sound from the East that they chanted loudly in yoga, their hypnotic voices emanating from dark doorways in the backstreets of Toronto, the streets that led to nirvana. "Do they have proof?" quipped Aidan. But maybe they're freeing themselves by entering into a new consciousness, I thought, interested nevertheless.

At the time, I was living in an old Victorian rooming-house in the student area of University of Toronto, where I'd secreted myself away after leaving Uncle Clive—he'd taken up with the blonde widow and I was in the way. I had fancied myself a sort of hippie. For the first time in my life I was doing something care-free, daring. I had a lover, and I was even risking pregnancy, since I wasn't on the pill. It didn't occur to me that being with Aidan was what was daring.

I still think about the old bedsitter, about Aidan's warm dark body, the pleasure. I look secretly at him as he sits across from me now at the formica table in our kitchen munching through a roti. I recall how he was, how we were in that rooming-house full of students. They hardly noticed him coming and going; they didn't care who he was or his nationality, assuming he was just another undergraduate. Perhaps that gave me false assurance.

The bedsitter itself was a large ugly room painted dirty pink, with a window to the side that overlooked the drains. Even so, I liked it very much because it was private—it was mine, secret. I had it all to myself. (At night, the pigeons settled on the roof with soft whirrings of feathers and low throaty coos.) The furniture was ancient: a double bed, an old oak desk, a hotplate, an old fridge that shook, a shared a communal bathroom. Entering from the street, you passed through a narrow passage with a small side table, where we left the mail. Steep narrow stairs led up to the second floor that I shared with Anya, a single parent who lived in the room next door with her young son. She informed me that a prostitute had been in my room before me. On the next floor up, in the attic, were three architectural students. On the ground floor was a middle-aged couple living together, Mrs. Madison and Mr. Kelner. Bills came for them, addressed separately—that's how I knew their names. The house on Sussex was certainly far from the segregated all-girls dorms I'd been used to at university in Wales, where the sign-in time had been set by the warden, a matronly figure, at strictly eleven o'clock.

Living like that, unmarried and answerable to no one, seemed like the way it should be, casual. Even so, I always knew that it wouldn't last forever. It was a little interlude in my life which until then had been full of studies, responsibilities, faithful attempts to fulfil Mother's expectations. Aidan couldn't understand why I'd moved downtown instead of staying in nice Willowdale. His parents were also bewildered, even suspicious. A young woman choosing to be alone in the inner city? Was that normal, or a bit weird? But I was fond of the neighbourhood. I washed my clothes in a Chinese laundromat on Spadina, where all sorts of dubious characters came and went with their quarters and bundles of clothes. Sometimes they talked to me. "You got a quarter, miss?" Or, "You got a place fer tonight?" I bought bread at a Portuguese bakery in the Jewish Market, as it was called, near Alexandra Street. There was an old synagogue nearby on one of the old streets, and on Saturday men in striped shawls with fringes huddled along with caps on their heads, holding the hands of young boys dressed in dark suits and white shirts without ties. One Saturday I ventured in. Two old men greeted me in the vestibule and motioned me upstairs. The women sat together on their own looking down over a balcony at the men below. No one seemed to mind—who was judging? An old lady pointed the place out in the Hebrew prayer book for me; the Hebrew script looked like little harsh hooks and strokes. I didn't want to say I didn't understand it, so I mumbled along, pretending. Gradually the low rhythm became familiar.

"But why on earth would you *go in there*?" Aidan was perplexed. (I'd wanted to feel what they felt inside the synagogue. But I kept my reason to myself.)

"Good God." My future father-in-law knocked back a whisky to steady himself. I was anxious that he might have other thoughts now about his prospective daughter-in-law. Even Mother-in-law looked concerned.

"Why did you *tell* them?" I was annoyed at Aidan, who just grinned.

"Well, why shouldn't they know?"

But it didn't stop me. I discovered the Italian community on College, a busy noisy street with trams, that Canadians call streetcars. There were a few cafés with awnings, dark and small, one called fancifully Capriccio, and another Arrivederci. One day I went in alone and ordered a cappuccino. I'd never tasted such coffee before, with foaming froth and a dash of exotic cinnamon. I was the only woman in the café. The waiter wore a long black apron and shouted in Italian to someone at the back, "*Sbrigati!*" The place was filled with Italian men playing cards at little tables, just like in Italy, I imagined. (Where were the women?) I hadn't realized that, just like the Jewish shopkeepers in the Market and their Sabbath, there was this Italian life all of its own quietly going on. Toronto was cosmopolitan. It was exciting to compare this new city to my little village in Wales, so staid and monochromatic. Everyone was Welsh in Ton-Y-Pandy. Everyone spoke the same language with the same lilt, ate the same food—fish or meat pie and chips—and looked the same: short stocky Celtic build, ruddy faces with some red in their hair. Everyone was a singer or a rugby player. "That's the gene pool," Aidan said.

Yorkville Avenue, north of Bloor, was the hippie hang-out. It was only blocks away, so we joined the throngs of sightseers every weekend to see the action. "They've never seen anything like it, either, in Toronto the Good," chuckled Aidan.

His hair had grown quite a bit by now and touched his collar, and he was sprouting a beard at my suggestion. I stomped anxiously along in new expensive Reebok sandals that most hippies seemed to clump around in—I'd discovered it cost money to be a hippie.

Yorkville was a seedy rundown place buzzing with excitement, what the French call *avant-garde*. The cheap rents attracted students and down-and-outs, beatniks and druggies; they had a name for everyone, when you thought about it. Old Victorian houses painted all sorts of colours had been turned into cafés and bars; poetry readings by writers you'd never heard of took place in the basements. They were offbeat and radical, their poems mimeographed, and there was lots of folk music. Gordon Lightfoot came, a new young Canadian folk artist that Aidan was drawn to. Sometimes there was a police raid, and hippies suspected of dealing drugs were carted off.

There was a line-up as usual at the Riverboat; it had red booths and was a popular spot. The Mynah Bird had skimpily dressed go-go dancers encased in glass, and gangs of ogling youths pressed against the window for a better look. Nothing much had really changed, I thought.

We pushed our way into the Penny Farthing and managed to get a seat in the window. It was packed. I was wearing my ripped jeans and long wooden beads, feeling like a hippie. There we were, together, part of it, blending in, I thought excitedly. Nervously I lit a cigarette. Eventually a waitress came over and partially leaned towards Aidan. She was wearing a bikini top—all the waitresses did, to attract business I thought. Aidan ordered two cappuccinos; they were expensive so we'd have to sip slowly. I was loving the psychedelic atmosphere—"vibes" the hippies called it. (You had to learn a new vocabulary to keep up with them.)

Someone began strumming "Little Boxes," the hit song on the charts, over and over.

It was about little houses made of "ticky tacky" that all looked the same, and about the people who lived in them, who all turned out the same. Then it talked about how their children then went to university, where they, too, "were put in little boxes" and "came out all the same."

"They've got it!" cried Aidan, really enjoying it. (He saw himself as a socialist rebel on the attack against Toronto the Good.)

At first, I thought it was funny and clever and right on, too. But then it began to irk me. I couldn't help thinking of my new Father and Mother-in-law's little veteran's house in Willowdale, and the rows of similar boxy houses on their street with old frame porches that they thought were wonderful—"Lucky to be here."

Was it really true? Were we all the same? I thought of Mr. Fong at the laundromat, and Rabbi Weiss, and Giovanni and Maria at Arrivederci, who were saving every cent to move out to a suburban box where, according to Aidan, Giovanni would change his name to John and Maria to Mary. It happened; it was common. Aidan had seen it before. (Fiona had wanted Deiter to change his name from Deiter Mueller to Dave Miller, and he'd refused—"*Mein Got!*") "But Giovanni is such a musical name!" I'd cried. Aidan pointed out, "When it comes down to it, he has to fit in—or else!" We didn't touch on how Father-in-law had gotten the name Gilmor. "If he'd had one of those interminably long Sinhalese names, like Mother-in-law's Goonesekere, "that officials couldn't get their tongues around, he wouldn't have made it past the gate-post," Aidan admitted. (In that instant I felt a querulous stab of betrayal. Would I have married Aidan if his name had been Goonesekere? I had to admit that Goonesekere would have made him someone else.)

I lit another cigarette, trembling. The café was noisy and full of smoke.

"You didn't *know* Toronto in the fifties, Selena, what it was like. It was awful without the immigrants." (Everything shut on a Sunday.) "It's these immigrants working all night in bars and cafés and bread factories, willing to break their backs, who are the ones really changing Canada," he added and I knew then he identified with them, heart and soul.

He leaned forward, staring at me intently. I had to understand that he had been a delivery boy at thirteen. He had worked for the pharmacy for twenty-five cents an hour, dropping off medications on his bicycle to seniors after school. The pharmacist, a German immigrant, had felt sorry for him. And then there was the part-time job he'd had at Dominion at age sixteen. His friend Rob had been given a cushy task stacking shelves inside, out of the cold, but the manager had given Aidan one swift glance and sent him out to the back entrance, out of the public eye, to unload trucks in all weather, for less money. Aidan invariably blamed this full square on the British Empire that had, after all, run the world.

I tried to look sympathetic. Yes, the Empire had had its day, I agreed. I'd heard his delivery-boy story before, but what was so awful about the Dominion tale was how Aidan, just a boy, had felt there must be something wrong with him, *and his friend had not.* "You never had to go through that," he'd said accusingly. "You were protected by your British-ness that you've always been proud of, that you identify with."

Well, I was proud of being Welsh in the way the Italian men at Arrivederci were proud of their heritage and would think nothing of suddenly bursting into song at the end of a game of poker—one of them had a good tenor voice. "*Torna a Surriento, famme campà!*" he would sing. And all of them would come to life. Or like that Italian woman carrying her vegetables on her head up Yonge Street in the fifties—that was me, too, in spirit.

"Such silly talk, Selena," Aidan had said affectionately, not taking it seriously. That was the problem.

"But that's the idea," he conceded warmly. "Italians singing arias in Trudeau's new multicultural society," he had pressed on excitedly. "Yes, your Italians in Arrivederci can sing '*Torna a Surriento*,' Selena, and still be Canadian!" That was the point; that was what was so revolutionary (the Anglo-Saxon guard stiffening in alarm). I was amused, and I lit another cigarette, enjoying it all, the thrilling ambience we were part of. A girl had come in dressed in black, with orange and pink streaked hair, metal chains, and a dagger around her waist. She had terrifying black eyelashes stiff with mascara that made her look as if she'd slit you open with a flick of an eyelash. But she was fascinating. "Lolo!" the hippies screamed at the back. I gripped my coffee, enjoying the moment. She may have been about fifteen.

Aidan frowned. He looked around and leaned forward intently again. "Do you notice something, Selena? These hippies are all *white*. White middle-class kids, probably with well-off parents behind them that they're rebelling against, that they'll fall back on when the novelty wears off. They'll likely end up at Daddy's firm—you'll see. Not like immigrant kids."

He meant well, I knew, but somehow the evening went *pthunk!*

The nights were getting chilly. Soon we'd be getting married, in Wales. As we walked to the bedsitter, the street was dark with heavy trees and foreboding, tall houses.

Aidan was concerned about getting an oil change on my old Volks. "This is what's important in life, Selena. And check the tires well before winter—this is Canada."

When we got in he made us an omelette on the hotplate and cut up little pieces of onion and garlic, mixing them in with a little Tabasco sauce. The old bedsitter glowed in a cozy way, the double bed sagging. "Tea?" He plugged in the kettle. Suddenly there was an ominous *thud* below.

Mrs. Madison came out into the passage and yelled up the stairs: "You fucking stupid bitch, you blow my TV again with that fucking kettle!"

I went out and called down towards the landing: "It's not my fault the cheapo landlord puts too many things on one fuse!"

"Who the hell was that?" whispered Aidan. He was rolling on the bed, trying to stifle his laughter.

"It's Mrs. Madison. She comes with the house," I said.

"Yes, that was a crazy place, Selena," Aidan laughs. He mops up the remains of his curry sauce with the last of his roti. The sun glints across the formica table and illuminates the little glass of flowers from our garden. The house is quiet. "I never did understand why you never got a nice bachelor apartment in Willowdale. You'd have been near your uncle and my parents if something went wrong."

I understand now that everything I'd loved about downtown was what poor struggling immigrants were eager to escape. They wanted to leave for Willowdale or Don Mills, with its clean-cut side-splits and carved lawns.

"Well, would you like to live in a crack house with rats and cockroaches? You were living in the nice part," Aidan says when I explain.

We mop up the leftovers and finish off the mango chutney on the side. "Hey, this curry and *dhal* was good," says Aidan, surprised. But he looks somewhat disoriented. His English wife cooking curry? Who'd believe it? Certainly not Mother in Wales. He grimaces.

I push back the memory of the wedding. The things that were revealed that day are still too painful to explore. They left me feeling conscious of myself in a new way. I felt like I had been separated from my friends, who had all married white boys—something I hadn't registered until we were walking down the aisle of St. David's Church side by side, brown and white. ("Ooh, he *is* dark, ain't he? She'll be 'aving picaninnies—terrible for Mrs. Jones," I'd heard a neighbour say in a titilated thrill. Poor Mother.) I tense. We seem to tacitly avoid Mother's name most of the time, which is sad. If it does pop up, Aidan winces slightly.

I put the dishes into the sink. "Here, let me, Selena. You do my essays for me." Aidan begins washing up. It's a tender moment. The heat drifts through the kitchen. There's a sultry stillness, just the swish of the water. The bedsitter and the hippies are fading into the past summer. We kiss. Slowly we mount the stairs to the bedroom, a little disoriented since the house is still strange. He tends to be shy, and therefore so am I. The sun is making pleasant shadows on the bedspread. I notice Aidan's exposed body, a lighter shade than his dark sunburned face and arms, as he undresses hurriedly.

Afterwards I join him outside on the verandah. He's put on a fresh T-shirt and shorts, his burnished skin glowing in the hot sun.

We stand together, proudly surveying the street and our little plot. Presently, a man with dirty blond hair comes out of the brick house opposite and stands on the porch in a singlet and underpants. His arms are folded, bulging with muscles. He stares across the street at us. After a while he turns abruptly and goes back inside, slamming the door.

4.

IT'S SOMETHING I SENSE, something about the way the net curtains twitch whenever we walk down the road, as if someone is peering from behind. But I never see anyone. Morton Road is still and silent in the early September heat.

The neighbours seem invisible, keeping inside their houses; *Beware of the Dog* signs are clipped on side gates where there are no dogs. Everything neat and quiet.

Our puppy Bosie is getting bigger. He's a big black dog, hinting at fierceness, even though he's really a softie. I was happy the day we got him from the pound; I'd always wanted a dog. We have him on a thick leash—I suppose it signifies "Danger, don't mess with us," like a warning—as we walk around the block, past the musty old cinema on Kingston Road that's currently showing Charlton Heston in *The Ten Commandments*. The owner of a small machine shop on the corner waves to us in his oily dungarees and says he'd like a guard dog like ours. Other than that there's little social connection. I'm lonely without it. Perhaps I'm missing the old downtown bedsitter and chats with Anya. No one has invited me in yet for a cup of tea, as they would in Wales. No one seems to want to know me here.

"I'm lonely," I blurt out, to my surprise. I'd knocked on the door of our next-door neighbour Ann Mainwaring, a middle-aged woman. I'm holding a letter addressed to her that has come to our house by mistake. "There's no one to talk to. Maybe we could visit for a cup of tea," I gush.

Ann Mainwaring frowns. "Oh dear.... Well, I'm a widow; I'm used to being on my own."

Her voice stiffens. I wonder if it's because of Aidan. *Am I being paranoid?* I'm more aware now of how the neighbours might see me—the white girl living with a brown man in the green house. "My husband and I just got married this summer," I offer.

An embarrassed look of dislike and confusion crosses her face. "Yes, I know. He's from India, isn't he? A Paki?"

"No, Ceylon—you know, where the tea comes from." I smile.

"And what did your parents say?" It's a naked question veiled with disapproval. I too now am foreign. She has the door open only a few inches. We have nothing to talk about. She takes the letter. "Thank you." The door closes firmly behind me. I'm surprised at how quickly tears come to my eyes. I hear the draw of a bolt.

As I turn away and stumble to the sidewalk, I feel a small thud on my back. Then another. A shower of painful pebbles and stones hit my shoulders and head. I put my hands over my face for protection, frightened. There's a scuffle behind the hedge, and a couple of sniggering teenagers call out "Pakis fuck off!" and run away.

"Aw don't cry, Selena." Aidan pats me awkwardly. There are bloody cuts on my face and one eye is swelling. He seems embarrassed. "They're just kids. They don't know what they're saying." But they do. They don't want us here, we're outsiders. I can't help but think of Mother.

It's Saturday morning, and we're meeting up with Scott and Darleene in the diner on Yonge Street, in Willowdale. Darleene cheerfully waves us over and we join them in the booth. The diner is fifties era, drab but comforting, like most places in Willowdale. The high-backed booths have red vinyl upholstery of another era, and there are the original jukeboxes you can flip through and pick out a song. Autographed photos of

Hollywood greats cover the walls: Cary Grant, Vivien Leigh, Clark Gable—"My mother is still in love with him," Darleene says, grimacing humorously. They give off a certain romantic gloom that Aidan and I appreciate. Someone has put on Elvis, crooning "Love Me Tender."

"Oh, *Elvis!*" drawls Scott in a mocking tone. He's just bought the Beatles' latest album, *Sgt. Pepper's Lonely Hearts Club Band*, which is already at the top of the charts and starts to hum, "Lucy in the Sky with Diamonds."

The windowsill is crammed with frowzy crawling plants. I light a cigarette, joining Darleene.

"So, congratulations to you both! Saturday is the big day!" I cry, echoed by Aidan. They had waited until Aidan and I returned from Wales. Darleene's engagement ring, an amethyst set in a circle of diamonds, flashes in the light; she's partial to amethysts, she says. They bought it at People's Jewellers in Willowdale. "Beautiful, Darl," I say. They have their gold wedding bands at the ready.

"Caught, now, Scott," teases Aidan. Scott looks pleased; he likes being like everyone else.

"You're awfully young to get married," I say again tentatively, "but it's so romantic." "Well, Ma was only eighteen when she married Daddy, and Daddy was twenty—like me," Scott points out defiantly. Apparently, Father-in-law had poured a whisky at the news of the engagement, trembling in the kitchen, proud as hell. Mother-in-law was more cautious. "Father Matthew says it can be good to commit oneself early before God."

"One advantage of marrying as students is that we'll get that cheap apartment at York in the married quarters," says Darleene.

She fishes in her purse and pulls out the congratulatory cards they've already received from friends, some of them humorous: *Weddings make all that stuff you want to do decent and legal.* The grooms are all white, something I would never have noticed before. (Before *what*? Before entering this new dimension.) *A Promise Forever*, says another.

Scott and Darleene are wearing identical denim jackets, emphasizing their togetherness, and Scott's hair is fashionably long, like a hippie. "Need a damn haircut," Father-in-law had growled.

"That's Daddy for you, antediluvian," Scott drawls again, amused. But Scott and Darleene are no hippies, though they're the right age—five years younger than us.

"Huh, spoiled brats!" cries Darleene. "There were some hippies in Bayview High, all snobs. We didn't mix with them." Scott says he and Darleene always knew *they* had to *work*. (They want a house in Willowdale eventually, and they'll be no doubt helped financially by Mother and Father-in-law.) It's interesting how attached to the old neighbourhood they are; how they want to be near Father and Mother-in-law.

"See, Selena," Aidan turns triumphantly towards me. "I told you immigrant kids stay close to home. They're smart like the Italians. Italian kids pool their earnings with their parents to pay off the mortgage, or buy food—one for all, all for one."

Scott and Darleene blink. This obviously isn't the conversation they had in mind, but Aidan loves the stories that seem to verify the image he has of himself: the dutiful, self-sacrificing, steadfast immigrant son facing racism. He tells the story of being a delivery boy again. "I gave all my money to Ma," he stresses. He was so sorry for Ma that he'd also helped her thread tiresome bead chains for two cents a foot in Mr. Green's basement in Willowdale in the evenings. Her employer, Mr. Green, hadn't made much from it himself. It was a small cottage industry—just his wife and daughter and himself and Mother-in-law, the four of them in the basement, toiling at the beads for a company downtown. He'd been kind to Ma, giving her cups of coffee and biscuits. Scott looks awkward at this, and Darleene nonplussed. Mother and Father-in-law recently bought him a little Dodge Dart as a graduation gift, so he won't have to stand on corners waiting for buses on the campus, especially in the winter. Scott wishes it was a bigger model, a four-door sedan; he complains that the Dart is like a matchbox. (Thankfully Aidan does not say "You're lucky to get it at all. I had to walk.") The bead chains are firmly entrenched in Aidan's consciousness; they made him a socialist.

"Well, Ma and Daddy have more money now. They pay for everything," Scott mumbles apologetically. He's never thought about Aidan working low-paying jobs as a teenager when they first immigrated. He was just a kid at the time.

"It's not your fault; it's the luck of the draw," I say quickly, wanting peace between them. I like Scott and Darleene. We're in-laws, belonging to each other now. I realize that Mother must have understood this from the beginning—that these in-laws are hers too. I admire Darl's ring again, grateful for the diversion. The cuts are healed on my face and there's only a slight bruise left over my eye. I don't want Aidan to tell them about the attack, but of course he does, giving me a quick defiant look. ("Why shouldn't they know?" he'd argued on the way in the car. Because....)

"*Really?*" says Scott. "*Stoned?*" Darleene gasps, which makes it worse. It sounds like something from the Old Testament, a condemned woman stoned to death. "Well, maybe it's not that serious," says Darleene tactfully.

"It only happened the once," I hedge.

"Well, you were crying," says Aidan, and I flush, feeling betrayed. I quickly light up another du Maurier and puff in agitation, trying to cover up my embarrassment. I frown a warning at him, which he pretends not to understand. (Sometimes Aidan's super-honesty feels more like an ambush. I know he's in favour of always telling the truth over taking hurt feelings into account, but at times it's too much.)

Curls of smoke drift past Cary Grant. Outside the window, the sun is violet and a swathe of shadow passes down the street, which is dun-coloured monochrome. "This is Main

Street Ontario," I say to no one in particular: one long line of billboards, awnings striped and faded, a barber shop, one other restaurant in a brown building, a ladies' hair salon, and the Dempsey Brothers hardware store on the corner of Sheppard that's been there since the year dot. A neon sign glows at Chancey Funeral Home on the other side, where Aunt Clarice had lain in her coffin. She'd always laughed at Canadian funeral parlours, so different to English ones; "mausoleums" she'd called them. "Then she ended up in one," Uncle Clive had said wryly. His humour had been macabre, to say the least. We were standing around in the deserted visitation room that smelled of wax and faded flowers and the dead; the children were half-asleep in a pew. The coffin was on a dais with Aunt Clarice inside. Her head had poked out of red crushed velvet, unrecognizable, features sculpted smooth as alabaster. Her nose was not her nose; her lips had been sealed. The place was empty and echoing, dim lamps inset along the walls. The Harrows hadn't been long enough in Canada before the accident—a mere summer—for any neighbours to know them, and it was Christmas. Then a dark middle-aged woman had shuffled in; she was wearing a sensible cloth coat and her frizzy black hair pushed out of her woolen hat. She was accompanied by a young man, equally dark, with a hypnotic gaze. "We're your neighbours from across the street, on Violet Avenue," he said. "I'm Aidan Gilmor, and this is my mother, Mildred. We're sorry for your loss, Mr. Harrow." Then Mildred Gilmor spoke up: "I went to typing class with Clarice in the fall. She was a very nice person."

Afterwards we'd stepped out into the winter, onto a bleak stretch of Yonge Street with the shops closed early. Christmas lights were swinging in the wintry wind, and snow was blowing in drifts against the sidewalks in the dusk. But it had happened. I'd met the man I was going to marry.

Darleene, listening, nods with a knowing smile. "Absolutely," she agrees. I hadn't hesitated to go to the movies with Aidan the next evening, even though the funeral was the following day.

Aidan recalls the facts. "The movie was *After the Fox*, a comedy starring Peter Sellers, and you never laughed once, Selena."

"Hey, that's when I had my first kiss!" cries Scottie, and he's so earnest that we can't help laughing.

Darleene looks gratified that he remembers. When she was in high school, she had her own room, like a little bedsitter, in the family basement. Her father put in a washroom down there for her, so it was self-contained, away from her mother. "Darleene did all the family cooking," Scott suddenly remembers. I don't ask why her mother didn't do it. ("It's obvious why," says Aidan later.)

"Other girls liked Scott." Darleene stresses this, perhaps trying to imply that she hadn't ended up with a nerd that no other girl wanted. It was grade twelve, and the students were pairing off, anxious to be "taken." "I had competition." She smiles. But he chose her.

"By the way, you look different, Aidan. I like your new hairstyle, it's neat."

Aidan looks self-conscious. "Selena made me brush it forward."

"He looked like Richard Nixon before, with his hair brushed backwards and glued down with vaseline." They laugh.

"And that new jacket," says Scott, admiringly. "You're cool, Aidan, at last."

"Well, Selena chose it, too." It's a lovely Harris tweed with velvet lapels and leather buttons—expensive. "My God! A bloody Englishman!" Father-in-law had cried when Aidan walked into the kitchen in his new togs, smoking a pipe. We all laugh again.

"But it's damn itchy."

I glance surreptitiously at Scott and Darleene. They are a "mixed" couple like Aidan and me, only not so noticeable. I never thought of it that way before. (Everything now is Before and After.) I wonder if Darleene has faced any sort of opposition from her family about the engagement. I hint at it subtly. "I guess your parents must really like Scott, Darleene."

Darleene sees through it at once. "Oh, they're not bothered by Scott's ... background," she says smoothly, giving me a quick knowing look of appraisal. "But our so-called friends sure are. Tell them, Scott."

"What's the big secret?" asks Aidan, suddenly curious.

Darleene makes a wry face. "Go on, Scott."

"About what?" he grumbles.

"Mike Lawson. *You* know."

"Oh, *him*. Some friend he turned out to be, damn racist...." Scott frowns. Perhaps he doesn't like admitting that he's not so white after all. He hedges.

"Oh?" Aidan looks interested. "You mean *you've* had racial problems?" he says disbelievingly, if bluntly. His fair-skinned all-Canadian brother?

"Well, you wouldn't *believe* what Mike Lawson said to me when I started dating Darleene in our last year of high school."

Mike Lawson lives at number 60 Violet Avenue, about four doors down from the Gilmors. Scott relates what he told Scott at graduation. "He said, 'You should be dating *your own kind*, Scott Gilmor, and leave our girls alone.'" Scott imitates Mike's petulant tone. "'Look at your older brother and that English girl, Selena. That's what happens.'"

Scott's face twists in chagrin. I feel a sick lurch. *Why can't people leave us alone?* He tries to laugh it off in front of Aidan, but the pain is evident. Aidan was always the one who had racial taunts directed at him. It was usually at the silly Catholic Church dances run by Italian fathers who didn't allow Black boys in. Later on, he was constantly teased at work, where his coworkers called him "Boy." Scott had managed to avoid all this, with his Canadian accent and olive complexion—he was Canadian, or so he'd thought.

"But what did you *say* to him, Scott?"

"I said, 'What the hell are you *talking* about, Mike? You, me, and Darl were in *grade school* together!'" Darleene grew up a few blocks away from Scott and Mike, on Park Street.

Scott and Darleene have instinctively kept this from Father and Mother-in-law, knowing it would hurt them. I agree, thinking that I certainly plan to keep the incident with the stones a secret, too, for I'm getting fond of them. Father and Mother-in-law really believe the neighbours like and accept them, and perhaps they do. Scott is the golden boy, in their eyes; he's the all-Canadian boy they're so proud of, the one who really blends into the neighbourhood. To them, his assimilation wipes out the colonial past, whatever that is.

"Well, I'm going to tell Ma and Daddy!" cries Aidan.

"No! Don't! Please, Aidan! Why make trouble?" I'm upset.

"They should know the truth!" Aidan purses his mouth, looking virtuous. He often needles his father, for some reason; there seems to be hidden antagonism there. He wants to expose the damn neighbours on Violet Avenue, and something deeper, perhaps: his parents' innocent trust and their annoying image of Scott as the Canadian son. That most of all.

"It's not your story to blab, Aidan," says Scott.

Darleene doesn't care. She's not as vulnerable as Scott and Aidan. This must be because she's a "real" Canadian, meaning she's Canadian-born, which counts for a lot. Mike Lawson will pass out of their lives. She's too excited at the prospect of the upcoming wedding and her First Communion to really let it matter. She's been converting to the Catholic faith this past year, as a catechumen, which means she's been learning the Sacraments of Initiation under the Rite of Christian Initiation of Adults. Her face flushes a pretty pink and her eyes sparkle. She wants to be close to Scott and to Mother-in-law, she says. Her parents, Jim and Mabel Kingsley, are getting a divorce, and I wonder if that has influenced her.

"Well, you'll have the backing of all the saints and angels of St. Raphael of All Angels behind you," I quip, but only Aidan laughs. Scott and Darleene take the Church very seriously. Usually the confirmation of new communicants is at Easter, but Darleene has special indemnity from Father Matthew to be accepted into the Church during the wedding ceremony. She hopes to model herself on Mother-in-law, she confides. She admires her stoicism in dealing with Father-in-law, who is, undeniably, a bit of a curmudgeon.

Darleene has taken a saint's name for her first communion, as is the custom, though it is voluntary. You take the name of a Catholic saint, she explains, waving her cigarette. She's chosen Teresa after gentle Teresa of the Little Flowers. I look at solid feisty Darleene with new interest; her choice tells me something about how she sees herself. Now she'll be bound to the ancient Roman Catholic Church that goes back to Constantine the Great. She's happy to share her saint's name, but she won't divulge the style of the wedding dress or the veil. "You'll have to wait and see," she says.

She and her mother have been looking at wedding dresses all year. They went to various couturiers and a store called Bridal Collections in Willowdale. "You have to book your dress early," she explains gravely. "You wouldn't believe."

I think about Darleene's wedding dress and bridal veil, secreted away under wraps in her closet, only her mother is allowed to see until The Day, The Moment. (Weddings and betrothals are bizarre rituals when you think about it; ancient rituals revolving around claiming ownership of young females.)

"Are you nervous?"

"Who, me? About getting married? No, but Scott is."

"Me nervous? I'm damn well terrified," says Scott, and we all laugh.

(You slip the gold band over your finger and you are different, different, forever and ever, you can never go back....)

5.

THE CHURCH SMELLED OF FLOWERS and incense and candles. "This is an important day for Darleene," Mother-in-law said. "She's also becoming a Catholic."

Father-in-law's younger cousin, Colin, had come from Listowel. He'd immigrated the same time as Felix, and had married a Canadian woman, Doreen, from southwest Ontario, old pioneer stock. They stood in the pew with their two children—another "mixed" marriage, as people call it, that I could observe, I thought, feeling a twinge of expectation. The wedding provided another opportunity for me to view new relatives. But this thought was soon overshadowed as the organ plunged into a chord and Darleene came shimmering down the nave in a white organza dress and a lace cap. "Aah!" everyone breathed, satisfied. She and Scott knelt before the altar, and Father Matthew made the sign of the cross, starting at his lips, the way Catholics do. He was a pale, fair-haired youngish priest, with a saintly sort of expression. At some point during the mass that followed the ceremony, a young acolyte rang a bell three times in the sanctuary as Darleene, "Little Teresa of the Flowers," took her first communion. Father-in-law began to sob, overcome with emotion. "Shh, pet, no need of sobbing," said Mother-in-law.

"Superstitious witchcraft," Aidan muttered, but not so loud as to spoil it.

The reception was held in the Gilmors' garden, since Darleene's parents were still in the process of divorce and selling their house. ("Bloody fools," muttered Father-in-law). He had set up a grand marquis in the back, and hired a Scottish bagpiper to march up and down, inexplicably playing "The Bluebells of Scotland."

Oh where, tell me where, has your Highland laddie gone?
He's gone with streaming banners where noble deeds are done
And it's oh, in my heart I wish him safe at home.

"*Aiyo,* what for bagpipes, Jack, pet? And why 'Bluebells of Scotland?'" Mother-in-law had chided, worried about the neighbours and the sound of the pipes wailing like a banshee over the hedge.

"To hell with the neighbours!"

Scott had objected to the Union Jack, so Father-in-law had taken it down. "Darleene's *Canadian,* Daddy!" Instead, an old Ontario ensign he'd gotten from somewhere held pride of place to satisfy Darleene's family, who were old conservative Ontario blue. The aunts were dressed in stodgy suits and bulbous hats, very Presbyterian. Father-in-law went about all afternoon, boasting, "My son has married a *real* Canadian!"

Colin, the younger cousin, is in his forties and much admired by the family. He certainly is handsome; he reminds me of Jawaharlal Nehru of India. (I wished Mother could have seen him.) He is intelligent and apparently used to take all the prizes at Holy Innocents School. He walked away with the English prize, the oratory medal, and he even gave the Latin oration. He was a favourite of the priests. Here in Canada, he is a chartered accountant with a big firm in Waterloo. He stood smiling, amused, next to Doreen, a heavy formidable woman, who looked as if she wished she were back in Listowel. Their two children, a boy and a girl, followed a pattern, I noted: one brown child and one fair, like Fiona's children.

The greatest shock was Lally, Mother-in-law's youngest sister, the only one from the Goonesekere side of the family who was present. Nothing had prepared me for the confusing racial difference between my mother-in-law and her sister. Mother-in-law was solid and stocky with a swarthy complexion, and comported herself with great dignity. Lally was small-boned, tiny like a little bird, her complexion was lighter and smooth as velvet, and her eyes were large and eloquent. Yet, they were sisters. She wore her black hair flowing to her waist. "Jan says he likes it long," she said, laughing merrily. Jan Weider, a solid Pole, had turned up wearing German hosen. ("Honestly!" cried Fiona.) Lally gave me a hug and a beautiful big smile. "*Aiyo,* Aidan's English wife!"

Their five children dominated the afternoon. Each one varied in colour, from dark eleven-year-old Suzanna to pale Alexander, age two. They seemed to fill the garden. Or was that because there were so many of them? The five Weiders ran uninhibited around the trees, and in and out of the bushes, playing tag. "Mind the bloody flowers, you kids," yelled Father-in-law, knocking back another whisky. ("Pet, pet, think of your liver.")

In contrast, Fiona's two children were shy and polite, calling their German father "Papa." Deiter seemed a nice man; it was a shame they'd separated, I thought. He and Fiona made a ravishing couple, with her dark Sinhalese beauty and his blond Teutonic looks. Quite breathtaking. (A reflection of Aidan and me, perhaps? Was that how people looked at us, too? As a dynamic mixing of the races?) Of their two children, Heidi was brown-skinned, and Hans was fair. The same racial pattern had emerged again. I couldn't help thinking of Mother and her warnings about genetics: "You don't know what you'll get in a mixed marriage, Selena." I had to admit Mother was right in this respect. One brown child, one fair—those seemed to be the odds. But why did it matter, really? (That was when Mother had said, "Of course it matters! What's got *in* to you,

Selena?") But when I realized that I would love whatever came, and it was simply natural, it was all right.

The evening began to wane. Scott and Darleene were given a round of applause. The sun sank behind the cedar hedge. Father-in-law got drunk with the bagpiper and lay passed out under the apple tree. *"Aiyo-o...."*

Now, Fiona and Aidan laugh and joke about the wedding and the collection of family characters. They love making fun of them. We're sitting in Fiona's dining room in her house in Richmond Hill, sipping Riesling. The table is laden with various German dishes, including *sauerbraten* and *Kartoffelkloesse* with real sour cream, as promised.

"Did you *see* Darleene's mother? Tipsy as hell, like Daddy. They make a pair!" chortles Fiona. Mabel Kingsley had swayed around the garden singing "Where oh where has my Highland laddie gone?" But I'd felt sorry for Mrs. Kingsley, who hadn't realized that people were laughing at her. "Oh, she's crazy!" Fiona cries dismissively.

"I like her," I say. "I like her zaniness." She knew all the movie stars going back to 1920. Her favourites were Katharine Hepburn and Humphrey Bogart in *African Queen.* I consider how different mother and daughter are. Darleene is stoic, solid, and practical, which must be why she's drawn to Mother-in-law.

I continue to learn more about my new family. "We visited Lally and Jan last weekend," I say, cautiously.

"Wha-a-t? You went to that hole? It's full of drugs."

"Lally told us a lot about the family that I never knew," says Aidan thoughtfully.

"Ughh. Ceylon is over in my life. Who cares a hoot over here about that crazy place? And Daddy's crazy too, always tuning in to *Voice of Ceylon*! I don't want to even *think* about Sinhalese and Tamils and their stupid riots. And Lally's a nincompoop marrying a Polack, even if he does think he's German."

"Poor Lally," smiles Aidan, "Granpa Delaney used to call her a simpleton, remember? He said she smiled too much."

I rather liked Lally and her family. True, their neighourhood north of Jane and Finch left much to be desired. Rows of new utilitarian cement-like blocks stretched to the horizon "like Tamil coolie lines," Aidan had observed. Coolie lines were what Tamil labourers lived in on the tea estates.

Lally's children had been playing outside at a beat-up play-ground belonging to the government housing co-op. They came running towards us as soon as they spotted Aidan, little Alexander toddling after them on chubby legs. They blended in with the neighourhood children, various West Indians from the islands or Canadian-born East Indians. Some of the girls were in flimsy saris, shawls fluttering around their heads. Lally's children had only stood out at the party because they'd been amongst predominantly white guests, I realized—just as they would in the Beaches. I imagined myself in a remote Indian village in Uttar Pradesh or in a back alley in Calcutta, and pictured how my whiteness would stand out in contrast. (Why was it different?)

"Auntie Selena, can I see your ring? Oh, it's beautiful! See Ma?" Eleven-year-old Sophie had grasped my hand as we sat on the sofa in the small cozy living room. "That means you belong to Aidan now and you can have babies together," she said artfully and somewhat precociously. "*Aiyo*, Sophie!" Lally chortled.

The diamond engagement ring and gold wedding band flashed in the light.

I turn to Fiona who's filling our glasses again—"Drink! Drink!"—and I say slowly, "Lally told us that Aidan's grand-mother, the one you called Amma in Ceylon, died after the birth of her last baby." Mother-in-law had been only fifteen years old at the time, and little Lally three. Later, Lally had gone to live at Weyweltalawa with Mildred and Jack after they married. "She said Amma had eight children, that she was locked up in Angoda, and that she died there." Hearing Lally speak, I knew at once that Angoda was some terrible place where terrible things happened. It was only later that I learned that it was the lunatic asylum in Ceylon. How was I to know I was hurtling a bomb into Fiona's dining room?

"Oh, my God! Lally told you *that*?" shrieks Fiona, highly vexed. "What did she tell you that for, the ninny?"

"Why was Amma sent there?" I turn to Aidan, who's looking uncomfortable. I have to ask; I have to know the truth about his Sinhalese grandmother, Amma. She was Mother-in-law's mother on the Goonesekere side. "Was she ... insane?" (I can imagine Mother's blood pressure, hear her remonstrations. "Well, they certainly kept *that* from you, Selena.")

Perhaps Fiona is right, and Ceylon is a murky, secret place of darkness, despite the images of bright parrots in jungle tree-tops and sacred sun-gilded mountains.

"Well, not exactly insane. She *went* insane." Aidan hesitates. Of course, there's a difference. "She became sort of like ... schizophrenic ... as far as I know. It all happened before I was born...." Aidan falls silent, embarrassed.

"They thought she'd kill the baby. She was attacking it— that's what I heard Granny say. I was only a little toddler, but I heard. They persuaded Granpa Delaney to send her to Angoda," says Fiona, in her forthright way. It was as though she was saying, *You may as well know everything—you're family now.* "Well, it's primitive over there, Selena. What d'you expect in a backward place like Ceylon?" Fiona shrugs.

I sip my wine cautiously. It sounds as if Amma had suffered from post-partum depression, treatable today with drugs. And yes, I understand how poverty and ignorance could lead a village woman into an over-crowded Third World mental ward, to suffer terrifying psychiatric treatments, chained to an iron bed—a destiny of hell. Because she'd had too many children in too quick succession. I think quickly. "Did anyone visit her?"

Fiona looks shocked. "God, no, I wouldn't think so. Mental illness brings shame on a family; the Sinhalese try to keep it quiet. Old Granny, that's Daddy's mother, said it was a break-down or something. Well, she was only thirteen when she married Grandpa." Aidan looks shocked and Fiona smirks. So Mother-in-law's mother, a Sinhalese village girl, had likely had her first baby at the age of thirteen or fourteen, and had died before age thirty after her eighth child, most likely from the shock to her system. I try to hide my dismay.

"Ma never likes to talk about these things. Remember when she thrashed Lally, Aidan?"

Mother-in-law thrashing her younger sister? I try to look calm. It puts Mother-in-law in a new light. She always seems so self-possessed and just. *But thrashing people? Sweet Lally?*

"Oh yes." Fiona turns to me, seeing my expression. "That's Ma for you. She isn't all she appears to be, Selena."

"Ohhh...." Aidan buries his face in his hands. "Don't remind me, Fiona. I still feel so bad about it."

"It was over a Sinhalese boy who liked Lally. He worked at the railway station in the mornings, where we caught the train to school—at Nawalapitya, you remember. Aidan saw them together, and then he, just a chubby little boy then, had run eagerly to Ma and told her everything as soon as he got home."

"I was a real little blabber-mouth," he says and sighs. "And then Ma beat Lally. I was begging her to stop, I was so upset. I was only six or so."

"She was mad because he was Sinhalese," says Fiona. "And rightfully so!"

"Oh, Fiona."

"Well, it's true, Aidan. She wanted better for Lally: a Eur-asian, a tea planter, one of us."

Aidan looks embarrassed. Then he galvanizes himself. "Thanks to the British," he says bitterly. "They made us ashamed of our Sinhalese blood." He glares at me.

I'm responsible in some vaguely related way, I suppose, as an Englishwoman, though I think it's ridiculous.

Fiona gives a sharp laugh. "I'm going to live my own life," she cries. "No one, not Ma or Daddy is going to tell me what to do." The divorce from Deiter is nearly settled. Now she can have friends over for dinner, go out to dances, and socialize, which Deiter always discouraged.

Heidi and Hans come in from the garden. Fiona had had children right away, one after the other, but had stopped at two. "I didn't want to end up like Lally, overridden with kids," she says in front of them.

"Did you bring Bosie, Uncle Aidan?" cries Hans.

"Sorry. Next time. You can come for a visit and take him for a walk."

Hans wants hot dogs and ketchup, or Kraft dinner. "See! I have the best German food and Hans will only eat hot dogs and ketchup, just like Scottie," cries Fiona. "Go back out in the garden to play after you finish, you two. And feed Mopsy in her hutch, Heidi."

"Can we have Mikey over?"

"Yes, sure. Now, eat, eat."

Fiona lives in the modern brick bungalow that Deiter bought when they first married. It had been a new subdivision in old Richmond Hill, built with young married couples in mind, back in the 1950s. Deiter had supplied the down payment with help from his family in Germany. I look around appreciatively. There's a large airy living room painted cream, with a big picture window, and a large "eat-in" kitchen in the Canadian open-concept style so different from closed-in British houses. On the wall is a hanging of a tamarind tree that Fiona had embroidered when she was a girl in Kandy Convent.

"It's lovely, Fiona!" I exclaim. "I like your German dirndl, too, by the way," I add. It's a relief to change the subject from disturbing family history.

"I got it in Germany years ago, on my honeymoon."

"Did you ever wear a sari, in Ceylon?" I'm curious.

"*Never.*" I'm concerned I've offended her in some way. She stresses with pride. "Daddy always bought us the best imported English clothes. Ma sometimes wore a sari to the club when the Sinhalese wives were there. But Daddy stopped Ma from wearing a sari in Canada." The neighbours had apparently been transfixed when Mother-in-law put on a sari one day and swayed down the driveway on Violet Avenue. "These foreign immigrants bringing down the tone of the street," Fiona gives a mocking imitation.

Deiter had been the tall, blond, blue-eyed, handsome European that Fiona had dreamed of marrying back in the convent. (According to Lally, Fiona always said she'd marry a white man. No Sinhalese for her. "But don't tell her I told you so," Lally had giggled. "Fiona's crazy.")

I wonder what Fiona's German in-laws had thought of her; I wonder how they felt about having a Eurasian daughter-in-law.

Aidan tells us that Deiter had once confided to him that Fiona had been quite different at first. She had seemed like a sweet submissive Asian girl, convent-educated. And then ... *Blitzkreig*!

Fiona gives a screech of laughter. "He said that? Oh, that's Deiter for you. He's all screwed up. I'm so glad it's over!" she cries.

The mournful self-pity of Deiter, this white man who'd obviously turned to her in need, was something she rejected vehemently with all the force of her Gilmor nature. "Ughh, he was always crying that no one liked him because he was German! I couldn't stand it." He hadn't turned out to be the superior, self-assured colonial type she'd so admired in Ceylon, the *periya dorai* with a fine horse and riding whip. "Oh, Deiter's a wimp, underneath."

"Well, it's not his fault about the war, Fiona," I say. "Deiter would have only been about two or three." (Like myself, though on the British side of the water. We were both war babies.) "I'm sure Germans were discriminated against and disliked in Canada after the war."

"Ughh! His family were Nazis! They had a swastika in the cellar. They still celebrate the Fuhrer's birthday—'Mein Fuhrer!'" she giggles. "I could tell you!"

She'll never go back to him; she's emphatic. It's over. "I'm a single parent now." She has two part-time jobs to keep her going. She intends to take Bookkeeping 1 at the Community College in the fall. She'd get a good job when she finished. "Just you wait and see."

There's something vigorous and brave about Fiona. She set her face to the wind. She would remake her life. For a moment, her eyes stare hard into the future as if looking directly into the face of truth. "Ach! Men," cries Fiona. "They're all the same, whether they're in a pinstripe suit or a sarong." A pained look crosses Fiona's derisive face and her lip quivers. "Oh, I don't care!" she cries, with a bravado that doesn't deceive anyone. "I'm having fun with Renata."

Renata is a new friend at her workplace, a divorcée from South America. She and Fiona go to the dance-halls and clubs together on the weekends while Mrs. Meyer, her next-door neighbour, looks after the kids. "Oh, we have fun!" Of course, Fiona is always being misconstrued by men. "They can't figure me out. They call me *chi chi*," she says bitterly. It sounds like a racial word, of racist intent, a specific code I've never heard in the small enclosed world where I grew up.

"Daddy wasn't always like this, Selena—fat and drunken, living in that squishy horrid bungalow in Willowdale," she says. "He was very high class. You wouldn't believe."

Yet his status means nothing here. "It's useless to say at a dance that my father was once *periya dorai* of a big tea estate," she fumes. "Men always take me for *Philippino!*"

"Actually, I hardly knew Daddy as a father—not the way Canadian kids know their dads over here," says Aidan; he too sounds bitter.

"I hardly knew Ma, either. I was sent to Kandy Convent at age four." She's gratified that I'm shocked. Sent to boarding school at *four?*

Aidan nods in agreement. His face has a pained, scrunched-up look. The conversation has suddenly shifted to something else.

As always, we return to Weyweltalawa and Madeniya, to the scenes of Father-in-law's bygone glory on the tea estates. But something had happened to that old colonial world when they came to Canada, something irrevocable. There was a sharp divide between how Fiona and Aidan had felt about their father in Ceylon, and how they came to feel about him in Canada. "Remember how *terrified* Daddy was of the furnace in the basement, that first winter?" Fiona screams with laughter.

That she dares mock Father-in-law.... I'm aghast.

But Aidan is chuckling, too. "Oh, my God, yes!"

"He thought it was a monster. It started up in the middle of the night, Selena—I think it was late October. The temperature outside had dropped below zero, only Daddy didn't know that, coming from the tropics."

Father and Mother-in-law crouched in wonder and terror, staring at the Thing in the corner of the basement, its huge metal tentacles shuddering and growling. There was an inexplicable smell of oil. Suddenly a roar and heat. "What the hell *is* it, Mildred pet?" Their father was frightened—it was incomprehensible. "Stand back, you kids!" Father-in-law peered cautiously at the steel octopus that suddenly shuddered again, the metal tentacles giving loud creaks. "Run, pet. It might explode."

Father-in-law called 911. In a matter of minutes, three police cruisers and a fire truck had roared up Violet Avenue, sirens blaring, followed by an ambulance with blinking red lights illuminating the houses and awakening the neighbours. They crowded outside on the road in silence, staring at number 80 and at Mr. Gilmor running around in his pyjamas.

"It's just your furnace, sir," said the fire constable. "It comes on in the fall. Are you the new occupants? Likely the real estate agent ordered a tank of oil for you. You'll get the bill in the mail."

Fiona and Aidan are rocking with mirth. Tears stream down Aidan's face, he's laughing so hard. "Poor Daddy. He was so naïve."

6.

O F COURSE, IT GOES WITHOUT SAYING that I'd never let on
to Father-in-law that his English daughter-in-law knows
all about the crazy furnace story and other humiliations. He'd
certainly feel shame, the once proud *periya dorai*. How he'd
broken down and wept, for instance, that first winter in Toronto
in 1956. His moustache froze, and a little row of icicles hung
down over his lip. Aidan remembers Father-in-law's fingers,
raw, red, and bleeding, swollen in painful lumps, unaccustomed
to minus twenty degrees Celsius. Fall had suddenly turned to
winter on Violet Avenue. Deep snow drifts appeared in the
driveway that Father-in-law had to dig out before backing out
his car to go to work in the morning, numbed to the bone. At
night, the two boys, Aidan and Scottie, squished together in
the little back bedroom, listening in wonder to Daddy's muffled sobs through the thin wall, as Ma said, "They're called
chilblains, pet. You have to wear *fur-lined gloves* in Canada."

What the hell had he done coming to this frozen bloody country? He mourned his life in the tropics. In Ceylon, the tamarind
trees were in blossom at Madeniya—a mass of violet-pink in
front of the estate bungalow—and cockatoos were swinging in
the bamboos. No one had told him about winter in Toronto.
Even more of a shock for the boys, cowering under their blankets, was Daddy sobbing that maybe they *should go back to
Ceylon* and take their chances with the new government, even
though he would lose face before the relatives. And then Ma,

to the boys' astonishment, hissed fiercely that if he went back, he went alone: she liked Canada, and she knew it was best for the children. "Look how well Aidan is doing in school."

Father-in-law seems to have suffered more of a shock than Mother-in-law as an immigrant. He'd gone through a personal revolution. One of his first jobs was at Steeles Company in Long Branch, miles from Willowdale. It was an hour's drive each way. It was a large factory that employed hundreds of people making parts for Avro Arrow planes for the United States, a big contract. He'd been lucky to get the job, a menial, junior position in the accounting department—the accounting skills he had gained as a tea planter in Ceylon had paid off.

Then he lost his job. Father-in-law had been shocked, ashamed to go home. The conservative prime minister, John Diefenbaker—Dief the Chief—had cancelled the Avro Arrow contract, apparently because of complications in financing. "Damn fool." Father-in-law had turned to his bottle of Black and White, which he stashed away in the garage behind tins of turpentine, and vowed to vote NDP from then on. This was not like losing his job as manager of a tea plantation, where his high position and the old tea planters' network had compensated him with an even better position overnight. He was now put on something called Unemployment Insurance—the "dole" in Britain. He'd had to line up with other men at a desolate office on Jarvis Street, in downtown Toronto—"As if I were some bloody coolie on the plantation," he'd grumbled to Mother-in-law. Some of the men were obviously drifters who had been out of work for a long time. They'd looked thin and hungry; they wore threadbare clothes and broken running shoes, and they lived in hostels.

Then Father-in-law had had his big chance: a government job in accounts for Ontario Hydro. A pension plan and a subscription to Blue Cross health plan was included. It wasn't an important position or terribly well-paying, but he was grateful, happy; he donated a portion of his first paycheque to St. Raphael of All Angels. "Always try to get a government job," he stressed to his bewildered children. "Security is better than a show-off salary." This from their former wasteful *pukkah* father of Ceylon?

"After his first day on the new job at Hydro, Daddy returned in shock," recalls Aidan, amused but rueful. We are snuggled up in bed, reminiscing about a past that I feel increasingly closer to. It means something for my marriage, for my understanding of my father-in-law. "Poor Daddy." On his first day, Father-in-law had politely said "Sir" to his boss, Mr. George Harasti, whom he was shocked to discover was no upper-class Englishman but a Hungarian immigrant from the 1956 revolution. He said, "Yes, Mr. Harasti, sir," and "No, sir," as in Ceylon.

Mr. Harasti soon put him straight. "What is all this 'sir' crap, Jack? Cut it out, you're in Canada now, not Buckingham Palace."

Father-in-law felt wounded. What had he done wrong? He observed, shocked, that his co-workers called Mr. Harasti "George." Father-in-law still identified with the great British Empire, but no one here gave a fuck. He laughed and cried back home in his humble Willowdale bungalow. "What have I believed in all my life, pet?"

There were all sorts of people in the office—Ukrainians, Poles, Lithuanians, Germans—and all sorts of languages. He began to recognize the harsh *zsch* sound of Polish and Ukrainian, and the clipped, clear, sometimes rough consonants of the Germans—"*Ach!*" His mind whirled. He hung on to his British tailored suits, his English leather shoes that pinched, his colonial accent, the Union Jack. "What the fuck, man? The British Empire? We had empires too. The Austro-Hungarian Empire, the Ottoman Empire," boasted a Turk from senior accounts. "We ruled Palestine first."

No one rose to attention to the strains of "God Save the Queen." No one listened to Her Majesty's message to the British people and the Commonwealth on Christmas Day. Everyone said that Canada should be a republic like the United States.

He couldn't understand the jokes. "Know what FIAT stands for? Fix-it-again-Tony." His colleagues chortled with amusement at their desks. "Hey, what do Italians shout when there's a fire? 'CONCRE-EE-TE!'" (It seemed when the bags of concrete arrive at a factory, the foreman shouts "concrete!" and the men run to work.) More mystifying laughter. Father-in-law managed a weak smile. He had no idea that Italians had built a concrete factory on Yonge Street in Willowdale in the fifties and brought in hundreds of poor immigrant Italian workers as indentured labourers, paying them peanuts. He didn't know that they controlled the construction industry. He didn't know anything.

But the greatest shock that first winter was the British car he bought, a second-hand Standard 8. In Ceylon, the Standard had been essential for tea planters driving around the hilly estates, where its steady reliable performance was renowned: "The British make the best bloody cars, no bones about it." Now the Standard wouldn't start in minus ten degrees. The bloody thing stalled in the driveway before he even backed out, broke down constantly in blizzards and white-outs, and skidded horribly on Toronto's icy roads.

"What the fuck are you driving that English shit-box for? Get yourself an American car for Chrissakes!" the men in accounts would cry. Feeling like he was letting down the English side, he traded in the Standard for a new, big American Chevrolet. It started right away in the morning, even at twenty below zero. He still couldn't believe he was living with temperatures below zero.

That first spring, Father-in-law was shocked to see white men digging and patching the roads in Toronto, like Tamil labourers. It almost hurt to see his former colonial masters bared to the waist, their pale chests and backs glistening with sweat as they dug cheerfully through the surfaces with picks, drilled through concrete, and lay tarmac like navvies. They sat unashamed on the curbs, next to Italian labourers, eating huge sandwiches and gulping something out of flasks, grinning at young white girls walking half-naked down the sidewalks to work—another shock. These girls were dolled up in tight skirts called "minis" that went down to just below their buttocks. He'd seen young Sinhalese and Tamil prostitutes on the back streets of Colombo, around Slave Island, but these were *white,* respectable working girls and women. No one seemed to notice or care. Mildred's skirts were a modest length at mid-calf.

Father-in-law stood swaying, whisky in hand, as an electricians' van parked in his driveway one Saturday morning. The company, We Light Up Your Life—had sent a young woman to fix some faulty wiring in the basement. She stood before Father-in-law, a thick leather band girding her waist bulging with tools, detector in hand, wires across her shoulders, smiling with confidence. "Hi there, I'm Heather." Father-in-law gaped at her as though she were a Martian that had descended through the willow.

"*Aiyo!* See, pet! I am telling you, women here can do anything. And see how young! She has been to technical college, got her papers."

"Well, as long as she doesn't bloody well blow up the house."

But it went deeper than that. Suddenly, in Toronto, the family had found themselves crammed together at close quarters in a small bungalow they couldn't escape. Father-in-law had cashed his Ceylon life insurance policy to come to Canada, using all the money for the down payment on the house.

They settled in to face each other for the first time.

Where were the servants? Fiona and Aidan recall watching Daddy having to pull on his own socks and polish his own boots. Daddy had to carry in bags of groceries himself from Knob Hill Farms, like a house servant. Ma was happy, grateful. "This is our own Canadian home, pet." They'd lived in grand bungalows on the vast tea estates in Ceylon, but it occurred to Aidan for the first time that Ma and Daddy had never actually owned any of them, not a stick of furniture. The Willowdale bungalow was the size of the old *kanake pulle*'s thatched house at Weyweltalawa, but it was theirs, said Ma. It had three small bedrooms the size of servants' quarters, a living room, and a kitchen. There was no dining room. No large netted verandah to keep out the mosquitoes, giant night moths, and bats at dusk. No stable or aviary. Daddy had always kept a collection of birds—cockatiels, a parrot, and peacocks—at Weyweltalawa and Madeniya. In the Willowdale bungalow there was one small bathroom they all shared. In Madeniya each bedroom had had its own enormous adjoining bathroom. And where was house servant to run their baths?

"You'll have to run your own bloody bath from now on," growled Father-in-law.

The children got on Father-in-law's nerves; they were under his feet all day until they went to school. He wasn't used to it, and they weren't used to him being around either. In Madeniya, he would depart for the nurseries at six in the morning, return in the mid-afternoon, take a shower, and then retire for his mid-day siesta. They had not dared speak to him or interrupt him. Now Daddy had to be at work all day, from eight in the morning to six in the evening, like a Tamil labourer. The two boys had to walk to school like other Canadian children. They did not need to be driven to boarding school—Daddy could not afford the fees now. They had to attend the free local government school like everyone else. None of the kids on Violet Avenue went to boarding school.

I try to understand how this issue of boarding school came to be such a sore point for Fiona and Aidan. They seem united in a deep-seated resentment about it, a burden that Scottie is free of. "He only went for one term!" they cry. Scottie got the best end of the stick there too. Mother-in-law held on to him as long as possible, keeping him with her on Madeniya until he was seven years old. (Aidan is very bitter and jealous about this. I try to grasp the loss he felt, but it's not the sort of thing one can talk about.)

So I'm shocked when, one Saturday, Fiona turns on Mother-in-law in the kitchen. She'd taken her shopping at Knob Hill Farms—"Better than that dirty Indian place she goes to!" Fiona disapproves of much of what Mother-in-law does and is embarrassed that Mother-in-law looks for cheap bargains like second-day bread and brown bananas. Nevertheless, she comes to Willowdale faithfully every Saturday to take Ma shopping, as a dutiful daughter. Then she accuses her mother of desertion.

"Yes, Ma! Desertion! I actually knew Sister Veronica better than you, as a kid. You're *still* a stranger to me—we just don't relate!"

Lately, Fiona has been reading psychology books about re-living personal trauma and alienation. Mother-in-law looks bewildered but quickly regains control and says evenly, "What is this silly talk, Fiona? That was thirty years ago. There is nothing wrong with you."

Aidan looks amused, sipping a beer, and keeping out of it for now. I concentrate on patting Tabby, the family cat, and rubbing her back.

"*You sent me away to that convent when I was only four!*" screams Fiona.

"What is Babsey-girl gurgling about now?" Father-in-law shuffles into the kitchen looking the worse for wear after a restless night, his belly bloated. ("If you drank less, pet.")

"Fiona says you sent her away at age four to the convent and traumatized her." Aidan smirks. For some reason, he likes to get at Father-in-law. I'm concerned.

"Ugh. That's how it was then, Babsey. How else would you have gotten an education up in those mountains? From the bloody monkeys?" grunts Father-in-law.

"Everyone went away for schooling, Fiona. Your daddy and I did before you, and Aidan and Scottie too—not just you," says Mother-in-law in her sensible way. Fiona ignores this; she doesn't like facts.

"I'm reading *psychology,* Daddy! *Woman Divided* says I'm cut off from my mother! That's what's *wrong* with me! *Sending me to that convent*!" She lets out a shrill and challenging scream, and Tabby leaps from my lap.

Father-in-law gapes. "Cut off? What the bloody hell is she talking about?"

"Oh, you just don't *get* it!" Fiona fumes at Father-in-law, who blinks in bewilderment.

"Fiona, you are a fine human being. Look how you are coping as a single parent with the children," says Mother-in-law patiently, even though she highly disapproves of Fiona's status from a Catholic point of view. She has discussed her daughter's situation at length with Father Matthew. Fiona's eyes suddenly fill with tears. "Oh, what's the point?"

"Good God. What is Babsey whacking her head against the window for, pet?"

"You see!" Fiona gesticulates to us. "Hopeless!"

Aidan grins, sympathetic to Fiona but really enjoying the scene.

"That's the bloody trouble with women reading books," Father-in-law grumbles.

The real change in the family circumstances happened when Mother-in-law finally got a good job as a counsellor at the Mental Retardation Centre in Toronto. It was certainly a step up from making bead chains in a basement. "A government job," boasted Father-in-law. It came with a pension like his and health benefits, thanks to the NDP.

She had to take night school courses in nursing to qualify, which meant that Father-in-law had to look after Scottie and oversee bedtime. (Fiona had left by then, having married Deiter at nineteen.) Aidan recalls Father-in-law: Now he was a bloody *ayah*, he'd grumbled, taking down a bottle of Scotch. "Jack, pet, you are not planning on drinking that in front of Scottie? Think of the example you're setting that child, in your new country."

"What am I, a bloody saint?"

"No saint, pet. A saint you are not."

"Ughh."

He switched off Scottie's light at bedtime. "Cleaned your bloody teeth, son? Okay, good night."

After a long day's work, Mother-in-law had to ride the subway home and, once home, she had to cook supper. Then on weekends, she had to vacuum, do laundry, scrub the kitchen, and wax and polish the parquet floors on her hands and knees, like former house servant number one at Weyweltalawa. She even cleaned the stained toilet bowl with a brush and Sani-Flush. "Now I am a *varsi vannu* as well." Meaning "shit-cleaner"— the lowest caste in Ceylon. This task was always relegated to the poorest Tamils.

"What the hell are you doing on your knees with a bloody scrubbing brush, pet?" screamed Father-in-law.

Mother-in-law looked up, her mouth twitching sardonically. Every married woman here in Canada did *dhobi* work—it was part of being a wife and mother—and apparently did not complain.

"It is good for me to experience all this, Jack pet, otherwise how else would I ever have known?" (What it was to be a servant. And what kind of mistress she herself had once been in Ceylon?)

If Father-in-law looked dazed it was because he'd had no idea what awaited them in Canada—his wife Mildred on her hands and knees with a bucket of slosh, servant number one. What the hell would he tell the relatives back home in Ceylon, and in Australia?

England did not disappoint. In the autumn of 1956, on their way to Canada, the family sailed across the Indian Ocean, up the Suez Canal, across the Mediterranean and the English Channel, and berthed at Tilbury Docks.

"Oh, they loved London, and England. We all did," Aidan gushes. His face lights up as always at the recollection. I never tire of hearing about it.

It was everything they had ever yearned for, from the little neatly laid out fields in patchwork squares—"Oh look! real hedges!"—to the great city of London itself. Home. So familiar, so honourable, exactly as they'd seen and imagined in books, the movies, magazines, *Times of Ceylon*, *Colombo Gazette*. They especially loved how polite everyone was. "Good morning" and "Good day to you"—English etiquette. Father-in-law was delighted by how well dressed the Englishmen were in the streets; he marvelled at the Englishman walking to the office in his three-piece pinstriped suit and bowler hat, carrying a furled umbrella, called a gamp, in case of rain. They quickly learned the two topics that guaranteed good conversation with the English: the weather and their dogs. The English actually dressed their poodles in little woolen jackets against the cold! "That's a boy. Come, Tupper!"

The streets were fine and broad, heavily treed. They went to Hyde Park and stood at Speakers' Corner, listening to some crazy man on a soap-box dressed in rags rant about wages and the damn monarchy—"Bloodsuckers, that's what!" Of course, that was the famous British free speech. No one got arrested.

They visited Marble Arch, gleaming white under drooping trees, the Strand, Picadilly Circus, Buckingham Palace. They watched the changing of the guard in awe. A flag flew from the ramparts showing that Her Majesty was "in residence." "Imagine! She's inside her palace right now, pet." Likely signing important state documents.

They stayed at Tilbury House, off Bayswater. The rooms were chilly; you had to put sixpence in the gas metre to warm them up. The maids were all white Irish girls, and they sang all day at their work.

Mrs. Crooks, the landlady, banged a gong every morning at eight o'clock sharp. Punctuality was of the essence—this was England, after all. They all sprang out of bed and rushed downstairs to the basement level where breakfast was served. It was a formal, dark, and intimidating room with a low ceiling; white linen tablecloths were spread on the tables with a flowery teapot in the centre, surrounded by straight-backed chairs. The walls had wainscoting, darkly varnished. Everyone whispered.

Those breakfasts! Thick rashers of bacon, eggs, baked beans, smelly things called kippers the English loved, sausages, and mounds of toast. And tea, Lipton's tea. From Ceylon.

"Well, you're a long way from home, aren't you then, Mr. Gilmor?" said Mrs. Crooks.

"This is home now." They felt like they belonged.

Everything ran like clockwork—the tube, the trains, the buses—not like in Ceylon, where the bus driver would suddenly stop for a toddy or run in to a mud-walled house to visit his *amma,* leaving the passengers stewing in the heat. The scent of autumn in London, the streets swept with raindrops, and the trees tall and gracious, spreading deep umbrage. Red double-decker buses went rumbling by. They took one and sat upstairs, and Lally screamed when she looked down. "We're going to topple over!"

"Oh, Lally!"

Then one morning, early, as Aidan stood quietly in the passage, he heard Mrs. Crooks through the glass door: "I don't mind the coloured family from the colonies upstairs—nice quiet educated people they are—but I won't tolerate darkies in my 'ouse for love or money."

"So what did your parents think when they arrived in Canada, in Toronto?" I was curious. (Their sojourn in England had told me so much.) I put on the kettle for more tea.

Terror. They'd shuffled out of Union Station with their luggage and stared up at the Royal York Hotel, a grim, rearing, obdurate building with rows and rows of small square windows like a prison. The street was dark, gloomy, without trees. Grim-looking landladies stood in a row holding placards—*CLEAN ROOMS $25 A WEEK ROOM AND BOARD.*

They stayed at a boarding house on Gloucester Street. Bed and breakfast and dinner inclusive. *Immigrants welcome*, said the sign outside. It was a tall three-storey Victorian made of grimy dark brick with gables and a fan-light over the front door. The street was dark and long with similar buildings on each side, tall and foreboding. But there were trees, heavy ones tinged with scarlet and gold called maples. At the far end, on Jarvis Street, were several Chinese boarding houses. They were cheaper, but they wouldn't allow guests with children.

The landlady was tall and thin, Polish with a Polish name they couldn't pronounce, something like Kracowskowski. She served them strange food, flaccid soups without a shred of curry in which dumplings and lumps of ham floated, and a Canadian breakfast—this was a stack of what she called pancakes, which looked like thick hoppers, over which they were to pour maple syrup, very sweet like Ceylon kitul treacle. They drank ovaltine before bed.

They ventured out. Yonge Street was grimy and narrow, filled with billboards and signs and funny little shops and masseuse parlours. No Marble Arch, no splendid fountains, no changing of the guard. They found University Avenue, which was a fine boulevard with dazzling white buildings, a statue of Queen Victoria in the park, and another one of a soldier from World

War I. At the head of the avenue was the Ontario Legislature, an old impressive building that reminded Father-in-law of the Fort district in colonial Ceylon.

The house was full of men, immigrants like themselves, looking for work. One was Albanian, another was Irish, and another Serbian. Father-in-law had to find work. He saw an ad in *The Globe and Mail* for work on a small farm in a place called Willowdale, in the north end of the city. He took the subway to Eglinton and then took a taxi. He'd put on his best pinstriped suit from London, and a bowler hat. He felt very English but a little foolish. It turned out that the job involved working in the fields and apple orchards, like a coolie....

That night Father and Mother-in-law knelt before the little statue they'd set up in their bedroom to the Virgin Mary and St. Michael the Archangel, and Father-in-law prayed with all his heart: "*Oh God, help us.*"

7.

"I'VE PUT THE COLOURED BOY from India in your class, Mrs. Gilmor." Mr. Mirrell, my principal at Hillside Public School, is obviously uncomfortable. It's well into the fall term and class organization is complete. "I'm afraid the other teachers ... well, just could not accommodate Rajit. I hope you understand," he adds quickly, in a low, apologetic tone.

Well, I am the new teacher on staff, which usually means one has to be prepared to be taken advantage of, so it's no surprise that he is adding an extra student to my class. Except that in this case I don't mind. "Of course, Mr. Mirrell," I say, perhaps too eagerly.

"Ah, well ... thank you. Good old British grit, eh?" He looks relieved.

Mr. Mirrell calls a special staff meeting first thing to discuss the changing demographics of Toronto and how they might impinge on Hillside. "Greeks are starting to move along the Danforth," he warns gravely. "And now ... an Indian family and Jamaicans at our own door-step. I'm afraid they just arrive whenever they please."

There's a stir of consternation. First the Italians, now the Greeks ... and now Blacks. Everyone blames the new low-rental building that the government put up over the past summer. It sits on a piece of previously vacant ground on the school boundary, supposedly in an effort at social integration. "It's been allowing in Blacks, Pakis, welfare bums, and God knows what from God knows where into the neighbourhood," objects Marlene Fisher. She teaches grade five in the junior division, like myself, and has swivelling eyes like a fish. Hillside is an elite uptown area in Toronto, part of an English-Canadian enclave of old money where the upper crust live and send their offspring to private school.

Mr. Mirrell holds out a roster. "Gladstone Williams will be in Miss Morton's class; his sister Yolande Rennie has been placed in Mrs. Evers' grade one class; Rajit Mukherjee will be with our new member of staff, Selena Harcourt-Jones, and his younger sister Saraswati—maybe make that Sarah?— will be with Miss Denby." He mispronounces Mukherjee as "Muck-jee."

Marlene glances at me sympathetically, even guiltily. She admires my stoicism. I've reacted calmly, welcoming Rajit into my class. The general consensus seems to be, "*Glad it's you and not me.*" Rajit's name will now be changed to Roger.

Gladstone and Yolande, the new students from Jamaica, and Rajit and Saraswati (otherwise known as Roger and Sarah) from India, are the prime topic of conversation around the staff lunchroom at noon.

"They have a smell," says Joanne Hammond. "Garlic. Ughh. And those spices they use! Immigrants just don't care how offensive their garlic breath is to others," she cries indignantly.

I'd thought Joanne was one person on staff I'd have liked to be friends with—I miss having girlfriends—but then she said, "I wouldn't want a coloured boy in my class." Joanne is a cheerful, fun-loving sort, with a reputation as a good teacher. Now I know, sadly, that she can never be my friend; she can never be introduced to Aidan. I'm disappointed. I feel cut off from the teachers, who consist mainly of young unmarried women, except for Marlene and a few other married women in other divisions that we don't mix with. Each teacher is expected to keep to her division, even at the lunch tables.

"The kids are already calling them 'Coffee' on the playground," says Marlene.

"Ohh. Do you think we should be letting them do that?" I demure softly.

"Well, what are we supposed to do about it? They don't *belong* here."

I murmur something about Trudeau saying we all belong here, and I cite his new multicultural society. "Everyone has come from elsewhere at some time or other," I add defensively, thinking of Mother and Father-in-law from Ceylon. ("Except for the Indigenous people, of course," I also want to add, but don't. The look on their faces stops me in my tracks.) At once there's a buzz: "*Trudeau?*"

"That communist!" cries Joanne.

"Him and that multicultural crap he's trying to force on us. Stanfield should have won the election." They must mean Robert Stanfield, the leader of the Conservative Party, now in Opposition.

These women are probably conservative themselves, dyed blue. Many of them actually live in the area—they are the wives of lawyers and businessmen and brokers. Maybe their mindset has to do with protecting their money. Most immigrants are poor.

"So, tell us about your husband, Selena. You never talk about him."

I fumble with my cheese sandwich as Marlene Fisher turns those pale fish-eyes on me. I try to convince myself that the question is not malicious. I'm still the relatively new teacher on staff at Hillside Public School, so it's natural for her to be curious; they all want to know about me and Aidan. But it's a question I've been dreading.

"Oh, well, he's … a Canadian, from … Willowdale."

There's a murmur of approval.

I'm lying by omission.

"Is that where you live?"

"No. We're ... um, in the Beaches area." Another murmur of approval: an Anglo-Saxon neighbourhood. (I know by now that "Anglo-Saxon" is a Canadian euphemism for white.) I instinctively keep it general and vague. I don't want my private life exposed to Marlene Fisher. Definitely not. My heart patters. "Do you have a photo of him?"

I gulp. "No, no. I don't carry photos in my wallet; it makes it bulge."

"Not even of your husband?" The married teachers carry photos of their husbands on them, I know; some even have framed photos of smiling spouses and children on their classroom desks. (Marlene's husband Dick has a thick porky face with hair slicked sideways like Uncle Clive's.) "Oh well, I'll bring one in some time."

To change the subject, I tell the teachers briefly about Aunt Clarice's death.

"Wow ... amazing. So what does Aidan do?"

"He's a high school teacher at a technical school in Toronto in the west end, near College," I say proudly. I'm careful not to give details such as the exact school name or street address.

"You mean in the downtown *core*? But that's a terrible place. I wouldn't teach there for all the tea in China," says Nesta Neilson, who runs the kindergarten. There are similar expressions of concern from the others, who lean towards me. I bite into my cheese sandwich. "Full of immigrants and beatniks and drugs and welfare bums."

"There's gangsters there."

I sense their opinion of Aidan plummeting; he can't be a very good teacher if that's the best the Toronto board has offered him. The area south of College in the inner city is indeed old and run-down, with its dingy bars and cafes and pubs, compared with orderly Hillside, I suppose. Aidan took me to see Brockhurst Technical during the summer. It's a typical big secondary school. It has long oblong buildings with high windows and large technical shops with revolving doors and special technical equipment. A group of teenagers in hoodies were swarming around some broken basketball nets, trying to shoot baskets, while various little kids climbed a jungle gym that had seen better days. It is very different from orderly Hillside Public School with its modern, brightly painted playground surrounded by upper-middle-class homes. The Hillside teachers never actually spend time in downtown neighbourhoods west of University and College. "Are you kidding?" They turn away; they've already lost interest and I'm relieved. I'm trembling all the same.

Alice Grayson's mother is waiting outside my door after the four o'clock bell. "Could I please have a word with you, Mrs. Gilmor?" She hesitates awkwardly.

"Of course," I nod. We sit down at my desk in the empty portable. Alice's desk is in aisle two, near the front.

"Look, don't misunderstand me, Mrs. Gilmor, but, well ... could you make sure Alice never sits next to the new boy, the coloured boy?" She utters this in a low voice I can barely make out. "I mean, I don't mind him being in the class, and maybe he's a nice boy—I'm not saying he isn't. It's just ... I don't want her ... sitting with him...."

"Rajit is from India. Yes, he's a nice boy. But I understand," I say. And I do, but I feel sick. "The boys never want to sit with the girls anyway, Mrs. Grayson, so you don't have to really worry. Sit with a girl?" I laugh it off, cowardly and conniving. I'm beginning to hate myself.

"Thank you. Oh, thank you, Mrs. Gilmor. I knew you would understand, being British."

What does that say for the British Empire that runs so deep in us WASPS? What are the parents saying among themselves, I wonder? What would they think if they knew that Mrs. Gilmor is married to a coloured man herself? Suddenly I feel weary. I have a headache. I hate my cowardice. *Why didn't I say "No way" to Mrs. Grayson?* I should have said, *"I'm married to a dark-skinned Ceylonese Eurasian myself. Mixed. So go to hell.*" The words would not come.

There's Rajit behind the portable again, after school. His eyes are filled with tears. He isn't a tough child like Gladstone, who gives as good as he gets. "You call me darkie? You mungie-cake!" *POW*. Besides, the boys have quickly discovered that Gladstone pitches a good mean ball in baseball, so they vie for him to be on their team.

"The boys, they shouting tings at me an' say they gonna beat me up. 'Go back 'ome, Paki,' they are calling. 'We don't want you.'"

Rajit's sister, Saraswati, crawls out from under the portable, her dress dusty and crumpled, her face streaked with dirt.

"You shouldn't go under there. It's dangerous, Saraswati. Oh well. Come along with me. I'll walk you across the field. No one is going to hurt you. You hold my hands."

"No, she's Sarah now, Miss G'lmor," says Rajit. "And I'm Roger."

"Well. I like Saraswati and Rajit—they're beautiful names."

Silence as Rajit absorbs this.

We cross the asphalt playground towards the playing field and their building on the boundary. "Does your daddy have work, Rajit?" Rajit is nine or ten, old enough to understand.

"Yes, Miss, he cleans big offices. An' in the day he work at A&W."

He's referring to the fast-food joint with the drive-by, likely the one on Yonge Street. He works two jobs, like many immigrants. I wonder if Mr. Mukherjee is kept at the back in the kitchen out of sight of customers, as Aidan had been at the variety store. He'd had to enter the store through the back door. Something unexpected opens up to me.

"What did Daddy do in India?" *Am I prying here?* But I want to know; I want to understand. Perhaps Rajit's answer will tell me something more about Father-in-law.

"Dada was a chemist, but he got to get his papers here, Miss Gilmor," Raji says seriously. I can't help realizing the experiences this little Indian boy has had, compared with the thoughtless boys on my street who threw stones at me and ran away.

As we reach the field, a group of boys watch from a distance. Saraswati's long plait swings like a snake down her back. Most of the staff and students have already left for home. Silence falls as we pass the boys; their eyes widen as we reach the low-rise apartment building. Yes, I suppose it is a blot on the landscape: a long, plain, oblong, brick building without flowers or bushes to relieve the monotony. There's some garbage around—a few cans of beer, cigarette butts—and the odour of marijuana floats in the air. (Hillside residents, like Marlene, are petitioning for a hedge to be dug in and a seven-foot fence placed around the building. One has to consider property values.) A line of washing is slung across a balcony; I can well imagine Marlene's blood pressure. Rajit points out their entrance, and I leave him and his sister at the double glass doors. Saraswati grips her Snoopy lunchbox, looking anxious as Rajit reaches up to press the buzzer on the intercom.

The children hang up their coats on the rows of hooks at the back of the room—a higgledy-piggledy mass of hats, scarves, jackets, and outdoor boots—and then find their places. Fall is upon us, and it's cold now and dark by late afternoon. They scrape chairs and slam desks. They don't realize it, but I'm fond of these trusting children; they have become dear to me over the past months, have become part of me. I talk to them about being kind to new students. "I want you to look out for kids from other countries, like Jamaica or India, for they don't yet have any friends and must be lonely. No following them after school or shouting mean things." I appeal to the boys to protect Yolande, for instance. "She's only in Grade One. I'd like you to be brave and stand up for her—and Gladstone and Raj if other kids attack them."

Rajit sits very still and attentive at his desk, his dark eyes large and luminous, thickly lashed like Aidan's. He could be the son I might have one day, I think.

"It's not us, Mrs. Gilmor! It's Tony Baker and his gang in Five B, in Mr. Randall's class."

"Oh, you said 'darkie' to Yolande yesterday, George. I heard him, Miss!"

"No, I never, Miss Gilmor!"

"I don't want to hear that word! It hurts Yolande. And I don't want tattletales. We are all friends in this school. Now, thank you everyone. I know I can rely on you, and especially you girls to be kind and friendly to Yolande and Saraswati out on the playground." I sweep an encouraging smile at the girls who sit stiffly in their seats, primped up in new wool leggings and smart fuzzy sweaters, their hair neatly plaited.

The strains of "*O Canada*" waft over the PA. "*Our home and native land....*" This is followed by the Lord's Prayer to be said in the classroom, and a psalm (at the teacher's discretion). The boys recite gruffly, open-eyed and staring around absently, their fists clasped; the little girls fold their hands properly, palms together, and their eyes are squeezed shut. Raj knows all the words. "*For thine is the–kingdom–the–power–'n'–the–glory–for–ever–'n'–ever–amen,*" they recite in a sudden rush, a trusting babble, led by me.

I've put off speaking to Mr. Mirrell about the incident in the school yard for almost a week now. I can't let it go, but I'm nervous and hesitant as I approach his desk. He has a big intimidating photo of his wife up front—it's the first thing you see—and another of his two little girls with blonde hair: his family. "Good morning, Mrs. Gilmor."

"I've heard them call Gladstone the n-word at recess."

Mr. Mirrell's mouth twitches at the words. "Well...?" He raises an eyebrow, as if trying to figure out the purpose of my visit. "What is it you want, exactly?" he asks.

"Well, do you think you could maybe bring it up in a meeting and ask the teachers to talk to their students? Tell them to watch out for the immigrant kids after school?" I mumble. I'm taking sides, putting him on the spot, I know. Mr. Mirrell is tall and lean, like a greyhound. I add—cunningly, for I've heard he has aspirations to become the next superintendent—"I mean, we wouldn't want a race fight at Hillside getting to the ears of the superintendent, or the newspapers, for that matter."

Mr. Mirrell's mouth tightens. "Ah yes. Well, I see your point, Mrs. Gilmor. I'll do what I can, but don't expect any converts." His mouth twitches again at his little jest. "We've never had nig—um—Jamaicans or Indians in this neighbourhood. Or government housing," he adds stiffly.

Later, there's the expected outburst from Marlene and the others around the staff lunch table at noon. "Damn lucky they are to be in this country!"

"What are we letting in?"

"And what sort of name is *Saraswati*, anyway?"

"Good for you, Selena. You're showing which side you're on." Aidan couldn't wait to tell Mother and Father-in-law in the kitchen that Sunday about how I'd confronted Mr. Mirrell. He was flushed with pride and enthusiasm as he recounted the events. "Selena really stood up to that racist principal, Ma."

"Well ... nothing much came of it." I was embarrassed. "I didn't do that much."

"Hey, you stood up for the right thing! That makes you part of the civil rights movement. Black Is Beautiful. You're right there with Jesse Jackson and Eldridge Cleaver, Selena!"

Father-in-law looked confused—his English daughter-in-law?

"Well, that is very good, Selena! See, pet." Mother-in-law nodded approval. "Just like Quintus in the old days. He was always speaking up for the Tamil labourers, Selena, confronting the British."

"Ughh. And now he's in jail in Colombo." Father-in-law knocked back a whisky.

Aidan had brought along *Soul On Ice*. "Read this, Daddy!"

"But…" father-in-law touches the book tentatively.

"I don't want to read any bloody *Soul On Ice*," he said. He planned to tune in to Voice of Ceylon and the latest riots.

"All I did was help a little kid," I said. I wasn't sure I wanted to be part of a movement either, but I was afraid of disappointing and crossing Aidan, especially in front of Mother and Father-in-law. I'd always been excited by Aidan's political fire, but he couldn't know the effect of Marlene Fisher's all-seeing eyes. He was giving them the wrong impression of me, for I hadn't stood up for what really mattered: Aidan himself.

Gladstone Williams and his half-sister, Yolande Rennie, continue to be a particular source of fascination for the staff in the junior and primary divisions.

The teachers unwrap their various strong-smelling bologna and salami sandwiches with dill pickle, heat pots of ravioli on the stove, and munch on salted crisps. The odour wafts around the lunchroom, but no one notices.

"*Gladstone?*"

The teachers are amused. "Likely named for Queen Victoria's famous prime minister, William Gladstone," says Marlene Fisher.

"Maybe his mother thinks he'll be prime minister of Britain one day." Chortles all round. "What! A tarbrush in Downing Street?"

"That's going a bit far, Marlene," I blurt.

"It's just a joke! What's with you Brits?"

Gladstone Williams and Yolande Rennie are half-siblings. The different surnames mean, of course, that they have different fathers, a fact not lost on the teachers. There had been no explanation as to why the grandmother in Kingston, Jamaica, suddenly sent them to Canada to live with their mother.

It's their different complexions that galvanize everyone. Gladstone's skin colour is about ten shades darker than Yolande's, which is a sort of beige. But it's her frizzy pigtails pulled tight all over her head like corkscrews, inexplicably blonde, that electrify Hillside. The ten pigtails sticking out all over her head, with ten pink plastic bobbles twisted round the ends, bob up and down and round and round whenever she turns. "Enough to make you dizzy."

"Mixed blood," Nesta Penmore sniffs. She turns up her nose and squishes her mouth.

The remark provokes more, seemingly endless, speculation. *Mixed, mestistos, half-breed, mulatto, coloured, Eurasian....* The words seem to burn the air in the lunchroom. I struggle to swallow my piece of brown bread, thinking of Aidan and Mother-in-law with their dark complexions, realizing just how my colleagues here would see them.

"Actually, Gladstone and his sister are West Indian." I suddenly find my voice.

"Well, Gladstone can barely read or write, West or East," quips Marlene. "He shouldn't *be* here."

"It's not his fault. He was working in the cane fields in the countryside all this time. Now he'll have a chance to learn, here in Canada. He'll have a chance to better himself."

"Are you a *socialist*?"

The teachers look at me, suspicious. They have only seen the tourist Jamaica; most of them go to the islands over Christmas or March Break and stay in the presidential or segregated resort compounds. They've never seen the "other" Jamaica, the one that Gladstone and Yolande were born to. And the India of the Mukherjee children is another mystery: yogis standing on their heads, mumbo-jumbo heathenism, strange temples covered with naked idols. To them, it is alien, a threatening culture being thrust into the heart of Anglican Hillside.

"And that girl Sarah and her brother Roger—their mother has a *red dot* in the middle of her forehead. Must be one of those

Hindus, I ask you!" Marlene is indignant. "She turned up at the office the other day wearing a long dress to the ground—a sari they call it—as if she's in India. In this weather!"

"And stinking of curry."

8.

MOTHER-IN-LAW IS SQUEEZING CLOVES of garlic using an old press—goodness knows where she got it from—while I grind turmeric in a pestle and mortar, a tool I didn't know people still used. We're like ancient villagers from a long time past, bent over our tasks. My fingers are stained orange and I smell of curry. I'm happy. Sunlight flows through the kitchen window from the wintry garden where the flowers are frozen, gone to seed; the vines on the trellis are limp by the door, and the willow is a spangled shower of icicles. The Union Jack hangs stiff as a corpse. But inside it's cozy. Father-in-law is smoking a pipe, and Aidan tinkers with Mother-in-law's broken toaster while Felix reads the world news in the *Star*, Tabby purring in his lap. Another pleasant Sunday in the Willowdale bungalow, one of many to come in my marriage, I hope.

"Good God, Mildred, is Selena servant number two, now?" Father-in-law bristles.

"Oh, I don't mind, really, I like helping."

"See, Jack pet, she enjoys it."

"Huhh!"

"You still have your old pots, Mildred?" observes Felix, trying to smooth over the dispute. He's come for lunch, as he often does. I suspect he may be lonely in his solitary one-bedroom apartment behind a synagogue on Bathurst Street, especially with winter approaching. Mother and Father-in-law are kind to him, always welcoming. Something about his long melancholy face and black clothes—black suit, white shirt buttoned to the neck without a tie, black homburg hat—makes him look like a Hassidic Jew. Aidan finds it hilarious. He chortles mystifyingly, rocking with laughter. I don't understand his humour, and I don't see why Felix goes along with it. He's good-natured about it, amused, maybe even pleased. He says his Jewish neighbours are kind to him, and that they give him good deals; they think he's Jewish too, which makes Aidan chuckle all the more. Felix goes on about how once, when he was sick, Mrs. Gould, the superintendent's wife, brought him a bowl of homemade chicken matzo-ball soup. What more could a middle-aged bachelor want?

Mother-in-law pats her pots. "Best thing I ever invested in, Felix. Excellent for curries, slow simmer." Indeed, the stove-top is loaded with the heavy cast-iron pots that Mother-in-law bought from a door-to-door salesman when she first arrived in Canada. She'd felt sorry for him, she says.

"Imagine! Your mother never so much as boiled an egg in Ceylon," says Felix, turning to Aidan and then back to Mother-in-law. "I remember your servant, Amara Gooneratne."

"She was a very good cook, Felix."

"Except when it came to animal flesh," Felix chuckles. "She refused to cook those paddy birds Jack and his planter pals shot that time. All the Buddhist kitchen help walked out, if I recall."

They laugh, and I'm fascinated by this sudden little snippet of plantation life. "Bloody rot," mutters Father-in-law. It's an incident he obviously would rather forget. "I think you had to get Ganesh, the Tamil gardener, to throw them into the pot and boil them. *He* didn't mind, being Hindu."

"*Aiyo*, a terrible thing, those poor little defenceless paddy birds, no bigger than sparrows over here."

"Ughh." Father-in-law knocks back a whisky, thoroughly disgruntled at a memory. He gives me, the English daughter-in-law, a quick, furtive glance, but I am careful to hide my amusement.

"Speaking of sparrows, Father Matthew gave an excellent sermon this morning on the topic, Selena. 'Not even a sparrow falls....'"

There have been several not so subtle hints, from time to time, that I become a Catholic like Darleene. They love how she kneels at the altar rail at St. Raphael of All Angels with them, side by side with Scottie. "You should hear Father Matthew preach, Selena," Mother-in-law murmurs. I quietly bristle. I draw the line at becoming a Catholic. (I could imagine Mother's wail: "Now they're making her a *Papist*.")

"Well, I'm sure Father Matthew is a good preacher," I say tactfully.

Aidan gives me quiet support, amused. "Religion is the opiate of the people, Ma. Just quoting Karl Marx."

"Hah!" goes Felix.

Father-in-law scowls at his oldest son.

I'm still undeniably Protestant. I suppose I'm non-conforming, whatever that means in the sixties in the West, with the churches suddenly empty. I think of the hippies filling the yoga centres and chanting "*Om, Om, Om*" instead of "Our Father," and I recall Nangi in her little white-washed chapel at home. Secretly, I feel that if I were to convert, I would somehow betray Nangi. Her old-fashioned devotion to Ebenezer Chapel unexpectedly touches some deeper fealty. "There's an old hymn Nangi loved to sing in Welsh," I murmur. "Something about the *frail wanderer in the wilderness*.... Nangi was a frail wanderer herself, if anyone was," I say with a wry smile. (I picture Nangi in her worn pinny standing outside her row house in the coal field waving goodbye to Aidan and me....)

"Poor old Nangi, she really believes all that stuff," says Aidan. I feel a jarring inside at this, but recover quickly, keeping my feelings hidden.

"Ughh, well, and why shouldn't she?" Father-in-law gives me a sudden glance and pours himself another whisky. "Aren't we all frail wanderers in the bloody wilderness?"

"Hah! Well said, old chap."

I'm relieved when Felix unexpectedly brings out a gift and hands it to me, changing the subject. "For you, Selena." Everyone looks. I open the package and hold up a small bible, surprised. A Protestant bible, the King James version. "My Tamil grandmother's family bible from Ceylon. It's been in our family for half a century, " says Felix proudly. "I want you to have it Selena. I have no children."

Now I'm bonded to Felix forever in a special way, and to this Tamil grandmother of his, whoever she may have been. For of course now I'll have to read it, as he expects. (Perhaps I will recite a psalm or two. I can still recollect one from school: *Blessed is the man that walketh not in the counsel of the ungodly....*) To Felix, I say, "It's a beautiful book. Thank you so much. I'm honoured, and I'll treasure it, Felix."

"I thought Tamils were Hindu," I say, tentatively. I might be on touchy ground.

"Oh no, no, many Tamils converted to Catholicism. It goes back to Portuguese rule. Sometimes both, Hindu and Catholic—same difference!" He and Aidan burst into their mystifying chuckles of amusement; they find this hilarious. "And even Methodist." More laughter.

"There are many beautiful white-washed Catholic churches in Jaffna, in the north of the island," says Felix. This was where his grandmother had come from. Jaffna.

I'm obviously supposed to know the ins and outs of colonial history. The British weren't the only desecrators, then. Tamils, I now understand, are an old Dravidian race of people from South India who've lived for thousands of years in Ceylon. They are darker than the Sinhalese, who claim to be of Aryan origin. It's important to know this, I think. I'm anxious. The Tamils came from India across the Palk Strait into the north of Ceylon. "Oh, Jaffna was very hot. Only Tamils could live there; only they could take the heat," cries Mother-in-law suddenly. "They are the Jaffna Tamils, or Ceylon Tamils as they were also called, highly favoured by the British."

"Yes, indeed. They got the top jobs in the judiciary and civil service," Felix recalls. "Not like the poor Tamil labourers on the estates."

That's the clue that I must get into my head: the Tamil labourers on the tea estates were exploited by the British, the underdogs in the colonial system. I suppose they are the reason Quintus Delay and now Aidan are socialists.

"Now that is a very old bible, Selena," says Mother-in-law, interested. She takes it into her hands reverently for a moment. "It goes back to when Jack's grandfather lived at Gampola—you remember, pet?"

Father-in-law scowls and turns away. He evidently does not wish to remember Gampola, for some reason.

The bible is small with a reddish-brown leather cover and a gold clasp. Someone has written on the fly-leaf inside: *Gampola Post Office 1892.* Perhaps Felix's Tamil grandmother?

And there is more to it, of course to the bible, its significance illuminating that other life of colonialism simmering among them that Aidan longs to challenge. A faded pressed flower has fallen from between the leaves, where someone must have placed it more than half a century ago. Perhaps Felix's grandmother, as a girl.

"Hmph. That belonged to my great aunt Kitty Subramanian. I remember her in the old days, as a child. Met her once, at Pennylands." Father-in-law breaks into the conversation. (So the Tamil grandmother had an English name: Kitty. It seems important but I dare not ask.)

"Kitty was lively," says Mother-in-law, smiling. So she had known her, too, as a young child.

The little bible has created quite a stir.

Father-in-law knocks his pipe gently, putting out the ash, and stumbles with a sigh to the bedroom down the hall. Time for his afternoon nap, the siesta, a vestige of old Ceylon and tropical afternoons. In Canada, he can only indulge in it on the weekend, for he's not yet retired.

Presently we hear the sleepy drone of the cricket commentary from his transistor radio, drifting through the walls. "Silly mid-off," he mumbles. England is losing to Australia; the fast bowlers on the Aussie side have gotten them all out. "Bloody Aussies," we hear Father-in-law mumble. Then silence. Before we know it, rumblings and snores and gasps. As I pass the open doorway on my way to the bathroom, I glimpse Father-in-law sprawled across the bed on his back, like a beached whale, his belly heaving and bubbles whistling from his sagging mouth. His shirt has fallen open, and the word LILY is exposed, a big purplish tattoo across his heart. *Lily*. Someone long past, still marring his chest. A rash moment of youth, perhaps?

"Never bloody well tattoo a woman's name in your flesh, son," he'd warned Aidan once, but the story behind it is not to be known. "Perhaps Jack found the past isn't so easily erased," Felix had murmured wryly. Poor Mother-in-law. She's had to sleep, make love, bear her children, live her whole life next to LILY. But Mother-in-law is phlegmatic, calm. "Yes, a foolish thing to have done."

Now I bring up her name, trying to sound casual. "I just happened to wonder…"

"Well, we British Eurasians tended to marry our own kind in Ceylon." Felix turns to me. Aidan's face has taken on a guarded look at this; he is sensitive. What do Felix's words exactly imply about such marriages?

"Eurasians wed Eurasians; Burghers wed Burghers." *Is this the unspoken code of colonial Ceylon?* Felix has no compunctions about family secrets. "Of course, there'd be exceptions. Jack, for instance. He fell in love with this Lily de Groot. Oh, she was a beauty, a fair Dutch Burgher girl with some Tamil blood," Felix recalls. But a Burgher, all the same. He'd actually known her. "Jack was only twenty."

Felix glances at Mother-in-law as if to see whether time obliterates pain. She studiously ignores him. Her chores over for now, she leafs through a *Dark Embrace* magazine with studied interest: *And then he swept me into his arms....* She's quietly partial to these stories of passionate affairs of sex, betrayal, and desire. I discovered a shelf of such stories in the basement one afternoon, tucked away in her sewing area. This is where she keeps her Singer sewing machine and a wicker work-box on legs full of embroidery silks and threads—a secret domain where she hoards her collection. *Sinhala Affair*, a paperback featuring a voluptuous young Sinhalese woman on the cover with a white buccaneer-type lover in the background brandishing a sword, was well-worn with dog-ears. I'd been bemused at this secret life that staid Mother-in-law seemed to indulge in. Perhaps it goes back to the lonely tea estates in Ceylon, when she thrived on such novels as an escape from loneliness and boredom. I realized how little I really know her. She continues to ignore us, though I'm sure she's listening to Felix.

"It was a long time ago. We were young men and women in the prime of life," Felix muses.

"What happened?" I ask, though I'm sure Father-in-law would rather I not know. Love and passion in the tropics, a time that has long since passed.

"Oh, the family was adamant against Lily."

Granny, old Sinclair Gilmor's wife, made Father-in-law go down on his knees before the altar in St. Lucia Catholic Cathedral in Colombo and swear he would never ever marry a de Groot. Then, at the Planters' Club in Hatton, he met Mother-in-law: Mildred Goonesekere Delaney, Eurasian Sinhalese, highly suitable. They knew each other's families, the Gilmors and Delaneys. (Mother-in-law smiles to herself as she turns a page.) So Father-in-law fell in love again and saw things differently.

Father-in-law still has a handsome face, lean and fair. "He could easily 'pass' in those days," says Felix.

"Daddy had a red moustache, too," Aidan adds proudly.

"Remember, Felix?" Red. Proof. Though still a Eurasian.

And there is a mystery here, a sudden lapse, the story not followed through. As the white English daughter-in-law, I feel somehow a vague assumed guilt, the very weight of colonial history, that silences me. (Yet, am I not, perhaps, the unattainable English girl in Ceylon that Aidan was able to attract in Canada?) Of course, it's not something I could ever broach or touch upon with him. It could possibly be hurtful; it would be a risk to bring it up.

"There's another book here somewhere that you must see, Selena." Felix goes to Father-in-law's book-case in the living room and pushes around at the books on the bottom shelf, then pulls out an enormous tome.

"You're not bringing that out, are you?" asks Mother-in-law, alarmed.

"Well, Selena should see it; she should know what it was all about." The British colonial empire in Ceylon. Tea.

"That racist stuff?" cries Aidan, also upset.

But Felix ignores them and shows me the book. It's thick. The covers are heavy, beautiful, and wooden with gilt-embossed lettering: *Impressions of Ceylon: Its History, People, Commerce, Industries, and Resources.* It's dated 1907—a very old book. It had obviously been written for new white administrative assistants coming over fresh from England to the Crown colony of Ceylon to rule the natives. It contained everything that someone like Sinclair Gilmor, Aidan's British great-grandfather, an adventurer and prospector seeking his fortune in Ceylon in the nineteenth century, needed to know. These photographs had obviously been meant to portray the Indigenous Ceylon natives that the white administrators had better be familiar with and that they were likely fascinated by.

We bring *Impressions of Ceylon* into the kitchen and set it down. I give Mother-in-law a surreptitious glance, but she's still seemingly immersed for the moment in *Dark Embrace.* I turn the pages carefully—they are gilt-edged as in the old days—and look at the photographs emerging from the past. This is the white colonial view of the Ceylonese, of my distant relatives-in-law, the people who are now my family. I'm shocked. The first photograph reveals a woman. *Sinhalese High Caste Woman*, says the caption, by way of explanation. She has her hair swept into a chignon and wears long earrings and many strings of beads round her neck. Had Amma, Mother-in-law's Buddhist mother, dressed like this?

There follows an example of a Sinhalese man, referred to in the caption as a bullock driver. He looks so much like Aidan that I am startled; he has the same broad, strong features and intense eyes. His moustache and beard have turned white (but he has the same fuzzy soft hair on his chest). Aidan frowns. Then there is a group photo of naked girls with small round brown breasts captioned *Tamil Girls*. They glower out at us. They look like Sinhalese girls, only darker. They have large beads and coins around their necks, and all of them are frowning. Felix quickly turns the page. The next image is of a fair-skinned woman—a Burgher, according to the caption. *Perhaps like Lily?*

Had Father-in-law read, or, worse, *believed* this stuff?

A slurry, breathy shuffle alerts us, too late. Father-in-law has come in from the bedroom and is looming over us. "What the bloody hell are you doing *touching my books?*" he screams.

"Oh, come, pet. They are just looking," objects Mother-in-law, looking up from *Dark Embrace*. "What for this palaver?"

"Here, let me see that!" Father-in-law snatches at the book and the offending photograph of the naked Tamil girls. "Bloody hell! Damn racist rot! Why are you showing Selena this?"

"Well, Daddy, you're the one who brought the book from Ceylon in the first place," smirks Aidan; he always likes to needle his father, catch him out.

"What the devil—?"

"Well, it's a valuable book, Jack. It's part of history," objects Felix in a reasonable tone.

"Whose bloody history?" storms Father-in-law; he's shrieking now, purple in the face. His white hair sticks out like wild stalks.

Mother-in-law is concerned. "Pet, pet, you'll burst a blood vessel."

"I should have thrown it to the bottom of the bloody Mahaweli Ganga."

Father-in-law staggers across the kitchen, hugging the book to his chest, and makes a big gesture of dumping it into the garbage. The spine splits, and pages of photographs loosen over the remains of curried chicken giblets. "There! Where it bloody well belongs." It's a shocking thing to do, surely, to a beautiful old book like that. It is likely valuable, an original part of the history of colonial Ceylon, and of the Gilmor family. It had been owned by old Sinclair Gilmor himself. And, of course, there's more to this, hidden in Father-in-law's pain. He pours himself a whisky, and glares.

He likely knows that Mother-in-law will salvage it, which she does. She kneels down and retrieves the book, flicking giblets off the covers. "There, see, pet, curry stain on it!"

"Grrrrr."

Apologies are in order.

"I'm very, very sorry, Father-in-law. We should never have touched your book without your permission. It won't happen again, I promise."

"Well said, Selena," cries Felix. "I was the real culprit, come to that, Jack, old boy. I took it down to show Selena old Gilmor's history."

"That bastard," growls Father-in-law, his usual endearment. But he is somewhat mollified by my contrition. Saving face is essential. Aidan smirks; he's enjoying watching me grovel.

"Now then, pet, it's history. Our grandchildren will appreciate it when we are gone; they too should know of their progenitor." Mother-in-law is soothing. "What for tempest in teacup? And on a Sunday. Think of Father Matthew at St. Raphael of All Angels...."

And so on, and so on, as they mumble and fumble through their Sunday. The familiar chatter is a relief, smoothing over Father-in-law's emotional fracas. "Damn Australian bowlers, Felix. They always go for the legs...." Father-in-law shuffles into the living room and switches on the Bush radiogram with its short-wave band that is his primary link to the colonial world: the BBC overseas service, the "pips" at one o'clock, Big Ben chimes, cricket Test Matches, Ceylon's latest massacres, and "anything else going on on the bloody island."

"Damn news, what with that bloody idiot Dudley Senanayake in power...."

"Cup of tea, Selena?"

Outside, on the flagpole, the Union Jack still hangs inert. Soon Father-in-law will don his khaki shorts and roll his woolen socks up to his knees and go out before dark. He raises the Union Jack, symbol of the British colonial empire, over the rooftop every weekend. He rolls it down at dusk on Sunday evening, holding himself erect as he gives the salute, trembling in the old colonial togs of another era. *What does it all mean?* I dare not ask.

I'll never understand him.

9.

SUNLIGHT FALLS IN PATTERNS on the parquet floors. Sparrows chirp in the laurels as I sip my tea one Saturday morning in the sunroom.

Something has subtly changed on Morton Road this year. *Or is it just how I'm looking at it?* Perhaps the neighbours have become used to the dark attractive stranger with a beard in the green-and-white house. They seem to accept Aidan and no longer turn and stare at us walking down the road. The woman who lives next door, on the opposite side from Mrs. Mainwaring, introduced herself to me one afternoon; she was digging mulch into her flowerbeds and glanced across the hedge with a nod. "I'm Greta Hegel," she said. "My husband and I came from Germany after the war." She has a slight German accent. She looks to be in her early fifties, blonde and trim. She said that our garden looks very nice now. That was all, but a beginning. The kids on the street have stopped their attacks. They stare hard at us as they pass by, looking from one to the other. One day when I was walking alone one of them whistled at me. I felt insulted but wondered if I was becoming overly sensitive. Would they have done it if I'd been married to a white man? They'd have respected me. I agonized about it, but then dismissed it. One or two of the boys love to pat Bosie; they say they wished they had a dog.

Another day, an old woman who lives in a brick bungalow opposite came outside on her porch and called to me as I went by. "I'm Nadia Woychuk. My husband and I are from Poland. Here forty years." She peered at me sympathetically. "I know what it is to be new immigrant, dear, foreigner. Don't take notice of neighbours. They mind themselves—no bother you." Am I a foreigner then? I've never thought of myself as such. I am somewhat taken aback, even amused.

The street seemed different after that—almost friendly, accepting. The houses now seemed quiet and cozy, not so anonymous. The front door at number 8 has been painted at last. Number 12 still has a crumbling, flaking garage, and half the tiles have been blown off the roof. I now know that an old lady, Mrs. Craig, lives in the old two-storey frame house further down. Her net curtains are grey and mottled with dust. She comes outside sometimes and stands on the verandah, blinking rapidly, leaning on a cane and staring down the street.

One of the families is Irish, with four kids packed into a tiny bungalow. They have broad Belfast accents. They don't seem to be able to afford to paint the side of the house, which is a bit dilapidated, the paint peeling away in patches. One day I told the mother my name and that I was from Wales and had been to Dublin. "Oh aye," she said softly, very shy. "The auld country." She said her name was Audrey and her husband was Bill. I told her we lived in number 39. "Oh aye," she said. I knew better than to invite her over for tea and a chat. I realize now that most of the neighbours are hardworking working-class people, likely struggling to pay off mortgages or the rent and raise their children; they have no time for socializing. They come home and just slump in front of the TV after supper. I see them sometimes as I walk by in the dark with Bosie, their outlines lit up on their sofas. They work in factories and trades, not unlike Mum and Dad, the neighbours I grew up with in my home village, or Nangi in the coal fields, I reflect. One particularly cold and rainy day, I saw Audrey trudge past our house. She was leaning into the wind, pushing a stroller and carrying a heavy shopping bag, just as Mum used to do.

That was when I thought of Mother as "Mum," like the other mothers on the street, before we moved to fancy "Fernside."

Mum shopped after work and caught a bus home, and then carried her loaded bags up the hill. We had no fridge—no one did after the War; that was something only wonderful Americans had—so our mothers had to shop every day. What a drudge. I'd run down the hill to help her.

So when Aidan hints that maybe we should sell and move to a more professional area in the Beaches, amongst people on our own level, I'm reluctant and surprised. A year ago, I would have jumped at the idea, but now I feel like we belong. "No, Aidan," I murmur. "I'd rather stay put. I like it here now, it's familiar."

Walking hand-in-hand along the boardwalk in the evening, like so many other couples, is pleasant: the crinkly planks of wood under your feet, the graceful row of willows bending over, the lake on one side, vast, changeable. The lawn bowling green and the knocking sound of bowls are so English, so familiar; this is where old men dress in whites playing the ancient game—another echo from my childhood. There's a kiosk halfway down where we can stop for a coffee. Yes, it's a lovely neighbourhood Aidan chose especially for me. I squeeze his hand.

"They had a bowling green up at Nuwara Eliya in Ceylon—a very English place upcountry, where the English planters lived...."

I can't help but notice how white everyone is. You can see the British genes, especially in the men, in the thick, broad, solid builds, the open faces, the curly brown or blond hair. They are very sporty, too. Everyone at the beach always seems to be out running like mad; walking their dogs; canoeing at the Balmy Beach Club; kayaking; or playing lacrosse, tennis, or volleyball on the sands. Aidan is not sporty—he has a permanent slipped disc in his lower back—and he says he never liked sports at school. I feel a vague discomfort: a man not liking sports? He likes politics and religion—attacking them, that is.

Every weekend the boardwalk is transformed and throngs with visitors; many of them are immigrants who speak their own languages and come from other districts in Toronto. They stand out—Italians and Greeks and a few East Indians and West Indians, mothers with children and babies, hefty bags in tow. Many are from the inner city and get off the trams at the Queen Street stop to enjoy the beach and the grass for the afternoon. Some spread out blankets on the grass and set up little pup-tents and picnics, the men-folk lighting barbecues and sizzling burgers, sausages, and chunks of lamb and goat on metal skewers mixed with something called jerk that they seem to love. Loud, jazzy, rhythmic music throbs across the lawns and sands. Everyone is having a good time, but needless to say all this does not endear them to the permanent residents. However, it's the only time Aidan says he feels comfortable among people, indistinguishable from everyone around him.

And then, there comes Marlene Fisher and her husband, walking directly towards us.

She disappears in the crowd. My heart is knocking painfully against my chest with that familiar sensation. The band strikes up "Roses of Picardy" in the bandstand across the park, its gay striped bunting fluttering in the sunshine. The song is an English one, of Nanny Harcourt's era, the sort favoured by Marlene. "That's a real old English melody, Aidan!" *Has Marlene seen me? Seen Aidan?*

"They used to play it at Daddy's upcountry club in Ceylon, long ago...."

On Monday, at the lunch table, the teachers chat about their weekends. Marlene says, "Dan and I were at the boardwalk yesterday. Wouldn't go there again—too many immigrants. They take all the parking spots or come by streetcar in droves—you can't stop them—and they babble away in foreign tongues. You wouldn't know it's Canada anymore. We'll stick to Lawrence Park from now on; it's much nicer."

She turns to me: "I saw you on the boardwalk, Selena, by the kiosk. Then you got lost in the crowd."

"Ohh?" I wait, my egg sandwich suspended. She turns back to Joanne, who wants to tell everyone about her date with a guy she met Saturday night.

That's all. I'm safe for another day. Though Aidan had been walking right next to me, he'd been invisible to Marlene—just another immigrant. *She'd not even seen him.* My heart continues to beat painfully for him. How can I face him over chicken *tikka* this evening? How can I smile and share *papadums* and *seeni sambol* as if nothing has happened? How can I face myself?

That night in bed I pretend I'm unwell again when he touches me and moves over me. It's as if Marlene Fisher and her pale revolving fish eyes are there at the foot of the bed, ogling us, watching, titillated, and smirking all the while. I can hear her voice in my head: *I always knew … mixed.* I turn away with a sigh sadly. "Oh, all right," he says softly in the dark. He is like that; he never forces you. It's what I like about him. We just lie in each other's arms. Soon he is snoring. My head is tight, my eyes squeezed shut. The lids are thin and taut with silent tears slipping out.

I thought my marriage could remain that way, a private fact to keep to myself at school. I don't want to have to face inevitable questions as to why I've married "outside of my race." Why does there have to be a reason? I cringe, conscious that I'm different now, in some way inferior.

I begin to cough excessively the day before a potluck party. "You sound really bad, Selena." So I conveniently take the day off. "Too bad you missed the fun, Selena. Mr. Mirrell has a gorgeous house." And what was Mrs. Mirrell like? Of course, that was a topic of interest round the lunch table the next day: Mabel Mirrell, the principal's wife. The spouse. Giggly comments and asides from the teachers. "He's so good-looking and she, well...." Of course, everyone is interested in everyone else's spouse, and Aidan is no exception.

"I'm not coming to your staff party?"

Aidan surveys me and my wrapped gift thoughtfully as I appear in the living room. I'm wearing a bright red dress and high heels, and my hair is waved for the Hillside Christmas party, which is being held at Mr. Mirrell's place, a grand home in Lawrence Park. A "surprise" wrapped Christmas gift—bath essence and powder—for the secret partner I'd chosen in the draw is tucked under my arm.

The fairy lights twinkle in our pine Christmas tree in the corner by the fireplace. Aidan carried it home from the lot on the corner and put it up on a metal tripod. We spent time together yesterday dressing it up with the fairy lights and tinsel and coloured balls, and then we put a flaxen-haired Christmas angel on the top. "A load of bosh—just magical thinking" he said. But it still looks pretty.

I hesitate. I have my answer ready: that this year the staff has decided it was to be teachers only. "No spouses or couples, Aidan." I affect regret, as if I'm bewildered. I feel mean and cowardly again. "Everyone decided to keep it to just staff this year—keep it simple," I lie. "Honestly, I don't really want to go." At least that was true. "See you later, Aidan, I won't stay long; it's a bore."

So I go alone and make sure I slip away early without saying goodbye. I feel lonely, disassociated from the merriment, the happy loud couples sharing the fun and festivities. There are screams of delight as teachers open their gifts—a roll of co-loured toilet paper that plays a tune, and even bright naughty Santa boxer shorts for Mr. Mirrell, accompanied by screams. Everyone is having fun. I try to meld into the background by Mr. Mirrell's Christmas tree. "No husband, Selena?" Mr. Mirrell smiles kindly. He and his stout evangelical wife Mabel are Presbyterians. I make the excuse that Aidan's own staff party is the same evening, so we'd decided to split up and go our separate ways.

"Too bad they've fallen on the same night." I pretend regret.

"Oh, that's a shame," says Mr. Mirrell. "We'd have loved to meet your husband. Maybe next time, at the end-of-year party." He smiles.

The next evening, Aidan takes me proudly to his own staff Christmas Party. It's at his principal Mr. Stanley's house in Toronto, a grand home in York Mills. The boulevard is lined with heavy trees and big turreted old houses, some with ivied walls. We have drinks. I'm dressed in the new red dress again and the stiletto heels, and I've washed and curled my hair. Aidan introduces me personally to his technical director and colleagues, to Mr. Stanley, and to the vice principal, Max Goldstein. They look surprised to see me—Aidan Gilmor's wife? Perhaps they were expecting an exotic Sinhalese woman. Everyone is interested in meeting me. "Wow! I never knew you had such a lovely wife, Aidan!" they exclaim. "Where have you been keeping her?"

"I love your English accent—you enunciate everything so clearly. Say 'Toronto' for us again."

The math teacher, Mel Chang, is from Hong Kong; the history teacher, Stephan Muriani, is Hungarian. He came to Toronto as a child, he says; some of his relatives were killed in the revolution. There are several Jewish teachers, a burly Scot who teaches baking, and a French-Canadian who's in charge of French. Even an Egyptian: Maryam Farzana. They reinforce the realization that I'm living in a secluded enclave in Hillside. This is the new, real, multicultural world beyond Hillside and the Beach that Mr. Mirrell and his teachers so fear.

I see how proud Aidan is of me, of my being his wife. His love for me is so evident in his soft words: "My vife." He says this to his principal with such innocent faith that I want to weep.

Instead, I say, "Yes, Aidan is a wonderful husband." His face lights up with pride. I can't stand it.

It wasn't all so congenial at the school, though. Aidan had told me how a few older teachers had taken the huff when a "Coloured" was hired, especially because he was being paid the same as the white teachers. Macaulay, the electrical teacher, took to putting his hands together at his chest like Gandhi and salaaming every time he passed Aidan in the corridors, saying *Namaste*. Aidan had deliberately laughed. "You're doing me an honour, Macaulay. Thank you." Another time Macaulay wrapped a towel round his head like a turban, stuck a knife in his belt, and strutted around the staff-room, guffawing and telling everyone that he was a "rag-head." Some staff laughed, others told him to cut the fuck out. "Don't take any notice of that SOB, Aidan. He's Neolithic."

Now Macaulay sidles up to me among the crowd, beer in hand. "So what's a nice white English girl like you—one of us—doing with a coloured," he hisses. "Married to an oil sheik," he cackles in a low hateful voice. I don't realize that this is an old racist stereotype that really amuses some people.

I know he's trying to get to me. I tighten. "Am I?" I quickly force myself to say innocently. "I wish I were, Mr. Macaulay! Yes. All those lovely oil dollars."

His face darkens, but it's what he says next that twists my gut. He leans close to me, his beery breath in my face. "Like a bit of brown cock to suck, eh…?"

"Oh, all the time," I respond lightly with a grin (essential not to give way to sickening horror).

Macaulay's face suffuses with mortification at my words. I've hit something, though I'm not sure what.

I glance across at Aidan, who's chatting happily to his principal. (Do people look at us this way? The boys on our street, for example? Is that what they think about too when they see us together?) I feel sick. I can't face myself. It's something I'll never tell Aidan—those words—and certainly not Mother.

That's the real shock. Of course, Mother had warned me about what happens to a foolish white girl who gets carried away and marries a foreigner instead of a nice Welsh boy. I just hadn't believed her.

10.

DARLEENE IS PREGNANT. "We couldn't wait!" says Scott. "We wanted to be the first." He laughs, pleased with himself. Time is slipping by, and it's hard to believe that he and Darleene are in their last year at York. Scott has a good job in the federal government lined up and waiting; he did well in his interviews. He's good-looking and articulate. Father-in-law is inordinately proud: "The *government*," he echoes, opening a bottle of Black and White.

The announcement creates another stir in the family. Mother and Father-in-law are excited. "The first Gilmor grandchild to be born in Canada!" boasts Father-in-law. He's quite cheery. The Union Jack flutters gaily at the top of the flagpole.

"Congratulations!" Aidan pats Scottie on the shoulder, and we both give Darleene a hug.

"Well, beat you to the mark, Aidan!" Scott chortles. Aidan blushes, and I'm embarrassed; we're so much older. "All in good time." Mother-in-law smooths over the awkward moment.

Fiona is bristling. "But Daddy, *Heidi* is the first grandchild— she's your oldest!"

"*Aiyo!* Yes, of course, Fiona. You are right," says Mother-in-law quickly, but it's Father-in-law's approval Fiona wants.

"Ughh. But this will be a *Gilmor*." Father-in-law pours himself a whisky. "Gin, old chap?" he turns to Felix, who has added his congratulations.

"This baby will be going back to great-grandfather Gilmor,"

Felix muses. Father-in-law scowls. "That bastard...."

"*Aiyo,* come now, pet."

Darleene remains composed, with that complacent look of pregnant women. She's done it. She will keep the Gilmor line going.

"Wonder what he'll look like. Beautiful, of course," adds Felix quickly, touching on a delicate subject indeed, as only he is free to do, for his geniality is so acceptable.

"It might be a girl," says Darleene reasonably. "A grand-daughter. As long as she's normal, that's what's important." Darleene gives the usual platitude.

"I'm sure the baby will be fair, like Scott," says Mother-in-law fondly. You can see the love and homage she feels for her youngest.

Scott looks proud. He's the centre of his parents' attention, in the lime-light. Aidan whispers to me, "The golden boy."

Fiona is irritated. "Daddy always singles out the fairest. Look how he favours Hans. Heidi sees it. D'you think she doesn't?"

"And Scottie," hisses Aidan.

"Ughh." Father-in-law stares at Fiona, this annoying daughter.

"Now, Fiona that's not fair to Daddy. Of course, he loves them both," says Mother-in-law quickly.

"That may be, but he *favours* Hans."

"Hah!" Felix flicks his ash into a saucer. He's enjoying this little maelstrom that Darleene's innocent pregnancy has aroused. Darleene looks bewildered.

"Of course, the baby could come out looking quite different from Scott and Darleene," observes Fiona spitefully, obviously determined to add fuel to the flames.

"Quite so," agrees Felix."

"What would you know about it, an old bachelor like you?" Mother-in-law bangs her pots irritably.

"I do have a modicum of intelligence, Mildred, and I can read statistics," says Felix. I think of Mother and the socio-genetic statistics that she regularly threatens me with in her letters.

Fiona smokes vigorously, puffing in and out wildly and waving her cigarette about.

"Look at Great Aunt Beatrice's son, Damian. She gave him away because he was too dark."

"*Fiona!*"

"Well, she did!" Fiona lets out a high, shrill laugh. She's just hurled a grenade into the kitchen again.

"Oh, my God, yes!" cries Felix.

Aidan gives a dark smirk. He sees what Fiona is up to.

"Bloody Beatrice!" Father-in-law stomps out into the living room and turns on the radiogram.

"What for bringing up that poor boy, Fiona?" objects Mother-in-law. "You weren't even born then."

"Granny told me, at Anewatte."

Soon we hear the low, serious tones of the *Voice of Ceylon* giving the latest riot in Colombo, drowning out the conversation. Mother-in-law shakes her head. "Pet, pet! Turn that down."

"I wonder if the baby will look like our side of the family or Darleene's," says Aidan. It's a natural enough question, but there's an edge to it; it could start things up again.

"Maybe both," says Darleene, unperturbed; she's modelling herself on Mother-in-law, always in control of herself.

I'm anxious. Does it matter what complexion Darleene's baby will have? I think of the teachers at Hillside, of Mother, and of that technical teacher Macaulay, and I know it does.

"Well, in a sense Fiona is right," says Felix. He's bemused at the dispute. "Aunt Beatrice did give Damian away because he was too dark, poor little devil. She and Uncle Nigel had two very fair little girls, as we Eurasians often do. Then Beatrice gave birth to this skinny little ugly duckling with furry black hair, a throwback to God knows what part of the family." Felix is sardonic. He twists his mouth at the memory, and I know I'm hearing a family secret that Aidan has kept from me. Felix had been a boy at the time, but he remembers. "My God, what a maelstrom that was! Turmoil broke out in the delivery room, and Beatrice shrieked in horror to the midwife, 'Take him away! I don't want that black beetle!' Wouldn't even breastfeed him," Felix recalls. "So they farmed him out to a Sinhalese couple in the village. But Uncle Nigel did pay the fees for Damian's education so he could attend Holy Innocents with Jack and me."

I avoid Darleene's eyes. I'm shocked at this, and surely she must be too. But the awful thing is, I'm not sure Mother or Marlene would necessarily disapprove of Great Aunt Beatrice.

"Oh, that's Ceylon for you. You wouldn't believe," cries Fiona.

"It wouldn't happen today," assures Mother-in-law, suddenly aware of Darleene.

I see the wistfulness on Aidan's face. He wants a baby, I know, a "baby bun." He whispers this at night, under the coverlet: Honey-Bun and Bunny-Hon and Baby-Bun, our new affectionate secret names for each other.

Fiona cannot let go of Kandy Convent. Ever since she read the psychology book *Facing Your Past: Overcoming Buried Trauma* by Nancy Delmontague, she keeps analyzing Mother-in-law.

We're sitting in the diner on Yonge Street again, on another Saturday morning. Fiona has left the two children with Mother-in-law for an hour to give herself a break. The place is a haze of cigarette smoke—someone is coughing—and the windowsills are frowzy with rolls of dust. But there's the usual congeniality, everyone talking and eating and smoking.

The same old waitress staggers under a loaded tray, a pencil stuck behind her ears. We order pancakes and bacon and coffee. Fiona flicks the jukebox and puts in a quarter. "Elvis is King," she cries, and chooses "Wooden Heart."-

"I hardly knew Ma." Fiona's brow furrows in a deep frown. "I was sent away at age *four*!" she repeats, as if it's news to me. Her voice trembles with indignation. "At least Aidan was seven when he went." It's unfair, I agree. Really strange. She's gratified by my support. I wonder if this might not be Fiona's unconscious need to be seen as a victim, perhaps in order to draw the sympathy and love that she feels she did not get from Father and Mother-in-law. (Of course, they must have loved her. She just doesn't see it that way.)

But Fiona presses on. Nancy Delmontague has apparently warned of the psychological dangers of being an eldest child. "Aidan and Scottie *superseded* me when they were born!" she screams. According to Lally, she used to whack Aidan across the head with a stick in the pampas grass out of sight of the bungalow—obvious sibling jealousy. Once, when I asked Mother-in-law about Aidan as a boy, she'd said, "Oh Aidan was the best baby, the best child. He was so good. And beautiful."

"I loved Weyweltalawa," sighs Aidan. "I was traumatized when Ma and Daddy sent me away. They don't understand that." There is pain in his voice. I'm taken aback. I struggle to comprehend all this. It seems so important to them both.

I take another drag on my cigarette and blow out thoughtfully. The old waitress shuffles by, fills our cups with steaming hot coffee, and plunks down a stack of pancakes.

Fiona has a screwy, desperate look on her face, as if to say *dare contradict me!*

Aidan looks sad.

I try to comprehend Mother and Father-in-law's motives. I recall Father-in-law's bewildered look at Fiona's outburst the other day—I'm sure he saw it as ingratitude—and Mother-in-law's hurt. She also seems bewildered by Fiona's concerns after all these years.

"Perhaps they had no choice, Fiona. As Father-in-law said, you were isolated up in the mountains. Would you have liked to go to the local Buddhist school with the village children and be taught in Sinhalese by the Buddhist monks?" I ask deftly.

Fiona shrieks, "God no! Can you imagine?" But her eyes flash dangerously. I sit well back. (She once cracked a plate over Deiter's head during a spat in a fancy restaurant.)

"To be fair to Daddy, you were only there for a year, until

you were five, Fiona," Aidan says. "Then you came back home and went to the little convent school at Hatton with Lally and me, remember? Remember the train we used to take? It stopped in the estate to pick us up. Until I was sent away to Holy Innocents. That's when you returned to Kandy Convent. I remember."

Fiona tosses this more accurate version aside. "Ma was having Scottie! That's why I was sent away so young!" she shrieks. She won't let it go. "I was in the way. And so were you, Aidan, but you were just too young to go to boarding school, that's all."

Fiona is hard and radiant in the truth she now sees clearly, thanks to *Facing Your Past* and Nancy Delmontague. "You should read it, Aidan."

"I didn't want to leave Ma and Daddy. I was traumatized." Aidan is still in his childhood, lamenting over and over about Holy Innocents. He seems broken by the experience.

It occurs to me that Fiona and Aidan have never left Ceylon in their heads and hearts; they never got over the experience. Only Scottie is normal in the sense that he's perfectly at home in Willowdale, in Canada; he doesn't remember anything else. Ceylon is a distant dream with a fairy-tale quality, not his country.

For a moment, I envy Darleene. She and Scottie just don't experience the same things due to Scott's light skin; that's the fact. They'll never get stoned. I try to change the subject.

"You know, I'd have loved to go away to boarding school as a kid," I say, suddenly. Of course, my idea of it is coloured by romantic schoolgirl stories featuring tall English heroines with long blonde hair tossed about their shoulders, and wearing cute short uniforms and panama hats with the school crest in front. It was all very aristocratic and superior; this was the power of these stories, of course. The girls were always having a "ripping good time" at their posh private schools away from their parents, as far removed from my humble local elementary school and Welsh village as could be possible, and from myself.

"Oh no, you wouldn't have," says Fiona witheringly.

Aidan looks hurt. He needs me to agree with him. "That's why we were sent away!" he cries accusingly at me, now. "Because of the screwed-up British colonial idea of family and … and … English status. This was what we 'coloured' colonials aped, like poor Daddy and Ma. . It's not like I even got a good education out of it," he adds bitterly. "Daddy paid hundreds of thousands of rupees for me to be abused and beaten and screwed by those priests. If he only knew—yes!" (I am stunned. So, at last I have some insight into his antagonism toward his father; he blames him, perhaps for not protecting him.)

Fiona makes a choking sound.

I tighten. I don't know what to say. It's another reality I can't relate to Ceylon, to a British colony. The abuse of children in a colonial boarding school seemed an anathema to the genteel British lifestyle I imagined and sometimes coveted.

"I was so upset and disoriented that I couldn't learn. And they kept beating me for using my left hand. They said left-handedness was the work of the devil. Father St. Sebastian kept forcing me to use my right hand. My brain couldn't cope. That's why I didn't do well in school— until I came to Canada. Canada saved me."

"But your cousin Colin did well there. At the wedding he told me he loved Holy Innocents," I say, pushing away Aidan's horrific revelation.

"*Colin was right-handed!* And he went home every weekend to Aunty Agnes who lived close to the school. The priests knew that. He didn't know what I went through in those Sunrise Cottages. No one did."

Aidan stabs his fork through a pancake, tears in his eyes. "I didn't find myself until I came to Canada, to Willowdale, and I was put into the technical stream at Bathurst Heights Secondary. That's when I came into my own, thanks to the tech teachers. The school was sixty percent Jewish then, in the fifties. Nate Levy used to take me home and his mother would feed me up." He smiles at the recollection. "She'd say 'Eat, Aidan, eat!' Oh, those blintzes and matzo ball soups! And we also got the extra Jewish high holidays! He chuckles.

"The teachers were good to me, too. For the first time in my life I heard I was smart—not dumb like Father St. Sebastian used to tell Ma and Daddy. 'He's fit only for ploughing the fields,' he'd say. No wonder they only saved up to send Scottie to university! But the technical teacher saw my drawing skills—about the only thing Holy Innocents gave me. The Sinhalese penmanship teacher let me use my left hand and I excelled at copying the Sinhalese curly script. It made me careful and detailed. Later at Bathurst Tech I graduated first place in architecture and drafting in grade twelve. Ma and Daddy were so surprised."

Fiona is listening attentively. "I never realized, Aidan." She has always thought Scottie is the smart one.

"No one does," says Aidan bitterly.

"But it's not his fault," I put in quickly. "You can't blame Scottie."

Aidan stares at himself, aged seven. He stands in the old sepia photograph, hands clenched. He's dressed in his new Holy Innocents uniform: stiff white shirt, striped school tie, khaki shorts down to his knees and long woolen socks up to his knees, and polished English leather shoes. His long curls have been cut. (I'd seen a little snapshot of him younger, about age four, splashing carefree in a waterfall at Weyweltalawa, dressed in little cotton knickers and vest, his fair curls clinging wet to his face.)

We're sitting in our kitchen, which is sunny and quiet in our house on Morton Road. Bosie is flopped at our feet, hoping for a walk.

The words tumble out: the dormitory in Sunrise Cottages, designated for the little boys up to age ten; being beaten by the priest on duty and shitting his nightgown in terror; the priest's sardonic laugh. He becomes that little boy again. He puts the photo down on the table, clearly in pain. Then a darker memory surfaces that he hadn't spoken of before: the Tamil assistant, The Man, who molested him when he was nine. Aidan doesn't look at me. I hear the clock out in the hall, the slow rhythmic thuds marking time, the time it takes to remember. "I didn't know what was happening, he came from behind, holding me tight."

The words echo, unreal. (So, it wasn't being left-handed that stopped his learning.)

"The other day I was watching this Chief of Six Nations on TV talking about being sexually abused in the residential school he was forced to go to. It changed everything, seeing him cry like that. A grown man cry. I got it. Finally I understood what had happened to me. He's a brave man to speak out, to say those words on television. It's called 'telling your truth,' Selena. I never said a word until now. Never told Ma and Daddy. Kids don't. The Man must have known that; he must have known that I wouldn't tell. That made it worse. And Daddy sent me there, unprotected. He wasn't there for me, never checked up on me, or the priests. I'll never do that to my kids. I'll be a good father!"

I'm taking it all in. Now I, too, carry this burden.

"You're not going to tell them now, are you? I mean, after all these years?" I suddenly feel anxious for Mother and Father-in-law.

"I might tell Ma one day, when I'm ready, but not Daddy. Not yet, anyway." He sighs. "He was so proud that his eldest son went to Holy Innocents."

11.

SUDDENLY WE'RE IN THE MIDDLE of a race riot. It's February 11, 1969. Protests have broken out at Sir George Williams University in Montreal; it's all over the nightly news. Six Black Caribbean students are occupying the ninth floor of the Henry Hall building. They claim that the biology professor is racist, saying he gives lower marks to Blacks than to whites on their term papers, even when they share the same work.

The daily newspapers are full of it: *rioters protest!* CBC newscasters and cameramen in Montreal move in to capture the latest scoop. Clips of a mass student rally cover the TV screen day and night, black faces yelling slogans into the camera. Pierre Berton, of the *Pierre Berton Hour,* gives his political opinion.

Apparently a committee was set up by university officials to look into the allegations. The hundreds of protestors in the audience—mainly students from the Caribbean and their supporters, some of whom were white—were rowdy and disruptive. "We want justice!" they chanted. "Order! Order!" called the clerk. "Could we have *order*?!" he screamed in the footage on the evening news.

Now, banners and placards are being waved both inside the building and outside on Mackay Street: *JUSTICE! MONTREAL ALABAMA. LIBEREZ NOS CAMARADES!*

It's deemed the largest student riot in Canadian history.

Father-in-law is agog. "What the bloody hell?!"

"*Blacks* are occupying the university's computer centre!"

warns the newscaster. They've taken the elevators and telephones out of service. The media, shocked, emphasize that this is an "act of civil disobedience" in defiance of the police, the courts of justice, and the university officials. It's been going on for two weeks.

"Good God!" Father-in-law stares at the TV in the living room. What's happening to Canada, his chosen country? He looks up, dazed, at Aidan and Felix.

Aidan is secretly enjoying this moment. "Good for them, Daddy!" The computer room on the ninth floor of the university is by all accounts ablaze; the Black students have locked themselves in and *set it on fire.*

"My God, pet! They've set the bloody place *on fire!*"

"Achh. Not a touch on a Ceylon riot, Jack. Over there they set *people* on fire."

"I don't think Selena needs to be hearing such things, Felix," observes Mother-in-law, with a threatening edge to her voice. She continues ironing stolidly on the kitchen table, stamping down on Father-in-law's shirt. ("Mind that collar, pet.")

It's unclear who started the fire. The police blame the students, but the students claim that the cops set it to force them out of the building, and, even worse, that they took away the fire axes.

Another news clip of Mackay Street, smoke swirling out of the upper windows. Police officers, the riot squad from Station 10—in full gear, with bulletproof vests and helmets—are at the ready. They're going to go in.

The alleged influence behind the riot is none other than Stokely Carmichael, one of Aidan's heroes, the leader of the Black Movement for Civil Rights in the United States and the "Black Is Beautiful" ideology. Apparently, Carmichael was guest presenter at McGill University three months before, speaking on civil rights with the support of the Negro Citizenship Association in Montreal, much admired by Aidan. He seizes the opportunity to remind us that when the Gilmors arrived in Canada they were still lynching Blacks in the U.S. There's a terrible silence. Father-in-law makes for the cupboard where the liquor is stowed away for emergencies. I feel sick, a vivid image of a noose swinging makes me weak; the words are cruel, but Aidan seems to relish the moment. It's forcing people—white people—to face up to things. He smirks.

"On the weekend, there's to be a big protest march in downtown Toronto in solidarity with our Black brothers and sisters. Of course, we'll be with them, shoulder to shoulder," he boasts, enthused. "You should come with us, Daddy."

"Ughh." Father-in-law's eyes bulge. "I cross two oceans and the bloody Suez Canal to end up in a Canadian jail?"

"Be careful, Aidan," says Mother-in-law. "You're not taking Selena, are you?"

"Of course I'm going—it's history," I say loyally. Aidan is so eager to do the right thing, so determined when it comes to racial abuse, but I'm beginning to feel that maybe it is the pain from his past that drives him to fight against injustice. (Of course, Mother must not know any of this; she'd cry "*Bolshies.*")

"Hey! They've set the place on fire," says Marlene. The teachers are taking a coffee break in the staff room.

"Mayhem!" echoes Joanne in horror, and the others follow suit.

"It's destruction of property." Now *that* can't be tolerated.

"That's what happens when you let in these niggers," Marlene continues. She sets her mouth and looks at me defiantly.

I stiffen. "I think it's time you drop that word, Marlene. It might even be inciting riots," I say quietly, threatening.

"Sir George Williams has always let in foreigners, every rag tag and bobtail from the islands," cries Joanne, stepping up to support Marlene. "That's the problem."

"It's always been hard for Black students to get into McGill," I respond. "They deliberately set the entrance tests too high. There even was a Jewish quota once, before the War."

This is met with silence. Most of them support quotas. ("What about the rights of our white Canadian students?") Marlene's lips form a tight line when I bring up Stokely Carmichael. She has only the vaguest notion of who he is.

"Well, Stokely Carmichael is the famous Black civil rights leader, and he was *invited* to speak at McGill University, Marlene."

When I say "Black is beautiful," Joanne rolls her eyes.

"And the protestors are hardly rag tags," I point out. "Roosevelt 'Rosie' Douglas is from a leading wealthy educated Black family in Dominica, and Cheddi Jagar is the son of the prime minister of Guyana." (I gathered these useful facts from Aidan.)

"Ughh, so they smash up the university that's been good to them?"

"As if a professor would deliberately give low marks," scoffs Joanne. "They've got some nerve! Lucky to be here in this country—"

"Send them back to where they belong!"

"These Black West Indian students are not the only ones to incite a riot in Canada," I say as evenly as possible, keeping implacable Mother-in-law in mind. "Whites have started racial riots too, right here in Toronto."

There's a stunned silence around the coffee pot. Now I'm in for it. It must be Aidan's influence. I press on: "What about the attacks on Jewish families living in the Beaches in the 1930s? And the race riot at Christie Pits? That was when the Harbord Jewish-Italian baseball team was attacked by the St. Peter's team at the park. It was worse in the Beaches. Jews were mobbed for walking on the boardwalk and letting their kids play on the grass. People even put up signs—*No dogs or Jews allowed*—and smashed the storefronts of Jewish business. It was like Kristallnacht in Hitler's Germany. I read about it in Hugh Garner's novel, *Cabbagetown*—he took part in it himself. And there are records in old Jewish journals of the time. Young Canadian Nazi gangs from the city set up headquarters at Balmy Beach Club of all places, waving swastikas on the boardwalk. They were part of the Swastika Clubs of Toronto. And no one stopped them. Where'd they get the swastikas from?"

I've said enough. Marlene is incensed; her eyes are bulging. The others look stricken. Everyone is listening, their sandwiches suspended, especially when I cite *Der Yidisher Zhurnal*. I could be Aidan, a troublemaker.

"But that's the past, ages ago, another generation. They were just kids, Selena. It didn't last long," says Marlene.

But the Jewish families sold their businesses and moved away all the same, I think but don't say out loud. Who could blame them? They quietly shifted to the other side of the city, up Bathurst Street, and clustered around the synagogues for security. Others settled in a more elite neighbourhood, which is actually located on the other side of the school. It was quietly acknowledged, like a tentative truce. But the fact is they're gone from the Beaches. Only an old synagogue remains, unobtrusive on a quiet street, a testament to the past. I think about how the Black riot at Sir George Williams will one day be forgotten, a footnote in Canadian archives. (Perhaps I now have some understanding of Father-in-law's weird obsession with the riots in Ceylon; perhaps he doesn't want them to be passed over, diminished, revised.) It's a battle.

After lunch, my students have their weekly library period to browse and check out books. Todd Milford, the librarian, takes me aside behind a bookcase. He's an unobtrusive, mild man with pale blue eyes and fair hair. He wears round rimless spectacles like Gandhi's for reading, which gives him a studious air. He also teaches grade eight math, in the senior division, so I seldom cross his path. He says in a low voice, keeping an eye on the students, "Selena, I want you to know that we don't all think like Marlene Fisher. She's old Ontario stock. Some of us understand what's at stake in Montreal and support the Caribbean students. And," he pauses with a wry smile, "my grandfather was in the attacks against the Jews in the Beaches in the 1930s. He took part in the Christie Pits riot too; a group of them on the St. Peter's baseball team beat up the Jewish kids on the Harbord team—though they got as good as they gave. The Jewish kids didn't take it lying down, and they had the Italian kids joining in on their side. It's not something I'm proud of."

"I'm glad you told me. Thanks, Todd. I always feel so alone, as if I'm under siege."

"You're not alone."

Over ninety people have been arrested in Montreal, including white supporters. The six original protestors are still locked inside the computer room. To the death!

"What the hell is going on, son?" Father-in-law sways about the kitchen, whiskey in hand. He thought he'd left this sort of thing behind in Ceylon. "*Black power*? What the hell is that?" he cries.

"You should have read *Soul On Ice*, Daddy," smirks Aidan.

We now know that the leader is from Dominica, from the Windward Islands in the Lesser Antilles. Another rebel is from Barbados, another from Jamaica. "Bloody hell!" cries Father-in-law, and downs his glass of whisky.

"It'll soon settle down," soothes Mother-in-law.

"No, it won't, Ma," Aidan insists. "The white supremacists are in it now. They've gathered on Mackay Street chanting 'Let the niggers burn!'"

"*Aiyo,* now that is going too far."

The white supremacists, some with bandanas over their faces, stare up at the ninth floor, chanting those hateful words; it's all on the news.

"I never knew we *had* bloody white supremacists." Father-in-law says, pouring more whisky into his glass.

"Well, I think it's probably true, Daddy—what they say. I bet the Black students do get lower marks," cries Aidan, eager as always for a dispute. "And they're fighting back, exposing the system. I know that some teachers at my school Brockhurst High regularly pass over black students for marks and awards, even in athletics."

I join in and mention that Gladstone and Yolande are always passed over even though they are the fastest runners and Gladstone is the best baseball player in the school. "It happens."

"But Aidan, why should a Black student get high marks just because he's Black?" drawls Scott, joining in the dispute. He and Darleene have dropped in for afternoon tea, and to show off baby Emily. Darleene sits down next to a pile of ironing, and cuddles her. "Maybe the professor is right and their work is *not* as good. Maybe they're just not as brainy."

The two brothers face each other: Scott with a university education and Aidan with a raw intelligence.

Father-in-law stares balefully at his favoured son, who is working on getting a Master's degree from a Canadian university. He should therefore know, but doesn't necessarily.

"Perhaps Scott is right," says Mother-in-law smoothly. "We don't know the full story."

"Oh, come off it, Ma!"

Darleene feeds Emily some scoops of milky rice, and Mother-in-law fusses over them. The baby was baptized by Father Matthew a week ago in St. Raphael-of-All Angels, to Mother and Father-in-law's satisfaction. They're very pleased with Darleene. She's pregnant again with her second. "Thought I'd get it over with all in one go," she smiles cheerfully. "They can play together." Emily is fair like her, with soft blonde baby hair and big hazel eyes, to the delight of Mother and Father-in-law. Scott likes to boast about little fair-skinned Emily: "There's no doubt who the mother of this baby is."

Mr. Mirrell calls an emergency staff meeting to deal with the crisis. Should our Black students be barred from school for their own protection?

"Mr. Mirrell, I'm worried about what's happening out on the playground right now." My voice wavers anxiously. "Only this morning on yard duty I heard kids in grade four taunting our West Indian students, repeating the words they're hearing on TV at night: 'Let the n... burn.'"

The ugly words resonate round the room. There's a squeak from Marlene and a gasp from the teachers, and my face turns red, but the words speak for themselves.

Mr. Mirrell looks flustered and wipes his forehead. I'm conscious of a definite wave of hostility.

"Let kids be kids. You can't be on their backs for everything," Marlene speaks up. "It will pass."

"I think Selena is right," says a male voice suddenly from the senior division. It's Todd Milford. "We teachers should take a stand and show that we won't tolerate any prejudice." There's a low mumble from the staff, but no one speaks out.

"I think we'll defer to the board on this," says Mr. Mirrell faintly.

In Montreal, the protestors have hurled thousands of computer tapes and white punch cards out of the windows of the ninth floor, like swarms of snowflakes descending on Mackay Street. They have done two million dollars' worth of damage.

Anne Cools from Barbados refuses in court to admit she's guilty of any moral wrong doing, and is sentenced to two months in jail. 'Rosie' Douglas from Dominica is given two years, and is to be deported later. The leader, Kennedy Fredericks, has fled to Tanzania.

"Serves them right," says Marlene at lunch. "I hope they all rot in jail."

"Tanzania? Just shows what we're letting in!"

"Darkest Africa."

"Why should Canadians pay for their expenses in jail? Deport the lot of them."

"And that includes Gladstone Williams and that half-breed sister of his, Yolande."

Years later, Roosevelt "Rosie" Douglas will have a brilliant career in politics, and eventually become Prime Minister of Dominica. And Anne Cools will be granted a pardon by the Canadian government. She will found the first shelter for female victims of violence in Toronto, and in 1984, she will be appointed to the Canadian Senate by Prime Minister Pierre Elliott Trudeau. But back then, none of us can even remotely imagine these things.

12.

"WHY DON'T YOU AND YOUR HUSBAND come to our bridge night Thursday evening, Selena? We still haven't met him; it must be nearly two years." Marlene turns to me at the lunch table. Now that the rioters in Montreal have been vanquished, the leaders suitably punished and put away, and the professor involved reinstated and exonerated of all charges, they turn their attention back to normal life—to me.

I've managed to evade mention of Aidan and my marriage, hoping it will not be noticed. But now the teachers are inviting us to be bridge partners, which I recognize as a gesture of friendship and acceptance. Despite our differences, they want us to be part of their social circle. I'm English after all, and so, they imagine, is Aidan. They think he's one of them. But can either of us ever be?

"You and your husband don't *play bridge?*" Disbelief. Everyone knows how to play contract bridge in their circle. "What does he like to do, then?" I bite carefully into my egg sandwich, trying to play for time. "Um, he … he helps out at the missions downtown."

They look bewildered. "You mean hostels for destitutes? Isn't that dangerous? He could catch something." There's silence as they absorb this new information. It implies that Aidan—and by extension me—might not be a fit for their social circle after all. Even though Marlene is a Baptist evangelical and does "good works" for the poor, it doesn't extend into her bridge parties, for which she will not be made to feel guilty, she says. She takes up her knife and cuts fiercely into a smelly sausage.

"So what do *you* do, then, Selena, in your spare time?" asks Martha, from primary division.

It takes me by surprise. I gulp my coffee. "Me? Oh ... *um* ... yoga, I guess."

"You mean stand on your head upside down and twist yourself into knots?"

"But *what for*?"

Quizzical faces turn in my direction. I tense. They're wondering if I'm into psychism. Or magic. Martha is suspicious—her father is a minister. For some reason, I'm an inexhaustible source of interest.

"Idol worshippers," she pronounces. She's particularly upset at the idea of no pews and devotees sitting cross-legged *on the floor*, staring at nothing. I suppose it might seem that way. Yoga is the foreign threat that is infiltrating the West, and even the Beaches. It is at their own backdoor, undermining the established Church.

"It's just exercises, really, and ... meditation."

Marlene looks concerned; this is not like saying the Lord's Prayer to oneself. I imagine that she would be alarmed at the sight of the rows of candles, little bowls of fruit and rice, and white scarves before the image of the Buddha in the Beach Sun Yoga Centre. But is it any different from a Christian Thanksgiving service with its sheaves of oats, turnips, and marrows at the sanctuary? Or from a Christmas service with crèches and statues of sheep and cows and angels round a mound of straw before the altar? But Marlene is not into inter-ecumenical dialogue.

Most of the teachers in our division, I know by now, are Protestant: Presbyterian, United Church (former Methodists and Baptists), and Anglican. They are all church-going and devout; it's part of their husbands' financial portfolios. (Marlene belongs to a Baptist Missionary Society that sends aid to Africa, so she's into converting.)

"You better be careful, Selena. It could be a cult," she warns darkly.

Another peaceful Sunday in the Willowdale bungalow. It's a relief to be away from the school for a couple of days. Mother-in-law is making a pot of tea, still wearing her church clothes.

"Selena's becoming a Buddhist."

"Noo!" Father-in-law puts down his beer, and the teapot drops with a thud.

Aidan grins.

I feel distinct irritation at him for exposing me—this is surely a betrayal. "Well, what for keeping it secret, if you genuinely believe in it?" he needles. He'd spotted my meditation niche on the bookshelf in our bedroom: a small clay Buddha, a little brass bell to ring three times to begin the practise, and sticks of special incense—the same kind that is apparently used by real yogis in the Himalayas and in the ashrams and temples of India and Ceylon. "It's all in your head," he'd mocked. "Magical thinking! You're going back to the stone age," which of course had spoiled any meditation. I'd blown out the candle, annoyed, and stubbed out the incense stick.

"*Buddhism?*"

Mother-in-law raises her arms in bewilderment, and Fiona snorts. I say, "Oh, don't listen to Aidan. I just go to yoga in the Beaches once a week. Lots of Canadians do." I try to downplay it and back-pedal, to Aidan's amusement.

"You bought a mantra from the swami for your next life."

"*Aiyo!*"

How I regret taking Aidan with me to swami's *darshan,* holy blessing, at the Sun Yoga Centre. Now he's using it to annoy and tease me. "I was just curious to see an Eastern ... holy man," I murmur, trying to calm down Father-in-law, who's opened another beer.

At the centre, there was blessed incense and sacred flowers in honour of the visitor, Swami Tissananda, from India. We sat cross-legged on the floor of the center with the other devotees. "Why are they sacred?" Aidan argued at the time. "They're not any more sacred than Daddy's petunias."

Sandra, our yoga instructor, invited Swami Tissananda to the centre to give the devotees the *darshan*. ("Ughh, and you give him dollars," hissed Aidan.) The devotees were mainly hippies and students—some of whom were dressed all in white with shawls over their shoulders—and a few seniors looking intense with joy.

Swami was not quite what I'd expected. He wore a saffron robe that was swirled around a big fat belly. (Shouldn't a yogi be thin from a holy bare-bones diet?) He'd just come from a visit to Ceylon, where he'd spent time meditating with the monks at Kandy Temple. It was part of a world tour—he was flying all around the globe in his jet, promoting peace, love, and yoga. He was giving out special secret mantras for devotees to meditate on for the rest of their lives; I had my fifty-dollar donation ready.

"See, Aidan? Swami has been practising Ceylon Theravada meditation, so he must be genuine," I whispered.

"Why must he be genuine just because he's been with Ceylonese monks? They're the biggest scoundrels on earth. Where does he get the money for his fancy jet when Ceylon is going bankrupt?"

"Shh! His holiness is speaking." A young girl wrapped in a white shawl turned around, frowning.

"*Om om, om namah shivaya!*" Swami had chanted in a loud magnetic voice. "It's no accident you are all here in Sun Yoga Centre this blessed evening, because we're all connected in spirit. *We've known each other before in a previous life.*"

Low ripples of exclamation. Along with everyone else, I was thrilled—though I was glad Father-in-law was not there, for he and Mother-in-law firmly believe in the resurrection of the body and life everlasting only once. We, however, believed Swami implicitly.

"Load of bullshit," Aidan muttered under his breath.

"*Om, om! Hare Krishna, Ram ram! Shanti!*"

A basket was passed around for offerings during the chanting. The hippies and young people tossed in their five- and ten-dollar bills. Some older adults, sobbing softly, wrote cheques. I dropped in a ten-dollar bill, changing my mind about the fifty-dollar donation for my personal mantra. "Are you crazy?" hissed Aidan. But I wanted to believe in Swami. I wanted to believe that this fat rollicking man was a genuine yogi, even though he doubtless couldn't touch his toes to save his life. I wanted to believe that if I meditated long enough on his secret mantra, I would annihilate Marlene and my own betrayals.

"She believes in reincarnation, Daddy," Aidan continues, enjoying himself.

"Good God!"

"That's not true! At least, not the way you're saying it."

"Huh, they're all fakes," cries Fiona, butting in. "We had Swami Michael teaching yoga in Richmond Hill—handsome young East Indian guy, with long black curls and Bollywood looks. Then he was found screwing the devotees, the young pretty ones, of course. He made off with all the cash, and the police still haven't got him."

Father-in-law is gulping, incensed at Fiona using the word *screwing* in his presence. He reaches for the whisky. This needs something strong.

"See! Now I've upset Daddy!"

Mother-in-law turns to me, ignoring Fiona. "You know, Father Matthew says be true to yourself and your God, Selena. I wish you had heard him this morning at mass." (Still hoping I'll convert, perhaps.)

"She's been writing to some monk in Kandy Temple."

Father-in-law pours himself the last of the bottle, his eyes still bulging.

"Pet, pet, mixing drinks is not good for the organs, the doctor says—"

"I take Andrews Liver Salts every bloody morning, don't I?" Father-in-law grumbles.

Mother-in-law turns to me, looking worried. Writing to a monk? That's serious. "But what for all this, Selena?"

"Oh, it's just someone who used to be at Kandy Temple called Nyanaponika. The monks sent me some little booklets on meditation. I was curious, that's all." I try to shrug it off.

In reality, I'd taken a chance and sent a letter—and a bank draft for twenty-five dollars, which must have translated into thousands of rupees—addressed to: "Chief Monk, Kandy Temple, Kandy, Ceylon." Then I waited and hoped for the best. Fine, pale, onion-skin booklets, just two inches square, had arrived forthwith along with a kind letter from a monk of the Bodhi Press, Kandy, likely a small local press.

I pull *Meditation for Beginners* out of my purse and show Mother-in-law; it was printed in Kandy by Buddhist Publications Society by Dharmawardene Gammanpila.

"But that is a big press of the monks. And Nyanaponiks was a famous monk," cries Mother-in-law. She turns the tiny frail booklet over in her hands. "Kandy Printers, Dalada vidiya, Kandy," she reads aloud. "I know where that is."

"You do?"

"Yes. It's not far from Kandy Temple."

I'm excited. Monk Khantipalo is suddenly real.

Father-in-law drains his glass, heaves himself up, and pokes quietly around the shelf under the sink where Mother-in-law keeps her cleaning fluids and floor polish. Behind a bottle of Clorox Bleaches-Whiter-Than-Snow he sneaks out a small bottle of scotch, glancing at Mother-in-law, and unscrews it behind her back. He takes a quick swig. "Damn monks."

"Now, then, pet. It's wrong to speak ill of anyone, Father Matthew says."

She reminds him that there had been good in Kandy, too,

like the kind old monk who had helped them with their papers to leave Ceylon.

"Ughh."

Mother-in-law is confused. Her English daughter-in-law turning to Buddhism while she herself had turned to Roman Catholicism, how many lifetimes back, in another era. The irony can't be denied.

"Well, Granga was Buddhist," taunts Aidan. He's enjoying his parents' discomfort and his newfound power to wield it, of course. I can see that a family history of betrayals—secrets I'm not privy to—has been unwittingly touched upon. Fiona smirks, also sensing her parents' helplessness.

"Yes, yes, that is true." Mother-in-law recapitulates the way she often does, keeping control.

"I used to go to the temple sometimes as a child, with my mother," she concedes slowly. "She took me on *poya* days, holy days on the Buddhist calendar—the time of the full moon. They dress in white and carry temple flowers with white sweet-scented blossoms. Yes, it is very nice."

Something implicit opens and closes. I'm sorry now that my curiosity about Buddhism has brought up feelings of regret and pain for them, for I'm fond of Father and Mother-in-law. "But ... you're still a Christian, Selena?" Mother-in-law is truly concerned.

"Oh, yes. Yes, of course. As far as I understand, the Catholic church is okay with meditation," I add slowly, cunningly.

"*Aiyo!*" Mother-in-law seizes at this. "That is true. We recite the rosary to the Virgin Mary. You may meditate on that, Selena, on Our Lady. She will answer your prayers!" *Pray for us sinners now and at the hour of our death....*

"Father Matthew says the rosary is the 'book of the blind'," says Mother-in-law, nodding, apparently quoting a saint.

Father-in-law settles down, clearly relieved. I'm still a Christian. Aidan grins. I think of Marlene and her fishy, sneaky eyes, the power I've given her over me. I am angry with myself.

"Mother Evangelica used to make us say the rosary at Kandy Convent at bedtime. But really, Ma! If you saw what Renata and I see."

I picture Fiona and her girlfriend Renata in some sleazy dive with flashing neon lights at the edge of the highway, next to a convenient motel in Richmond Hill.

Her eyes flash. "Ughh, these guys are wimps. Dagos and wops and pakis on the prowl behind their wives' backs, looking for a quick screw. Then they go to Mass and say the rosary. Oh, could we tell you!"

"My God!" Father-in-law gapes again. He's trembling.

Fiona laughs shrilly. "It's true, Daddy!"

"That's racist!" cries Aidan, embarrassed.

"Fiona, what for this silly talk? Sit down with Selena and have a cup of tea." Mother-in-law attempts to smooth things over. She pours the tea.

"I don't have time for cups of tea in my life, Ma! I came to borrow your sewing machine. I'll return it next Saturday." She wants to fix up a pretty but old dress for Saturday night. She and Renata are going to the Red Hot Hop.

"Ughh, what did we do wrong, pet?" Father-in-law buries his face in his arms, as usual, after Fiona leaves. In Ceylon, Fiona would have returned home with the children to be under Father-in-law's protection after a divorce. But here in Canada, the bungalow and his salary are too small. Father-in-law weeps, perhaps at his loss of power, his inability to protect. And the bloody way his daughter says *screw* all the time.

"Where the hell is Felix when I need him?"

The fact is, Father-in-law always weeps easily. Just the thought of Fiona going through that divorce from Deiter annihilates him. Her self-will, her daring defiance. "Forked lightning," Felix calls her.

"Jack, pet, what for tears. Father Matthew says to count our blessings. Our sons are doing well, and Fiona is a good mother despite her faults. And we have another grandchild on the way, and two good daughters-in-law."

I can't help tightening at the thought of my betrayals, my lack of courage concerning Aidan at school, the one I should most defend. Worse, Mother-in-law pats my head. "Selena is a good daughter to us, pet, and a good wife to Aidan, so loyal. He's lucky to have her."

Aidan looks pleased; he smiles at me. I'm his.

I hear Father-in-law mumbling awkwardly, without looking at me: "Yes, a damn good daughter-in-law. Why the hell you make her wash dirty dishes in the sink, and chop up chicken livers like a bloody servant, I don't know."

Their loving voices blur in the usual soft grumbling. This is what their marriage comes down to, their intimate retaliations and banter in the darkening afternoon, comforting, assuring. I feel their warmth and faith in me, and Aidan's pride, and something twists inside.

It's the same kind of wrench I'd felt when little Brian Sven waited for me one afternoon after the bell at school. He'd looked anxious and excited, edging up to my desk. "Miss, can I show you somethink?"

Brian Sven has white-blond hair, Nordic blue eyes like glass, and pale skin. His face is solid, his lips arched. A sturdy, kind boy, well-liked by his classmates, no trouble. Shyly he'd pulled out a worn wallet from his pants pocket. "I got something special for you ter see, Miss."

It was a well-thumbed photograph. He thrust it into my hands. Against the shadows is a Black man, tall and thin with frizzy tight hair, a jazz player I presumed since he held a clarinet in his hands; he'd half turned to smile at the camera. A few other Black men were visible in the background playing instruments—a bassoon, a piccolo, and something else. They seemed to be in a nightclub, you could see smoke rising in wreaths and faded people at a bar. "That's my dad."

He observed me closely. Something was happening to me

that Brian couldn't see. I quickly expressed delight, admiration. "Well, how wonderful, Brian! You're a lucky boy! A musician for a dad?"

Brian smiled. "He plays the clarinet, Miss, in a band out west. Vancouver. He's famous."

"Really? What's his name?

"Lightning Riley. He got a band, Lightning Riley's Band. They're on tour right now."

"Do you"—here I'd hesitated, but the boy had his photograph—"ever see your dad, Brian?"

"My mom and I are going out west ter visit him in July. My mom is Swedish." That accounted for his Swedish surname; she'd given him hers.

"So that's where you get your blond hair from. Is it the first time you'll be meeting your dad?"

He nodded. "Since I was a baby. He had ter go off and work at his music. He writes to me sometimes and we talk on the phone."

"Well, I'm happy for you, Brian."

I prayed this was not going to be a big disappointment for him. I wanted it to work out. I wanted this absent jazz guy to love this son, maybe come to Toronto and live with him. And I wanted to protect Brian from the Marlenes and Joannes and Mr. Mirrells of this world. I couldn't bear that he might have heard the ugly supremacist chanting in Montreal and come to realize something very deep and ugly about the dad he loved.

But who was I to have such fears and hopes? To judge? "Well, you know Brian, it's a very busy life being a musician, a performer. Your dad likely has to be on the move all the time." What a phony platitude. I could hear my voice bleating. Brian knew at once.

"Oh yes, Miss. That's why he can't see me too much." He'd said this with such innocent faith and love that I longed to put my arms around him.

He pushed the photo back into the wallet, our secret. Then

he left, shutting the door quietly after him, the boy that he is. But something had happened. Had that been the moment? Were Mother and Father-in-law and Brian the turning-point? I suddenly knew what I had to do. I'd always known.

It's the end-of-year party at Mr. Mirrell's house again. Another potluck and BYOB. I have a six-pack ready, and a cheesecake. I wear a new summer dress and sandals. I've washed and curled my hair; it glows, falling in a blonde sheath to my shoulders.

"You look lovely," says Aidan. He takes me in his arms. He's dressed in a fresh light open-neck shirt and summer pants for the party. A deep brown V of bronzed skin peeks through his shirt. Everything is going to change this evening—everything between us and inside myself. It already has. I'm going to face something—I'm going to reveal who and what I am—and *I don't care*. This *is* who I am. And now Mr. Mirrell and the teachers will know.

"I'm sorry, Aidan, about everything ... not taking you to my staff parties." Not acknowledging you, keeping you in shadow, that dark place, that otherness. "Pretending you couldn't come, all those times. I lied."

The words hover. The truth.

"Aw, Selena, I knew all along. Did you think I didn't? Of course, I saw through you.... But you weren't ready. It was hard for you. I understand, honest."

What else wasn't I ready for? "I'm such a coward...."

"You're not, Selena. You're brave. You married me, didn't you? You did more than Daddy did with Lily."

He hugs me to him, his Honey-Bun. "I'm sorry Bunny-Hon," I murmur. Honey-Bun and Bunny-Hon. "Isn't it time we had a little Baby Bun?" he whispers. He's wanted a baby for such a long time. Something, a veil of illusion perhaps, seems to part in a rosy film.

We get into the car and Aidan turns on the ignition. We're off to the staff party, together. Anything could happen now.

It's Mrs. Mirrell who opens the door. She's stout and short, decked out in chiffon and pearls, like the Queen Mother. "Ohhh?"

We're shown into the Mirrells' recreation room at the back, Aidan and I together, hand in hand. The teachers and their partners are gathered around. They turn, startled. The low, pleasant hum of conversation stops.

13.

MOTHER IS COMING OVER. "It's time," she writes, some-what ominously, in her letter. I'm anxious. I think about the relations she will meet. As fond as I am of Felix, I'm not sure what Mother will make of him, in his black macabre clothes; she's sure to see him as Svengali. And then there are the mix of children, now close relatives by marriage: Heidi and Hans, not to mention Darleene's two baby girls. Mother is sure to take note of the startling difference between them. Darleene had a second baby recently, and they named her "Kimberley." It had been easy to spot her in the nursery wing at the hospital, her little brown face nestled in her bassinet amongst the rows of white babies. "Funny, isn't it," Darleene said obliquely from her bed in the maternity ward, "how the genes fall each time." I know Mother is not in favour of me having children. ("You don't know *what* they'll come out looking like, Selena.") Now Mother will see for herself. But is it so terrible? And then there's Fiona's hair. She cropped her beautiful shoulder-length locks close to her scalp, like a nun. She couldn't have picked a worse time to cut them off.

"Good God!" Father-in-law gaped as Fiona came in through the kitchen door. "Now I've got a bloody *bhikkhu* for a daughter."

"My new look, Daddy. My new life." It seems her girlfriend Renata was thrown out of El Mocambo and went back to Ecuador with gangsters in pursuit. "No more men for me.

That's it! I'm finished with the jerks." She was wearing a dark pantsuit and a crisp white shirt, very business-like.

Fiona has been reading *The Feminine Mystique*. "Betty Friedan says to hell with housework and being a slave to a man, Daddy."

"Since when were you ever Deiter's slave?" murmured Felix, who'd been watching the interaction, bemused.

"Betty Friedan says statistics show married women are unhappy. They need to throw off the image of themselves in the glossies—the girly magazines, Felix—and get out there and have careers. We're confined by our sexual, biological role, and we have to challenge it."

Father-in-law's eyes widened; he was offended by the word *sexual* in his kitchen. He knocked back another whisky, trembling. "And who the hell is Betty Friedan?"

Despite my anxiety, when Mother comes through the arrivals gate at Pearson Airport, my heart leaps for joy. *Mother! Mum, oh Mum!* It's been over three years since the wedding.

"Well, it's certainly a lovely big place you have, Selena," Mother says, settling in. The house is pretty, with its white-frame siding and green gables. She glances at Aidan. "I see you've grown a beard, Aidan."

It's now curly and deep black. He's trimmed it into a Van Dyke, which makes his rounded face look more angular, more European (less Ceylonese). "You've certainly changed."

"Thanks to Selena."

Aidan looks abashed. He's still not completely comfortable with his new look. He complains regularly about the English tweed jacket. "It's itchy. Why do I have to wear it?" He adds crossly, "And why should I smoke this damn pipe?"

"Oh, you look good with it," I coax.

"Here's your room, Mum. I'm sorry it's so small." But it overlooks the backyard with the large oak tree in the corner. I've put a bunch of flowers on the windowsill.

"Well, I'll only sleep in here," says Mother gracelessly.

But later, downstairs, she turns to me. "You've gone to a lot of trouble in my room, Selly." She tries to hug me. I feel awkward.

Over tea the following week, Mother waits for me to confide in her about the intimate details of my marriage. She gives hints: "So ... how are ... things between you and Aidan ... okay?" Lightly prising me open. At once I close up tight like a clam in the sand.

Once the initial excitement has died down, there's less to talk about. Mother quickly grows bored and restless here on Morton Road. We don't *do* anything, she complains, except walk the boardwalk with the dog. She notices my little altar in the bedroom and eyes the Buddha suspiciously. "You're not becoming religious, are you Selena?"

We're walking along the boardwalk again. Mother is flashing flirtatious little smiles at every older unaccompanied bachelor walking his poodle. "I think he's *looking* at me, Selena."

"Don't you have friends?" she asks another time. She means friends of my own. I pretend to dismiss it, but the question drops like a ton of cement.

"It's summer, all the teachers I work with are on holiday or live far away, Mum," I evade. The fact is, after I appeared at the party with Aidan, the teachers became distant and awkward. They stopped talking freely about the immigrant children in front of me, and began sending each other significant looks, like a code. Eventually, Marlene broached the topic of Aidan's colour. "Well ... he's certainly a darker hue. What is he, then?"

When I said "Eurasian," there was silence as the teachers tried to guess exactly what that was.

"Like ... *mestizo*?" enquired Marlene finally, sweetly.

"Yeah, you could say that, Marlene."

Mother would understand Marlene's view perfectly, I realize, feeling uneasy.

"And you never see any neighbours about." Mother looks

disgruntled. She expects to be invited into people's homes for morning tea, just like I had at the beginning. "They're all out at work, I guess," I say weakly, thinking of Mrs. Mainwaring next door. She'd watched Mother and me walk past the house, and she'd quickly twitched her net curtain.

"But you don't seem to have any *fun*, Selena. Don't you go out dancing?" She saw the square dancing in the park the other evening as we strolled yet again down to the boardwalk. Dancers twirled merrily in a bright circle on the grass; the women were in swirling skirts and coloured blouses, the men in jeans with bright neckerchiefs round their throats. "One and two and dosey-do...." There were a couple of fiddlers and an accordionist. It did look fun.

"Aidan doesn't dance."

"Well, you could go."

"Oh, I wouldn't do that without him."

Mother tossed her head. "I did anything I wanted in my marriage."

"I know."

"Look, one of them is waving at you."

It was Todd Milford. "Oh, he's a teacher at my school." I waved back, smiling.

"He *likes* you, Selena."

"Oh, don't be silly, Mum." I'd laughed. Mum and her old fantasies about me, again. Todd was twirling a woman around, bending gallantly. He was wearing a bright red dotted neck-erchief, and he looked debonair. I was surprised. It certainly was different from how he looked in the library, bespectacled and nondescript. "He's looking at you again! He's waving. He *like*s you, I'm telling you. And he's nice looking. He looks English—blue eyes and fair hair."

"I think he is. Well, just born over there—he's been here all his life. He's Canadian."

It struck me then that Todd was the type of fine Englishman Mother would have liked me to marry.

"You know, Selena, you're becoming far too serious. You'll get age lines early around your eyes if you don't watch it."

She opened her purse, took out her compact, and dabbed her nose with powder. "Now how about a glass of wine and a ciggy back home, ducks?"

"Oh, do we *have* to?" Mother frowns, wrinkling her nose.

"Yes. They're Aidan's parents, and they don't live far. It would be an insult if you don't visit, Mum."

"By the way"—I hesitate, bracing myself—"they might call you 'Mrs. Harcourt,' Mum, instead of Jones. I used to go by Harcourt as a teacher to differentiate myself from other Joneses on staff."

"Oh well, it doesn't matter. It's only *them*...." I wince, but am relieved, nevertheless. Mother lights a cigarette and offers me one. I take it gladly. We puff thoughtfully. Mother gives me a quick, penetrating glance. "Don't like 'Jones' then? Well, I didn't myself when I first married Daddy."

"Oh, it's not that...." I lie. How guileful I can be.

She dresses up. "There's no need to be fancy, Mum." I know that Mother-in-law will likely be in a plain skirt and stiff ironed blouse. But Mother insists on wearing her new sundress that shows off her bare white shoulders, chest, and arms. She puts on high strapless sandals and a string of pearls.

"Will I do?" she titters at the mirror.

Mother turns out to be more knowledgeable about Ceylon than I've given her credit for. She knows about the social background, the mixed colonials, the difference between a Eurasian and a Dutch Burgher, all things she's gleaned from her work with overseas students in the Social Science department. She's quite coquettish with Father-in-law, calling him Jack. "Just call me Jack, Myrtle." So she does.

"And do call me Myrtle, Jack, and Mildred too, of course. Don't let's stand on ceremony."

"Hmph."

"Drink, Myrtle?"

"Well, I can be tempted, Jack."

I realize how much Mother comes alive in the company of men. She's very tall, with long legs like Marlene Dietriech, which she flashes shamelessly as she sits in the armchair in the living room.

"Wine? Beer? Whisky? Your choice, Myrtle."

"A glass of red wine will do nicely, Jack. Thank you."

"Nothing for me, pet," says Mother-in-law dourly.

Mother looks askance at Mother-in-law. Heavy, solid, sensible Mildred Gilmor is not to Mother's taste. Her dark brown face contrasts unfavourably with Father-in-law's light golden complexion and with Mother's fair skin and blonde curls, a result of Clairol ash-blonde rinse.

Mother-in-law has made a mild chicken curry and rice and a little *dhal*. I'd told her that Mother sometimes ate Indian food at the university. We move to the kitchen and squeeze around the table. The conversation turns to Canada and how wonderful it is. Mother-in-law brings up her friendship with Aunt Clarice before her death. Mother looks upset. "I hadn't realized you knew her."

"Oh yes. We had become friends. She was a very nice lady. Her death was so tragic; she was so young."

Mother is nervous. Emotional expression is not "done" in our family. How dissociative and strange this must seem to Mother and Father-in-law.

"If only Clive Harrow hadn't brought her out here," she says bitterly.

"Oh, but Aunt Clarice loved Canada, Mum!" I say quickly. "She loved Willowdale and her Canadian house. She always said it was so open." And she'd loved the summer, the long, bright, hot days filled with sunshine. It was a change from dour Aylesbury.

"Oh, well." Mother is a little taken aback. "Thank you anyway for helping out, Mildred and Jack," she says awkwardly.

Father-in-law puts a record on his gramophone, an oldie. "Oh, that takes me back years, Jack.," Mother coos. It's Jack Miller and his band, Boogie Woogie, music she must have danced to in the thirties, just as Jack had done perhaps in the upcountry planters' clubs in the old days. Father-in-law blinks, shifting to a time when he and Mother-in-law had been young.

This must be the sort of English conversation that Father-in-law had been familiar with in the old colonial days. Mother smiles and preens at Father-in-law, tipping her glass, as though she were an English colonial *memsahib* up in the hill clubs of long ago. But I'm sure Aidan is offended, not by Mother, but rather by the snobbish superior class she represents and that Father-in-law is acknowledging.

"Another glass of wine, Myrtle?"

"I can be tempted again, Jack," Mother titters coyly.

This seems to take Father-in-law back to that other era again, a time when ladies tittered at such things. He gallantly bounds into the kitchen.

Felix has arrived. He appears in the doorway like a figure from a Russian novel, his black overcoat like a cape of darkness. But he's gallant and gracious; he offers Mother a cigarette from his gold case and says, "Now, where has Selena been hiding you? You're such a beautiful woman—like mother, like daughter." Mother gives Felix an astonished look, taking in his black clothes and his melancholy face, but she graciously accepts a cigarette. Felix bends elegantly forward and lights it for her.

Finally Scottie and Darleene arrive with the babies, followed by Fiona and her two children. Fiona looks as if she's been scalped. Mother gapes but of course reserves comment. It couldn't be worse. Little blonde Emily is wriggling in Scottie's arms, wanting to be put down, while the new baby Kimberley is sleepy, her dark head nestling against Darleene's chest.

"Kimberley follows my side of the family; she looks a lot like Amma," says Mother-in-law, taking the baby off Darleene and into her arms. "And how is little Kimberley today?" She tickles the baby's chin, and she opens her eyes, large, black, lustrous. I pray she does not go on to explain that the dark skin is from the Goonesekere side of the family.

"Amma is Kimberley's great-grandmother in Ceylon on Ma's side of the family," explains Aidan to Mother. Mother looks mortified. She quickly puffs at her cigarette.

"See how the genes come down so strong," laughs Fiona. She gives a high, nervous sort of laugh. Hans and Heidi ask to play with the tape recorder in the bedroom. They, too, present a stark contrast in looks, a genetic fact that has not escaped Mother's notice.

It's clear that Mother is in shock, especially when Darleene calmly parts her blouse and starts to breastfeed, the baby's brown face turned against her white breast. Mother looks bewildered. Heidi comes back from the bedroom. She seems suddenly so dark, like Fiona—like Darleene's baby. Then Hans follows—so fair, with deep green eyes. "We're thirsty, Grandma." The two gather up cokes and go outside into the garden where Father-in-law has set up a badminton net for them. Mother moves back into the living room.

Fiona is hissing at Mother-in-law: "Don't you have *cake*, Ma? You can't serve Mrs. Harcourt *wadis*."

"Can I do anything?"

"Daddy and your mother are shooting up a storm in the living room, Selena," giggles Fiona.

"I'll make more tea," I offer to give Mother-in-law a rest. "You join the conversation."

"What for silly social talk, let them enjoy themselves their own way." And I am struck by how dour Mother-in-law can be.

Fiona is bemused at Father-in-law and Mother. "She's like the English ladies at the old planters' club," she laughs.

Scott looks impressed. He hardly remembers club life in Ceylon—it was so long ago—but I sense at once how important the club must have been to my in-laws, isolated as they were up in the tea hills, cut off from social intercourse. Afternoon tea on the lawn of the Hatton-Eliya Club, where Father-in-law was not welcome: *Whites Only.*

"Oh, rather!" says Felix. "But there were ways of getting around all that. I often went to the horse races at Nuwara Eliya in August, with my Colombo friends...."

"You were a man about town, Felix," says Mother-in-law unexpectedly.

Felix laughs. "Long gone, those days."

"Nuwara Eliya, with its great English houses and gardens that Mother could have fit into very well indeed," smiles Fiona. Perhaps Mother is the sort of mother she would have liked.

We sit down round the table, cramped together.

Mother-in-law has cooked Brussels sprouts, which gives rise to all sorts of unexpected comments.

Father-in-law recounts humorously the time he tried Brussels sprouts at Madeniya; he brought them back from Nuwara Eliya for the servants to cook, and they didn't known what to do with them. "We spat them out, stinking things, but the English loved them."

"Yes, it was funny, really," says Aidan. "Daddy making a fool of himself in front of the servants, spitting out the Brussels sprouts that had cost nearly a thousand rupees, trying to be 'English' in every way."

Mother makes an effort at a smile. "Yes, they're not to everyone's taste. You have to be brought up with them."

There's a sudden silence.

"Oh, quite so, quite so." Father-in-law helps himself to another tot of whisky, and lights a cigarette. "Another glass, Myrtle?" Father-in-law sways, grasping the red wine.

"In colonial times, he would have been decked out in a white tropical suit and dashing white silk tie and homburg hat," says Felix. "He would be cutting a dash amongst the Eurasian ladies of the Eurasian club that allowed Eurasians and whites."

Mother looks years younger; she's enjoying herself. Father-in-law, too, has a sparkle in his eye.

"Jack is the one in the family who most resembled his grandfather, Sinclair Gilmor," says Mother-in-law unexpectedly.

"Show Mrs. Harcourt-Jones the family album, Ma," urges Fiona. "She should see the relatives."

Mother looks as if she'd rather rumba with Father-in-law in the living room. Nevertheless, she affects interest as Mother-in-law gets the family album from the bedroom and spreads it open on the kitchen table. We gather around and I feel a certain dread. The photographs are old, small, and black-and-white, and they're glued to torn cellophane pages. They are ordinary family photos of the Gilmor family; Father-in-law's relatives peer up at us out of the past.

"That's Jack's mother." She's a stout fair-skinned Eurasian in western dress with a string of pearls round her neck.

"Oh?" says Mother. "No sari?"

"Indeed not! Jack's family all wore the latest fashions, western clothes from England," says Mother-in-law, indignant.

Mother is silent.

"And here's Gilmor, Sinclair Gilmor." He's the original White British colonial who came to Ceylon in the 1880s seeking his fortune—Ceylon tea, jewels, rubber, hemp. He's Father-in-law's grandfather and Aidan's great-grandfather. He sits on a horse in riding togs, whip in hand, sun helmet glinting on his head, surrounded by his hunting dogs. A tall grand handsome man in his forties with a blond moustache.

"Ughh, the bastard!" scowls Father-in-law. He stomps out of the kitchen.

"Oh, pet!"

Mother raises an eyebrow and glances at me. She's taking it all in, of course.

"And here is Granny," says Mother-in-law with reverence and pleasure. She was Sinclair Gilmor's wife, Aidan's great-grandmother. She's wearing a sari (which must indicate that she was a villager) and her hair is bound back tightly and decorated with a string of jewels. Her dark skin is smooth, her lips full, her eyes curved like a Burmese.

"Fiona looks like her," I say without thinking. Fiona screams. "Everyone says that!"

"She had ten children by Sinclair," says Mother-in-law.

"Heavens!" Mother lights a cigarette and glances quickly at me again, as if to say *See*.

Aidan laughs. "She always said, 'Be an Englishman!' to Daddy."

"They all did well," continues Mother-in-law. "Old Sinclair provided for them."

"*Provided* for them?" queries Mother. She's so alert to dangerous little pitfalls.

"Well, Sinclair went back to England in the end, to his English wife." Mother makes a choking sound. "He had his furlough and … never returned," says Mother-in-law calmly, as if this were simply to be expected, which it was. "You know how it was in those far-off colonial times; relationships were looser. They didn't, well, get formally married so to speak, it was accepted. It didn't matter so much then." She pauses enigmatically. Mother-in-law is trying to tell Mother something; she's trying to be honest about the Gilmor history, Jack's origins.

"Well, it certainly mattered later on," Felix cuts in drily.

Father-in-law, who has been listening in, swirling his whisky, scowls. "Damn right!" His lip quivers; his face is flushed. He stomps out into the living room again.

Mother is bewildered by the electric change in atmosphere.

Fiona gives a nervous hoot. "Now Daddy is upset, Felix."

"Well, the Ceylon Citizenship Act of 1948 changed everything," Felix goes on thoughtfully to Mother. "That's when the shit hit the fan, as Canadians like to say," he observes wryly. "It suddenly mattered. Not being married, that is."

"That old Mr. Gilmor had not married Granny. That's what it was all about," says Aidan. "And Daddy was affected."

"Oh, we all were, ultimately," says Felix. "It meant Jack and a lot of us Eurasians couldn't apply for citizenship or passports. You had to prove registration of the father's line going back three generations and Jack—a lot of us—couldn't do that."

At last I understand. And so does Mother. She shoots me an *I told you so* look. ("I warned you about this family.")

"But he did give the children an education, Felix," Mother-in-law objects reasonably. (Mother rolls her eyes.) "The boys went to good private schools, and the girls went to Kandy Convent or Methodist College. The children used to call his wife in England 'English Granny.' She was a good woman. You know what she did, Myrtle? When old Sinclair died, she reverted all his money and tea estates in Ceylon to them. Everything. She said it was theirs by right. That's how they became rich and went into the tea business. It was a fine thing she did."

"It was the *moral* thing, Ma!" Aidan is indignant.

The old photos have roused a storm of memory. Father-in-law is pacing the living room, the disenfranchised alien of his birth country. "Damn bloody act!" That was why he must have left. He'd had little choice, based on shame. The Ceylon Citizenship Act of 1948 had exposed the Gilmors, particularly his questionable grandfather, Sinclair Gilmor—the "bastard" in the photograph, astride his fine horse, whip in hand, gazing out.

Mother makes another choking sound.

Mother and I are alone at last in the house on Morton Road. Aidan made an excuse to take the dog for a walk.

"Well, the Gilmors are nice people—especially Jack—I'll admit. But..." Mother pauses. She lights a cigarette. "Ciggy, ducks?"

"Oh, okay, thanks." I guess what's bothering her before she starts speaking.

"That story about the great-grandfather, Sinclair. What balderdash!"

"What d'you mean?" At once I'm on the defensive.

"Well … that old Sinclair Gilmor, the old geezer, and that woman in the sari. 'Granny!' He was just using her for sex, for God's sake. His *country wife!* Tell me another. She was just for sex." Mother's lip curls contemptuously.

"They had children, Mum!"

"And they weren't legal. Not registered before the law. *That's* the point! Did they think I didn't see that?"

What is Mother saying? But I know. I know what she's implying.

"Well, then. Wasn't that wrong, then? Wrong of him to use a poor Sinhalese girl without intending to marry her?"

Mother stares at me.

"Wrong?" She butts out her ciggy viciously in the glass ashtray. "Sometimes I just don't understand you, Selena."

I think of Father-in-law's flushed face, his shame as he'd stomped out of the kitchen, the constant "bastard!" about his grandfather. I'm beginning to understand something very sensitive.

Mother takes up the attack again. "And Darleene's babies … and Fiona's two kids…"

"You mean Heidi and Hans?"

"Well, whatever they're called. There's such a *difference* between them, Selena, and between Darleene's babies. They're like two separate *races.* I wonder, does Hans have trouble in school, having such a dark sister? Well, kids are mean, Selena, because they're totally honest—face it. Do the kids taunt him, you know? Do they compare…? And what on earth has Fiona done to her *hair?*"

Mother's questions are natural, I admit. I think of the teachers' comments at Hillside, not to mention the kids' taunts on the street that time. If Mother only knew…. Perhaps Mother is thinking about any "mixed" grandchildren she herself might have one day. She could be genuinely concerned.

"I know what you're thinking, but the truth's the truth, Selena. Aidan's family are *coloureds, mixed,* the whole lot of them, and you can't see it. Oh, I know Jack is nice-looking and could pass. But really, Mildred? That complexion, that dour expression. And that cousin, Felix or whatever he's called. Those clothes, and that nose. There's Jewish blood there all right." Mother purses her mouth.

"Felix was a tea taster in Ceylon, Mum. He had a good position. And Father-in-law—Jack—was a leading planter. They're both honourable people. I've told you, Aidan's father was highly thought of."

I thought highly of him. I think of Father-in-law and his old quaint colonial adherence to the past, his faithful allegiance to the Union Jack. "That tatty old thing hanging on his flag-pole—what *on earth* is that all about?"

"It's the Union Jack."

"Well, I *know* that."

"I think he brought it from Ceylon. Felix said he's fond of the tradition."

Mother takes out her powder compact and dabs her face.

"Let's have a cup of tea."

"Look, Selena, face it. Face the truth. You're going to have mixed-blood offspring like Darleene if you have babies with Aidan. The laws of genetics don't lie." Her sociological research at the university comes to the fore. "It's not too late to get out of this. End this marriage, for God's sake, and come back with me. Now. There's loads of teaching jobs in Cardiff. After all, you've only been married a few years, and it's not as if you have any children to consider."

There's a swarming sensation; I'm suddenly feeling smothered, struggling for the words that will not come. For the fact is, I'm pregnant. The pharmacist has just confirmed it, and I was planning to tell Aidan in the privacy of our bedroom later, at a special moment. I'm going to have a baby.

14.

IT'S SNOWING AGAIN. Icicles stiffen like frozen candles on the branches of the willow and on the window ledge of the bungalow. The cedars are bundled up, wrapped in snow even though it's spring. But the forsythia is radiant, its tiny twigged flowers bursting open, golden before leaf. "Bloody weather! Call this spring?"

Father-in-law is gurgling into his drink, standing at the window. Early morning had been watery grey. "Nothing like the sunrises of Madeniya," he growls. "Remember sunrise, Mildred, pet?" The first pale flush before tropical dawn, the hue of the buds of the tamarind tree before they opened, then the oranges and reds and molten golds flowing over the mountains, the freshness and innocence of the world before life stepped in.

"What for tears, pet?" sighs Mother-in-law.

It's 1972, an auspicious year according to the Buddhist astrologers. Polly, our baby daughter, is already one and toddling around, holding on to my in-laws' furniture. With her blonde hair and blue eyes, she's the apple of Father-in-law's eye.

"Uh-huh." Father-in-law has been tuning in to Voice of Ceylon again. ("What for following those old politics, pet?")

But it seems that the Prime Minister, Mrs. Bandaranaike, whom Father-in-law invariably calls "that bloody woman," has changed the name of Ceylon to "Sri Lanka." Sinhalese. "Damn bloody fool."

"Yes, yes, pet. It was on the CBC world news."

Father-in-law knocks back a scotch.

"The name is no longer that of a colonial crown colony of Britain, Daddy. It's a republic," cries Aidan, excited.

"I bloody well know that! The damn radio speaks of nothing else. *A republic.*"

"The Socialist Republic of Sri Lanka, Daddy." Aidan rubs it in. "Everyone is now a Sri Lankan (except the estate Tamils, the labourers, of course—they don't count). No more Eurasians, British, or Dutch Burghers—they're all in the past now."

"Ughh. What are we, then, bloody ghosts?"

"Come, now, pet."

"What does 'Sri Lanka' mean?" I ask innocently.

"Well, *sri* means holy or venerable, and *lanka* means country. So, Holy Country," explains Mother-in-law.

"Holy bloody country, my arse." Father-in-law knocks back another whisky and glares defiantly all around. "Talk about *ahimsa*. The Buddhists won't kill a bloody mosquito but they'll hack a Tamil to death."

Ahimsa, I know from my yoga class, is the doctrine of non-violence.

"Now, is that fair, Daddy?" cries Aidan excitedly, ready at once for a verbal sparring. "What about the Christians? 'Turn the other cheek and pass the ammunition.'"

"Ehh?" Father-in-law gapes.

"*Aiyo.*" Mother-in-law glances apologetically at me.

"Well, I think you should fly the flag of Ceylon, Daddy, in honour of the event, and of Prime Minister Bandaranaike. There's that old one still in the basement in the tea chest you brought from Ceylon."

"Ughh."

Nevertheless, Father-in-law complies, mumbling and muttering. For Prime Minister, Bandaranaike—"that woman"—has declared the end of old British "Ceylon." Single-handedly, she's thrown out the Queen of England—a president is to rule in her stead—and sent the entire bloody British Empire to hell.

"Good for her!" Aidan enthuses wildly. I've never seen him so excited.

Felix smiles and raises his customary glass of gin in a mock toast, "To Mrs. Bandaranaike, her Royal Sinhalese Highness."

Father-in-law puts on his fur-lined hat and gloves, goes outside, lowers the old Union Jack, hoists the Ceylon flag, and salutes. There! An orange lion wielding a sword—or perhaps it's a dangerous-looking Kandyan knife—tail flicking ominously in the spring light, holds pride of place on the flagpole. This constant switching of flags has been going on for years. I'm still the English daughter-in-law and know better than to ask why. The Union Jack symbolizes the British Empire, otherwise known as "the damn bloody British," and I'm still not sure where I stand in my relation to Father-in-law after five years of marriage. (Aidan's dark glistening skin next to mine on the white sheets on our wedding night so long ago ... this is something at the heart of our marriage that has not yet been resolved.)

Sirimavo Bandaranaike had the distinction of being the first woman in the world to be a prime minister, back in 1960, Aidan reminds us.

"Ughh, sympathy vote," snorts Father-in-law.

I'd been at university at the time. I'd barely paid attention to the newsflash on the BBC: "First woman prime minister in the world"—an image of her had flashed across the screen: a woman in a sari with a dark, square, heavy, Asian face—"wife of former prime minister SWRD Bandaranaike of Ceylon, who was assassinated..."

Her husband, SWRD Bandaranaike, who was prime minister before her, had indeed been assassinated. (The BBC world news and the *Voice of Ceylon* had been consumed by it. "*Assassination rocks Ceylon!*") He was shot to death. By a monk. A Buddhist. The *bhikkhu* had simply walked into Tintagel—Bandaranaike's private residence on Rosemead Place, Colombo—and shot him through the chest. It happened on September 25, 1959. He died the following day. ("We got out just in time, thank God," mutters Felix.)

I didn't take much notice of that, either; we'd only just gotten our first television in our house in Pen-Y-Pandy, and I was consumed with *Anne of Green Gables*. I was still in high school. SWRD had attended Oxford in his youth, the commentators had eulogized; he'd apparently shone in the Oxford Debating Society, and had gained the attention of Anthony Eden, later Sir Anthony. Well, nothing to do with me. For me at the time, Ceylon was merely some tropical island far away in the Indian Ocean that provided us with boxes of tea. Now here were sudden shifts, hidden depths, a disturbing beauty, volatile.

For Prime Minister Bandaranaike has shown herself to be ruthless, if necessary, and perhaps that's what has shaken Father-in-law. Amongst other things, she has nationalized the banks and insurance companies, and is now in the process of taking over the tea estates owned by British, European, and wealthy Sinhalese companies, a move that will result in serious losses in profit and investment. Madeniya and Weyweltalawa, Father-in-law's former estates, are to be run cooperatively by Sinhalese managers. "What the hell do the Sinhalese know about bloody tea planting?" growls Father-in-law.

"Dick-all," agrees Felix.

"Well, Jack, pet, the Sinhalese are as capable as any Englishman of learning to grow tea," points out Mother-in-law calmly.

"Huh! And who's bloody well going to pluck the tea-buds? They've driven the Tamil labourers back to bloody India." Apparently a third of a million Tamil coolies had been shifted back to Tamil Nadhu, where they'd come from a century before in the first place, thanks to the "bloody act." He is referring, again, to the Ceylon Citizenship Act of 1948, which seems to link the coolies forever to Father-in-law in some way.

It's now 1972, and the "Insurrection" of last year, which began in April 1971, is still haunting Ceylon. ("My God, they're throwing Molotov cocktails, pet, at Government House! And bloody homemade bombs.") Prime Minister Bandaranaike had herself been threatened with assassination by the Sinhalese rebels. (But they were on her own side! I just couldn't understand Ceylon politics.)

"Damn goons!" growls Father-in-law.

In reality, they were poor, hungry, rural Sinhalese youths looking for better jobs. Prime Minister Bandaranaike was moved to Temple Trees for safety. "You remember Temple Trees, Mildred, pet." The Ceylon prime minister's country residence.

Then the young Marxist rebels turned to crime to fund themselves. Father-in-law tuned in to hear about daring bank robberies: the Badulla bank robbery, the Ambalangoda robbery, and the York Street bank robbery in Fort, where Father-in-law had once kept his savings in the old days. Tamils were being dragged, terrified, out of classes at the University of Ceylon; the Sinhalese rebels were claiming that the Tamils had always been favoured by the British during colonial times and that they had been given the first university seats and the best posts in the civil service. It wasn't fair. "Damn rot," cries Father-in-law. "They were just smarter." The antagonism between Sinhalese and Tamil went far deeper, of course.

"Oh, back to 1948 and that Ceylon Citizenship Act aimed at the Tamil labourers," murmurs Felix. "But everyone's forgotten that. Do those young rebels even *know* their own history?"

"Ughh!"

All this despite Prime Minister Bandaranaike's ongoing friendship with Pierre Elliott Trudeau. Mrs Bandaranaike was invited to Canada on a state visit in October of last year. A photo of Trudeau salaaming to her, his palms pressed together in deference at his forehead, had drawn vituperations from Father-in-law. "Damn bloody fool!"

Now Prime Minister Bandaranaike has declared another state of emergency, an old British tactic.

"Hell!" Father-in-law screams from the living-room. The bloody radio has conked out again.

The new Sri Lankan flag, as it must now be called, flutters in the breeze—bright reds and orange, with emblems and crests. "Mother Lanka" is the new slogan of the country.

Polly squirms in my arms and shakes her toy rabbit. "Little Bunny," says Mother-in-law, wagging its ears, and Polly breaks into a smile. "*Aiyo*! See, she knows me, pet."

"Pollywogs," gurgles Father-in-law proudly, tousling her curls.

Polly, with her golden curls, blue eyes, and rosy pink cheeks, is his favourite grandchild. I was elated and relieved when she was born last year. A secret weight had lifted. Mother had been overjoyed. "A granddaughter!" she'd cooed. "She looks just like Selena" she'd boasted, no doubt, to all her neighbours at Fernside. Mother had flown out at once for ten days, ostensibly to help me, but in reality "just to see." And she'd not been disappointed. "She's absolutely darling, an English rose."

Father-in-law had also been delighted. He'd rung every relative in Ceylon and Australia. "Who'd have thought I'd ever have such a fair granddaughter, with *blue* eyes?" he'd boasted. "Cornflower blue, no mistaking. Not in Ceylon."

I'd proudly taken baby Polly to show the teachers at Hillside Public School, a time-honoured tradition. "Wow, well … she's … gorgeous!" they'd cried, surprised, clamouring around the carry-cot. I lifted her out, my little Pollyanna-Popsicle. Soft, new-born, blonde fuzz covered her head. She opened her startling blue eyes. "She's one of us," said Marlene, surprised, approving. "She's so fair."

Mr. Mirrell was also pleased. He'd been taken aback during my pregnancy when I'd had to admit that no, I wasn't sure what colour the baby would be. "Good Lord, not *know*?" A teacher of his not knowing what *colour* her baby would be? It was unthinkable.

Even the neighbours on Morton Road opened up in a pleasant way. "A baby on the street—how nice! It's been a few years!" exclaimed one woman smiling and stopping to look at Polly in her pram. One day Audrey, the Irish woman three doors down, knocked on the door and handed me a gift: a little Irish woolen cape and bonnet—"for the babby," she said, as shy as ever.

"Oh thank you! Come on in and see the baby, I'll put the kettle on." To my surprise, she did, shuffling in.

"Ah, a sweet bobby baby," she said.

"Yes, well, you never know what you'll get in a marriage like ours," I joked honestly. I felt I could confide in her.

"Oh aye," she nodded sympathetically. "I know what you mean, *begorrah*. We had awful trouble Bill and me getting married in Belfast—Protestant and Catholic you see we was."

"Really?"

"Oh aye. Escaped just in time. They was coming to tar an' feather us, mixed marriage you see. Why can't we all live and let live in peace I says to Mother Mary."

I'd not thought of a Protestant-Catholic couple as "mixed," to be condemned.

Then one Sunday Felix came by the Willowdale bungalow to see the baby. He, too, was charmed by Polly. "A beautiful granddaughter, Jack. And look at those baby blues!" And then he let slip, in his casual way, "Well, Jack, you came to Canada so the children could marry white people, and you certainly succeeded, old chap."

There was silence. I carefully continued to sip my tea, gripping the cup and stirring in a little jiggery, as if I hadn't heard. A cup of tea: the refuge of the British, restorative through all crises, from bomb attacks, blackouts, flying zeppelins, and wintry storms, to sudden words that incise themselves like steel blades within the heart. Aidan turned away, embarrassed.

Pure leaves from sunny Ceylon, said the caption on the tea caddy in front of me. There was a tiny picture of mountains and an estate near Nuwara Eliya, and a tiny smiling tea picker, a Tamil woman with a nose ring, her sari pulled up over her head like a hood to protect her from the burning sun. She carried a cane basket of pickings strapped on her back, as she picked from dawn to dusk. *The champagne of teas, the elixir of flavour....*

15.

"**D**AMN FOOLS!" Trouble in Sri Lanka again. More riots, more killings. *Set on fire ... children burn to death... mutilated....* The reports are endless.

"What's going *on*, Selena?" Mother writes urgently, as if I should know. "Do the Gilmors have anyone over there? I warned you." (Marrying into that dangerous family.)

Father-in-law was crouched over the shortwave radio, tuning in. He always wanted to hear about everything firsthand. He spoke both fluent Tamil and inferior Sinhalese.

"Jack, pet, pet," Mother-in-law called towards the living room. "*Aiyo,* switch off that radio. Aidan and Selena have news. There's a new baby on the way, a new grandchild for us!"

I was expecting our second child. But I was apprehensive. Each birth seemed to coincide with an uprising in Aidan's native land, which was full of horror these days.

"Uhh?"

"Bloody country." Father-in-law lurched in the doorway, whisky in hand. He was wearing a singlet vest pulled over his sagging potbelly, long khaki shorts, and long wool socks to his knees—his usual Sunday garb once church was over, a vestige of British colonial days. Mother-in-law still wore her church clothes, dark pleated skirt, simple blouse, old-fashioned lisle stockings, and brogues.

"Beer, son?"

"Did you hear, Jack?"

Father-in-law gurgled something appropriate about my pregnancy and the coming baby, due in December. His fine hair stuck up like chicken feathers and his fair face was flushed with urgency. The truth was, he couldn't wait to tell us about the latest machinations of Prime Minister Bandaranaike and her Sri Lanka Freedom Party, SLFP. ("*What* bloody freedom?") "It's a coalition with other parties, including the bloody communist party," he muttered.

"Jack, pet, what for all this silliness? What is Mrs. Bandaranaike to us, here in Canada?"

Father-in-law ignored this remark. An election was imminent in Sri Lanka, an important one, it being 1977. He knocked back his whisky indignantly. He was very excited. Prime Minister Bandaranaike's government might fall at any moment. In fact, Prime Minister Bandaranaike was doomed according to all the astrologers and soothsayers. "Hah!"

Just then six-year-old Polly peeked around the doorway. "Mommy! Daddy!" she cried. She was cuddling her doll, Jasmine. It had a brown face, black hair, and dark eyes that opened and shut when tilted.

"Damn doll." Father-in-law scowled. "You should buy her a white one, pet."

"She doesn't want a white doll. She likes that one."

Polly had been playing with Jasmine in Aidan and Scott's old bedroom where Mother-in-law kept the tape recorder and toys for her five grandchildren. "Did you have a good time staying with Granma and Granpa, Pollywogs?" I gave her a big hug.

"Oh, yes. Mommy, I maded a tape of me an' Jasmine talking and singing with Granma."

"Rascal," said Father-in-law affectionately, tousling her curls, as always. I couldn't help but think of my sister-in-law Darleene's eight-year-old daughter Sarah, fair with hazel eyes like Darleene's. And her other daughter Kimberley, dark like Mother-in-law, with long thick eyelashes and a rough mop of thick black hair.

I noticed how Father-in-law favoured the fairest grandchildren: Hans, Emily, and now Pollyanna. What would my second baby look like? Of course I would love him or her dearly, whatever the complexion, I knew. It would make no difference. Still. Would he be dark, like Aidan? It was only natural to wonder, I told myself. Perhaps very dark, with black eyes. Sinhalese. (I couldn't help but think of Mother and her dire warnings about genes and "mixed" babies: "Throw-backs, Selena.")

Prime Minister Bandaranaike has lost the election. She's been kicked out. Humiliated.

The old United National Party that Father and Mother-in-law had apparently voted for in former Ceylon, swept back into power in August with a huge majority, hopefully boding well for our unborn child. "It's an absolute landslide!" Father-in-law gloats, elated that Mrs. B. has had to step down. "It's her own bloody fault."

Excitedly he unfurls the "Ceylon" lion flag. It returns to pride of place at the top of the pole, the lion's tail jauntily twitching over the roofs of Willowdale in honour of the new prime minister, Junius Richard Jayewardene, or J.R., as he is called. He's from a prominent Sinhalese family, like the Bandaranaikes and Senanayakes, and is a graduate of Colombo Law College. Jayewardene's mother had converted from Catholicism to Buddhism, a politically significant gesture that I have difficulty comprehending. It hardly registers with Father and Mother-in-law. After all, Mother-in-law herself had switched from being Buddhist to Catholic after Amma's death.

Jayewardene has vowed to have Mrs. Bandaranaike charged with corruption. She'd refused to dissolve parliament for the past two years, misused funds, indulged in nepotism, and incited an insurrection. She is to be banned from holding government office for seven years. "Well, that effectively shuts her out from competing in the next general election," observes Felix drily.

"Ughh."

But Sirimavo Bandaranaike is apparently not a woman easily dismissed. Those flashing demonic eyes that Father-in-law deplores—"damn devil eyes"—and dominant fieriness are features I'm now connected to, as to Sri Lanka itself, by marriage, our children by blood. A violent place, throbbing with intrigue.

"But what is she to us, pet?" Mother-in-law asks again. I go outside and wander down the garden with Polly, collecting gooseberries and currants, while Aidan has a beer with Father-in-law. It's a typical Sunday afternoon at the Willowdale bungalow. My belly is swelling with the coming baby, a brother or sister for Polly. She cuddles her doll, pretending to feed her. It has a tiny plastic milk bottle that fits into the brown lips. "Take, take all you want, Selena," calls Mother-in-law through the open window. Old Mr. Sweetley, who lives next door in number 82, looks up skywards as his wife Muriel brings in the washing off the pulley line. He wonders sometimes about the coloured neighbours next door. He once whispered to me across the fence that he's concerned they might be communist infiltrators.

"That orange lion again, Selena. *Socialist Republic of Sri Lanka*. I know what that means: Communism." But he admits that Jack Gilmor is a nice enough fellow—he drives a Buick—and Mrs. Gilmor, the dark one, is a harmless person. She wears ordinary Western clothes, which is to say, dowdy. "No weird saris for her or red dots in the middle of her forehead like them Hindus," he says, nodding. She goes to work somewhere downtown Toronto; he often sees her waiting for the bus to the subway on Finch Avenue. So he knows they're not immigrant welfare bums.

I fill the basin with berries and then stop for a rest. Father-in-law's cherished flowers are profuse with colour, revealing themselves. Summertime in Father-in-law's garden: the clematis sagging over the trellis, the hum of bees. I feel the baby give a kick, reminding me of family ties—"foreign ties" Mother likes to quip.

"Bloody hell, Jasmine," Polly chides her doll.

"Hear that, Jack, pet? See what you are teaching that child."

"Ughh."

Father-in-law has joined us on the grass and collapsed into a deck chair, where he dozes off. He lets out a sigh, bubbles of spittle dribbling round his lips. A profusion of pinks and morning glory trails round the porch and trellis, tendrils of sweet peas. The Queen Elizabeth tea roses are in rich, deep bloom. A cardinal sings, long liquid notes resounding from the top of the apple tree. The Ceylon lion waggles over the roof. "Granpa fatty-belly," giggles Polly, and pokes his belly.

"Wha-at?" He jerks awake, and Polly runs off with her doll.

Aidan hovers, a dark figure suddenly against the sunlight as he stands at the kitchen door. "Don't spend too long in the sun," he warns us. So we troop inside, into the cool kitchen. Mother-in-law has switched on the fan, and Aidan takes Polly in his lap and reads her a favourite childhood storybook of his that he brought from Ceylon, *The Long Long Magic Beard*. ("I used to read this on rainy days out on the verandah.") It says inside: *Ceylon Printers, Kutagastota, Ceylon, 1947.* He reads softly: "Mr Sugunasiri was a very old man in the village of Warakapola. He wore an old dhoti and a turban round his head, and he had a very long beard...."

Jaywardene is busy quelling riots instigated by the Janatha Vimukthi Peramuna, or J.V.P., young Marxist Sinhalese communists that had first risen up against Prime Minister Bandaranaike. They are still around stirring up trouble. He ends the state of emergency that she had put in place, a policy that the citizens had hated throughout the island. He promises to acknowledge the Tamil language on a par with Sinhala, a compromise Mother and Father-in-law approve of. This pleases the Tamils and angers the Sinhalese, especially the monks. ("There's a stir of resentment within the Buddhist ranks," reports *Voice of Ceylon*.) The "Sinhala Only" Act, passed by

SWRD Banadaranaike in 1956, had made Sinhala the foremost language in the country, and the monks want it kept that way. What is wily Jayewardene up to? He assures everyone that it's simply to calm things down, restore normalcy to the island, encourage foreign investment. Who wants to risk money in a riot?

"See?" cries Father-in-law. "A man in charge."

But Mother-in-law doesn't trust Jayewardene. (I suspect she has a sneaking admiration for Mrs. Bandaranaike.) "Jaywardene is an old dog," she says. He's been involved in Ceylon politics for a long time. He was Minister of Finance, for instance, in the 1950s when Dudley Senanayake was in office and cut the rice subsidy for the poor that he'd promised never to touch. Riots had ensued, followed by a *hartal*. "Now you remember *that*, pet."

Father-in-law sways. "Ughh, yes, the *hartal*. Whole bloody island shut down."

"*Hartal* is a Tamil word meaning 'general strike' or 'work stoppage,'" explains Mother-in-law. The police (or was it the army?) had moved in to the square in Colombo; there was violence and people were killed in the streets. Dudley Senanayake, who couldn't stand the sight of blood, had taken off, hiding out in a naval ship in Colombo harbour until it was all over. Of course, he had to resign in the face of such ignominy.

Father-in-law's eyes glaze. "You remember it, son? The *hartal*...?"

Aidan winces. He would have been about to turn twelve, just going into adolescence at Holy Innocents College, locked up and desperately lonely—though Mother and Father-in-law know nothing of that, of his true feelings. They are part of the many confidences whispered between us under the sheets at night.

"I-I don't remember, Daddy. I was at school."

The truth is, Sri Lanka's economy is in dire straits. The GNP is dropping, rubber prices are down, and even tea, the mainstay of the economy, is suffering. Prime Minister Bandaranaike had effectively nationalized the estates and the rupee and sterling companies when she was in power, with their consequent demise. Now Jayewardene has to turn things around. First, he turns to real estate. He has plans for a vibrant new Sri Lanka, a tourist mecca: towering high-rise hotels along the coasts, replete with central air, kidney-shaped swimming pools, and all-day buffets for the Europeans who like to eat bacon and eggs, smoked salmon, and prawns non-stop. And signs on the beaches: *NO TAMILS, NO FISHERMEN, NO LOCALS.* The goal is to attract zillions of tourist dollars and revitalize the economy. But of course, he has to get rid of the Tamil fisher-folk first; they are still there, shitting up the sands, their shaky thatched huts taking up space on the pristine beaches. Prime property. The developers rub their hands in anticipation. Jaywardene is their man.

Mother-in-law frowns, perhaps sensing betrayal. Aidan joins in: "See, Daddy! The fisher-folk have been there since time immemorial, and now they're getting evicted." He senses a duel of words with his father. Polly fingers the picture of the old village man, Mr. Sugunasiri, in her daddy's old storybook, tracing his long beard that runs through the village, over the stream and the paddy fields to infinity....

The baby shifts inside me and kicks, perhaps alarmed at his future grandfather. Another three months, and he'll be in this world.

"Yes, you're right, Jack," observes Felix. "It was the Ceylon Citizenship Act that set it all off."

"And then that bloody 'Sinhala Only' Act that came after it." Father-in-law purses his lips and glares. The special measures that followed had been the reason the Gilmors left Ceylon. It's a story that defines them, sending secret signals back and forth in the drama of their lives. Aidan had been too young at the time to fully understand why the family had suddenly left Ceylon after the citizenship and language acts. Sinhala had become the important language of the country, but the Gilmors spoke English. Buddhism was suddenly the favoured religion, and they were Christians. Being Sinhalese was what was foremost, and they were British Eurasian.

"We were on the wrong side of history, old chap." Felix sighs wryly.

"Ughh!"

"I wasn't a citizen in my own bloody country," says Father-in-law bitterly.

"It's no longer our problem, pet," says Mother-in-law patiently. "We're here, not there." (Can't he understand that?) "What for opening old wounds?"

"It *matters,* pet!" Father-in-law explodes, gulping down another whisky.

"Ah, history. If we do not learn from it we are doomed to repeat it, or something like that," says Felix enigmatically. "Who said that?" The blossoms have fallen silently from the apple trees, covering the ground like melting snow. Summer is coming.

Father-in-law stares. "*Achmillai, achamillai, acham enpathu illaye....*" The ancient Tamil words roll off his tongue. I've long known that Father-in-law can speak Tamil, a language he loves. The tea planters used it to communicate with the labourers and pickers, but it's a thrilling shock all the same to hear the strange undulating syllables, *Achmillai, achmillai....*

"*Fear I have not, fear I have not,*" explains Felix, who has understood the words, being part Tamil himself.

"Vasudevan was a great Tamil poet, Selena. He wrote that during the height of British imperialism when he was a rebel. Damn brave of him, I'd say."

"What for Jack reciting Tamil poetry, Felix? It's long gone." Mother-in-law eyes them both with exasperation. But it's surely an important moment. The poem has touched on something. (What were their lives like before? When they read Tamil poetry?)

"Damn scoundrels!"

Father-in-law gurgles over his whisky as Felix recalls some-one called Saviamoorthy Thondaman, the leader of the Tamil labourers in the old days and the president of the Workers Trade Union Congress. He would go around the plantations at night teaching the coolies all sorts of things—insurrection, how to put an *x* on a vote. Quintus, Mother-in-law's commu-nist brother, was a follower of Thondaman and accompanied him at night.

"Crazy times when you are young," says Felix with a sigh.

"Oh yes, Quintus was very much involved with labourers' rights!" agrees Mother-in-law.

"First they take away your language; then everything else follows. Thondaman said that," murmurs Felix. There's silence.

Father-in-law stumbles out of the kitchen to the bedroom. He can't take any more.

"You know, Aidan, your father was a very good master and loved his Tamil labourers," says Mother-in-law finally. "He got the owner of Madeniya to provide a new set of clothes for them every year at Christmas. He had a school built for the workers' children on the estate. And he was very upset when the labourers lost their voting rights after the Act."

"And then he lost his own rights," says Felix drily. "It was a bad time for us Eurasians once the British left."

We can hear low rumbling snores from the bedroom. Father-in-law's siesta.

"The Catholic Church certainly didn't like Buddhism replac-ing Christianity as the chief religion!" says Felix.

Aidan looks perplexed. "I only really remember Ganesh, the Tamil gardener at Weyweltalawa. taking me fishing."

"Ah, now!" Mother-in-law breaks in. "Jack gave him his old pipe when we left, and he wept bitterly."

"What happened, then?" I murmur to Aidan, nestling under

the blankets. "Why didn't you all speak Sinhalese? It's your language, too."

"Same reason why you don't speak Welsh, I suppose," Aidan retaliates. "Ma and Daddy and the priests spoke only English to us. What happened to your Welsh grandfather? The one who was gassed in the trenches?"

"I don't know; I never knew him. Nangi always spoke in Welsh about it to the old miners. I couldn't follow the words; I was too little. I only understood what Nangi said about him later, when she used English. She said he was gassed in the war and died later in his fifties. The gas had burnt his lungs."

We marvel at the fact that both of us had lost our native tongues. Now Nangi is dead. She passed away the previous summer in her little house on the hillside. With her has passed away the last of the Welsh language in our family. It follows the demise of the great coal fields, the collieries gone. So it was with me, and so it is with Aidan, with the loss of Sinhala. The language has passed away from the Gilmor family here in Canada. Our children will likely never speak either tongue, and we *don't want them to*. That is the truth. They will be "English Only" Canadians. Like Scottie.

The months pass full of waiting, expectancy. *I wonder what the new baby will look like*, writes Mother tentatively from Fernside, and is irritated when I reply *I don't know*. I can't help tensing. I'm thinking of Mr. Mirrell, my old principal, and his earnest intention to "keep Hillside white."

Suddenly it's fall, and the apple trees turn a deep russet hue in Father-in-law's garden. Flocks of birds gather on the washing line and make forays into the berries. The garden moves into winter mode in November. The remains of Father-in-law's frozen turnips at the bottom of the garden stick up like pokers. A sheet of ice coats the lawn, and snow powders the Ceylon lion above the roof.

My time is near. I'm seized with apprehension, excitement,

and anticipatory dread. I've taken the usual leave of absence from my teaching position, received the obligatory kind gift from the staff at Hillside: a baby change-table. I also got some pointed opprobrious looks from Marlene; it's clear that she thinks I am taking a reckless risk by having a second baby. Who knows what it might turn out like this time? The troubles of Ceylon pale in the face of the sudden chasm that opens within, the throes of tribulation my body undergoes, the throbbing pain as my thighs part. Aidan rushes me to hospital and calls Mother-in-law to look after Polly.

"*Aiyo*, Jack, pet, pet," she says, putting down the phone. "Turn off that silly radio. Selena has had the baby—our *sixth* grandchild, imagine! A boy."

It's happened.

He's tiny and beautiful in my arms, with dark, dusky skin, a mass of fuzzy black hair, and curved eyelids—unmistakable. They have come down four generations, a gift from his Burmese great-great-grandmother. We name him Rupert Owen Gilmor.

He looks Sinhalese, with Nangi Jones's nose.

16.

"WELL, HE *IS* DARK, SELENA, but not *that* dark...."
Mother scrutinizes four-year-old Rupert as we sit on the sofa together. "And at least he's good looking, in his own way."

"Aye, he's an 'andsome lad," says Dad amiably.

"Well..." Mother lights a cigarette. "There *is* a big difference between them. It's undeniable," she continues. "Polly's so fair." She'd frowned when she saw them running through the fountain in the park, brown Rupert and fair-skinned, ten-year-old Polly, splashing about side by side.

Mother has come over for a visit, ostensibly to see her grandson for the first time since his birth but in reality to see how bad the catastrophe is. She's brought Dad with her this time. Seeing him again, and feeling his big comfortable body hugging me, I forget everything.

A big hug for Aidan.

"Welcome to Canada ... Dad."

"Aw, son, call me Cedric, mun, at your age."

"Oh, I can't do that...." Aidan's British colonial upbringing reared up; he was horrified.

Mother was dressed in her finery, a new homemade dress edged with black broderie Anglaise, new shoes, and a new purse. "We had a wonderful flight, didn't we, Cedric? Good wine."

"Didn't know you were moving through the air, mun."

It's taken them a few days to settle in. Daddy admired the

house—"Lovely place you got here"—and the garden. It's not as large as Father-in-law's garden in Willowdale, but it is pretty, a mass of flowers with a hedge all around and a large oak tree in the corner under which Aidan has put up a playhouse for the children.

Dad was amazed at the size of Lake Ontario. "That's a lake, you say? Bigger than the ocean, mun."

We took them for a walk along the boardwalk at sunset. Daddy stared across the vast grey pink-tinged water. He was used to the small curving bays and coves of Wales, with sheltering towering cliffs, crashing waves, and vast tides that went out miles and miles.

"I told you, Cedric—it's a freshwater lake. It's one of the biggest inland lakes in the world I think. And it hardly moves, just a few inches."

Mother was obviously going to be Dad's tour guide for the duration of the trip. She was enjoying herself with Daddy as a companion. She linked her arm in his. Daddy blushed happily. I'd never seen them so happy. Polly ran happily ahead with Bosie on the leash while I pushed Rupert in the pushchair.

"Papa, do you want an ice cream?" Polly called.

"Listen to the Canadian accent," marvelled poor Daddy.

Polly slipped her hand in Mother's. "I love you, Nana."

"Nana" had brought her a girly pre-teen makeup kit, bangles, a necklace, a pretty toilet bag, and British girl magazines for her eleventh birthday, which was coming up soon. "Oh, this is fun! You're always such fun, Nana," she had said.

We gave Mother and Dad our bigger bedroom because of the heat, and we slept downstairs in a small spare room off the hall.

"Lovely 'eat," said Dad with a sigh. He loved the sun, like all poor sun-starved Britons. He lay in the deck chair in the back garden in the full sun, soaking it in, an alien activity to Aidan and his family. They never sat out in the sun or sunbathed. "I've already got my tan," Aidan joked. Mother rolled her eyes and twitched her mouth, glancing at me.

When we're alone, she broaches the subject of Polly and Rupert. "Don't get me wrong, but how do the kids see Polly? How do they treat her at school? Do they call her names?" She looks worried. "I mean... having Aidan for a father and Rupert for a brother. Do they notice?"

Only that morning, early, Mother had come to me in the kitchen, bewildered. "Selena, there's a *Chinese* girl at the door wanting to come in...."

"Oh, that's Lin Yu, Mum, from next door. She's come over to play." Ann Mainwaring, the old widow, had moved out to a nursing home and sold the house to the Yus a few years ago. They had four young children. Lin and Polly were buddies, I explained.

But then Mother saw Winston, a West Indian boy and his small sister wandering in the backyard. "They were taking Rupert's toys!" she said indignantly. "They never even asked to come in!"

"Mum, that's just Winston and his sister Samantha. They live in the apartments behind the church, on the next street over. He's in Polly's class at school. It's okay. He comes over all the time. He's a nice boy, really Mum." Mother shut her lips tight.

Then they all played together happily, splashing in the plastic pool Aidan had set up for them in the garden, squirting the hose at each other. Mother was silent again, no doubt contemplating the mix of skin colour: brown, white, golden-beige, black. "It's like the United Nations here," she observed wryly, with good humour.

"Trudeau's multicultural mosaic," grinned Aidan, startling her. He sipped his beer.

"Aye, they all play nicely together," said Dad, oblivious to the undercurrent.

Later, puffing thoughtfully in the living room, she coughed and said slowly, "Look, Selena ... I know things are different over here, and maybe it's not my business, but ... d'you think it wise to encourage that black kid, Winston or whatever his name is, to play with Polly...? I mean, you have to think of when they'll be older ... in their teens."

"Think of what?"

"Oh, you're so *obtuse* at times, Selena!"

The Upper Beaches and Morton Road neighbourhood has been changing. The old people are dying off and "ethnic" families are moving in. Even Hillside has a smattering of new immigrants, who are not necessarily living in the low-rent apartment buildings. A well-off Pakistani family has bought a big house on Maydew Crescent.

I had visited the teachers with baby Rupert just after he was born. There had been a distinct buzz in the lunchroom as I came in and lifted him out of the carrycot. "Well, he *is* different from your other one—Polly, isn't it?"

"Mixed marriage," someone murmured.

"Is he, well—what was that word you used, Selena?—a *Eurasian*?" asked Marlene sweetly.

"Yeah, that's right. Mixed," I said boldly.

But then Marlene said slowly, "You know, Selena, I must say I do admire you, really, bringing in your baby like this, so proud of him." I nodded, deciding to let it pass.

"Oh, we have all sorts here, now," added Joanne drily. She'd stared at Rupert. "Look at the eyelashes on him!"

In the mall on the Danforth, a few new stores have tentatively appeared with exotic East Asian dresswear for women on display: graceful saris, gauzy *shalwaz* and chemises, loose, billowy pants, and floating scarves. One day, a Pakistani woman dressed in a tunic and pants, with a gold stud in her nose and a scarf flung across her shoulders like a noblewoman, came gliding down the aisle of the mall, pushing a little boy in a stroller. A tough-looking youth, a skinhead dressed in a black shirt and dungarees, turned and glared at her. He was with a girlfriend.

"Paki!" he hissed, disgusted. "Why do they let them in?"

I stopped and turned. "Hey, do you *know* what paki means? It means 'holy.'" The sight of his gaping mouth set me giggling, a nervous reaction. What had gotten into me?

"Oh, leave her, Rick, the fucking, crazy bitch," said his girlfriend, pulling at his arm.

Mother tugged at mine. "Why get *involved?*" she hissed. "We have them in Britain, too." She seemed a little frightened.

"Because it might be Rupert one day, Mum." The woman in the sari had disappeared.

I was surprised at myself, that I'd dared to confront someone like that. It brought back the disturbing incident last summer at Sauble Beach that of course I've kept from Mother. Sauble Beach, a little tourist spot on Lake Huron, seemed to be a lovely place. We'd decided to rent a cottage there for a week at Leigh's Lakeside Cottages. Mother and Father-in-law had enjoyed themselves at Sauble earlier that summer; they had gone camping in Wildwood Beach Trailer Park. We'd visited them for a day—it was only a two-hours' drive from Toronto—and found their little beat-up trailer under the trees at their site. Father-in-law was lounging in a deck chair with a beer, Tabby was prowling on a leash, the other cat Dimples was curled up asleep, and Mother-in-law was cooking chicken curry over a campfire, unperturbed by the eighty-five-degree heat. The odour of curry had wafted through the pines. Father-in-law loved the Canadian wild and usually ventured much further north into Muskoka, Georgian Bay, and the Haliburton Highlands. He spent the winter poring over maps and calling Parks Canada to reserve campsites as far into wilderness as he dared. Wildwood Beach Trailer Park in Southwest Ontario was the closest he'd ever been to town; he usually went off the beaten track. Father-in-law was very convivial when camping. Aidan told me once that it reminded him of his hunting trips in the wilderness and jungle of Ceylon. He'd make friends with all sorts of people—"Come on over and have a beer!" One year he'd met a professor of forestry from Calgary, another a magistrate; they simply gravitated, intrigued, to this odd old couple from colonial Ceylon cooking curry in the outback. We thought we'd have a wonderful time, too, in a cottage there.

North Sauble was residential and quiet; private and rental cottages were sprinkled among the evergreens and maples near the falls. It was far from the strip, which was at the other end of the beach, with its motorbike gangs and teenagers, jazzy beach-front shops, fast-food takeout spots, and blaring ghetto-blasters from the young crowd. Our end of the beach was peaceful, or so we'd thought; it was a long white beach of golden sand dotted with families, a curving bay, and a long line of breakers rifting the shore.

We quietly settled on the sands among the other families, who were all white; in fact, I soon noticed that everyone everywhere was white. I sensed a certain alarm from the families close to us as we undressed and changed into our swimsuits and walked to the water's edge. We dipped our bodies in, and I thought I saw other swimmers move their children away from Aidan. Afterwards we rubbed ourselves down with towels; it seemed as if everyone was watching Aidan patting his brown bare back and chest with a towel—such an intimate gesture. We helped Rupert make a sandcastle. Again, I sensed a certain reserve from the families sitting near us. I recognized two mothers, Jean and Hilda, and their children who were renting the cottage next to us. I'd chatted to them over the fence only that morning. They had told me that they had lived in Brampton, part of the Greater Toronto Area, but had moved to Owen Sound, not far from Sauble "to get away," Jean had confided. She had said slowly, "Brampton used to be a lovely place in the old days, quite English."

"But not anymore," Hilda had cut in, her face tightening. "Immigrants. All those Indians moving in, taking over, buying up." Brampton and Bramalea—dubbed *Bramladesh*—were being expanded, I'd heard, and a number of East Indian and Sikh immigrants were taking advantage of the low house prices and interest rates there. It was the same in in Agincourt—dubbed *Asiancourt*—which was north of us, in the east side of Toronto. Just then Aidan had come outside with Rupert. The women immediately gave each other a look and went back inside.

Now they were ignoring us on the beach. Polly said sadly, "They won't play with me, Mommy." Aidan took her for an ice cream at the little café at the edge of the esplanade while I played with Rupert. I soon decided to join them, but as we approached I could see Aidan outside the café, surrounded by skinhead types, with shaved heads, metal chains, knives, and big black Doc Martens.

"What the fuck are you doin' with that little girl, Paki?" I heard. Something clenched at me, a rush of intense loyalty. I must protect him and Polly.

"Please don't hurt Daddy," I heard her say. Polly was gripping Aidan's hand.

"What d'you mean? She's my *daughter*!"

I ran forward. Aidan seemed relieved to see me.

"Oh, Mommy!" The skinheads turned, stunned. Then their faces turned into sneers as they realized the four of us were together, a "mixed" family, something they hated. As the men stared at me intensely, I forced myself to say lightly, "Let's have a coffee inside."

They watched through the window as we sat on bar-stools and ordered drinks and hot-dogs, hoping they'd get tired and go away. What they seemed to hate most was that we were there in Sauble Beach, enjoying it like white people. They growled that it was *their* territory. ("Get the fuck out!") You could see the tattoos on their arms—weird crooked symbols, eagles, angels, and crossbones. (Mother would have had a fit. "I warned you.")

"They're fucking everywhere. They're even here now," one of them had muttered, grieving, under his breath. He seemed young, perhaps twenty, with bright blue eyes. On the radio the other morning, I'd heard an interview with a skinhead of the Western Guard in Toronto who seemed bitter, anguished. "Indians have India and the Jews have Israel, and *they* don't let nobody in they don't want, but we the white race let in everyone, all the browns. That Trudeau and his cronies, it's like they want us to be a minority in our own white nation till there's nothing left of us, for *us*." His voice jerked over the radio waves from an unconscious place; what was he *saying*? Now there was this skinhead in Sauble, outside a wooden café in the sand, dressed in his working-class togs and metal chains. We could feel his hatred and contempt for us, for me especially—I was the one who had broken faith, betrayed them, betrayed my white race (one of their slogans was *Give birth to as many white babies as possible!*). But our children were already created, the new mixed race.

Things were already changing, even as this young punk wanted the old Ontario of the past—all white, with white children playing in the golden fields and white beaches of yore—all for himself. (This is not unlike the Sinhalese longing for the return of the Kandyan throne of their forefathers in Sri Lanka, I suppose.) And now Aidan and I and our offspring were there in Sauble Beach spoiling the myth, taking the last dream away from him. For a moment, I could feel his loss, his desperation. I remembered the voice on the radio: "...endangered species in our own nation," "WANNA TALK TO A RACIST? WELL, I AM A RACIST!" A sudden dial tone from the caller. "And that's Contemporary Exchange for today, everyone, on Country Radio. Join us tomorrow for...."

I still find myself trembling at the memory of something I hadn't known was everywhere. In that moment, I knew what was important, but I also understood how much safer we were in the city, as though Toronto's many immigrants were a bulwark I could rely on. I was frightened now of this rural environment, full of gentle-looking farms and quiet villages. "Let's go back to Toronto!" I said. I wanted to leave at once and forget the money, but Aidan was stubborn.

"No, we're staying. We've paid for the week. Why should we leave?"

"They might come after us, find our cottage, and attack us...."

Mr. Leigh, the owner of Leigh's Lakeside Cottages, was amused. "Ah, don't worry; they'll not come here. The police are on to these skinheads and punks," he assured us calmly. "They don't want tourists scared off." He was a kindly older man, making a summer seasonal living out of renting his cottages; he shut down his business at Thanksgiving. He had lived in the area all his life, he told us. "Of course you wouldn't want to take a job out here—that's a different kettle of fish, Mr. Gilmor," he added apologetically. "There's a Klan element here—in Wiarton (which we'd thought was such a sleepy old town), Owen Sound down to Kitchener-Waterloo, and Hamilton. Plenty of white supremacists, swastikas, National Front sort of stuff. Bad for business if they get violent." He gave a pathetic, wry grimace. "No sir, you don't want to mess with them."

There was something out there festering, a menacing undercurrent that must be kept from Mother. ("Now we have skinheads to deal with.")

Of course, I say nothing about any of this. I glance at Mother as she lightly powders her nose, sitting in the easy chair; she has no idea. Not that Mother isn't knowledgeable about the skinheads around Cardiff—it's surprising what she's aware of these days. "Oh we've got skins, haven't we Cedric?" she said lightly, poking fun, not really getting the implication. I don't want to worry Mother. For the first time, I sense the truth behind her needling, her warnings, ugly and threatening. But the uglier thought is of the white people moving from Toronto out to the countryside to be as far away as possible from us, from Polly and Rupert. They go "up North," as they call it, or "out to cottage country," to get away from immigrants instead of trying to live in harmony together.

"You see them on the streets, these punks and skins—I don't know what work they do—with their shaved heads," Mother is saying. "They wear bracers and button-down shirts and steel-toe work boots (to crunch you in the face), and call themselves the working class." Dad nods.

"Not any working class I ever knew," he adds. "Terrible, mun, on a Saturday night, after the pubs shut. You aren't safe outside."

Mother is more concerned about the riots in Sri Lanka; the old Empire is always more riveting and fascinating for her colonial generation, I suppose. In her letters, she's been sending regular snippets of information from the British newspapers about every riot and massacre. *BBC News is still the best in the world, Selena. See what is happening over there, now that the British are no longer in power?* she'd write. Of course, it was essential to burn these letters or hide them from Aidan in order to keep peace in the home. Mother seems to tacitly understand; however, it's best she keep her colonial opinions to herself in front of Aidan.

While Polly is in school, we often take a stroll along the boardwalk. I feel safe, though the area has its own murky history of violence against Jews, long forgotten. It's a lovely day; Mother enjoys the sunshine in her fancy sundress. "It would be raining in Cardiff right now," she says. Dad and Aidan walk ahead, happily discussing the working class in the old days, unions and such. Mum and I link arms, and I push the stroller. "Well those two seem to get along like a house on fire," she observes.

"Well, you know how fond Aidan is of Dad."

At once I regret the remark. Mother's face clouds in confusion, hurt. "Yes, I know," she says, embarrassed. She loosens her arm and lights a cigarette, her fingers trembling. Carefully, after a while, she says in a small voice,

"You know, Selena, I only ever wanted the best for you and

Betsy. You have to realize, when you brought Aidan over for the first time to get married, Dad and I were unprepared. We're not terribly educated people; we both left school at fourteen. Oh, I know I've done well with what little I had..." (as I try to protest). "Nanny didn't believe in higher education for girls. She'd have preferred I help out in Dada's business, but I had other ideas. My speed was eight-five words per minute, and my shorthand was fast, so I got good jobs for a girl. And then my secretarial experience got me the plum job of personal secretary to Professor Reisling at the university—that and my good legs. I was only eighteen when I met Daddy and got married. Then there was the war and all the bombing. I used to be so terrified, crouching under the staircase with Betsy in my arms. And the long lineups for food, the shortages during the war; all the food went to our boys at the Front. You and Betsy didn't know what milk and eggs were; you were raised on powdered eggs and powdered milk. So ... it was important to me and to Daddy that you did well at school, that you got every advantage possible. When you went to university, the first one in the family, I was so proud. We all were. I just wanted the best...."

"I know, Mum, I understand. Honest." I realize this is Mother's way of saying she's sorry about what happened at the wedding. I'd like to give her a kiss and a hug, but it would be too emotional; we weren't brought up that way. In fact, Mother has remarked on how much I hug and kiss Polly and Rupert. Is it good for them?

17.

FATHER-IN-LAW WAS VERY EXCITED at the thought of meeting Dad. "Mr. Harcourt is coming over for dinner with Myrtle, pet. Get out the silver, for God's sake."

"Oh! But there's no need, really." I was alarmed. "Dad is just ... ordinary."

"And fish forks and knives, meat forks and knives, pet..."

"But really!" Dad's diet is basically British fish and chips, but how could I say that?

Mother-in-law nevertheless proceeded to get out the old tarnished silver that the family had brought from Ceylon. She began polishing it frantically with Silvo. "We must have the best for your father, Selena."

"By the way, Daddy, it's not Mr. *Harcourt*." Aidan grinned, enjoying my discomfort, as usual. "It's Jones. Plain Jones."

I realized that Father and Mother-in-law implicitly expected Dad to be a replica of Uncle Clive, a fine Englishman. I know they'd admired Uncle Clive, with his impeccable manners and private-school education. He spoke French. He was a metallurgist. I pray that Dad won't drop his aitches. I imagine him saying, "*Appy to meet yew, Mr. and Missus Gilmor.*"

The meeting is even worse than I'd anticipated.

Father and Mother-in-law are dressed in their Sunday best. Father-in-law sports his old Holy Innocents school tie. They rise to greet Daddy and Mother in the kitchen as though they are greeting the King and Queen. (Daddy scrunches up his nose at the strong smell of curry, which I now take for granted.) He quickly covers his discomfort and smiles, holding out his hand.

Father-in-law looks somewhat taken aback, perhaps at Father's open-neck, short-sleeved shirt, his short stocky Celtic build, and his scarlet-red sunburn and cheery face—he's not the long lean pale David Niven type Father-in-law had no doubt expected.

Mother is fluttering, oblivious. "Oh Jack, Mildred, this is my husband, Cedric. Wonderful to see you both again." Mother is dressed in a flowery new dress, a tinkly necklace, and open-toed sandals—very swish. She's touched up her ash-blonde hair colour.

We cram into the tiny, familiar kitchen. Father-in-law lights his pipe, bemused. "Drink, Cedric?"

"Ah, no thank you. Don't touch the stuff."

"Ughh. Cigarette, then?"

"Don't smoke."

(Please God, don't let him say he was a weightlifter.)

"I was a weightlifter—South Wales middle-weight champion—when I was younger. Got to look after yewer 'ealth."

"A weightlifter?" If Dad had said he was a navvy on the railroad Father-in-law could not have looked more surprised.

"That is very good, Cedric," says Mother-in-law approvingly. She glances reproachfuly at Father-in-law's bulging belly. "See, pet."

Mother-in-law puts on the kettle for a nice cup of tea. Tea is truly the saving grace for every occasion. How grateful I am for its essence and warmth, for the excuse it provides to change the conversation at any given moment. "Just a little milk, thank you, Mildred."

Daddy tactfully asks to see the garden—probably a ploy to get away from the curry smell—and he and Father-in-law go outside. Daddy has an inborn working-class suspicion of any "foreign" food. (He's convinced that Chinese food contains chopped thumbs; he claims that one was found by a customer in Cardiff in his chop suey.)

Soon Daddy and Father-in-law are sitting on the lawn chairs under the apple tree discussing sports, a safe topic. "English football? Gone right down after the World Cup of '66, mun." England had won in extra time. What a celebration! They'd lifted Geoff Hurst onto their shoulders.

"Winning goal after ninety minutes o' play." They switch to cricket.

"Remember Compton ... and ... Ramadeen?" ("Cricket, lovely cricket, at Lord's where I saw it," had hit the top of the British charts.) Daddy tactfully agrees that some fine cricketers have come out of Ceylon, too, in its time.

They discuss which team would win this year's Ashes. "Oh England, mun," says Daddy. "They got a fast bowler now...."

Mother-in-law has made an "English" meal, starting with fried scallops—in order to use the fish knives, I suspect. This is followed by roast beef, Yorkshire pudding that has fallen flat like a crumpet, Brussels sprouts (the English like these smelly things), mashed potatoes and gravy, and apple pie and ice cream for dessert.

Father eats sparsely. "Yew gone to a lot of trouble here, Mildred. But fish an' chips would 'ave done me fine." Mother-in-law is nonplussed. The sprouts are mush.

Fiona arrives with Heidi and Hans. Then Scott and Darleene come by especially to meet Dad, bringing their two girls. Dad shakes hands all around and says "Pleased to meet yew." I can see he's disoriented by Fiona's shorn head. ("What 'appened to 'er 'ead?") Later, Fiona says, "Selena's father is very nice and kind, of course, but he's sort of like those British soldiers in the war in Ceylon, isn't he?"

Scott and Darleene do not seem to notice anything untoward about Daddy, for which I'm grateful. Daddy's face has turned even brighter red by now from sitting in the sun. "I can see you get sunburned fast, just like me," says Darleene with a smile.

Dad whispers to me as we leave, "Ooh the smell of curry in that 'ouse is something awful, Selena. Don't know 'ow you stand it."

For the first time, I think Dad has doubts about my marriage. How could I have fallen for a curry eater? Aidan overhears him, and grins.

"Well, Dad," he says, "British cooking has smells too, like bacon and those awful things ... kippers, you call them. Ugh, really awful stink to us."

"Oh, aye, they smells something terrible," says Dad affably. "Unless you like them."

"You going my way?" It's Todd Milford. He's appeared this summer in my yoga class. He has his yoga mat rolled into a special long carrier-bag that slings across his shoulder, like mine. He walks beside me, matching my stride. I'm meeting up with Aidan, Mum, and Dad on the boardwalk. I can see them in the distance sitting at the kiosk having coffee, Rupert slouched in his stroller licking an ice cream. Mother turns, catches sight of me, and gives a wave.

"That's Mother," I say. "My parents are over on a visit from Wales."

"Oh, interesting. Lovely place," Todd smiles. I realize with surprise that he's quite nice-looking in a lean, aquiline, English way. He's not wearing the round wire spectacles he has on at school. His blond hair is turning grey.

"You're from England, right?"

"Me? Oh? I don't remember it. I was just a baby when we left. I'm Canadian."

We've reached the tennis courts. "I turn off here." He nods. "I live in the duplexes now. I moved to Balmy Beach to go kayaking; it's a good spot. I can put my kayak in the water in the early morning before dawn and paddle across the lake."

I never thought of a librarian as being sporty, but why not? He laughs. I feel like he can read my mind.

All the duplexes have balconies with window-boxes filled with flowers, making them look like Swiss chalets.

"It's so pretty."

He bends down and plants a gallant peck of a kiss on my cheek, grazing my lips. "See you." I'm electrified; it's like a little shot of lightning, grounding me instantly. It means nothing, of course. The men do it all the time in friendship at Sun Yoga. I'm annoyed, for some reason, disconcerted.

"Who was that?" asks Aidan sharply as I join him.

"Just someone at my school. I don't really know him. Hi there, Rupert-Bear."

"Oh? For a moment it looked like that nice Englishman we saw square-dancing when I was over last," says Mother.

The lake is flat, pale blue, deceptively calm.

"Englishman?" frowns Aidan, lighting up his pipe.

"Just an English guy Selena knows." Mother lights a cigarette.

"*Mum!* I don't *know* him."

"I thought you did," says Mother innocently, enjoying the confusion. She puffs on her cigarette, as if casual.

"He's a twerp!" Aidan bristles. "I've seen him around with a kayak."

"Well, he seemed very well spoken, that time we met him. He's very English, tall and fair. We just saw him giving you a naughty little peck, Selena," she teases, really enjoying this.

"Now then, Myrtle," warns Dad. He knows Mother.

Aidan turns to Mother, furious. A seagull swoops down, ravenous, to swipe our muffins. I brush it away wildly.

"I know what you're getting at by 'Englishman, tall and fair, and all that crap," sneers Aidan. "I know what you're implying: I'm not English like him, not white enough. Never have been," he adds bitterly.

"Tha's going a bit far, Aidan, mun. She don't mean it. You know Myrtle," says Dad soothingly. "Dun't upset yourself, son, just when we're leaving." Dad gets up, "I'm going to the lavatory," he mumbles.

Mother smirks. She's still enjoying herself; she loves to needle. "Well, if the cap fits," she murmurs.

"*Mum!*" There are times I hate her.

Perhaps it was the smirk. Aidan flushes and clenches his fists. "Oh, go to hell!"

There's silence. "Seagull got muffin, Mommy!" Rupert reaches out his chubby hands, laughing.

"Naughty seagull," I say. I'm relieved when Dad comes back and Mother says they'll catch the bus to Kingston Road and then walk to the house by themselves. "We know the way." Dad looks relieved. He hates scenes.

"That was damn rude, Aidan. Mum doesn't deserve that."

I put Rupert in the playroom off the kitchen and switch on his train-set. The little train goes chugging along the track, around the floor, past pretend villages and shops, hooting and whistling. I face Aidan. He looks shame-faced but defiant. "Well, look what she said to me, deliberately needling. She had it coming."

"Poor Mum."

"Poor Mum my arse. She's a harridan and you know it. And talk about trust. What's going on with that guy, kissing you like that? We *saw*. Suppose you saw me kissing a woman on the boardwalk when I thought you weren't around. What would you think?"

"It was nothing, a peck on the cheek. He was just being friendly. Honest, Aidan."

The kiss that opens passion suddenly without warning, shooting through you like a delicious flame. What's happening? It was nothing.

"You don't love me. Never did."

The words were like the sudden swell of a breaker and then the swift undertow.

"Of course I do. Bunny-Hon…"

"Don't you Bunny-Hon me. That's over." Snarling.

I feel inexplicable anguish. But he's right about one thing: Bunny-Hon and Honey-Bun belong to our youth, a time of innocence.

"You just used me," Aidan hisses.

"Well, I could say that of you too. What about all those essays I wrote for you to pass your technical courses to get into teaching?" That was back in the sixties. What am I talking about? I'm bringing up things from a decade ago. Snatching for words.

Intense, his heart heaving. "You saw me, a decent innocent human being, trusting. And you were clever. Cunning. Like all the English. They knew how to manipulate in the colonies, pitting one group against another. That's why you wanted me to have a beard—it was to hide my Sinhalese features, wasn't it?"

("No! No!" Yes, yes.)

"And you wanted me to smoke a pipe like a fucking Englishman." He grabs his pipe off the mantelpiece and throws it against the fireplace; it cracks and tobacco flies out in puffs all over the grate. "And those fucking itchy English tweeds you made me wear. All to make me a fucking Englishman when I'm not!"

"I ... it's not true. It wasn't like that; you're misconstruing."

"You saw that I was better than your family. Yes! My father had a high position in Ceylon; he had a thousand labourers under him, servants, his own horse. But your mother's all screwed up—*you're* screwed up, from a screwed up fucking country, *Great* Britain. Great my arse. I see that now.

"And all those fucking news clippings your mother keeps sending about the war: *Tamils found hacked to death in Trinco, Sinhalese retaliation, Sinhalese girls found raped with ears cut off, Ceylon army accused of.....* What is going *on* over there, Selena?"

He mimics Mother. "What she should be asking is *why* the Tamils and Sinhalese are slaughtering each other, brother against brother. She should be asking about what the British did, bringing in a million Tamil labourers and putting them on tea plantations, just so she could have her fucking cup of *tea*.

"Your family would be nothing in Ceylon, nothing, but for their white skin." Aidan's eyes are bulging.

"Dad's family would never have been *sent* to Ceylon in the first place! Don't you get it? They belonged in the coal mines digging coal on their hands and knees, and fighting at the front, gassed and shell-shocked for their colonial Empire, just like your father's Tamil coolies slaving on his plantation."

There's so much here, depths below depths.

"You betrayed me...."

"No, you betrayed me."

We stare wildly at each other. I'm actually clenching my fists as if I'll hit him. What has happened to mindfulness and calm abiding? For a moment Aidan is thrown off balance.

"My Welsh grandfather was a coal miner. He couldn't even read and write. He's going to rule the empire in Ceylon with Lord Soulsbury and Lord—Lord Donoughmore? Unlike *your* father with his high position and fancy house and servants and horses. He did well out of British colonialism, didn't he?"

I've hit the mark. The truth. The look of anguish on Aidan's face tells me that. He looks sick. At once I'm sorry, sorry for the whole rotten colonial world.

"You don't understand ... you don't understand how it all came about, he had no choice," bleats Aidan.

"He had a choice," I cut in, decisive, relentless. "Your father could have chosen to be a simple accountant in Colombo. Or, he could have chosen a lower salary and an ordinary house. He didn't have to go into tea...."

What do I know? Do I have a clue what I'm talking about? There's another world here I'm not privy to, their world. My words are faltering through sunlight....

The toy train shrieks as it dives into the miniature tunnel and comes out the other end gaily intact; Rupert squeals with delight.

"Aw, let's go for a walk and meet your parents at the bus stop...." Aidan says, his shoulders suddenly slumped.

We call Bosie out from under the table where he's been hiding, and make a fuss of him. "Good dog, nice dog, let's go walkies." We allow Rupert to help hold the leash for a while as we go down the road together. Walking the dog is a way of declaring a truce, a useful barrage in a crisis, like a cup of tea. The English and their tea; the English and their dogs....

18.

WE PAY ONE LAST VISIT to Mother and Father-in-law before Mother and Dad fly back home. It's likely to be Dad's last visit. He'll not come to Canada again, he confides. He says that life here is "too awful, mun, too fast," compared with Wales.

"Well, we're in a backwater, that's why, Cedric," says Mother.

"No backwater, mun. Wales is beautiful; it's the best place on earth,'" Dad cries indignantly. We arrive at the bungalow and park under the willow tree. Tabby runs to greet us meowing loudly.

"*Bloody hell!*"

I'm not sure Dad will be able to cope with this: Father-in-law sagging over his shortwave radio in the living room as we troop in, tears streaming down his cheeks. British men just do not cry like this; they bear whatever comes, even death, like men, stoically like Uncle Clive. What is going on? Obviously something has happened—perhaps a terrible slaughter in Sri Lanka?

"Five hundred thousand Tamil books and sacred manuscripts in Jaffna, gone," weeps Father-in-law, looking dishevelled, his fresh short-sleeved shirt hanging loose, open and sodden. His *Lily* tattoo is exposed, moist and glowing across his chest. "Destroyed."

"What for tears, pet? We never even ever *went* to Jaffna," says Mother-in-law, irritated. "Look, Cedric and Myrtle are here to say goodbye. They're going back to Wales at the end of the week."

"*I* went there as a boy, with Uncle Henry," Father-in-law flares, indignant.

"Where's Jaffna? What is Jaffna?" I ask.

"It's the Tamil area in the north," explains Aidan. Felix intercedes. He knows Jaffna well from his courting days in Ceylon. "There's a Strait of Mannar up there, where you cross to India to Tamil Nadhu, Selena. There's a beautiful lagoon and beautiful kovils in white. There are dazzling white Catholic churches too, for many Tamils are Christian. But it's like the desert there, so hot that nobody wants to live there—only Tamils." Though this, of course, is not the answer we need.

"A hundred thousand sacred books, burned to the ground. The beautiful Jaffna library," mourns Father-in-law. It was an act of Sinhalese revenge against the Tamils, retaliation for who knows what.

Dad is surprisingly sympathetic, despite Mother's remark: "Oh, well, they're always at each other's throats over there, aren't they? Yes, I'll have a cup of tea, Mildred, thank you." Dad turns to Father-in-law.

"Aye, tha's a desecration, mun. Terrible thing to do, ter burn books. Books is precious." They certainly are in the Welsh coal fields and blackened valleys of the old miners and in Nangi's collieries and Welsh chapel. It's considered an abomination to burn a sacred book, even a Tamil one. "Us Welsh miners venerates books an' educashun, mun."

Father-in-law gives him a gratified look.

Mother rolls her eyes deprecatingly at Dad. "Oh, Cedric, what would *you* know about it? You and Nangi can't even read!" she says flippantly, with an amused laugh.

"Oh, he *can,* Mum," I cry. There are moments I hate her, she can be so mean to Dad.

Dad looks wounded. I know that it's likely that neither Nangi nor Grandad Jones could read or write. "Well, Grandad could sing, hymns anyway, all the miners did in their choirs," I say stoutly. Mother stares. We so rarely mention Grandad Jones; he died so long ago.

"What good is singing hymns to anybody?" she snorts. "It didn't stop the closures of the coal mines."

"Oh Myrtle," Mother-in-law intervenes. "Father Matthew says a good hymn sung sincerely can do more than we dream of."

Mother looks ready to convulse.

"Well, coal is thing of the past," she insists. "Mrs. Thatcher is seeing to that all right! She's closing the pits; the writing is on the wall. She's out to kill the unions now she's prime minister." I wonder why Mother likes to needle Dad so much. He rises to the bait, while Father-in-law gapes, bewildered. (Is the decline in coal in Britain not unlike that of tea in Sri Lanka?)

"They'll always need coal, mun," says Dad defiantly, ignoring Mother. "She's a tough nut. Thatcher the Milk Snatcher they calls 'er." He nods and adds, "The kids used to get a free third of a pint of milk every day, in school, in little glass bottles."

"Oh, yes, Cedric," Mother-in-law surprisingly joins in. "She took the milk away from those poor British children in the schools."

Mother snorts. "*That* was when she was the minister of health! Well, the school kids didn't need it anymore. The war's been over for decades, Mildred."

"Next it'll be coal, now that she's prime minister. There's signs everywhere: *Back the Miners and Keep the Pits Open*. She got the miners' union against 'er." Dad turns to Father-in-law.

"Ughh, Mrs. Thatcher!" Father-in-law growls dourly through his tears. Another bloody woman in charge.

Mother rolls her eyes and lights a cigarette.

"Bloody turmoil everywhere." In both Britain and Sri Lanka, I reflect.

"It's the end of the Empire. That's why, Daddy," says Aidan, and Father-in-law scowls.

"It's this damn war going on between the Tamils and Sinhalese ... damn fighting." He trembles again and knocks back a whisky. "And burning bloody libraries is the result."

"Aye, just like 'Itler did. There's conflict everywhere; there's war and killing all over the world, Jack," Dad agrees. "Like the Great War, only there wasn' nothing *great* about the 'Great' War. It's the young uns I feel sorry for. Sent to the front, just cannon fodder they are, poor buggers, and they dun't even know it till they gets gassed an' tortured an' loses 'alf their legs an' worse. An' what for? Just to fill the pockets of the toffs."

Father-in-law stares. "By God, Cedric. You're damn right!"

"Well, pet, Father Matthew says we are to live our lives wherever God has placed us."

"Ughh."

It's a strange sort of goodbye. Father-in-law sobs as he shakes Dad's hand and gives Mother a peck on the cheek, which at once revitalizes her.

"Your father is a very good man, Selena," says Mother-in-law quietly, with a sigh. No doubt Father Matthew would approve of him.

19.

THE TAMILS HAVE TO TAKE AN OATH: the Oath of Allegiance to the single state of Sri Lanka. Of course, the Tamil MPs have refused. They have consequently been expelled from the House by Jayawardena. It's that word *single* that they object to; they want dual acknowledgement of both Tamil and Sinhala languages. "Damn well right," snarls Father-in-law, pouring himself a whisky. "Ceylon's going to the dogs!"

"It's not *Ceylon* anymore, Daddy. It's Sri Lanka." Father-in-law scowls, as usual.

A conflagration of bottled-up resentment erupts against Jay Awardena and the government that had begun under Prime Minister Bandaranaike. The Sinhalese Janatha Vimukthi Peramuna—or JVP—youths are rioting again against the government, hurtling homemade bombs and Molotov cocktails at Government House, demanding jobs and university educations. Where is it all going to end?

In 1979, Jayewardene invoked the old British Anti-Terrorism Act, always a useful ploy to repress rebels, and they haven't forgotten. It was followed by Emergency Regulation 15A, which allowed police or soldiers to make arrests without charge and to bury or cremate victims without having to first identify who they'd killed. Suddenly people could just disappear, and they did. There was no accountability. Tamils say it's directed at them. The Sinhalese JVP *knows* it's directed at them. Deadlock.

Father-in-law turns up the *Voice of Ceylon* on his shortwave radio and presses his ear close. "Shh...." There's rioting, pillaging, raping, burnings—outright rampage. "Damn goons." No one really seems to know what's going on, or why. Who is to blame? Everyone, it seems. Who can deny responsibility? The Sinhalese blame the Tamils; the Ceylon Tamils blame the Sinhalese; the Tamil labourers don't count. The governments of the West are too focused on Iran, the fall of the Shah, the oil crisis, and mad Khomeini to care about a forgotten little island that hangs like a sapphire at the foot of India.

"They are calling it an insurrection of the middle class, Daddy."

"I never knew Ceylon *had* a bloody middle class." There had been the rulers and the ruled; and Father-in-law had belonged with the rulers.

Jayawardene granted himself new powers as "President For Life." ("Good God!") Even Father-in-law is taken aback.

"I told you, pet, about that man," says Mother-in-law somewhat smugly.

Meanwhile, in Toronto, Tamil refugees hold a protest at Queen's Park, the Ontario legislature. It seems that the Tamils in the north of Sri Lanka around Jaffna have formed a rebel group known as the Tamil United Liberation Front, or TULF, soon to call themselves the Tamil Tigers. They are going to give as good as they get from now on, they vow: rape, murder, conflagration. The leader is just a seventeen-year-old kid called Velupillai Prabhakaran ("My God, Mildred, pet!").

Aidan knows of Velupillai through his students at Brockhurst Tech. Dark Tamil youths, first refugees from the civil war in Sri Lanka, have been appearing in Aidan's drafting classes at Brockhurst Tech. The Toronto school board had deemed technical courses more useful for such immigrants to learn practical skills, which would lead to more job opportunities.

They couldn't believe that Aidan was from Sri Lanka, that he was born in Kandy. "*Ill!* No, sir!"

"Yes. My father was a tea planter."

"No! *Unmiakava*? Truly?"

They clustered around him. "You Sinhalese, sir? You Tamil? You're no Tamil."

"I'm Eurasian."

Meaningless. Aidan tried to explain the old reality of being "mixed" in colonial Ceylon: half British, half Sinhalese, half Dutch, half Tamil, half Portuguese.

But the students seemed to know very little about the colonial era; they didn't know about the tea estates or about the half million Tamil "coolies" imported by the British to work the plantations back in the nineteenth and early twentieth centuries. They weren't even aware of the Ceylon Citizenship Act of 1948 that had denied them suffrage. What had happened to history? (It can happen: history can be be erased, I fear.)

Saviamoorthy, one of the boys, confided in Aidan that his family hadn't liked the Tigers. They secretly hadn't supported the leader, Velupillai, calling him a "stupid *muttalh*," an idiotic teenager. Saviamoorthy's Tamil grandmother—his *Pattiy*—used to have a pass to go free by rail all over the island, in the old days under the Sinhalese. Then the children were forced to join the Tamil Tigers. "We were afraid all the time, sir. If you didn't join, they kill your family."

Aidan is despondent. He feels as though everything he remembers never existed at all; yet Tamils and Sinhalese are killing each other like crazy.

The Tamil protestors outside the legislature are demanding that the Canadian government do something, speak out at the United Nations. "*EELAM! EELAM!*" they shout; the evening news shows footage of them chanting and waving flags. Aidan tells me that Eelam is the part of Sri Lanka in the north that the Tamils now want for themselves.

"*Eelam*?" cries Father-in-law. "What the bloody hell are Canadians supposed to do about it?" "A *satyagraha* here in Toronto!" He's bewildered.

"But this is Canada. What for *satyagraha* here, Jack, pet?"

Confused Canadians, not sure what side they are supposed to be on, watch in dismay. What are these hordes of dark swarthy men with names longer than the tongue can recite doing in the Canadian mosaic? Something is catching up with Mother and Father-in-law; the past, whatever it was they'd thought they were leaving behind in Ceylon, is right out there at Queen's Park. Father-in-law reaches for the scotch and slumps in his chair at the table.

"You know what it is, Daddy," urges Aidan. "It's the whole rotten system that you were part of, that you hated deep down. Yes! Being master, *periya dorai*, over those poor Tamil labourers on the estates. Deep inside your psyche, you knew it was immoral. Because at heart you're a decent human being, Daddy. Honest."

Father-in-law begins to sob, as he invariably does on these Sunday afternoons in the Willowdale bungalow, especially when it's rainy and misty outside. He sobs deeply, his shirt stained with tears and whisky and whatever else he's sloshed inside himself to forget his past forget the unforgettable....

Meanwhile, Junius Philip Jayewardene is to be addressed as *Devi Yanse*. Your Excellency.

"Bloody fool!"

More fresh graves have been found by villagers. Weeping Sinhalese and Tamil mothers protest in the streets of Colombo, asking: "*Where are our sons?*"

"In prison, being tortured," says Uncle Neville.

His wife Miriam buries her face in her hands. "Don't, oh don't, Neville."

At last I'm meeting Neville Delaney, Mother-in-law's revered, Cambridge-educated older brother that I've heard so much about. He and his wife Miriam are returning from a visit to Sri Lanka, where they went to find out what's happened to Quintus. They've stopped over in Toronto on their way back.

They live in Portland, Oregon, the closest thing Neville could find to Ceylon, he tells us. It has mountains, the ocean, wild forests, and a milder climate than Canada.

They sit at the kitchen table. Neville is tall and broad-shouldered with a stocky build. He has crisp, curly brown hair that is greying, and light greenish eyes. He wears a French Basque beret that gives him a distinguished cosmopolitan air. Miriam is small and fair with narrow features and piercing eyes behind round wire glasses. She's obviously intelligent and somewhat sardonic; yet another Cambridge graduate, her field is molecular science.

"How long has it been, Jack old chap? 1956...?"

There were hugs all round when they came in, and more tears from Father-in-law. "Damn rascal," he said affectionately to Neville. He ignored Miriam. She's the woman he had The Fight with forty years ago on Normandy Estate, on his father-in-law Titus Delaney's cocoa plantation.

"He still hasn't forgiven Aunt Miriam," whispers Aidan. "How ridiculous of Daddy to hold it against her after all this time."

"That is *so* Gilmor," says Felix, amused. "They take their feuds to the grave."

Miriam, Jewish, outspoken, irreverent in her twenties, had apparently dared to mock the Catholic Church and the Pope. Father-in-law had taken off in his Morris Minor, incensed, churning up clouds of dust, leaving Miriam stranded on the cocoa plantation.

"Whisky, old boy? Gin for you, I know, Felix."

Neville accepts a tot on the rocks. He's delighted to see Father-in-law again, and especially Mother-in-law, his sister, and Aidan after so many years. He's also excited to meet me, the "English daughter-in-law," and our children, Polly and Rupert.

"Miriam and I always knew that Aidan would turn out well in the end," he says obliquely.

There's another Aidan here that they all know about, the one they keep in their memories.

We sit around the kitchen table, squished in.

I look curiously at Neville and Miriam: a "mixed" couple married in Ceylon well before our time. I long to ask many questions; I especially want to know how Miriam's German-Jewish parents had felt about her marrying Neville back in the 1940s.

"So what is happening with Quintus? Is he still in jail?" Mother-in-law is worried. Quintus was the daredevil, the communist younger brother, the rebel. He was a follower of Thondaman, the leader of the Tamil labourers.

"Sri Lanka is not the Ceylon you knew...." Neville hesitates before telling us that Quintus is in prison and that he has been transferred to Welikada. "Sorry, Mildred. It's best you know."

"*Welikada! Aiyo!*"

"My God, Neville."

They obviously know the place. Welikada Prison, in Colombo, was built by the British in colonial times. I've seen pictures of it in the old Ceylon tourist guides: *Welikada, oldest biggest maximum security prison of colonial Ceylon dating from 1841....* The pictures showed high walls, a large sandy compound, and chains. Amnesty International has released graphic reports about what happens within its walls, within its many cells. "Everyone knows about the torture that goes on," says Neville. "Rumour has it that sixty top agents of the Israeli Mossad were sent to Ceylon to advise on torture techniques, not that it was needed."

"*Aiyo!* To be tortured!" Mother-in-law's eyes fill with tears; I've never seen her show such distress. Father-in-law knocks back another whisky. The only hope is that Britain, the old "mother land," grants Quintus refuge. Neville has been in touch with the British embassy to plead for Quintus's release, citing Britain's old commitment in 1947 to ex-colonials. After all, Quintus is still a British citizen.

"None of this would have happened in Ceylon if SWRD Bandaranaike hadn't been assassinated," says Neville bitterly.

"Damn monks!" Father-in-law knocks back yet another whisky.

"No! What you should be saying, Daddy, is 'damn British Colonials!'" cries Aidan. "The Sinhalese and Tamils are both victims—don't you see? They're turning on each other while the British get off scot-free."

Neville gives a deep, approving laugh, and Miriam smiles wryly. "Good for you, Aidan! Chip off the old block, eh, Jack?" He means Aidan's grandfather, Titus Delaney, another rebel.

"Ughh." Father-in-law gapes at this contentious son he conceived from his own loins.

"And that Union Jack you're always flying, it has nothing to do with us Gilmors anymore." Aidan is getting vehement. "We're Canadian now, Daddy!"

Mother-in-law takes up the refrain, the magic word "Canadian," the talisman protecting everyone, myself included, from the past. "Yes, what for Union Jack, pet?"

"I'll bloody well fly the skull and crossbones if I want!"

Neville gives Felix a wry smile, as if to say, *Same old Jack, the Jack of the great tea plantations, periya dorai.* The colonial past that they all remember, that they were all part of, is gone. Neville sighs. "No more Normandy Estate—it was expropriated by the government under Mrs. Bandaranaike's nationalization scheme. Even Madeniya…" Here he hesitates.

"Madeniya?" explodes Father-in-law.

"Afraid so, old chap. It's a rubber estate now, run by a Sinhalese, hell of a nice chap…"

"Bloody hell!"

"The tamarind tree's gone, too. Sisera said it went long ago."

"My God!"

Mother-in-law is stoic. "What for tears, pet? Even trees cannot last forever."

"Ughh!"

Felix has been listening intently. Now he breaks in: "What about Mama and Dada at Pennylands? What's happened to our old estate?"

Neville looks melancholy. Aunt Bella and Uncle John were Felix's parents, and Pennylands had been a most beautiful estate. He and Miriam had visited Felix's parents on an earlier trip before they passed away. They were part of the relatives who had been "left behind" when Father-in-law sailed away on the *Stratheden* in 1956, over a decade before. Auntie Bella and Uncle John had said then, "It's not for us to leave now, we're too old. Our lives are lived." Aunt Bella had sighed. "Ceylon is our home, Neville, come what may. You and Felix and Jack save yourselves."

At this, Felix starts to cry. It's an awkward moment. Father-in-law trembles and knocks back a whisky. "Oh, come now, chap."

"I'd never have left Ceylon, I'd have stayed with Mama and Papa on Pennylands, but for ... what happened to ... to Cyril in '58," sobs Felix.

I am at last beginning to understand. Mother and Father-in-law have surely changed; they are other people now, and the past belongs to the people they can never be again. Everyone seems to know about the 1958 riot, a race riot that occurred in Colombo and in Tamil settlements across the island. Sinhalese gangs had attacked Tamils in reprisal for the Tamils' murderous attacks on them. Rumours had circulated about gangs roaming Colombo looking for Tamils. "Ahh, yes, that poor friend of yours, Felix, Cyril Coomaraswamy...." Father-in-law needs another whisky to get through this. "That was a very terrible thing."

"They used axes ... and homemade swords...."

So this is the real reason why Father-in-law sponsored Felix: so he could leave Ceylon after the slaughter, after what had befallen his Tamil friend Cyril. We all shudder. Tears stream down Felix's dark cheeks. "That was the end for me...."

He sobs softly. Cyril had been dragged, screaming, from the Colombo office midday. Later he was found down a well, his head severed. "There was nothing I could do. I was terrified. I hid in a cupboard," sobs Felix. "I didn't try to save him. I saved myself."

"There, Felix, have a cup of tea," says Mother-in-law soothingly. "It was not your fault."

"By God, the bloody country has a lot to answer for! Here, have a whisky. It'll do you a lot more good Felix, old chap, than a bloody cup of tea. Pull yourself together."

No one mentions Lily, Lily de Groot, the inspiration for Father-in-law's tattoo, which is fading now to a lighter hue. ("It's not your fault what happened to Lily, old chap," Aidan had heard Felix murmur once to Daddy. What was one life left behind, among so many during the exodus?)

"It's done, now, Felix," says Neville softly. Miriam still has her face hidden in her hands, weeping quietly.

Father-in-law begins to sob now too, a deep wracking grief that shakes his body. He stumbles outside onto the porch; we can see him through the storm door. "Oh, Lily," he howls. "Lily, I betrayed you." Father-in-law beats his head. "Ohh, poor Mr. Saeed ... oh what they did to him, too, and to his little grandson...."

"It wasn't your fault; we were already here in Canada, pet." Mother-in-law calls through the half-open door, but it's no comfort. Father-in-law tears at his hair.

"Poor, poor Mr. Saeed. I couldn't save you or your grandson!" he sobs. "Oh, Mr. Saeed!"

Neville and Felix look bewildered. "Who was Mr Saeed?"

Mother-in-law shakes her head. "I don't know. Likely one of the Mohammedan merchants in the Pettah; he was friends with a number of Muslims."

"And you know what they used to do to them," sighs Neville. "Pull down their pants and...."

Miriam covers her ears.

"Terrible, oh terrible, what they did to his little grandson," Father-in-law howls.

It's obvious that Lily de Groot and this Mr. Saeed and his grandson were part of the terrible events of the 1958 riot. Father and Mother-in-law and the children had already left Ceylon two years before, in 1956, saving themselves just in time. They'd had to leave Lily and Mr. Saeed and Felix behind. And that is all I will ever know, for no one is ever going to tell Aidan and me what happened.

20.

FATHER-IN-LAW IS GETTING OLD. I can see it. His hands are faded and trembling, and his belly heaves. His legs are swollen with dark blue varicose veins; his swollen feet blackening into a weird colour. He wears only slippers or sandals now, even in winter. He calls out from the bedroom, "Mildred! Come! Pet, pet!"

I hover in the doorway. "She's gone to Dalah's Market with Aidan and the children for groceries," I tell him.

"Ughh." Silence. Then: "Well, come in and help me, Selena. Stop standing in the doorway like a bloody ghost. Help me with my socks … please."

He indicates his feet, ugly purple-black smelly lumps, swollen and contorted. I bend down on my knees at his feet and heave the socks up, bit by bit, over his heels and up to his knees, panting.

"Well, thank you, Selena." He hesitates. "You're … a good woman."

Something settles inside me. The years in my marriage level out in some way; they become acceptable after all, comforting. It may not be the passion I'd anticipated with girlish fervour, but it has matured. I've survived this long. I can go on, it's not an unpleasant feeling.

"What's he up to now?" We jump out of the car and join a small group of neighbours gathered under the willow. Father-in-law is on the roof of the bungalow, seemingly trying to pull down the Union Jack. "Bloody flag...." His voice is carried in the wind.

"D'you think Mr. Gilmor should be up there, at his age?" asks old Mr. Sweetley from the house next door, worried. He's nearly a hundred himself by now. "Be careful," he calls up, his voice wavering.

"Pet, pet, *aiyo*, what is this foolishness? You are young man no longer," cries Mother-in-law, craning her neck.

"Daddy! Dad, I would have gone up there for you," Aidan calls up, concerned. We edge closer.

He's trying to free the flag from the TV antenna, where it's gotten twisted in the wind. "I'm taking the bloody thing down forever so the whole of Willowdale, the whole bloody world, will know which bloody side I am *not* on," he growls.

"Mind you don't kill yourself, pet." Mother-in-law is worried the roof will cave in. She's made *tilapu* curry for supper, she says.

"Bloody hell!" cries Father-in-law to the neighbourhood. We crane our necks further.

"Watch you don't *fall*."

He stands defiant against the clouds, like a prophet from the Old Testament, white hair streaming. "Granpa is Luke Skywalker in *Star Wars* now," says eleven-year-old Rupert, looking up in wonder.

"Silly," says superior seventeen-year-old Polly.

"What's he *up* to?" says Felix, frowning. "What the hell is he doing up there?"

The enormous Union Jack flaps suddenly in the wind, freed from the antenna. "Ah-h-h." Everyone breathes a sigh of re-lief. But suddenly it twists and twirls around Father-in-law's feet. He stumbles, entangled, his hands grasp at the air, and a second later he loses his footing and comes hurtling down, head-first, over the roof, wrapped in the Union Jack, and lands with a thud on the concrete. Everyone gasps. *Oh, Father-in-law! Father-in-law!*

Mother-in-law rushes forward, arms outstretched, too late. "*Aiyoooo....*"

PART TWO

CEYLON, 1947...

21.

IT WAS THE LOVELIEST PLACE in all the world: Weyweltalawa. Upcountry, in the Kandyan hills, it was poised three thousand feet above sea level. One had to negotiate twenty-two hairpin bends, with a nine-hundred-foot drop in one place, Daddy warned them. Peering over a precipice, one saw, far below, the rusted car wreck of a heedless driver—invariably an Englishman—who had met his fate going too fast and possibly drunk. The lonely tea estate stood at the top, peering through mist.

Drifts of hills floated in a fine constant rain, a thousand streams and waterfalls trickling and tumbling over mossy boulders, through deep forests. The winding Blackwater River, tributary of the Kelani Ganga that came out in Colombo, passed by the tea factory and then meandered through the deodars. There was a pool in the forest, one of many, shaded by tall ferns and clumps of bamboo. Aidan loved wandering in joy among the deodars with his little fish-net, not too far from the bungalow at first, then braver and further. He was nearly seven and Ganesh, the old Tamil gardener, accompanied him, carrying the pail.

Ganesh was only too glad to have an excuse for a break from the hard task of weeding Memsahib Mildred's flowerbeds in the burning sun. "*Sinna matya*, little master, go fish," he murmured, amused. He was fond of his *sinna matya,* as Aidan well knew.

Ganesh was toothless and had very dark skin, blue-black, and a deeply wrinkled face and hands. He usually wore a span cloth or a loose *dhoti*—which he wore the Tamil Hindu way—unless he was going to pray down by the river, at which time he would don a sarong that Daddy had bought him in the store at Ginigathena. Daddy had inherited Ganesh with the tea estate when he became assistant manager.

Ganesh showed Aidan how to make little watermills out of bamboo and twine pulled from the long vines that hung in festoons from the twisting tree limbs overhead. Aidan set the watermill inside the waterfall and played for hours, watching the wheels whir round and round in the current until they splintered and fell apart. He never tired of this, standing in the shallows in his undershorts and vest, (his fine English clothes cast aside on the rocks), barefoot like a village boy. The soles of his feet were tough and calloused like theirs; not even a red centipede could pierce them.

The pool was so cool and limpid in the dappled shade, ringed with all sorts of flowers: bright pinks and reds and mauves, coreopses, violets, shoe flowers that drooped like coloured paper bells from the bushes, and delicate frangipani petals floating through the air, temple flowers the Buddhists favoured. The eddy was dotted with small blue glimmering lilies; The Sinhalese called them *nil mahane*—"a sleeping girl's unopened eyes at dawn"—in the poetic way they had.

Silence hung strange and sultry in the heat of noon. Alien ferns, prehistoric and waving, towered over him as he stood listening, just a small boy in the sunlight, the dark shadow of Ganesh looming. Swaying lianas and curtains of mosses and fronds festooned the boughs; it was a place of flowers and fragrance and waterfalls. Rain fell softly, invisibly, plastering his hair to his forehead and soaking his little English vest and drawers. A thousand more waterfalls splashed gaily over deep black rocks fringed with grasses in the deep silence. The Muslims called it *paradise* in the Holy Book (though the Buddhists said "Chosen Land"). It was the Garden of Eden with the Tree of Knowledge of Good and Evil in its midst. This was where two Angels were said to hover, if one had the eyes to see, overpowering in their holiness. A certain drooping flower with a spotted open beak and tiger stripes was also there; if you but touched its petals they gently closed and you felt the sucking—open and close, part of the mystery.

A snake slid into the water. Aidan knew not from where, only that it had been there all the while. A myriad of small tropical fish, their colours sparkling and iridescent, squirmed out of its way, perhaps part of the same Good and Evil. He dipped his net quickly beneath the surface and caught a net-full.

"Ah, Aidan, *sinna matya!*" Ganesh smiled encouragingly.

On the way back, they passed the path that led to the village at the other end of the tea estate. But Ganesh would not take that path. He shook his head. He reminded Aidan that he was Tamil, a Hindu, a labourer working for the British masters, and those villagers were Sinhalese.

The sun had broken open in the sultry sky, following the mists and rain showers; there were sudden bright gleams of lovely blue, fresh breezes from the hills light with the fragrance of acacia and frangipani. The peaks of the highest mountains gleamed in the distance—Adam's Peak, over seven thousand feet, Hatton, and Nuwara Eliya—like a mirage. They trudged wearily and happily back to the Gilmors' bungalow, the big estate house at the end of a drive bordered with laurel.

Aidan left the bucket of fish behind the outside kitchen, and then forgot about it; it was found much later by the Sinhalese servants who muttered at the dead fishes floating belly-up, their eyes turned inward, for the house servants were Buddhist and kept the *tripitaka*, the three treasures of Buddha. All was *dukka*, suffering, to be appeased by following the holy *dharma*. Everything had its spirit and was not to be wantonly destroyed. *Aiyo!* Now the spirit world was offended.

22.

M R. PETER DE GROOT, whose name signified at once his
Dutch Burgher heritage, was the insurance agent from
Colombo. He regularly came upcountry to sell policies or
collect premiums from the tea planters who had already con-
tributed to a plan. That day, he had calmly manoeuvered the
twenty-two hairpin bends in his battered old Austin 8 to reach
the estate bungalow of Weyweltalawa. Jack Gilmor was one
of his clients; he had purchased a life insurance policy. (Jack
had felt indebted due to his long-past broken engagement, brief
though it had been, to Mr. de Groot's daughter, Lily.)

Peter de Groot was an older man in his early fifties, tall
and fair-skinned like many Burghers and Eurasians. His eyes,
however—dark, deep, flashing Tamil eyes denoting some gene
from the "other" side of the family—gave him away, according
to the people who put stock in such things (which was practically everyone on the island). How dark- or light-skinned you
were; how fair, tall, or short; if you were Sinhalese, Muslim,
Hindu, Afghani, or mixed—it was all a matter of intense
scrutiny. A sort of fanaticism for identification had come to
the island with the British, who kept important records and
censuses of such things. Mr. de Groot's grandfather had come
by way of a sloop from Amsterdam in the old days. He had
been a dealer in hemp and spices; he'd even owned a small
coconut and cinnamon plantation at some point in time,
which he had subsequently lost in the British takeover. Aidan

understood that first there had been the Portuguese invasion, which had happened a long time ago. They'd been mainly interested in spices, mostly cardamom and cinnamon, and religion, specifically Roman Catholicism. They'd taken over the coasts, destroyed the Buddhist shrines and *dagobas*, and erected Catholic churches in their stead—hundreds of churches dedicated to the Virgin Mary that still dotted the coastlines. They'd also left behind, of course, a slew of half-Portuguese offspring with names like de Silva and Fernandes. The Buddhist monks in particular had not forgotten; they were reminded at every holy shrine to the Virgin.

Then had come the Dutch, and with them law and order and Protestantism. The island still had Dutch law, despite the British takeover. But it was always who was in power in the moment that counted. Now, that was the British—Rule Britannia!—and the de Groots knew it. Nevertheless, Peter de Groot was a most welcome visitor in these lonely hills.

He had brought with him his youngest daughter, Esmé, to play with the Gilmor children, as he often did. She was a pretty little thing, barely ten, with a quantity of fair curls tumbling to her shoulders. (The older daughter, Lily de Groot, was the one who had once been an object of Jack Gilmor's affection—in his extreme youth, he would hasten to add.) A passing phase, he called it, an infatuation, madness. It had been back when he hadn't understood what the word *love* meant, when he hadn't known what he was doing. Lily had been a beautiful young girl of sixteen, fair like her father, with long blonde hair. But a Burgher. No match for a Eurasian like Jack Gilmor, who was of British descent. It was not as if the de Groots were a rich Burgher family either, highly positioned in law or government or high finance and living in Cinnamon Gardens. Peter de Groot was a mere insurance salesman from a poorer district of Colombo. The de Groot grandfather, old Simon, barely spoke a word of English. He still sang *Het lieve Faderland* for God's sake, and he worshipped at the Protestant Groot Kerk in Colombo. (The Dutch had not endeared themselves to the English Catholics. They had called the Catholic Church a "whore," amongst other things.) So a liaison with a protestant Burgher was reprehensible. Granny had made Jack go down on his knees before the altar in St. Joseph's Catholic Church and swear he would never ever marry a de Groot, certainly not Lily. Then he had met Mildred, Mildred Goonesekere Delaney, another Eurasian, at the local planters' club. Their families were known to each other; they played tennis at the same club and they were both Catholic—on such coincidences was a love match—true love—inspired, though the astrologers had said otherwise.

Unfortunately, in a moment of fervor, he'd had LILY tattooed forever across his chest. It meant Mildred had to make love, and sleep every night of her married life, next to LILY. Oh, the insanity of love!

Jack ordered the servant to bring two toddies for the men, tea for Mildred, with a little jiggery, and cool slices of papaya sprinkled with cinnamon. The children were sent outside to play, with fourteen-year-old Lally in charge. She was Mildred's youngest sister, but the children viewed her as a cousin rather than an aunt. Though she was the oldest cousin, she was the silliest, said Fiona; Lally would scream at anything.

They went at once to the waterfalls and the Blackwater pool, leaving Daddy and Esmé's father behind puzzling over percentages and premiums. The girls, Fiona and Lally, were decked out in pretty English frocks imported from England; Esmé's dress was worse for wear, too tight and with tears. (Mama would kindly give her one of Fiona's hand-me-downs before she left.) The boys went barefoot to their delight. Little Scottie trailed his *kootee*, an old stuffed rabbit split at the seams, that he insisted on taking everywhere. "What a baby," mocked Fiona. "Silly *kootee*."

"Don't make fun of him, he's only four and a half," said Aidan, and at once Fiona grabbed a big stick to hit him.

"Oh, don't hurt Aidan, you'll kill him!" cried Lally, and Aidan was certain that was what Fiona intended.

The sun broke out from behind a cloud, hot and dizzying. Soon the forest enclosed them, but they were unafraid. They moved through waving giant ferns. High in the tree tops the hanging parrots squawked and whistled upside down and bright turquoise parakeets swooped. As soon as the children got to the pool, Aidan and Scottie tore off their shirts and vests and waded in, splashing and calling out. Fiona, the older sister, already imperious at ten and the real boss despite Lally's superior age, stood superciliously apart, too old for such horseplay. "Miss Boss," Ganesh called her, though not in front of Mama and Daddy.

Esmé de Groot, thin and vibrant, tucked her dress into her knickers and joined in the fun. She was barefoot like the boys, while Fiona and Lally wore uncomfortable English sandals that pinched, as befitted the daughter and niece of a tea planter. Esmé was darker than Fiona despite her fair hair. Aidan thought she might be some distant cousin. The de Groots were related in some way to the Van der Meers, who were distant relatives on Mama's side from half a century ago. Did that make them cousins of sorts? Fiona knew. (Fiona knew everything.) They were not supposed to discuss such things—Esmé's complex relationship with them, and her older sister Lily's affair of the heart with Daddy, which had happened years before the children were born and which had been secretly divulged by the servants—but they did.

"Oh, the fishies!" cried Esmé, delightedly. "So *schoon*, all the colours!" She scooped eagerly with her outstretched hands, caught a larger one, and dropped it on a rock where it beat about helplessly. Soon it stopped gasping and was dead.

"Now you'll come back as a fish in your next life," said Fiona. "Or a worm that a fish will eat in revenge. It's your karma," she added triumphantly. Esmé looked frightened and began to cry. Scottie came over to her. He was the youngest, the baby brother everyone made much of; he was always loved and petted and given in to. He was the fairest of the three children, with pale beige skin like Daddy's but with thick, black, straight Sinhalese hair. (Aidan's hair was soft and silky, falling down his neck in light brown curls, but he was dark skinned, taking after Mama's Goonesekere side of the family, everyone said.)

Scottie got up on a rock to be level with Esmé's face. "Don't cwy, Esmé," he said. "I'll be a fish too. Then we can be marry." And he leaned over and kissed Esmé on the lips. "Now we be marry."

"You're not supposed to, " said Fiona quickly. "She's a Burgher. I'm telling Ma."

"What's *that* supposed to mean?" demanded Esmé, turning to Fiona, clenching her fists. Fiona slapped a frond against the rock and waves rose in the pool, making Aidan's little boat rock. Aidan was playing with it in the waterfall. Scottie looked confused.

"We don't marry Burghers."

"Oompa is as good as any of you!" cried Esmé.

Aidan watched his frail leaf boat swirl in the current, getting a battering from the rocks, but he was listening intently.

"You're ... Tamil. Half, anyway," cried Fiona.

"Well, what about Samira?"

Esmé's eyes glittered. The words slithered out of the past, like snakes: *Got you, Miss high-and-mighty Fiona Gilmor.*

"Samira doesn't count. Her mother was just *country-wife.*"

Not to be spoken of. Now that she was almost eleven, Fiona understood that much. An illicit liaison long ago between grandfather Owen Gilmor—Daddy's father, who was long since dead (of drink)—and a Sinhalese servant girl, now an old woman, had resulted in Samira, the illegitimate, unfortunate offspring of the affair, and therefore Daddy's half-sister. She still lived in the village somewhere, near Gampola. Definitely not to be spoken of.

Fiona trembled with indignation. She would like to slap

Esmé de Groot's face. Lally gaped unhappily. She always wanted everyone to smile and be happy. She was supposed to be in charge. But Fiona drew herself up on the rock and said imperiously: "We're *British.*"

And that settled that.

"Now there'll be trouble." Scottie and Fiona would be sure to blab everything. Lally plodded miserably after the others, her long black plait swinging. She did not look like her older sister, Mildred Gilmor, the children's mother. She looked like Amma, the mother she could barely remember, with her soft, rounded Sinhalese face. She had lived since age four with Mildred, who was more like a mother to her than an older sister. Jack Gilmor had taken Lally under his care for his wife's sake when they married. What would have become of Lally if Jack hadn't taken her in? An orphanage, or worse.

Once Mr. de Groot left early with Esmé—he wanted to make it down those hairpin bends before dusk—Fiona, of course, told Mama everything. But there was Scottie prancing about the living room defiantly shouting: "Me kiss Esmé! Me marry Esmé!"

Mama's mouth tightened. A look of alarm. "That's foolish talk, Scottie. Stop it!"

And, of course, Scottie shouted all the more. "Me marry Esmé, marry marry Esmé, kiss Esmé!"

Mama actually whacked him across the legs with the *Ceylon Times*, the only occasion Aidan ever saw her strike him. Scottie stopped in his tracks, shocked. Then he jumped around the living-room again, knocking over the rattan screen. "Will so! Me an' Esmé be marry, *kiss-kiss-kiss!*" He was the beloved child, the last child Mama and Daddy would have, and he was highly favoured.

"Rascal!" Daddy would chuckle. Scottie was always up to no good: he put salt in the sugar, confusing kitchen servant number two; he dropped crick-cricks in Father Balderelli's thinning hair; he slipped a gecko into Fiona's bed, sneaking in under the mosquito net; and he refused to eat Ceylonese food. Imagine, not liking *seeni sambol*, which everyone else adored, or hoppers for breakfast! "Not like hoppers?" everyone cried. He would eat only imported cereals from England—his favourite kind was corn flakes—and English beef and potatoes or hot dogs for lunch instead of chicken curry and *dhal* with *roti* like everyone else. "A right little Englishman!" chuckled Felix, Daddy's cousin. "But a spoiled brat."

"Well, you could talk," muttered Mama, annoyed. Felix had had a servant accompany him to Holy Innocents School to wait on him when he was a boy boarder. He'd had "English-only" food specially cooked for him. No *dhal* and *roti* for him. It cost Auntie Bella and Uncle John a fortune, but he was their only son.

Scott Gilmor got away with murder, the relatives all agreed, and something should be done about him. But it never was.

23.

"A BAD BUSINESS," agreed Father Balderelli. He was wearing the white robe and cassock of the Dominican Order. A simple wooden crucifix hung around his neck. "Of course, Jack, he can no longer partake of the holy sacrament...."

The two men were talking about Ritchie Thompson as they sat comfortably out on the screened verandah at Weyweltalawa after sunset. Thompson was the new planter in the district, a novice when it came to tea. He'd been giving it a go, though. He owned Braeside, a fairly large enterprise of two thousand acres consisting mainly of tea and some rubber.

Jack knocked back another whisky. Aidan could see him through the screen, legs crossed, leaning back leisurely in the rattan armchair, puffing his pipe.

"Nice chap, really, Father. Damn shame..."

Thompson had committed an unforgiveable sin for a white man in Ceylon: he had married a Hindu girl, a Tamil. Not a high-caste, wealthy Tamil, even, or a sophisticated city type with a good professional career—many of these Colombo Tamil girls were slim and pretty—but a mere labourer from the coolie lines on his estate. What had he been thinking? It was the talk of the club among the planters. If Thompson had merely had her as a mistress or concubine, or even a country wife on the side, they would have understand. God knew there were hundreds of such furtive liaisons all over the island, their offspring filling the convents and orphanages. (Here Jack felt uncomfortable, his own father's shame sweeping over him.) But to actually *marry* her, confer upon her legal legitimacy, land ownership, and citizenship (in this case British)? It was incomprehensible. A betrayal. British honour, the flag, the king! The planters and their wives were all a-buzz with it at the club. The women whispered of nothing else, gossiping fiercely over afternoon tea and *petit fours*.

"Another whisky, Father?"

Thompson had driven to Colombo, by all accounts, to the Muslim jewellers in the Pettah, and bought a gold ring with a huge gem for the engagement, along with other necklaces, bangles, and bracelets. Ceylon gems, rubies, and emeralds galore. Then he had gone through with it. A marquis had been raised on the grounds of Braeside by the labourers. A Hindu priest had been brought in, and *neem* paste had been smudged on Thompson's forehead. He'd even come in riding, Tamil-style, through the estate on the back of an elephant!

"That's carrying it a bit far, surely?" Father Balderelli could not help a wry smile.

The fact was, Thompson was one of hundreds of British soldiers who had been posted in Ceylon during the war. And World War II had changed everything. The common British soldiers had been the bane of the tea planter population, which very much fancied itself English gentry—and who knew otherwise? But the British soldiers were something else. With their common parlance and easy, friendly ways with the Ceylonese populace, the young soldiers had shown the villagers another side of the British that the Sinhalese had never suspected existed. The soldiers had mixed freely and openly with the villagers; they'd liked them. Hungry for female affection, and, on a deeper level, for women's warmth—missing the families, mothers, sisters, and girlfriends they'd left behind thousands of miles away—they'd reached out eagerly to the Sinhalese folk, joking and laughing with them. They tried to learn words and phrases in Sinhalese; they got drunk on toddy and arak, and lay sprawling, drunk, in the sandy dust outside the huts. These white men had scoffed at the so-called English gentry, the tea planters. "Ain't nothing aristocrat about them toffs," they'd laugh. "Most of 'em would be nothing back in England, we can tell you." Their mockery resulted in the intense chagrin of the planters at the club, and the delight of the Sinhalese. "Them and their fancy clubs—'arf of them wouldn't make it through the door back 'ome."

Jack Gilmor had been bewildered. And now here was Thompson—he had "gone native," as they said at the club. He was letting down the side.

Of course, Thompson was not invited to be a member of the Nuwara-Eliya Club, even though he was white. He was not a gentleman. Thompson did not seem to care. "Snobs," he said to Jack.

Even worse, Thompson, a white man, had a propensity for shitting outside in the open behind any bush like a coolie, shocking the field workers. Only the other day, Ethel Henshaw, wife of Eric Henshaw—*sinna dorai* of Netherlands, the next plantation over from Weyweltalawa—had been out walking in the grounds of the club with Bessie Matthews. The two women were shocked to come across Thompson "in the act," as it were, a pair of bare, rounded buttocks like two moons shining in their faces from the other side of the fence. His estate bounded club property. The man had not even had the gentility to cover himself, but had nonchalantly stood up, pants around his ankles, and grinned. "Got caught short, I'm afraid, ladies." To which Mrs. Henshaw and Mrs. Matthews had responded, of course, unflinching, as admirable English women: "Good day, Mr. Thompson."

"Aah," said Father Balderelli tactfully. "Yes, I do see; most unfortunate."

Yet the man had sent out gilt wedding invitations to everyone in the district. Ignored, of course. Not one tea planter had attended the ceremony except Jack and his wife Mildred. They had done so out of sympathy and shame, though somewhat bewildered and embarrassed. They certainly had not stayed for the alien festivities. Jack was an usher at his church, St. Francis of Assisi, in Hatton. He had done his Christian duty out of instinctive kindness.

Thompson had come one evening to the Gilmors' bungalow, crying to Jack and Mildred. "Why didn't the blighters come to my wedding? Why don't they like me?"

He'd laid down his head on the dining room table and sobbed like a small boy. What to say?

"Ah, buck up, man." Secretly, Jack had been shocked to see a white man cry in such a fashion. "Have a whisky. It's not so bad."

But it was. Jack knew well about that sort of ostracism from his childhood, when that bad business had happened with his father and that village girl. Father had been fired. The whole incident had darkened his boyhood, blotted out happiness. No happiness after that. A social outcast, that's what Thompson was now, foolish fellow.

"Yes, well…"

Father Balderelli hesitated. "Poor chap," he agreed cautiously. Jack Gilmor was a generous benefactor of the Catholic Church, and Mildred was a member of the Solidarity of the Blessed Virgin Mary (not to be taken for granted these days). Who knew what the future held for the Catholic Church in Ceylon if the threats of the Buddhists held true. The Buddhist monks were planning to end funding to the Christian churches—now labelled "foreign"—once Independence came and they took power.

Jack was fond of Father Balderelli, and the priest was always a welcome guest. Father was extremely poor, like all the priests of the order of St. Dominic in the district. Jack had once given Father Balderelli a pair of his shoes—they had the same size feet—and one of his old pipes with a pouch of tobacco. He felt sorry for the priests. Their robes were threadbare. They were truly given to the vow of poverty. Some of the older priests, including Father Balderelli, spoke sadly of their home towns far away in Italy and Belgium that they would never see again. Tears would well up in Father's eyes at such times. A terrible thing, really. Blessed Father would die far from home in this foreign land, his name engraved on a tombstone, like so many others before him, in the catholic cemetery at Hatton.

Jack knocked back another whisky, and the two men puffed their pipes, drawing in slowly. The aroma of tobacco drifted in the cool night air, melding with the sweet smell of the acacia blossoms and frangipani. There was the usual incessant whirring and buzzing of night insects, the blurp of toads, and the soft scream of night jars beyond the verandah screens. And an occasional screech of God knows what in the outer darkness.

Father Balderelli was smiling to himself. He was thinking of the little boy in his catechism class that morning. It was a mixed group of boys: some Sinhalese, some Tamil Catholics from better-off families, some very poor Sinhalese boys from the villages. He began recounting the little episode to Jack now, in the dark warmth from the glow of the hurricane lamp. All sorts of nightly flying insects, some brightly lit like sparks, and giant moths were beating themselves to death against the glass or knocking themselves unconscious against the screen, blinded, trying to reach the light.

"I asked the boys, Jack, 'What is the meaning of dogma?' And this little kid, must have been about five or six, said, 'My dog ma had four puppies, Father.'"

The two men laughed softly. A heavy mist had floated up from the valleys and the drifts of clouds had moved over the hills. It began to rain, a thick swishing through the bamboo.

"Ah well, I must be off." Father Balderelli pulled his cowl over his head. He made the sign of the cross. "The Lord be with you, Jack."

"And with you, Father."

Jack called Ganesh from the outhouse to bring a lantern and

accompany the holy Father on his way. They paused at the doorway; the night was now filled with the sound of drumming; the nightly tom-toms were beating in the darkness far off across the hills and estates—*th-rum th-rum*—the heartbeat of Ceylon. Things were stirring on the island. Independence was coming, political, social change. But some things never change.

24.

THE RED SANDY PATH evocative of his fishing afternoons with Ganesh stretched pleasantly through the trees. It wound its way to the edge of the estate and eventually came to the small Sinhalese village. It was hidden in mist among coconut palms and thick bamboo. Daddy had shown him the village once; it was a small encampment that had been there forever. Before the tea estate. Before the British, with their guns and ships and battles and discipline, glory and destruction. Since an incomprehensible time that Aidan could hardly imagine.

Now that he was nearly seven, Aidan walked alone through the forest, unafraid. He was aware that everyone on the estate knew who he was. He was dressed in pleated khaki shorts like Daddy and a short-sleeved English cotton shirt buttoned down the front. Soon he passed by the plantation, row upon row, mile upon mile, of tea bushes. They grew in neat tidy rows with narrow red sandy paths between them so the tea pickers could move around. The tea was planted in contours that had been shaped into the hillside, which was dotted with Tamil workers, women and children, their *kangeni,* in charge. (Tamil men did not pluck tea; they did the heavy work of the fields). The *kangeni* was an old, fierce-looking man who watched from under a tree, whip in hand. He was thin with a cloak around his shoulders, but the women had only loose shawls from their saris to pull over their heads against the beating sun. Up and down the rows, they worked, plucking tea buds, from dawn to dusk. Aidan felt a pang of sorrow, especially at the sight of the coolie lines where the labourers lived; they were long, ugly, cement blocks of living quarters with hot corrugated tin roofs. There were openings in the walls for doorways. Frightening. There was only a single room allotted per family, and they were dark and fetid. He was not allowed to go near them. He shuddered.

In contrast, Daddy's house, the big estate bungalow, was large and spacious with white walls, a teak shingled roof, and deep verandahs. Besides the beloved tamarind tree, there were three fruit trees in the front: a grapefruit tree, redolent with round yellow-green fruit no one bothered to pick, not even the servants; a mango tree, hanging with ripe golden mangoes, the ground littered with dropped fruit; and a guava tree. Daddy loved its fruit and the servants brought him a fresh guava each morning for breakfast. Then there was the winding drive, shaded by laurels and acacia.

But the coolie lines weighed on his heart. The women often cooked outside communally, bending over fires even during the monsoon. (Where did they defecate? Daddy had put in a request for the owner, Van der Meer, to put in cess pits for the sake of hygiene, to no avail.) Aidan often heard the drums and wailings far into the night from the encampment. Eerie mournings. Tamil labourers were Hindu, a strange religion. Daddy had once taken the children to Kataragama to see the fire-walking—bare-footed Tamil yogis treading in trances over red-hot coals. Nothing happened to them. He'd seen it. But it was not for Christians to try, not even Father Balderelli. (Our Gods are more powerful than your Gods.)

The white tea factory stood high on the hill, where Daddy went each morning, setting off on his BRS motorbike. That was where the tea buds were collected from the labourers by the bushel, treated by the tea maker, and transformed into tea. Daddy knew all about that, and Aidan would, too, when he grew up and became a planter. Sometimes Daddy took him inside, and the workers, donned in protective hats and gloves, would bow to Aidan as well, calling him *podi mathia*, little master. It was a vast airy place, deliberately dimly lit to protect the delicate tea leaves. There was a deafening roar from giant revolving fans that kept the tea cool.

He hastened on, and soon he passed by the cremation ground where the Tamil coolies burned their dead. He knew about it; he had watched the ceremonies once, from a distance. "What for looking at such things?" Fiona had said crossly, trying to pull him away. Lally had just stared, round-eyed, wonderingly. And that night, under the mosquito net, curled up in her safe snug bed, she had said she was scared of Hindu spirits. "Silly!" Fiona had cried in the dark, "Holy Mary and Jesus are tons more powerful than their spirits—just ask Father Balderelli."

Aidan understood her to mean "heathen" spirits. The Hindu women laid out the dying body facing the east, with a lamp lit at the head. Ganesh had told him this, in a low voice. ("Not for Miss Fiona to hear.") After death, the head was turned to face south, towards the mountains behind the deodar trees. The big toes were tied together and a cloth was tied around the head. There was burning of incense—you could smell it rising like a mist over the fields—and chanting to Aum Nama Narayanaya, one of their great spirits. Later, they raised up the dead body and put it on a big funeral pyre of wood sticks. Aidan had seen the grass and sticks stuffed underneath the body set alight by the oldest coolie who had to be a male, usually the son (which was why boys were so important to a family, Daddy said). You could smell it for weeks afterwards, all over the plantation, the sweet acrid scent of sandalwood and eucalyptus they sprinkled over the corpse. Then they took the ashes to the pool in the Blackwater River, which was black and ran behind the tea factory. It provided water to Weyweltalawa and the other estate on the far side,

Netherlands, which belonged to Mr. De Jurgen. He was the owner and manager there—*periya dorai*—and he also owned Weyweltalawa. Then a few days later, after the funeral, and on a special day, the Tamil coolies went down again to the pool in the river with their headman. He was like a priest with long, knotted, tangled plaits down his back, a painted face like a mask, and a special mark on his forehead. They went into the pool and bathed themselves; he had seen it, with his own eyes, hiding behind the bushes. There was a low humming of prayers, "*Om Hari Krishna*," accompanied by chanting women and children who held burning candles. It was very beautiful; it felt like it was taking place at the edge of time, immemorial. With a child's instinctual knowledge, he felt it was so. *Immemorial* was a word that was also on the stone wall of the Convent of the Sisters of St. Euphrasia, in the hot sun, dedicated to Sister St. Euphrasia herself. She was one of the Catholic saints that Mama and Daddy worshipped. Then the Tamils said more prayers in their language: "*Kadavulh ungalhI aseervadhipparaha....*" Daddy said that meant "May God bless you."

"You should not be around the cremation site, son, even watching from far away. You are too young, and it is very private for them. Don't watch again."

It took a long time for a body to be completely burned.

"What happens to the bones and teeth, Daddy?"

"What a question!" laughed Fiona.

"Aaah!" said Lally, and her eyes turned huge and dark, like liquid. She crossed herself.

"Silly!" Fiona tossed her head.

"Everything turns to ash and dust, and returns to nature, where it belongs," Mama explained.

"To Brahma," said Ganesh, when Aidan asked him the next morning.

Aidan was fearful, despite the bright sunlight.

And a great grey heron rose from the pool on silent wings.

Parakeets flashed, emerald and bronze, through the innocent tree tops of the Garden and the Tree of Good and Evil, the holy Tree of Life, where the two Angels hovered with folded wings that Aidan still had the power to see.

He walked on, happy and alone. No Ganesh today. He could meander at will, knowing he was safe as the son of the *sinna dorai*. He had no fear of the villagers, being half-Sinhalese himself and *podi mathia*. But all the time, even behind the sunlight, was a sadness, for he knew they were there, the other ones, the dark-skinned coolies with their thin bodies and worn rags. The women pluckers out in the tea bushes had wrapped woolen shawls over their heads and shoulders to protect themselves from the burning sun. They worked all day from sun-up, when Daddy cleaned his teeth and took his Andrews Liver Salts, to the setting of the sun over the hills, and Aidan felt very sorry for it. They had no break; that was what made him sad. "They don't have midday rest on cots, Daddy, and a whisky," he cried.

"Yes, well they are used to it, son. They're coolies and the field work has to get done by muster."

Their houses weren't pretty, as in a cosy Sinhalese village, but ugly. The Tamil women huddled together in the cement doorways of the coolie lines looking miserable, the smell of their South Indian spices wafting up over the rows of tea bushes and into the forest. "Say '*Vanhakkam*,' son, when you meet a Tamil. It means 'Greetings,'" said Daddy, who spoke fluent Tamil as well as Sinhalese. But English, of course, was his language, for he was the boss—little boss, or *sinna dorai*, as the Tamils called him, until the time he would be promoted to big boss, or *periya dorai*. Aidan knew all this. And he knew that he, too, one day, would be a *periya dorai*.

He was approaching the Sinhalese village. He took care not to take a shortcut across the terraced paddy fields. The paddies had little crabs in the ankle-deep water that pinched, and horrid bloodsuckers, and once, a small snake. Lally had screamed "Snake, snake!" Fiona had scoffed. "Oh, don't be silly Lally." But there had been little snakes slithering round their toes. A village man plodded behind a bullock through the paddy, tossing his whip as in olden times; he kicked the bullock's balls to make him go faster. A bent old woman went by carrying a huge bundle of firewood on her back. Before he knew it, he was approaching a red sandy clearing in the forest under tall coconut palms. Cocks crowed and a dog barked; he could smell the sweet incense from fires burning and the cooking of pleasant spices. He was going back in time; part of him—the deeper, unconscious part—understood this.

"Ah, *podi mathia* is here!"

An old woman, very old, with wrinkled brown skin, smiled as he approached. She was sitting at the entrance of her hut, which was small and cool, with a thatched cadjan roof, mud walls, and a dung floor. She brought out a king coconut and slashed it with a knife; out trickled coconut water, fresh and sweet. He sipped eagerly.

"*Ganga pattiys, mah-vah.*" He thanked her using the Sinhalese he had learned at the convent school, the alien language rolling over his tongue.

"*Aiyo!* He speak Sinhala!" she teased. She wore the Sinhalese-style sari, with a short bodice and bare midriff; the sari folds had been thrown over her shoulders and drooped down to her feet.

Villagers gathered amiably around him; it was big boss Gilmor's eldest son, the little Englishman. They grinned and ran their hands over his fine, imported English clothes with pleasure—the khaki pleated shorts like Daddy's, the short-sleeved white shirt buttoned up nicely.

Of course, they knew him. They knew more about him than he did himself; they knew his origins, back to old great-grand-father Gilmor, another era. They remembered the old boss Gilmor, Aidan's great grandfather, riding through the forest on horseback with his rifle and dogs. They knew of the family's disgrace; they knew of Samira, of course, for they knew her mother, Srimathi, and the village she had come from near Gampola. They knew that Srimathi had been old Gilmor's *see-yaa*, country wife. It was so long ago, but they remembered, with an ancestral memory. They knew also of Lily de Groot and Jack Gilmor's broken engagement, and they knew that Mildred Delaney (who was a Goonesekere on her mother's side) was "second choice."

"You walk long way, *puddi pu-thaah*." Little son.

He sat on the ground outside a hut, cross-legged, a very pleasant feeling, he noted. The hut was built of coconut-palm thatch and bamboo. The floor was hard; it was pressed cow dung, but it smelled sweet. Chickens pecked in the dirt while parakeets and bulbuls whistled, fluttered, and swooped outside. It was cool in the shade of the trees. Women sat around in the clearing, grinding spices—coriander, cinnamon, turmeric—as they must have done in Great-Grandaddy's time, using old stone pestle and mortars.

Aahch-chee took his hand and led him inside. In the corner of the hut he could see a small shrine, with a small brass Buddha, vessels of water and rice, and some flowers and incense sticks. He instinctively bowed, lifting his palms to his forehead as he'd seen the Buddhists do at the temple in Kandy, where Mama had taken him, once—oh, long ago—to take *sill,* as Mama's mother, his *aahch-chee*, must have done (before they'd taken her away). The villagers knew of her, too; they knew that she had been locked up in Angoda and gone insane inside those walls. Oh, everything! They knew that the Gilmors had ordered Aidan's horoscope drawn up at birth, according to custom, by the Buddhist priest-astrologer. And a good thing too, yes! Good righteous karma, following the holy *dharma*. The horoscope had been drawn up in the temple the day he was born, and it was locked in the safe in Daddy's office off the bedroom, the horoscope that foretold his fate. "Nonsense!"

Grandpa Titus Delaney had cried. "Don't fill the boy's head with superstition." But Mama, despite being a Catholic, kept the horoscope, carefully rolling it in bamboo.

Every night Mama and Daddy knelt by their bed and prayed to Jesus and the Blessed Virgin, and Mama whispered the rosary. The power of Mary was surely greater than that of any Buddha, since she was white. "*Blessed art thou among women and blessed is the fruit of thy womb, Jesus.... Pray for us sinners now and at the hour of our death.*" Nevertheless, Daddy gave a big donation every year to the Buddhist priests at Kandy Temple, for dead *Aahch-chee*'s sake, Aidan's Buddhist grandmother. The villagers knew that, too.

Young boys ran naked through the clearing with sticks, chasing each other. "Mind the devil bird don't catch you!" the adults shouted at them in Sinhalese, laughing. He recognized *ulama*—it meant devil bird—but mostly they spoke too fast for him.

Their skin was the same as his, glowing brown. They had the same big dark eyes with thick black lashes. They had the same hair, except that his was light brown and soft and curly, (that would be from the "British" side). He felt a jolt of recognition. They were the same. This was who he felt he surely was. And yet he was not Sinhalese. They were chattering and laughing at him. He could only guess what they were saying; he did not really know his own language. He was conscious of being superior, of being British and Christian. He tried so hard to be a good little Englishman and please Daddy. And yet when he saw a real English boy—the Henshaws' son, Martin, at Netherlands, who was home on holiday from St. Thomas School in Colombo—he saw the difference. Martin once called him a "native."

He sipped his coconut water in the shade of the palm-tree hut, reflecting happily on how slow and peaceful village life was. Part of him vaguely envied his unknown half aunt, Samira, who lived permanently in a pleasant village like this one. Of course, he would never speak of Samira, not even to Mama. Already, at seven, he knew there were things that just could not be said.

25.

DADDY HAD BEEN OUT HUNTING for a few days. He had left at dawn with his rifle and guns, food supply, water flasks (plus a couple of bottles of whisky), and a couple of beaters, including Ganesh. (The Sinhalese servants refused to go hunting, even for Big Boss.) He had met up with his comrades from the club, Dawson of Haven's Rest, Carstairs of Killarney, de Silva of Balmoral, and Uncle Ted, the only one of Mama's brothers who enjoyed a day's shooting.

Mama's other brothers, Uncle Neville and Uncle Quintus, sided with their mother's Buddhist background, following the doctrine of non-violence, even though Amma was long dead. The men, all tea planters except Uncle Ted, who managed a small coconut plantation, had transferred to Carstairs's big land rover. Daddy loved the jungle, which was several hours away, in the hot interior. The strange dry scrublands had sandy desert-type vegetation in which one could suddenly came across ancient statues toppled in the undergrowth, fallen long ago— perhaps centuries ago—amid the silence. Monkeys screamed at their presence, and the strange pristine quality of a certain loneliness and wildness excited him. No tigers or lions roamed Ceylon, but usually the men bagged a good amount of wild fowl—butagoyas, big birds that made good tasty curries—and smaller mammals, or an occasional deer. Daddy had once shot a leopard in the interior around Anuradhapura (a sacred place, in the eyes of the Buddhists). It had enormously increased his status in the eyes of the planters. The mighty, spotted, velvety carcass had been strung across the roof of the car, a trophy, when the hunters returned. The Sinhalese servants had backed away in silence, muttering prayers, as the carcass was carried into the outhouse, the macaws screeching. But Mama refused to have the skin hanging in the house, so Daddy had had to be content with donating it to the club, where it held pride of place over a stone fireplace. Daddy's reputation as a man, a planter, and a hunter had been established upcountry. ("Jack Gilmor, you know, killed a leopard—damn good shot.")

But they had not had a good day's hunting that day. It happened on occasion. The men had had to content themselves with shooting foraging birds, tiny little things that were a nuisance in the paddy fields.

When he returned, Daddy tipped out several sacks of the dead birds, hardly the size of sparrows, on to the floor of the outside kitchen. His comrades grinned ruefully and lit cigarettes. The Sinhalese servants muttered angrily and walked out, refusing to touch them. "*Aiyo!*" They went home to the village in protest.

"Bloody fools," grumbled Daddy.

It was not the first time the servants had rebelled. When Daddy had brought back king crabs from the fish market in Colombo, their claws manacled, the servants had backed off in horror, refusing to boil them. Aidan could remember that terrible hiss of death as they squirmed and then, the next instant, were boiled alive. *Aiyo!* Who wanted to come back as a crab in the next life?

It was left to Ganesh who, being Hindu, had no compunction about boiling anything dead or alive, to finally throw the twisting crustaceans into a pot of salted water. There had been a faint scream as the helpless crabs bubbled instantly; then it was over. But Aidan and Lally had felt sick. Lally cried, but Fiona had scoffed. "Baby! They can't *feel*, Lally!"

"But then why are they screaming? The poor things!"

The little dead birds lay in a mound on the floor of the outside kitchen. But who would have the task of boiling them? The children watched with interest as Mama rounded on Daddy in a fury.

"See, Jack, pet. What for killing such innocent little birds?! You big men with your big guns killing God's little creatures," shouted Mama. The children were shocked and frightened, but also curious. They had never seen Mama so angry.

"They're damn pests in the paddy," Daddy said. The two planters agreed, smiling. Women. "There's plenty more out there, Mildred, dear."

The men were staying over for the night. The bungalow was large, the bedrooms spacious. His parents regularly had visitors staying over, mainly relatives such as Felix and Uncle Neville and his wife Miriam, sometimes for a month at a time. The men settled down in the rattan armchairs out on the verandah for drinks. "Whisky for the sahibs," called Daddy to house servant number one, "and a jug of toddy." Ganesh left to get some Tamil women in from the lines to pluck and cook the birds. (First you boiled them so the feathers could be plucked easily.) The men were making a night of it. Freshly caught paddy bird curry. "Make it hot!" Daddy said in Tamil to the women who arrived with Ganesh from the lines. He used local Tamil to speak to labourers.

Mama refused to eat the curry, and she forbade the children to partake in eating the flesh of the desiccated little birds. Aidan listened carefully. It was the first time he had been made aware of two cultures: Daddy's white, Western, animal-killing Christian way of life, and Mama's non-violent Buddhist beliefs. He felt himself guiltily siding with Mama.

"Oh, you, Mildred!" mocked Daddy. "You're like that brother of yours, Neville." (Uncle Neville used to go out before dawn and scare the animals away before the hunters got started. Aidan had seen him once. "Don't tell your father.")

That night Daddy and the planters had the runs. They were

still groaning and clutching their stomachs in the morning and could not eat breakfast, not even a hopper.

"Those bloody birds must have eaten something poisonous, man."

"Ughh, I was shitting all night," moaned Daddy, clutching his belly. He had deep dark circles under his eyes. "Bring the Andrews Liver Salts," he ordered the houseboy.

"Serves you right!" laughed Mama. The Sinhalese servants nodded in dour satisfaction; Big Boss's karma. All is *dukka*.

26.

"*A*MMA," SAID SISTER ST. VERONICA. "Mother." Her prim tight face in its wimple-bound head-dress peered sternly at the children. With a steel-tipped pointer she tapped the blackboard on which were written rows of Sinhalese and English vocabulary words, side by side.

"*Amma*. Mother," they repeated in unison.

"*Tata*. Father."

"*Tata*..."

Beyond the small convent school window lay the sandy playground and the sounds of the small town nearby: the hooting of a train, the beeping of motor cars on the dusty road, the crunch of bullock carts and wagons, and whirring of cicadas high up in the tall trees. The world.

The classroom smelled of whitewash and incense. It wafted from the chapel through the open doorway along with the smell of curry and garlic that the children exuded. The school was attached to St. Euphrasia Convent, and the day began and ended with prayers and intercessions to the saint and the Blessed Virgin in chapel. On Sundays, Daddy and Mama took them for Mass at the church in Hatton. Very English. They had to look their best: white gloves and little veiled hats for Mama and the girls, and stiff starched shirts pressed by the *dhobi* for the boys, plus long hot prickly socks and stockings and uncomfortable stiff English shoes that pinched. "*Laudate per diem in coeli....*" intoned the Belgian priest. Outside, afterwards, the air smelled fresh from the breeze from the hills as if something was swept away.

"*Sthoo-thiy*. Thank you."

"*Sthoo-thiy*. Thank you."

Sister St. Veronica began swaying slowly up and down the aisle, her long white robes heavy and lilting.

A framed portrait hung on the wall. Aidan thought it was of His Holiness Pope Pius XII, but he could not be sure. His Holiness had a grim tight face, too, like Sister St. Veronica. He wore red and he had a small funny beanie cap on his head and a crucifix hanging down his chest. Sister St. Veronica bowed slightly whenever she passed him by.

"*Brinjal*. Eggplant."

"*Brinjal*. Eggplant."

"*Ulama!*"

Some said the hawk-eagle; it was a bird of ill omen. Aidan often heard it shrieking at night....

Of course, no one actually *spoke* Sinhalese at the convent school. The children were not there to talk to each other in the language. In fact, they were punished if they were caught. "English only!" snapped the nuns. If they heard a Sinhalese boy chatter in his language on the playground, he was cuffed across the neck. (Some ambitious villagers sent their boys to convent school, desperately paying the fees from their pittance.) The local Buddhist school in the village had blown down in a storm years before; the Buddhist priests had not had the money to rebuild just for poor villagers in the mountains.

The students sang, in their thick colonial accents, "*God save our gra-a-cious King.*" That was His Majesty King George VI. "Thank God for His Majesty across the ocean in Buckingham Palace," said Sister St. Veronica. And for his queen, Elizabeth, at his side, a fat lady in a tiara. And then they sang "I Vow to Thee My Country" (not the country of Ceylon, of course). This was Sister's favourite hymn.

I vow to thee, my country,
All earthly things above,
Entire and whole and perfect,
The service of my love....

It went on more about love: *The love that asks no question,
the love that stands the test....*

What was the question? What was the test he had to endure?
Aidan's brow puckered. For Daddy, of course; for England
and King George.

Aidan knew that eventually he would be going to the big
boarding school in Kandy, Holy Innocents College for Boys. It
was Daddy's old school and he called it his *alma mater*, and it
would therefore be Aidan's as well. Fiona was to be a boarder
again; she would join Lally at Kandy Convent, now that she was
a "young lady," said Mama. Fiona had already attended the
convent as a small child, barely five years old. It was Mama's
old school, but she had not been a boarder; Granpa Delaney
could not afford such a luxury. She had attended school as a
day scholar like her brothers Neville and Quintus, and had
boarded with relatives in town on the Goonesekere side of the
family, an uncle and aunt Goonesekere and their five children,
distant cousins.

Meanwhile the children still walked with Lally through the
estate in the early morning after a breakfast of hoppers and
fried eggs and *sambol*, to catch the train to Nawalapitya, where
the local convent school stood near the small town of Hatton.
They caught the train at Kotagala. Scottie was too young for
school, of course, so he stayed behind with Mama; he got
to have her all to himself. There was a simple whitewashed
waiting room with a thatched roof and a small office at the
little Kotagala railway station. The station guard was a young
man of about twenty named Tissa Gooneratna. He blew a
whistle and waved a flag when it was ready for the train. He
was a Sinhalese; they knew that from his name. He spoke a

little English. He wore a loose white *dhoti* shirt and sarong, and he often went barefoot.

He liked Lally. Who didn't? Lovely, happy, smiling Lally with her long black curls loosened from its plait and her crooked, shining teeth. They stuck out a little in front making her lips stay open; it looked like she was always smiling. Tissa let Lally ride for free. He teased her: "*U-blhah u-dhaa-sah-nahk.*" Good morning now, lovely Mees Lally Delaney.

Lally giggled.

He smiled with his big shining white teeth. His ancient god-like profile turned in the morning sun.

Aidan looked at Lally, in her neat white blouse and grey pleated school skirt, with new interest. Miss Lally.

"Are you going to marry Tissa, Lally?"

"Ohh!" screamed Lally, laughing, hiding her mouth behind her hands. "You are terrible boy, Aidan!" But she was giggling delightedly. Fiona frowned and reminded Lally that Tissa was not *pukkah*.

That day Tissa slipped Lally a gift as she stepped up on the steps of the train. Was it a ring? A gold bangle? A love note in Sinhalese? Lally's Sinhalese was better than any of theirs.

"*Ko-ho mah-dhah* today, Mees Lally?"

"*Aiyo!* Tissa. *Hon-dhin in-nah-waah,*" giggled Lally, blushing and smiling.

"I'm telling Mama," said Fiona. "You'll get in trouble."

Because he was Sinhalese, of course; Aidan understood this, and it troubled him.

But even he did not expect the outpouring of wrath that Mama displayed when she found out what had happened. "His name's Tissa, and they were speaking Sinhalese to each other, Mama," Fiona whispered when she got home from school.

Mama turned on Lally. "Cheap! You low cheap hussy of a girl! Making free with a Sinhalese man you do not even know!"

Mama took Daddy's riding whip, made trembling Lally, whose face was already pouring with tears, stand on a chair, and whipped her buttocks and legs. Ma raised the whip and swung it ferociously against Lally.

Fiona smirked. "I told you."

"Oh, don't hurt Lally, please, please, Mama!" cried Aidan, sobbing. He tried to grab the whip. Scottie began to laugh at Aidan.

"Teach you a lesson! Flirting with a low station boy! A Sinhalese! Letting us down after all we've done for you ... only fourteen ... reputation...."

Aidan, Fiona, and Scottie could hear Mama's raised voice, harsh and unfamiliar from behind the verandah screen. They'd been sent away, ordered to stay out of it. They heard Lally's piteous sobs, as did the servants who were watching through the out kitchen screen door. "Mistress's sister in big trouble," they said. "Beaten like a servant."

After that, Daddy began taking Lally to the club socials. She was fifteen now, so she was old enough. One of the planters, Richard Fairclough—Eurasian, very respectable, the assistant manager of Moorings—became interested in her. Lally came home full of the excitement of her new life; she forgot about barefoot Tissa Gooneratna in his sarong.

27.

THERE WERE DAYS WHEN THE MISTS and clouds hung so low that the bungalow seemed to disappear. The clouds were huge, soft billows like giant puffballs, through which one heard the clear call of the coucal. Weyweltalawa seemed to be floating in a bubbling cauldron of cloud, eerie and lonesome. The bungalow floated away, far far up high, up to heaven. Daddy and Mama went about mournfully, glum and dour, especially Mama. "It's so damp," she complained, drawing her English woolen shawl around her shoulders.

"Bloody rain."

Sisira, the servant boy, shook Daddy's boots out—smart leather ones brightly polished by Ganesh—in case any spiders and scorpions had taken up residence there. Then he helped Daddy pull them up. Daddy was off to the tea factory, which was somewhere out there through the swirling fog. He looked very smart in his newly pressed khaki pleated shorts, starched open-neck shirt with a flowing English tie, and long ribbed socks to his knees. *Pukkah* Englishman. Aidan's heart swelled with love and pride.

The southwest monsoon rains had come early that year. It rained for about eighteen hours per day, enough to wash away the roads on the estate. Torrents of rain swept in waves, drenching the labourers and the plantation, and filling the paddy fields far below where the village nestled (the soil would be perfect for planting rice later). Tremendous gusts shook the bungalow and the laurels, the spigot was ripped off the rain pipe, and the chickens huddled in the hen house. Everyone was afraid of the thunder and lightning; the servant girls ran about screaming with their hands over their ears. The bridge at Perediniya was swept away, as was the little wooden bridge at Ginigahena, where Mama shopped for groceries and household stuff. Fish reputedly swam in the grand hotels at Nuwara Eliya, which was under water. In the jungle, ancient stone gods lay submerged.

Some days the electric storm passed them over; peering out through the verandah screens, Aidan could see the mountains opposite, across the hills, lit up with lightning. Electric bolts struck the rubber trees, illuminating them ghostly white and toppling them over row by row like matchsticks.

"I no fear 'lectric!" shouted Scottie, clutching his *kutee* all the same.

"Little rascal!"

Then silence, but for the ticking of the grandfather clock in the vestibule and the rush of rain. They were isolated, locked in. It was too wet and dangerous (who would tackle those hairpin bends?) even to go to Ginigathena for kerosene. There was just enough left for the lamps in the living room in the evening. Not a soul for Mama to talk to all day except servants, mere villagers. Mama sighed, opened her organ, and took to playing hymns, plaintive melodies. Soon the strains of "*Abide with me, fast falls the eventide*" drifted sadly through the living room and out beyond the verandah only to be lost in the fog. It was a melancholy hymn of another era, of wars they hardly knew. Mama, her thick hair cut short in waves, was dressed in an English skirt, a cardigan, and a blouse with a lace collar and a diamante pin on her left breast pocket like Princess Elizabeth. The servants in their damp saris peered through the lattices. "*Aiyo*, Mistress playing organ."

Rain fell in sheets.

It washed against the aviary where Daddy had all sorts of birds—little finches and bulbuls, parakeets and love birds—at the back of the bungalow. A bedraggled peacock screeched through the mist. "*Aiyo*," went the servants. "*Anja ululu*, like devil bird!"

"Oh, for goodness sake," said Mama.

The rain turned into a black wave of water, swishing over the lawns and the driveway. Somewhere through the mists, the pluckers were still picking tea, moving like phantoms, their saris soaking and sticking to their cold miserable bodies, their bushel baskets slung on their backs. Aidan recalled the coolie lines and the corrugated roofs. Surely rivulets of mud and foul water would be pouring through the cracks today. It made him sad to think about it.

"They'll be all wet, Mama."

"Oh, they're just *coolies*. What are you crying for?" said Fiona scornfully. She was looking forward to Kandy Convent. Daddy had told her that a tea plantation was no place for a young teenager, and she was too old now for the little convent school in Hatton. Mama had been silent, twiddling with the knobs of the radio, trying to get the BBC overseas world news. Only a loud crackling and hiss had emerged.

Left to themselves during the monsoon, the children played "indoor" games, sometimes with the servants. They lounged on the floor on piles of cushions, reading their imported English comics—*Beano*, *Dandy*, *Children's Own*—while the houseboy, Asaf, brought them glasses of Lanka lime and packages of English Smiths crisps. Card games followed, then dominoes, except that Scottie knocked down all the dominoes just as Aidan had them all balanced. Fiona soon tired, saying that she was too old for such games. At Kandy Convent, she was to learn to be a proper English lady with beautiful English manners. She had a vague idea that she would one day marry an English planter like Daddy and be mistress of a tea estate with her own servants to do her bidding.

Aidan took out his pots and pans, a child's kitchen set that Felix, Daddy's cousin, had once brought him, amused at his interest in cooking. He went into the out kitchen, and Mama ordered the servants to let him cook. Bemused, they let him use the pestle and mortar to grind spices. "*Podi pu-thaah*, little son, *u-yah nah-vaah*, cook, cook," they said, laughing.

"That's the work of a servant girl," mocked Fiona, peering through the screen door. "And you a boy!"

"Watch your tongue, Fiona," said Mama sharply.

"I like cooking," said Aidan.

"*Podi*, cook," smiled the servants.

Towards the end of the monsoon, when the rain had begun to lighten, Felix drove up for a visit to show off his latest car and girlfriend. Everyone brightened. He invariably brought toys for the children from the Pettah bazaar in Colombo, plus jewellery and trinkets for Fiona now that she was a young lady, he teased. Aidan received a penknife with a corkscrew attached, which he loved, and Scottie got a toy train.

His escort was a tall beautiful Tamil girl with big breasts, a beauty named Kothai Chandrakanthan. She was a city girl from Colombo. She smiled coquettishly at Felix.

"*Maalai vanakkam, varavaerpu*, Miss Chandrakanthan," said Daddy, showing off his fluent Tamil.

She brought her palms together to her forehead in a *pronam* and bowed slightly. "*Vanakkam iya*, Meester Gilmor. Please to call me Kothai."

Fiona was entranced by Kothai's brilliant red Western dress with a slit at the side, and high heels. She wore makeup; her eyes were ringed with dark *khol*, making them appear huge and sultry, and her full mouth was swathed in deep red lipstick. "A *vesi*," hissed the Sinhalese servants, grinning; they disappeared behind the lattice doors, but not before Mama heard. Mildred's mouth tightened. She looked hard at Felix, who unconcernedly lit a Peacock cigarette from his gold case. He offered one to Daddy.

Felix often brought girlfriends up to Weyweltalawa to stay

overnight. They were invariably Eurasian, very smart office types dressed in Western clothes and stiletto heels, their thick hair straightened and styled, and their dark skin lightened with special cream. No sari-clad women for him. ("Bloody useless," Daddy would say afterwards of the stiletto heels, "Where the hell does she think she is, the casino?")

Felix had grown up on the loveliest estate, Pennylands, where Auntie Bella and Uncle John still lived. It had a beautiful white tea planter's bungalow with a cupola, sloping lawns, and a circular driveway, and it was surrounded by English flower beds. The previous owner, an Englishman called Gerald Swan had planted lovely English flowers: gladioli, lupins, pansies, narcissi, phlox, tea roses, and climbing roses over the trellises. It was lovely, so lovely that you felt you could sink into those flowers for their loveliness. Everyone said the estate had the best view of Hatton and Adam's Peak. (Hatton was very *pukkah*, very English.) There was afternoon tea and cricket on the lawn, and the men dressed in whites. Oh, rather! But Felix was nonchalant, especially when Daddy urged him to take up planting and maybe take over Pennylands when the time came.

"What for me as a planter, Jack, man?" he exclaimed, laughing. He was very tall, over six feet, and thin, with small dark eyes, thick black hair, and sharp features; you could see the Tamil blood showing, Daddy once said. Felix's maternal grandmother had been Tamil (a Catholic Tamil, so that was all right).

"It's a lonesome life, planting, isolated up in these hills, with only ghosts for company," he had said once when Daddy brought up the subject. "And who is there to marry? A Eurasian from the club if I'm lucky. Or I could take a Tamil coolie girl as a country-wife." (Many single tea planters did that.) "Besides," smiled Felix, leaning back in the cane chair with urbane ease, "I have a good life in Colombo."

He was a tea taster for Carson and Cumberbatch, one of the leading British tea companies in Ceylon. It was a very prestigious job in the industry, as Jack well knew. Felix spent his days in a clean white air-conditioned office in Colombo imbuing sips of the finest teas from all over the island, swirling them round on his tongue in an expert way, and pronouncing judgement. He could tell a Nuwara Eliya tea—the "champagne" of teas—from a Ratnapura or a gold-tip.

Plus Felix loved jazz, particularly the jazz scene in the Colombo bars and smart nightclubs. He loved expensive clothes, jewellery, and fine shoes, not to mention fast women and fast cars. He had a small select apartment in a pleasant part of Colombo not far from Cinnamon Gardens with a man-servant, a cook, and a *dhobi* to do his laundry. He belonged to the Colombo cricket club. Tall, handsome, with a public-school education, he had somehow wormed his way into the fashionable Colombo set. He even received the occasional invitation from British colonials to Nuwara Eliya, to the races in May. What more could a bachelor want? As such, he was privy to all the gossip of the elite Europeans about the illicit love affairs of dignitaries. (Everyone knew of the affair between Lord Mountbatten's wife, Edwina, and Pandit Jawaharlal Nehru in Calcutta. "So much for the partition of India," the joke went.)

Felix mentioned Lily de Groot, now Mrs. Lily de Saram, whom he had bumped into in the Pettah bazaar with her son Petr. She had married an ordinary accountant, it seemed, a protestant Dutch Burgher like herself—an acceptable union for a Dutch Burgher girl with little money. Old Simon de Groot had died and left a small inheritance, which had enabled Mr. de Groot to send Lily's younger sister Esmé to Kandy Convent. (As a Dutch Protestant, she was excused from Mass.) Silence followed this.

Then Jack said softly, "Hell, man, the past is past, Felix." He poured himself a double whisky.

"Not for me, Jack, old boy. Gin is my drink."

The conversation turned to Felix's brand-new car, the latest model. He had driven up in his mini-coupe, taking those hairpin bends at top speed and raising up a storm of dust on the winding estate road.

Kothai smiled and said nothing. She sipped her *palmyrah* toddy.

Later, when dinner was well over, she retired, pleading fatigue. The servants had just brought out more drinks on a brass tray with thin chocolate wafers for mistress and the lady guest. The tropical night had long fallen (darkness fell each evening at six o'clock sharp—you could set your watch by it). Kothai chose to join the children in their room. The bedrooms were enormous. There were six beds in Lally's room alone. Lally was at the convent, so Fiona had the double bed to herself. Scottie and Aidan had single beds each. There was another double bed by the tallboy—Kothai chose this one—and two more single beds for guests. Yet the room was still spacious. The servant was ordered to make up the bed and bring fresh towels for Miss Chandrakantham, which she did with ill grace, not liking to serve a low-country Colombo Tamil woman. She could tell from the brightly painted face and lips that the visitor was obviously a *vesi*, but who knew what caste? Later, in the darkness, Aidan heard the tread of servants' feet outside on the verandah and saw the glow of kerosene lamps bobbing through the lattice. He heard Mama turn on Felix.

"How could you bring a girl like that here, Felix? With the children, Fiona especially?" she hissed.

Felix evinced surprise.

"The servants knew what she was right away." Mildred could not bring herself to say *vesi*. "I heard them whispering 'call-girl.'"

Felix laughed.

"Oh, come now, pet," said Jack.

"Kothai's no call-girl! She works in a lawyer's office as a stenographer. She's a good Catholic Tamil girl. Just because a girl wears Western style and a bit of lipstick doesn't make her a *vesi!* These backward villagers ... they have likely never been to the city."

Mildred was sure she knew different. Gradually Aidan drifted off to sleep to the muted sounds of the adults' voices—talking now about the upcoming election and the surety of Senanayake and the UNP winning big time—and the clink of glasses and low laughter. Soon Daddy put on a record on the Bush gramophone he'd bought in Colombo. Aidan could hear the tunes of the thirties, which Daddy loved, through the walls: *Ain't got nobody to love but you....*

Presently Aidan heard the muffled, familiar voices of Daddy and Uncle Felix: "Another gin, old chap?"

"Well I think I will, Jack, old boy...."

How much time had passed? Then darkness closed in, and Aidan's eyes drooped heavily. He heard the rumbling of Tamil drums far off down in the coolie lines behind the tea factory. Then there were long strange wails stabbing the night, a sudden shriek out there, beyond the verandah. The hypnotic drumbeat continued, the Hindu mystery. He touched his scapula at his chest, given him by Father Balderelli. He was to wear it next to his heart, always—it was part of the bone of a saint, but he forgot which one—to make sure he was safe. Anxiously, he whispered the prayer of St. Michael, "*Do thou O Prince of the Heavenly Hosts cast into hell Satan and all the evil spirits who prowl throughout the world...?*"

In her bed, under the mosquito net, Miss Chandrakanthan lay on her back, very still, her eyes wide open, hard and bright.

Yes, Jack had chosen well in Mildred Delaney. He congratulated himself. (Lily de Groot was now a distant dream, ephemeral, a reckless moment of youth.) Mildred Goonesekere Delaney, to be exact. The "Goonesekere" denoted her mother's high Sinhalese Kandyan caste, which had been the highest of the royal castes in Ceylon. That was before the British deposed the last king of Kandy, Sri Vikrama Rajasinha in 1815, who was designated a tyrant (a monster) by the British commander.

Their families had known each other socially well before Jack had even met Mildred. And that was important. Mildred's older brother, Neville—a brilliant fellow who had won a scholarship to Cambridge and was now a top engineer under the Colombo Plan, working on the projected project at Gal Oya Dam—had been in school with him at Holy Innocents. Not as a boarder, like Jack, but as a day scholar. Not that Neville had ever dared approach Jack Gilmor at school; Jack came from a well-off tea-planting family. The Gilmors had money that had come down from old colonial Sinclair Gilmor. By comparison, the Delaneys were poor. Neville's father, Titus Delaney, though well-respected upcountry, was only the manager of a cocoa plantation, and he'd only managed to secure his position with the help of his benefactor, Emir Van der Meer. Cocoa was very good in its own way, but it wasn't comparable to tea. Tea was king. Neville recalled his own worn clothes at Holy Innocents, the second-hand uniform that was too tight for him, compared with Jack's superior togs. He'd certainly been a dapper dresser. But the Gilmors and Delaneys, nevertheless, were of the same Eurasian class. They frequented the same clubs and churches, and they knew each other through playing cricket and tennis and running plantations.

The fact was, Jack liked Mildred's family better than his own. He'd recognized and admired a certain quiet camaraderie that the six brothers and sisters had for each other, their loyalty and lack of jealousy. They all rejoiced at Neville's opportunity at Cambridge, even though Mildred had also won a top place in the Cambridge matric exams; she had ranked first in the country. But there was only enough money to send one child, and, naturally, the eldest son took pride of place. But Mildred bore no grudge, due perhaps to the early Buddhist influence of her mother, Una Goonesekere, which stressed acceptance. Jack admired that enormously. His own family—his mother Violet, and her sisters, Bella and Agnes—were absolutely virulent in their petty gossip and grudges, imagined slights and tempests. Especially cousin Felix's mother, Auntie Bella. Her predilection for revenge extended even to the mynah birds and crows that roosted outside the prayer room at Pennylands. Evening was the time for reciting the rosary at Pennylands, and the family and any visitors were expected to kneel before a statue of the Virgin Mary for the recitation, while the crows and mynah birds squawked and screeched outside the French windows—loud raucous quarreling, not unlike the three sisters. Auntie Bella would expel a sharp breath, seize the rifle that she kept by her side, and in one swoop march outside and shoot dead the "damn bloody crow" on top of the pepul tree. All the while, the family continued chanting their prayers to St. Michael: "*To thee do we cry, poor banished children of Eve....*"

That was Aunt Bella, killer of crows, reciter of the rosary; this was the type of family Jack came from, despite their money.

The only one of his relatives Jack really loved was a distant cousin by marriage, Tommy Wickramasingha, a lorry driver in Colombo. Whenever he spied Jack driving his Austin 8 through the crazy Colombo traffic he'd slam on the brakes of his "Ceylon Transport" lorry, jump out in the middle of the lanes, cars honking madly all around, and open his arms wide, his belly rippling like jelly. "Jackie-boy! Jack Gilmor, by God! *Sinna dorai*, hah hah hah!" He'd grip Jack to his big sweaty chest with joy. Jack would have also slammed on his brakes and jumped out for Tommy's embrace, in the middle of the thoroughfare, barely avoiding a goat.

"Jackie, my boy!"

"TOMMY!"

"*Ko-ho-mah-dhah?* Look at you. You looking the real swell, man. Big English *pukkah* sahib."

Jack didn't care if Tommy was grimy, covered in grease and dust, and smelling of curry and *seeni sambol*. His clothes and hair were sodden with sweat and he wore a loose crumpled *dhoti*, rumpled sarong, and thick sandals. Jack loved to reminisce with Felix about such meetings with Tommy; the two of them spoke often about what an incorrigible rascal Tommy Wickramasinha had been. He and Felix sat out on the verandah in the evening, smoking.

"Remember Tommy and the brouhaha at Galle Face Hotel, that time, Felix?"

Felix gave a low chuckle. He loved the tale of Tommy's outrageous prank—what Eurasian didn't? It had been the talk of Colombo at the time: how Tommy Wickramasingha and his Ceylon Transport buddies went to the Galle Face Hotel, stripped down for a lark, and jumped naked into the outdoor swimming pool before the shocked white Europeans and their gracious wives sipping cocktails on the patio. Tommy and his friends had shamelessly exhibited their well-endowed brown swinging *lingah-yah* cocks, turning their bums and farting at the *memsahib* ladies in their cool dresses and strings of pearls, to the horror and indignation of the waiters and maître d'. "*Ahm-mah-tah hu-kahn-nah*! Fuck! Get them OUT!" management had screamed. "Grab that *Wickramasingha, bal-li-geh pu-thaah*!" Son-of-a-bitch.

"Ah, those were the days," sighed Jack, tears running down his face for laughing.

Felix was nearly choking.

Other than Tommy, he admitted, he liked nothing better than to keep as far away as possible from his side of the family. Perhaps that was why Jack had put twenty-two hairpin bends between them and himself, observed Felix, in his droll way.

The men enjoyed another gin and whisky, respectively.

Felix touched tentatively again on the subject of Lily de Groot; after all, gossip was the life-blood of the Eurasians up in the hills. Jack sighed. The fact was, Lily de Groot had fallen gently out of his life long ago. Sweet, pretty Lily. She was very fair—this was her greatest asset, of course—but she was insipid next to vivid, strong-minded Mildred Delaney, a Goonesekere and a Catholic. Lily could never have fit into his life, as his mother and aunts—the three sisters together—had pointed out. Marry a Protestant in the Dutch kerk? Good God! It mattered then, that sort of thing. Lily had faded away with her stiff, pale Dutch Reform religion. Mildred Delaney and her brothers had taken over, and her strong, individualistic father, Titus Delaney, a known character upcountry. Titus had never remarried, never taken up with another woman after his wife's death, though plenty of village girls had been offered. This was something Jack had admired deeply.

The Delaneys took no part in the English upcountry set at the Hatton-Eliya Club, that English clique to which Jack tried so hard to belong. Why ape the English? They'd laugh at the thought. The youngest brother, Quintus, was more vehement: "They can go to hell!" He'd refused to stand for the "King" at the club, causing a ripple of indignation among the English planters.

One could not but help admire the chap.

All the same, Quintus might outrun his luck one day, thought Jack anxiously of his rapscallion brother-in-law. Jack recalled Quintus spouting his views over a toddy the other week at the inter-club cricket match in the exclusive Hatton-Eliya Club: "Colonial buildings?" he'd cried recklessly. "Blow the lot up!"

"And pray what would you put in their place, Delaney?" Henshaw, Jack's colleague in tea planting, had drawled. "A statue of Buddha reclining on the ground?"

Eric Henshaw was *sinna dorai* of Netherlands; he hadn't taken young Quintus Delaney's threats seriously, of course. Usual guffaws of amusement rose from the English planters.

"Why not?" Quintus had cried. "We're a Buddhist country, after all. Why not a statue of Rajasinha in Old Fort?"

Mahendra Rajasinha had been the last king of Kandy.

More chortles of derision.

"What, that bloody pervert?" Rajasinha had once ordered children to be beheaded, and their mother was forced to grind their heads in a rice mortar, Henshaw reminded everyone. (He'd also captured and mutilated British merchants and strung their genitals round their necks.)

Unfazed, Quintus had retaliated that all was fair in love and war. That was all very well, but some of the planters had glanced warily at the rambunctious little Eurasian upstart. Who knew what the future held after Independence. The Quintus Delaneys of Ceylon might soon be the ones in power.

But blowing up Old Fort, the heart of British Imperialism and His Majesty King George? That would be going too far.

28.

PERHAPS IT WAS THE COMING Independence of Ceylon, slated for February 1948, and the end of British colonial power, that made Jack decide to take the children on a trip around the island. It was the fashion, just then, among the English planters, to take their children through British Ceylon "for the last time." In particular, they wanted them to see the "cultural triangle" in the wilderness of Anuradhapura and Polonnaruwa, and the famous coasts of Ceylon, before it was too late. Hambantota was a favourite beach resort of the planters; Henshaw called it, "Ham and Tot," unaware of the stiffening frowns of the servants. In the jungle, the English children would exclaim in awe and surprise as they came upon rearing images of alien, heathen gods and goddesses who had had their own powers before the British had arrived. Imagine, the natives erecting such impressive edifices, such vast waterworks! Water tanks which could rival the old Roman underground waterworks— not to mention the aqueducts and bathing pools of the great Europeans—revealed a hidden superior culture of ancient "Serendip," emerging from the mists of time. Such an advanced civilization was undreamed of by the British. The tea planters and their prosaic, well-brought-up children could only gape, bewildered, and take snapshots with their Brownie cameras.

Daddy wanted his offspring to have the same advantages. The Gilmor children would not be left wanting; they would be equal to the English children. Of course, they would not exactly be viewing *their* country, but *the* country of Ceylon—this magnificent, alien Sinhalese place they were necessarily and enigmatically linked to by birth and blood, but from which they were strangely disassociated. And so they set off at dawn, crammed into the Austin Standard 8. Scottie sat on Mama's lap, clutching his *kutee*. Aidan, Fiona, and Lally squeezed into the back seat. "I can hardly breathe," Fiona complained.

Lally screamed at every hairpin bend on the way down. "Oh, *Lally*," everyone laughed. "Just shut your eyes."

Lally was afaid of everything. The way the full moon hung in the sky over the deodars on *poya* days. "What for being afraid?" the others asked. She didn't know; she only knew that there was nothing holding the moon up in that vast abyss. It might fall out of the sky into nothing.... "You really are the silliest nincompoop, Lally."

The British had built a trunk road right across the island, from Colombo to Batticoala. Confronted by a wall of rock, they drilled right through it; the British blasted their way through any damn thing. "You have to admire the Scottish engineers," said Daddy.

"Well, pet, what about the great Sinhalese kings from a thousand years ago? The ones who built the tank around Anuradhapura? Neville says it's the greatest engineering feat of all time. He says they were far ahead of the rest of the world, including Europe, and he should know, being Cambridge educated."

"Yes, yes, Mildred, pet. But that's different."

After a stay overnight in a rest-house, they reached Anuradhapura itself, and then the secret caves of the Buddhas at Mihintale. The children tingled with excitement at the strange stone creatures in the jungle; they stared at them, entranced, much like any English child looking at foreign wonders on this foreign island. They were unaware that it was their own culture they were looking at. The gods and goddesses at Anuradhapura and

Polonaruwa were so strange, surely heathen, certainly not like the images of Christian angels at Father Balderelli's church in Hatton. Fiona frowned. These images showed bodies writhing one over the other in mystic pyramids, reaching for empty nirvana, the goddesses holding snakes, tridents, and strange stone birds in their multiple hands. The Gilmor children stared innocently at these mysteries; to them, they were traces of an bizarre un-Christian people of long past.

"Oh, Mama, not another statue," Fiona complained. "All those arms and legs are giving me a headache." Scottie had his *kutee* gripped close to his chest, a powerful talisman.

"But these are historic artifacts, Fiona."

"There's a smell…. It's creepy."

They were in the deep, cool, dappled caves at Mihintale, away from the searing heat outside. Rows of seated and lying silent Buddhas, so very still, filled the cavern. "But they are wonderful," breathed Lally, fearful.

"Oh, you would think that!" scoffed Fiona.

"*Look on my works, ye Mighty, and despair!*'" murmured Daddy, all he could remember of Shelley's great poem, "Ozymandias," from his time at Holy Innocents.

Then, ah! The coast at last! The children were eager to swim, to escape the muggy heat of the interior. Sand and water, sun and fish: Arugam Bay.

Long graceful coconut palms leaned like swans' necks across a white sandy beach, toward the sea, and bright breakers crested over the water. The family changed on the beach among the palms. There were no change-stations, but they didn't care. Changing outside made them feel like they belonged there, like they were part of the sea and the lives of the shore fishermen around. Mama had forgotten her bathing costume, so she wrapped a large towel around her naked body and tucked it in at her chest. "Mama, how can you bathe like that? Like a villager?" cried Fiona.

"It's how our women have always bathed." Mama meant the Sinhalese. Unashamed, natural.

Tamil fishermen dotted the coastline. There was at once an oily acrid odour of fish. A flat plaited *cadjan*, standing on stilts which were stuck in the sand, held rows of *tilapu* laid out to dry in the hot sun. At evening, Tamil boys fished, balancing delicately in the tide, each one curling his legs around his own pole.

The sun went down in a flame of gold, as if swimming in fire.

As Daddy drove further north up the coast, there were fewer Sinhalese signs on shops and kiosks, until they finally disappeared. They heard Tamil spoken now. There were noisy shops and loud, blaring Tamil music. Women in bright red and purple silver-gilded saris moved slowly along the sandy streets, balancing baskets on their heads amongst goats and bedraggled chickens. "Ugh," said Fiona.

Clusters of huts formed little impromptu fishing villages along the sands; the odour of drying fish hanging in rows up and down the sands wafted over the beaches. The fishermen had built thatched huts to live in temporarily, as was their custom during the high fishing season. Some of the huts teetered at the ocean's edge. They were houses built the old way—on stilts—moistened with ocean spray.

A Tamil woman with grey hair drawn back, and wearing a bedraggled sari wet with brine, was crouched over a brazier, cooking outdoors in the sun. She was cooking in an ancient way, following the tide and the moons.

"*Maalai vanakkam*," said Daddy, wishing her good evening. "*Eppati irukkinga?*"

"*Nallaa irukean. Varavaerpu.*" The old woman smiled. She offered Daddy *tilapu*.

"No, *romba nandri*."

"*Romba nandri,*" repeated Aidan. He knew it meant "thanks" in Tamil.

"Good, son," Daddy said approvingly. "This is a way of life," he observed. "Be glad you are seeing it now before it disappears, and keep it in your heart."

Along the beach were a few shoddy hotels that bought fresh and dried fish off the Tamils. In the sand were strange brightly painted statues of St. Anthony, or the Virgin Mary with beads round her neck, encased in glass.

"Ughh, the smell," complained Fiona again, holding her nose. "Where do they go to the toilet, Mama? There's no toilets."

The fishermen came around and motioned helplessly at Jack and the sky. "*Nanga anavavam?*" they beseeched him. "What will become of us, when Independence come?

The town of Batticaloa was Tamil, but there was also a very old Muslim settlement; it was established when the Arab Moors had come to Ceylon in the eighth century to trade with—but not to conquer—the Sinhalese. They'd come without their women and had settled on the coasts, many of them intermarrying with the locals, something that had been done then. It had been a looser society. "That kind of thing is unthinkable today," said Jack. (He pushed back misgivings, rumours he'd heard about the intended fate of the Muslims at Independence: "They will get their throats slit....")

Daddy bought Fiona and Lally a gold bracelet each, one from a Muslim vendor and one from a Tamil. "Here Babsey," he mumbled. "And you, Lally girl." He loved to call Fiona "Babsey," her baby name. Fiona laughed and blushed, pleased.

"Oh, thank you, Daddy! Thank you, thank you."

"So beautiful!" cried Lally, overwhelmed.

The afternoon shone.

They had reached Colombo. The colonial city lay before them like a wrinkled old dowager, tottering in the sun. Aidan felt dazed by the crazed cacophony of noise; the tremendous bustling crowds along the pavements; the jostling cars, motorbikes, sedan chairs, and rickshaws; the hundreds of vendors shouting their wares from the gutters; and the many beggars, street sweepers, and bullock carts. The streets were full of glorious confusion. The air smelled of strung-up rotting meats, diesel oil, dung, and curry, all melded together into a sultry stew. He wiped his forehead with the clean English handkerchief that he kept in the top pocket of his white sailor-suit; it had been freshly starched before dawn by the old hotel *dhobi*.

The city teemed with sightseers and people of all castes and colours, pushing through the thoroughfares. Amongst the crowds the occasional Afghani stood out, whirling down the pavement in long robes and a turban. The man seemed over seven feet tall. "*Aiyo!*" cried Lally, clinging to Daddy.

"They're the money lenders," said Daddy.

A trumpet blared from an alley. A goat pissed, murky pee sizzling down the gutter. A few prostitutes hung back in dark shadowed alleys.

A long black car passed slowly by, the windows curtained. Aidan knew there were Muslim women inside, hidden from inquisitive eyes like his own.

A great and terrible city, British colonial in essence, with grand, old, colonial buildings. Daddy drove through a poorer section with different sorts of streets—run-down, and full of billboards and tawdry shops. They passed a sign, *Slave Island*, nailed to a corner store with a rusty, corrugated iron roof.

"Daddy, were there slaves?"

"A long time ago. Under the Dutch."

That was all right, then.

"Crocodiles were kept in Beira Lake to stop the slaves from swimming to freedom."

"Oh, Daddy!"

Lally began to cry. "There aren't any *today*, Lally," scoffed Fiona. But Lally was crying for the slaves.

"Cwocodile eat you up, Lally!" cried Scottie.

They moved through a ramshackle district bustling with

life; there were dark doorways where Sinhalese and Tamil *vesi* loomed, though Jack kept that from the children. Mr. de Groot and his family lived in a respectable, if small, house not far from the neighbourhood. There were mosques and minarets, and Aidan heard the *muezzin*'s long high call for midday *dhuhr.*

Old Fort, at last. This was the district Daddy really wanted Aidan, as his eldest son, to see. It was the centre of colonial Ceylon, their heritage. Fiona perked up.

Great old colonial buildings with pillars and ornate cornices erected by the British, or taken over from the Dutch era, still stood in the sun. Jack drove proudly by the British Governor's house, partly hidden behind a façade of trees, an important historic building that Aidan should know about. It was called "King's House," Daddy said, and it belonged to His Majesty King George VI at the moment. Again, Aidan and Fiona swelled with pleasure at the importance of the British; with their British heritage, they were invincible. Other than Old Fort, Jack didn't really like Colombo. "It's a dirty, hot, steamy place," he'd complain. He loved the cool upcountry, the loneliness.

Yet the city was captivating. The day was so innocent; this quivering moment, with the white heat shimmering over the monuments of the past, was to be held in memory forever. For no one could foresee the cataclysm that was to befall the island. No one could predict the events that were about to engulf them all.

The afternoon was given to the Pettah. It was the oldest part of the city, near Fort Railway Station. Rank and fetid, the Pettah bazaar reeked of rot and the mildewed water from the monsoons; it soaked into the crumbling little shops that tottered up and down narrow humid alleys. Odours of dried fish and strung-up animal carcasses wafted pungently throughout the district. A dead dog lay in the gutter, covered with flies. Mama held her nose and kept a firm grip on Scottie's hand. Fiona and Lally covered their mouths. But still the Pettah district swarmed with tourists and visitors, who were there just for the experience. ("Miss the Pettah? Not for the world!") It was everyone's favourite place for bargains at cut-throat prices. Thousands of people of all types and races ambled through its famous cross-streets and alleyways. In Pettah, you could get everything and anything.

Now that Aidan was nearly seven and had reached the age of reason, said Daddy, he was allowed to accompany him to visit his Muslim acquaintance, Mr. Saeed, who had a store in the Muslim sector. Mama and the girls and Scottie went off shopping for bales of cloth. Mama liked to sew in the lonely evenings at Weyweltalawa. Then she planned to visit the great Cathedral of St. Lucia, the biggest on the island.

Old Mr. Saeed was a carpet merchant. His store was one among many on the narrow street. They found him sitting under the awning of his small shop. He was short and plump with a cherubic face and quizzical, kind eyes; Mr. Hazeem, his partner, was tall and thin and sad. Mr. Saeed wore a buttoned, collarless jacket in the style of Jinnah, the Muslim leader, and a smart black fez on his head. Over his jacket he had donned a wool vest, which he wore with cool, loose, cotton pants. Daddy was dressed in a European white summer suit and tie, with a smart topee on his head, very *pukkah*.

"Ah, Meester Geelmor, Eenglishman!"

Jack liked Mr. Saeed and their conversations together. He seldom missed a visit when he came to Colombo. They invariably had discussions on the day's politics (that came first), as well as philosophy and religion—all sorts of topics. He got along well with Muslims, and he even knew a few holy Arabic words.

The men greeted each other, pressing their palms together at their hearts and bowing. Aidan copied, bowing to the old man.

"*Eli eleishon, Akbar eleishon,*" said Daddy

"*Inshallah.*" Allah be praised.

Then the men spoke English, alternately switching to Tamil,

for like most Muslim merchants Mr. Saeed spoke fluent Tamil. Tamil was the language of business and commerce. They sat on chairs under the awning, and soon Daddy lit his pipe after first asking Mr. Saeed's permission. Aidan curled up on a low stool nearby. Though the Muslim proprietor professed not to smoke or drink himself, keeping to the law of Islam, there were exceptions made for "Meester Geelmor, sahib." Behind the doorway, Aidan could see into a long, dark, musty interior where rows of beautiful woven carpets hung on long bamboo rods. A man in black Muslim garb was bent over a counter serving a customer. Mr. Saeed's wife was nowhere in sight.

First, Jack commiserated with Mr. Saeed about the situation in the newly created country of Pakistan—"A bad business," he agreed. Jinnah, a tall, dark, thin man, head of the All India Muslim League, had pushed for a separate country for the Muslims during talks with Nehru, resulting in the Partition of India. Despite appeals from Lord Mountbatten and Gandhi for unity, Nehru, Jinnah, and Mountbatten had finally agreed to divide India into two separate countries on August 17. Nehru was to be prime minister of the India Union, Jinnah the first Governor General in Karachi, and Mountbatten the new British Governor General of the India Union. All hell had broken loose. Mr. Saeed bowed his head in mute acknowledgement. The new Dominion of Pakistan, East and West—"May Allah be blessed"—was torn in two, he mourned, and the Sikhs were caught in the middle.

The partition of India into two countries, India and Pakistan—"Mountbatten's hair-brained idea," growled Jack—had cut the Punjab right down the middle, between Lahore and Amritsar. The western half was allotted to Pakistan, the eastern half to India. (Everyone, it seemed, wanted a slice of nice fertile Punjab.) What had been in his Lordship's head? But the British always played off one side against the other, the old "divide and rule" policy. "Bloody hell!" Aidan pretended not to hear.

Mr. Saeed waved his arms towards heaven. True, the Muslims now had their own country, Pakistan, which meant "Holy Stan," or "Holy land." "*Pakistan Zindabad!*" Long live Pakistan. "*La Ilaha Illallah,*" Mr. Saeed cried. What is the slogan of Pakistan? There is but one God; He is Allah.

But there was nothing holy about the massacres between Hindu and Muslim that had taken place after Jinnah's call to direct action, on August 16 of the previous year. It had been a disastrous day; the astrologers had predicted it. Muslim gangs had slaughtered Hindus and Sikhs in Calcutta—over a million Sikhs would be slaughtered by the end of Partition—and then, of course, there was the reprisal: the Week of the Long Knives. "It was said that little Muslim boys were held down and their stomachs carefully sliced open, the skin folded back, their little testicles and penises lifted out, and—"

Mr. Saeed shuddered. Meanwhile, the *Ceylon Times* and the British Pathé newsreels in the cinemas were showing footage of the carnage every day. Not even Ghandi could stop it. "Ah, these children!" he'd reputedly cried. Twelve million terrified men, women, and children were on the move, frantically trying to cross borders to escape slaughter. Mr. Saeed beat his breast. Trains had arrived in towns, drawing silently into the stations, their carriages filled with massacred Muslims or Hindus; people were hanging over seats and out of windows: women with their breasts sliced in the madness and unfortunate men with their genitals mutilated. There were no survivors. This, of course, necessitated more revenge: more rape, mutilations, slaughter, pillage. Muslim fathers beheaded or drowned their daughters to save them from being dishonoured. Mr. Saeed quivered. "But the will of Allah be done—Allahu Akbar—may His name be blessed." The British called it a bloody fiasco; they realized their mistake too late.

The men glanced suddenly at Aidan, concerned, but Aidan pretended not to be listening. In truth, he had not fully grasped such terrible words.

Mr. Saeed sighed. He was thankful to be safe in Ceylon under the British, whatever one may say of them. Ceylon was a far more equable country, and it was slated for the following year, when the Sinhalese majority would hold power. The British had promised to protect the Muslims, but no one really knew what would happen. The Tamils were already protesting against the Sinhalese, against the inevitable prospect of a Sinhalese majority. It was Tamil versus Sinhalese in the new parliament. "And where will that leave the Muslims?" asked Mr. Saeed suddenly, raising his arms again to heaven. "We are a tiny minority, caught in the middle. What will happen to my little shop and to my grandson?"

Jack agreed the whole bloody world was going to pot.

The men's talk moved on to religion, Christianity in particular. This was Mr. Saeed's favourite topic. Aidan sat very quietly, sipping spicy Indian tea from a tall glass. It had had been brought by a young boy with a gay red fez perched on the back of his head: Mr. Saeed's grandson, Naem. Aidan listened intently, with a certain excitement, for it seemed that Mr. Saeed believed that Jesus, whom he called "Yuz Asaf," did not die on the cross after crucifixion, but fainted. He had then been spirited away, along with his mother, Maryam, out of Palestine to Kashmir, India (which was now supposedly part of Pakistan).

"And why to Kashmir, Meester Geelmoor?"

Jack looked startled.

"Because," emphasized Mr. Saeed in earnest, spreading his hands, "many Kashmiris were descendants of Bani Israel, Sons of Israel who go back in antiquity to Sam, son of Noah, who lived in 4000 BCE. The Kashmiris are one of the ten lost tribes of Israel. One only has to look at many Kashmiris today to see that," persisted Mr. Saeed. Many a foreign diplomat—Sir Francis Younghusband for one, who was an Englishman and therefore given to rational judgement—had noted the Jewish features of many Kashmiris. "The women are tall, handsome, and full-breasted," murmured Mr. Saeed, "with beautiful, dark, elongated, semitic eyes." Also, many Kashmiris, it seemed, slept naked during the night, like the Israelites of old.

Mr. Saeed knew all sorts of fascinating facts about the ancient world. Jack puffed at his pipe, acknowledging his friend's erudition. Apparently, many Hebrew words had been absorbed into the Kashmiri language, such as *ajal* for death, and *achor,* which meant "to cause grief."

Naqat—hate.

Zabel—slaughter.

There was silence. The hot white sun moved slowly across the awning. Waves of heat and the stench of offal arose, mingling with the sounds of the tight crowds pushing and shuffling by like hordes, busying themselves among countless tables, stands, stores, and kiosks for food at bargain prices. Trumpets and horns blared from bands advertising wares. Bullock carts and cars rumbled by, and rickshaws darted in and out of traffic like pesky flies. A small procession passed by led by a Hindu holy man; he was half naked with plaited hair, blue paint streaks on his face, and a bright red *bindi* on his forehead to ward off evil spirits. Long skewers pierced his flesh. His followers were clapping and crying joyfully: "*Jai! Jai! Jai!*"

The afternoon swayed.

Mr. Saeed had reached the climax. Lowering his voice, he insisted that Yuz Asaf—"on whom be peace"—was *never taken bodily up to heaven.* He had lived for another hundred and twenty-five years in Kashmir with his Israelite ancestors, and was finally buried in a tomb on Khanyar Street in Srinagar. The ancient, sacred stone sepulcher had a hole for a window and a low square entrance; Mr. Saeed had photo of it. "Meester Geelmor, you could visit the sepulcher yourself, for a healing," he said. Lord Irwin, Viceroy of India, had even come to see the tomb for himself in 1939.

Jack relaxed. He was now on familiar ground. The Viceroy of India.

"All this was common knowledge up to the third century AD," continued Mr. Saeed, "at which time the Catholic Church began to change course and hide the truth of Yuz Asaf from the Christians. The Vatican deliberately kept them in ignorance, encouraging them to believe in supernaturalism that was popular with pagan Christians, to have power over them."

Jack tapped his pipe against the leg of his chair. This was heretical, of course, but he was too fond of Mr. Saeed to offer any protest. Besides, he was enjoying himself; he was intrigued. (Naturally, he would not divulge any of this to dear old Father Balderelli.)

The sun began to sink over the harbour, a huge violent crimson ball. It was time for Jack to take his leave and pick up Mildred and the children from the cathedral. The hundreds of stalls—many of them shabby and sagging with hanging bloated carcasses of meat and thousands of flies—gave up their wares. A mangy dog slipped behind a stall. A goat brayed. Hundreds of shoppers at the Pettah were bathed in a golden-red glow, like a mirage. The *muezzin*'s call for evening prayer, *al-maghrib*, quivered across the bazaar from a minaret, while in the Buddhist and Hindu temples and *kovils*, monks and priests would be lighting small golden lamps for *puja* and ringing bells. The sun suddenly disappeared below the horizon in a molten smear, the way it did in the tropics, and a violet darkness descended, against which Brahminy kites slowly wheeled.

The Indian Ocean, now darkest indigo, swelled against the embankment; it was the greatest ocean, the deepest in the world.

At Krewal Matton, in Kashmir, there was a sacred well that the Kashmiris called *Chahi Babel*. Over it hung two mysterious angels, upside down—"the angels of death," said Mr. Saeed. Their faces were averted; no one knew why.

29.

J ACK ANXIOUSLY ADJUSTED HIS BOWTIE. He disliked these perfunctory social visits to the Henshaws' bungalow as much as Mildred did. They were not as formal as Sunday dinner at the club—where black bowtie, black cummerbund, and black pants were *de rigeur*—but they were still sufficiently daunting.

As assistant superintendent at Weyweltalawa, Jack was lower in rank than Eric Henshaw, who was a tall, lean Englishman with greying hair, always swept briskly off his face, lean features, and a beagle nose. Henshaw was much favoured among the planters. He had been *sinna dorai*, assistant superintendent, at Netherlands, but he'd recently been promoted to temporary VA, visiting agent, while Riordan was on furlough. It was a position Jack himself had coveted and felt he deserved, as he was Henshaw's senior in terms of years of service. Henshaw's promotion meant that Jack now had to call him sir: "Yes sir," "No, sir," "Three bags full, sir."

The Big Boss, *periya dorai*, of both plantations was Damian De Jurgen. He owned and managed a number of tea estates upcountry, including Netherlands and Weyweltalawa. (He also dabbled in hemp, rubber, and gems). His bungalow, the largest and finest on the Netherlands estate, had gently graded, descending patios, circular lawns, a tennis court, an aviary, and summer house replete with charming fretwork. It was at a distance from Henshaw's humbler abode. De Jurgen also had a large fine house in Cinnamon Gardens, Colombo.

He was a beast of a man. Word had it he'd "crucified" some coolie over at Putalagola. He had shackled the naked man to the cross-bar, forcing him into a spread-eagled position, like an X, and had him flogged to death and left hanging in his shit. They always crapped out of pain and terror, the urine and shit running down their legs. His screams had apparently carried across the estate, terrorizing the labourers—the whole point of the exercise, of course.

There'd been a bit of a kerfuffle, afterwards, at head office in Colombo, but it had passed.

"Don't be soft on them, Gilmor," De Jurgen had urged when he hired Jack. Bloody bastard.

Jack frowned at his reflection in the mirror. He re-adjusted his bowtie, which was perched like a silly little bird at his throat.

Mildred had put on a sari, which was rather daring, but he appreciated her unspoken intent, admired her for it, even. They were to bring the children, who provided useful topics of conversation when needed.

Netherlands was the closest estate to Weyweltalawa in these remote parts; it was on the other side of the river, shrouded by forest and hills. They left early in order to arrive before dark.

Netherlands was a much larger outfit: fifteen hundred acres with a yield of over a thousand acres of tea, and a thousand Tamil labourers. Jack and Mildred drew up as muster was being called. Gangs of dejected, miserable-looking coolies stood by the hundreds, lined up in rows, on a large muster ground in front of the tea factory. The women pickers were in separate columns. The *kanganis* were taking roll call, while De Jurgen stood up front on a dais, twitching a whip.

"Kataraswamy, Mahahnanda..." droned the *kangeny*, first division.

Jack idled the car, watching in horror. A more wretched-looking lot of men had never been seen. Their matted hair was hanging to their shoulders or wrapped in turban rags. They were half starved—the lowest paid of the labourers—with rags on their backs. Some had a skeleton-like appearance, ribs sticking out from lack of food. He knew one bowl of rice a day was the subsistence allotted by De Jurgen. Others had missing fingers, toes, ripped ears, and scabies. And deep weals across their backs.

De Jurgen saw no need for a dispensary for coolies, nor for a school for their whippets.

A big, rippling man with powerful biceps, De Jurgen's glistening body shone with sweat under his fine, unbuttoned shirt. He was a man of many appetites, besides violence. It was common knowledge that he brought back women—mixed Tamil or Sinhalese, their ethnicity was irrelevant—from the brothels of Colombo for weekends (not unlike many a bachelor planter at the club). But De Jurgen was also partial to taking young Tamil girls plucking tea—he favoured thirteen-year-olds—for his use, to the ill-repressed resentment of the families.

He began striding up and down the rows at will, lashing out, striking buttocks and shoulders. "Stand straight, I say!" He dared not whip the women and girls—at least, not before the men. There would be instant rage, howls of fury, fearless reprisal; perhaps he knew it.

Staring through the windows of his car, Jack watched mutely, stunned, as though it were a scene from purgatory—Dante's Inferno, Ceylon-style. The raised whip, the cowering coolie instinctively raising his arms, the eerie, violent panorama. He seemed to see the entire British Empire, the whole colonial fantasy, pass before him in a wave of coolies working from dawn to dusk, lured over by the boat-loads from Tamil Nadu, South India, by the *kangenis*. They came across the Straight of Malacca to Ceylon as indentured servants, in everlasting debt to their *kangany*. He saw the line of power, its hierarchy: the *sinna dorai* obeyed the Big Boss, *periya dorai*, who in turn was answerable to the visiting agent, the mighty VA, assigned by the "company" in Colombo, which put up the money in the first place. They wanted a return for their investment. Profit:

that was the operating factor. Everything depended on tea, its yield, its amount and flavour. Tea decided your position, your income, your promotion, your furlough, your life and death. The best "upcountry" tea was sent to Britain; the rest to the colonies and Third World.

This secretive, other world of coolies, kept separate—apartheid—from others in Ceylon, submerged in its own Tamil language, Hindu religion, customs, and food, formed a separate reality from the Sinhalese, who rarely saw them but knew they were there. These imported Indian "coolies"—as they were called—were a British commodity living at the other end of the plantation, far from the traditional Sinhalese villages. The Sinhalese villagers could not know, but Jack did, that there were over a million imported Indian labourers on the plantations labouring, living, and dying in their midst. The Tamil coolies existed in a suspended state at the edge of a violent beauty, coming alive at night like animals emerging from their lairs, while planters, their wives, and their children slept in their locked bungalows, the Sinhalese servants at the back.

The profits of tea were for the British—the English, the Irish, and the Scots—and the few "mixed" Eurasians whom they allowed, cautiously, into the fold as planters (English public school education a must). Eurasians, like Jack, were part of a larger nebulous system; they shared the profits they worked so hard for, unlike the Tamil labourers with their allotted scant wages.

The estate lands had belonged to the Sinhalese, and the villagers were not going to cooperate with the British proprietors or let them forget. So they waited from the sidelines, resentful, insolent, biding their time.

He felt Mildred nudge him. "Shouldn't we be on our way, pet? What for the halt?"

He blinked and veered the car slowly back to the main drive, which was bordered by the usual laurel, acacia, rhododendron. Eventually they came to the familiar, gracious oval before the front portico. Henshaw's bungalow was on a much grander scale than Jack's, because Netherlands was a larger, more productive tea estate than Weyweltalawa. On three levels, with a teak, shingled roof, Henshaw's home was graced with grounds that boasted rolling lawns, circular rose beds, and gardens filled with English flowers, Ethel Henshaw's favourites. They were the same varieties that appeared on every tea estate: roses, dahlias, columbine, wall-flowers, Sweet William, gladioli, and pansies.

A little mandarin tree, fully laden, hung by the door. Wild scarlet bougainvillea had unexpectedly taken over the porch, frothing in brilliance.

Henshaw knocked back a Scotch on the rocks in the luxury of his drawing room, pleased with himself. His new position as VA, temporary though it was, gave him certain advantages and additional experience over Gilmor for any future promotions.

He thought Gilmor a decent chap, actually, even if he was "Eurasian" (as these half-castes called themselves). That said, one only went so far with them, and one had to be sure to guard one's daughters. His wife, Ethel, agreed. She was a solid woman in her late forties, with tight permed gold-tinted hair. Mixing of the races was never a good thing; it was necessary to keep a fine line, the finest. One but thought of that deluded Englishman, Thompson. (Not that Ethel Henshaw would admit to a flaw in a white man in front of the natives; loyalty was of the essence.) But the thought of that ignorant Hindu girl ensconced in Braeside, mistress of the domain—intolerable!

Of course, custom dictated that he must invite the Gilmors over once in a while; it was the expected sort of thing. It was important to get along (and sound Gilmor out), Eric Henshaw thought Jack Gilmor had VA potential. He was fluent in Tamil, for one thing, which would be useful in an emergency. A good planter, too. He produced good yield for the company, Carson and Cumberbatch, whom they both served. And Gilmor was a damn good shot. He had bagged a leopard up at Anuradhapura, one season. Not a bad looking chap, either, quite English-looking—a "sun-burned Englishman," he'd chuckled to Ethel. Mildred Gilmor, Jack's wife, was a different kettle of fish. Obviously Sinhalese, her face was pitted from smallpox that she had likely caught as a child in the village. Her thick, frizzy, black hair was cut short like a European. And that assortment of children they had—all different, not even looking as if they came from the same father. The girl, Fiona, had slanting eyes that had been passed down, apparently, from some Burmese great-grandmother—a "country wife" Mildred had said once, without a twinge of embarrassment, as if proud of the fact.

The servant motioned Jack and Mildred into the living room. Mildred Gilmor had turned up wearing a sari, Sinhalese-style, with a bare midriff, her dark brown skin glowing between the bodice and the wrap-around skirt. Well. What was that intending to show? A little spirit of Buddhist nationalism, now Independence was drawing near? Ethel Henshaw stiffened.

Aidan quietly observed the etiquette. Mama did not like visiting the Henshaws or any of the English planters and their wives, Aidan had often overheard her say so. She sat on the Henshaws' sofa before a stone fireplace—the English loved their fires—while Aidan and the other children played behind a screen. They had been told to play nicely and not bother the grown-ups.

It was a spacious house, like most planters' bungalows, with a large, gracious living room. French windows led out on to a stone-flagged patio, which descended to the lower levels and eventually to the rose garden and circular lawn. Another large French window opened on to the screened verandah, where a servant slept on a charpoy, and there were the usual comfortable, deep rattan armchairs (where Eric Henshaw liked to have a quiet smoke).

The teak floors were highly burnished, noted Mildred and Jack, and the walls had fine coverings, likely from Colombo's finest stores. Over the hearth was a boar's head; the boar had been shot by Henshaw on a hunting trip in the interior. Jolly good!

"Whisky, old chap?" asked Henshaw smoothly.

"Er, yes. Thank you, sir."

A faint, amused quirk of a smile passed over Henshaw's lips.

"I think we can dispense with the 'sir' this evening, Jack."

Of course. How foolish of him. He was always so overly eager to please, obsequious. Of course Henshaw saw it. Jack cringed at himself.

He was certain Henshaw had cut him at the Hatton-Eliya Club the other day. Jack had hoped Henshaw would sponsor him so he could gain the full membership he longed for. The Hatton Club was exclusive, elitist, limited to white Englishmen and Europeans—all the more reason Jack wanted in. But Henshaw had pretended not to see him, had gazed right through Jack as he approached eagerly with an anxious smile. "Oh is that you, old chap?" he had said to another member, and had passed on to join the president, who had been near the fireplace.

Mildred sat silent and stiff, a morose expression on her face—that Eastern inscrutability, thought Ethel Henshaw irritably. How did one talk to such a woman?

Apparently, she had played a good game of tennis at the club. "That was in my younger days," she said quietly. "Actually, I don't really like 'club' life...."

Mrs. Henshaw was astonished. Not like club life? Not like card parties and the delightful amateur theatricals they put on? It was jolly good fun. Not like bridge parties, croquet, and afternoon tea? She and her friend, Nettie Matthews—surely Mildred knew Nettie—had sung a duet in one variety show, a somewhat naughty ditty from music-hall days. "*A little of what you fancy does you good!*" Ethel Henshaw stopped short at the forbidding gaze of Mildred Gilmor. She had forgotten that the other woman was not eligible to participate, her husband not being a full member.

"Tea, Mrs. Gilmor? May I call you Mildred?"

She struggled for some topic of conversation and settled on the Gilmors' trip across the island. For a while they talked of white beaches and turquoise waters, elephants, and the strange wonders of Anuradhapura. Mildred was careful not to give further offence, even though Ethel Henshaw referred to the great Buddhist edifices as "idols." She sipped her tea.

The infernal drumming had started up somewhere out there in the forest, in the far distance. Mrs. Hemshaw had made a point of locking the windows, what with all that *tom-tom*-ing going on. "Who knows what it means," she hissed at no one in particular.

She explained to Mildred that the native drumming and unholy chanting started up every night. They were sending secret messages across the plantations, she was sure. "It was ancient, almost heathen, when one really thought about it." (It was then one realized one was isolated, lost in the wilderness, a small band of English surrounded by the dark peoples, a darkness which at any moment could....)

There were dainty silver spoons, Wedgewood china, and petit fours brought from the English shops at Nuwara Eliya.

"When I was a girl at Wellipatte, my family all played musical instruments, especially in the long evenings," Mildred said in between sips of tea. (It got dark early in the tropics, as Mrs. Henshaw well knew; the darkness fell like a curtain, each night, at six.) "My father, the children's grandfather, Titus Delaney, made violins and other instruments in his spare time. He had a cocoa plantation, which was easier to run."

"Oh." (Well. Some of these natives were quite clever, in their way.)

"Mildred's brother, Neville Delaney, is a Cambridge man," inserted Jack proudly. "Won a scholarship to Cambridge, ended up in engineering. Works on the preparations for the Gal Oya dam project." Senanayake had promised—one of many election promises—to build a large dam at Gal Oya, a supposedly magnificent affair that would create a reservoir to provide water for the Uva province. It was in the dry zone, and the Gal Oya reservoir would provide irrigation. "Damn good job." Henshaw would know of it.

"I say," said Eric Henshaw, impressed. "Another whisky, old chap?"

Mrs. Henshaw recalled now that Mildred Gilmor had another brother who was not quite so impressive: Quintus Delaney. He was known all over the island as a rabble-rouser. It must be the same family. A Marxist—no, a Trotskyite!—supporting Thondaman, the workers' leader trying to get the Tamil labourers' vote, and the *Lanka Sama Samaja,* or some such thing. The coolies were, unbelievably, going to be allowed to vote in the election! (Most of them had never held a pen in their lives.) She'd heard about this Quintus Delaney at the club. It seemed he went around the estates with Thondaman, inciting the coolies to ask for higher wages, clothing, even *toilets.* The usual piece of cloth the coolies had worn for half a century was no longer good enough. (Many of the men wore just a span cloth; they were half-naked out in the fields under the hot sun, but then they were used to it.) Quintus and Thondaman also demanded itinerant dispensaries for the women. What for? One regularly saw them plucking tea in the terraces, with huge wicker baskets on their backs held up by bands of cloth across their foreheads. What were their heads made of? Concrete? Ethel took a sip of tea.

"You know, Quintus was always interested in social injustices, even as a little boy," Mildred observed, in that calm, objective way of hers. "He once saw a planter whip a coolie and tried to stop him, and he was only about seven or eight years old at the time." Her voice hesitated. Mrs. Henshaw bristled. (Really! This woman was too much.)

The conversation turned to the trouble going on, the strikes and protests that were taking place in Malaya right then. Jack realized that the English planters, of course, felt a definite camaraderie with the British rubber planters there, who were really up against it; they were receiving threats of attacks from communists out on those lonely rubber estates (and Ethel Henshaw knew what that was like). "There have been over three hundred strikes this year," Eric said. "I heard it on the BBC overseas service. It's just paralyzing the rubber plantations. Rioting bands of Indian coolies armed, no less, with *spears,* good God, and stones, bottles, machetes, lead piping, what have you, were threatening the British planters."

"There will be murder, one day," muttered Mrs. Henshaw. "Mark my word."

She looked cautiously at Mildred Gilmor, as though she might be concealing a Kandyan dagger in the folds of her sari.

There was some kerfuffle going on behind the screen the far end of the room, where the children had been told they could play. Scottie, the youngest, obviously spoilt, had been teasing Sinbad the parrot: "Say 'Bugger off! Bugger off!'" Aidan, the quiet one, admonished his brother.

"You shouldn't say that! That's bad, Scottie. You'll get it from Daddy." But, of course, he would not.

"Rascal!" laughed Jack, humorously.

"Oh, Sinbad knows worse than that, Jack, from the fellows at the club," said Henshaw, laughing. The men were smoking Rainbow cigarettes imported from England—all the rage.

"What a good child Aidan is," Ethel Henshaw observed to Mildred, to change the topic.

"Oh," Mildred replied evenly, "he's always been a good little boy. When he was born the Buddhist priest drew up his natal chart—in Pali, you know—and he called Aidan 'a lamp to the world.'"

Ethel Henshaw was astonished. (What did one say to a remark like that?) And it had been said so matter-of-factly, with no shame at such hocus-pocus. These people would run the country according to horoscopes and the phases of the moon!

The talk had turned to Ceylon Independence—the threat of it, depending on which side you placed your bets on—and the upcoming election.

"They'll not survive without British law and order," Eric was saying. "Lord Soulbury will make sure of that. His Lordship is in the process of creating a new constitution for the island: the Soulbury Constitution." He flicked his ash into the fireplace.

"Indeed," agreed Jack. "Think it will go through, sir?"

"Bloody well looks like it. India's already gone that way, what with Nehru and that Gandhi fellow and his sit-ins and salt marches." Lord Mountbatten had given in and divided India—that very month, August 1947—into two countries: India on one bloody side of the Punjab, and the Muslims on the other; the Sikhs caught in the middle.

"One house, I hear, will have the front door in India and the back door in Pakistan, sir."

"Hah!"

"All that blood flowing, Hindus and Muslims at each other's throats and worse to come, you'll see. Same old struggle."

"But it won't be like that here, sir, surely?"

Ethel Henshaw shivered. Perhaps it was time to send their girls, Patricia and Isabel, and son, Martin, back "home" in the care of the Foresters, who were leaving Ceylon on the next ship. Home. England. A brief, presaging chill passed over Ethel Henshaw. Far from England being a "green and pleasant land," she recalled cold, damp, dark rooms in London, and the prospect of a reduced pension.

The general election in Ceylon was set for September; it was only a few weeks away. General suffrage had been granted by the British Soulbury Commission back in 1943. *Everyone* could vote now, even the illiterate, ignorant labourers. Insane! No one knew how that would work out, in the long run, but the Sinhalese were thrilled. It meant they would automatically be the majority, with seventy-five percent of the populace. The Tamils were anxious. They stood to lose the most. "They suddenly found themselves a minority, like the Muslims," observed Henshaw, puffing at his pipe. "No one is worried about the coolies. They don't count; they're not even citizens of Ceylon." While not worried, Henshaw maintained a certain stoic distance, for now.

There was something unreal about the population voting for a brown-skinned Ceylonese prime minister. Don Stephen Senanayake—the planters called him "Don"—was a sure bet to win the election. He would be Ceylon's first Sinhalese, non-white prime minister. He was a Buddhist, but he had been at the elite English school, St. Thomas Anglican School, in Mitwal, where their own son Martin was a pupil. "Don" was also a wealthy man. The Senanayake family had invested astutely in real estate and also had rubber and plumbago plantations, which put them in the *goigamas* class, like most of the Sinhalese in power in Colombo. It boded well for the English planters who, of course, would not be voting.

"Yes, I think Senanayake and the United National Party, the UNP, will likely take it," said Jack cautiously. He, too, felt disoriented; though, unlike Henshaw, he was secretly excited at the prospect of a Ceylonese prime minister ruling Ceylon, running the show for the first time. Though he wouldn't be completely in charge—trust the British for that! There was to be an English governor general in control over the prime minister.

Henshaw took a deep gulp of whisky and stared hard, for a moment, out into the night. Burma had also opted out of the British Empire. Burma! And Malaya had followed. Now, Ceylon.

He wondered how safe it was to confide in Gilmor. He wasn't one of the "boys" at the club.

"Will you stay on, sir?" enquired Jack, and at once he knew he should not have asked.

Henshaw shifted his gaze into the distance, the way the

English did when they had no intention of giving themselves away. Indeed, Henshaw was perturbed. He had no bloody intention of sticking around in Ceylon under Buddhist Sinhalese rule. (Good God—the Sinhalese lion flying at the ramparts at Government House!)

The drumming seemed to rise in intensity in the far distance, out there in the darkness beyond the bungalow. The dense tropical night was lit only by the moon, a violent beauty.

"It's full moon tonight," observed Jack Gilmor.

"*Poya* day," said Mildred quietly.

Again, Ethel felt a strange presence. These moon days actually meant something to these natives, Buddhist and Hindu alike. Mrs. Henshaw was vaguely aware of primitive peoples ruled by the moon. That Sinhalese *Esala perahera* that the Buddhists held every year in high summer in Kandy, for instance; it was a gaudy affair, a tourist "must," with Kandyan dancers wearing gruesome masks with their tongues sticking out, loud chanting, and the beating of drums and cymbals. A sacred tooth, which the Buddhists actually believed was from the mouth of Buddha over a thousand years ago—the fairy-tales these people swallowed—was carried aloft on a jewelled, heavily decorated elephant, everyone bowing as it passed by. (And these people were to govern themselves?)

"Strange beliefs, these Sinhalese have," she could not help but say.

"Well, no stranger than Christians believing Jesus rose from the dead—I mean, to a Buddhist," said Mildred Gilmor calmly, with a slight twitch of her lips.

Mrs. Henshaw stiffened. (The nerve of the woman.) "I would hardly compare the resurrection of our Lord Jesus Christ to a supposed tooth of a Buddha," she said stiffly.

Mildred saw her mistake, too late.

"Speaking of religion, there's talk of the Buddhist monks, the *bhikkhus*, stirring up the Sinhalese against the Tamils and causing trouble at Independence," said Henshaw cautiously.

Jack sighed. Religion was the incendiary device that always seemed to ignite the passions of the entire country of Ceylon. (Besides, he wasn't sure himself what was going on.) The Buddhist monks—the *Sangha*—were up to something, according to Quintus. Some so-called scholar-monk, Walpola Rahula, had written an insidious Sinhalese book urging the monks to be "Buddhists in revolt!" and to get out of the seclusion of their temples and into politics.

"Buddhists in revolt?" queried Henshaw, somewhat anxiously. It would be like the Archbishop of Canterbury calling Anglican priests to arms. It was not that Henshaw favoured the Tamil coolies, or had any particular love for them. It was a question of economics. The tea companies might lose money, God forbid. "Buddhist interference has to be put a stop to, Jack."

"Yes, I'm afraid it's the 'new' rebel *bhikkhu,* sir," sighed Jack cautiously. A far cry from the simple, saffron-robed monk of the past with his begging bowl.

"Bit of an oxymoron, wouldn't you say?" said Henshaw, with a sardonic twist of his mouth.

That was the problem with Ceylon: there were too many bloody religions to deal with. It was a national obsession. Give him England every time, where everyone was just Christian.

"Another whisky, Gilmor?"

"Speaking of the Tamils and religious customs," he continued, turning to Jack, "De Jurgen and I were wondering, old chap, if you could help us out with a little problem with the coolies, you being fluent in Tamil and all that."

Jack had always known he was useful to De Jurgen in this matter. De Jurgen and Henshaw, and many white European masters, knew only command words in Tamil; they only knew how to give orders to the coolies.

It seemed the Tamil labourers on Netherlands were upset over the new ruling about the use of the pool in the river that ran behind the tea factory. Ethel and the ladies from the club had decided they'd like to use it to bathe in. It was a charming place, shady with tall tamarind trees and other sultry foliage bending over, providing privacy for the *memsahibs*. There were large slabs of stone in the river, forming a ring on which one could stretch out and laze in the filtered sunlight, or slip into the water like a fish. Yes, an ideal site for the ladies. But the coolies from both plantations had long used the pool for depositing the ashes of their dead after cremation, and for bathing themselves after five days, according to their custom. De Jurgen wanted that to stop. He had already given orders to the *kangenis* on both plantations. Henshaw feared revolt.

"Naturally, it would be unpleasant for the ladies if…"

Mrs. Henshaw shuddered. Just the thought of swallowing dissolved ashes of dead Hindu bodies while bathing made her sick to her stomach (not to mention sharing the water with those dark greasy Tamil bodies).

"Why can't they bury their dead, like everyone else?" she remarked irritably. "I agree with Mr. De Jurgen. What if we all went around throwing the ashes of our dead into the rivers of the world?" She added fretfully, "Unhygienic."

Henshaw nodded. The damn stench of those cremations from the cremation grounds, seeping all over the estates was another sore point. It had to stop.

"We-ell, I'm not sure, sir. Er, Eric. There might be trouble. I think it has to do with their deep belief in reincarnation, that sort of thing."

"*Reincarnation?*"

"The soul leaves the body at death and needs to return to earth again to enter another body, sir. So if the old body is still around rotting…." His voice petered off.

The Henshaws stared about, alarmed, as if Hindu spirits were walking about Netherlands and Weyweltalawa waiting to slip into a body. God knows they put up with all sorts of voodoo-like beliefs in this country—not least the utterly prehistoric fashion of the women putting rice into the mouth of the dead body to feed him in the afterlife—but were they expected to share a pool with reincarnated spirits and the great unwashed?

Just then a high, blood-curdling screech echoed through the living room from the deep dark deodars and forest beyond. The Sinhalese servants ran in from the outside kitchen. "*Aiyo!*"

"Oh, Daddy!" cried Scottie, darting into the living room area followed by Aidan and Fiona. They were excited and frightened.

"*Ulama!* Devil bird! Meester Henshaw, Master! *Podya Mathi Ulama! Ulama!*"

There was another blood-curdling screech, followed by weird cries as of strangulation emanating from the darkness beyond the French windows. Mrs. Henshaw clutched her bosom. "Oh, God!"

The servants trembled, holding on to each other, wide-eyed, excitable. Aidan understood it was a bad omen, especially during a full moon, on *poya* day. The devil bird was the Ceylon cryptid; some said it was an eagle owl, others a serpent eagle or Brahminy kite. Whatever it was, it was a portent, evil in intent, signifying the descent of a curse.

"Nonsense!" said Henshaw.

But the next day, Daddy got fired from his job.

30.

THE DAY STARTED OUT like any other. The houseboy, Asaf, knocked on the bedroom door at five o'clock in the morning and brought in tea, sliding the tray under the mosquito net. He glanced sideways at Memsahib Gilmor, tousled and flushed under the sheet, a hint of breast exposed.

"Good morning, *sahib*."

Jack followed the usual routine: he showered, shaved, and changed into his usual, freshly laundered khaki shirt and shorts that came to the knee, and his long English woolen socks. He knocked back a glass of fizzing Andrews Liver Salts; the English planters took their salts seriously—best thing to clean out the insides. Then he was off with his tiffin box, which had been prepared by the servants, containing a roti with hot chili spread, papaya slices, a few *wadis*, and a flask of tea. He was at muster ground in front of the tea factory by six o'clock.

Right away, he sensed that something was amiss. The nursery *kangeny*—usually an outsider who was employed for six months for the care of the seedlings—was taking muster, and the chief *kangeny* was nowhere in sight. A quarter of the field labourers were missing, though all the women tea pluckers were present.

The roll call commenced. The men were standing miserably in their rows with that early morning weariness on their faces. They seemed on edge today, tensing as each name was called out. Jack himself supported a few of the families financially, secretly giving them wages taken from his own salary to provide them with clothing and food. That morning they answered in a surly way, muttering in low voices, avoiding Jack's gaze.

He ignored it for the moment. Low clouds drifted over the hills, and mynah birds squawked from the tree tops. With the roll call completed, he commenced giving orders for the field work to the KP, or field supervisor, a position always held by a Tamil. The women and girls were assigned to the lower terraces for plucking, and the old *kelavens*, elders too old to do field work and logging, were allotted roadside drainage clearance, an important task. Water that did not flow properly into drains caused overflow onto the roads and subsequent buckling, which, in turn, could cause sinkholes big enough to topple a lorry loaded with tea.

After muster he entered the information in the muster book in the tea factory's head office. Since it was the second day of the month, he had to calculate the balance of wages for each worker, and prepare the requisition for cash to pay the workers to the nearest cent, before the tenth. The requisition was then sent to the head office in Colombo. (As *sinna dorai* he drove to the city each month to collect the wages.) Many of the workers were indebted to their *kangeny*—poor devils. They had to repay the cost of the "journey" to Ceylon, transportation money from when they had been hired back in India. The debt became never-ending, and Jack could do nothing about it. (There were well-founded rumours that the *kangeny* extracted sexual "favours" from the women in lieu of money.)

Then he met with the KP, Kumaraswamy, also factory superintendent, and his assistant, Mr. Veeralaitham. They were responsible for the actual process of turning the hundreds of bushels of leaves, which were brought in twice a day by the pickers, into tea.

"*Vanhakkam,* Good morning, Mr. Gilmor, *sinna dorai.*"

"*Vanhakkam,* Mukanda."

The tea factory had five floors, each one responsible for a different facet of the tea-making process.

Jack respected these Ceylon Tamils, as they were known all over the island. A different breed altogether from the "estate" Tamils, who had been imported from India a century ago as indentured workers. The professional Ceylon Tamils belonged to the country as much as the Sinhalese, and mainly occupied the province in the north, the Vannu, and Jaffna peninsula, where it was very hot and dry. They were businessmen, accountants, and lawyers who had been trained to work for the Ceylon civil service (according to the resentful Sinhalese). They were intelligent, well-educated, and well-spoken in English. Most of all, the Ceylon Tamils were loyal to the British Crown, to which, they realized, they owed everything. They were therefore highly favoured by the British.

The labourers in the field, not unlike the Ceylon Tamils, also understood the system; they understood who was master, unlike the Sinhalese, who simmered with ill-concealed resentment, (and were therefore more dangerous). The Sinhalese did not forget that the land had been expropriated by the British with the help of their cheating Tamil *chetties*. It was important to understand this, Jack thought. How cleverly the British divided and ruled.

Where he himself stood—as racially mixed: part British and part Sinhalese—was always precarious, resting on the whims of the owner and master, De Jurgen. For who was he? Who was Jack Gilmor?

That morning he'd planned to check the weeding and tree lopping accompanied by Mr. Kumaraswamy.

But again, he sensed that something was wrong. The workers were clustered in shifty-looking groups here. In the distance, down by the coolie lines, Jack could see a knot of men with the *kangeny* and head man, a man akin to a shaman who served the labourers, as they could not afford a proper priest. They'd had to make do with a homemade temple, or *kovil*, made of bamboo, vines, coconut leaves. Even these unassuming structures had now been banned by De Jurgen. He had had the one on Netherlands burned down. ("Nothing but bloody breeding-grounds for insurrection.")

"*Naraham*! What the bloody hell is going on?" Jack yelled at the workers.

Though, of course, he had already guessed: it was a rumble over De Jurgen's cremation order. All night the Tamil drums had been pounding urgently, sending messages all over the district. The loss of their pool for the holy sprinkling of ashes, not to mention the ire of the head man, was not to be taken lightly, a fact that De Jurgen and Henshaw could not understand.

"Get to bloody work!"

He rode his motorbike down to the fields of nursery beds, where weeding had commenced. The *kanakapulle* was already there examining the work, which was a delicate operation, like everything to do with growing tea. Some of the workers were using scrapers to loosen the weeds.

"God damn!" Jack yelled in Tamil to one old man, a *kelaven*, who should know better. "*Nilli sorondi!*" The use of scrapers had long been banned; they loosened the surface soil, causing erosion and consequent overflows in the river and streams. "Use *eetie pick*, you bloody fool!"

The old *kelaven* cringed before Jack. Instinctively he raised his thin, bony, discoloured arm beseechingly to protect his face, a motion Jack had seen so often from De Jurgen's workers. If De Jurgen had been there—as he often was, accompanying his assistant manager on his rounds—the old man would have gotten a good thrashing right then and would have been docked a day's pay. So Jack raised his stick—just to show he could. If he couldn't discipline three hundred labourers, how would he ever get promoted to a big plantation like Netherlands, with a thousand coolies under him?

"*Ennal mudiyadhu, sahib*," begged the elder. Of course, the man had no extra money to buy an *eetie*.

In that instant, Jack hated his job, hated Weyweltalawa, and hated being under De Jurgen's administration. He hated the whole rotten business of it. And he hated himself.

God, the reproachful look on the man's face. He was afraid of him, the *sinna dorai*.

The sense of foreboding continued, though on the surface work continued as well. He had his tiffin break in the field with the KP, slipped back to the bungalow at noon for lunch and a shower, and then took his midday rest.

Jack returned to the factory in the late afternoon to observe the weighing of the afternoon green leaf and write the pluckers' chits. He entered the small check roll, feeling uneasy. He was not surprised to get a sudden phone call from De Jurgen. The phone was in the factory's head office.

"Come as soon as you can," yelled De Jurgen down the party line; half the district was listening in, of course. "Trouble with the bloody workers."

Jack jumped on his motorbike and went back to the bungalow. He pulled on a jacket and a hard topee hat for bullet protection, and took down his rifle and a gun.

"Stay inside with the kids," he ordered Mildred. The Sinhalese servants were cowering behind the doorway of the outside kitchen for protection. Ganesh appeared with a pitchfork and a machete in his hands. Jack decided to take the car for added protection. Ganesh jumped in the back, ever loyal, ever brave.

It was dark by the time they reached Netherlands. Long bands of coolies were trudging up the drive. They had walked for miles, trudging for hours from Weyweltalawa to Netherlands, taking the back paths that they knew. There was a low dirge of muttering as he passed by. Some shook fists. *"Suhainthram! Thavivam anavankda eruthi krikia pana, suhanthram vandum!"* They wanted their sacred right to dispose of the ashes of their dead.

A large angry crowd stood pushing against De Jurgen's bun-

galow, waving torches that flared orange-red, illuminating De
Jurgen and Henshaw and the front of the house. Many wielded
machetes and pitchforks. De Jurgen stood on the portico steps
with his hunting rifle. Henshaw was next to him. He had a
gun. He fired it into the air. Peacocks and other roosting birds
rose screeching from the roof.

The crowd dropped back, then surged forward again. They
had hurricane lamps and more torches, which illuminated their
worn faces. They stood in their rags around their head man.

They were shouting that they wanted their cremation rights,
suhainthrami. "We want cremation rights We want our ancestors' ashes honoured in the pool! It is our right!"

"*Suhainthram! Suhainthram!*" Rights! Rights! they clam-
oured.

Jack pushed through the throng. "Careful, *sahib*," said
Ganesh.

"Thank God, you've come!" gasped Henshaw, giving Jack
a hand and hoisting him up on to the verandah. Jack caught
a glimpse of Mrs. Henshaw behind the locked windows. She
was clutching her bosom as usual. "Oh God! Oh God!"

"What are they saying?"

De Jurgen's shirt was wrinkled with sweat that ran down
his face and chest.

"They're saying they want to cremate their dead as they've
always done and put the ashes in the pool. They say that it's
their right."

"Bloody hell it is!" cried De Jurgen. "Damn bloody insurrection is what it is! I'd hang the lot!"

"May I speak with them, sir? I think I could calm them down."
An idea had occurred to Jack.

De Jurgen nodded. There was no time to waste. This could
get ugly. (One thought of those rebels in Malaya who had shot
two British planters to death in an insurrection recently. It had
been the talk of the club.)

The workers started up a chant as they recognized Jack,

pressing forward with their flares. "Boss Gilmor, Quintus Delaney brother. Quintus Delaney good good man. He tell us to strike. Quintus! Quintus!"

The labourers fell silent as Jack began to address the head man. "Boss Gilmor, *sinna dorai* of Weyweltalawa speaks."

Jack salaamed to the head man, bringing his palms together at his chest and forehead.

"Namaste," he began, speaking in Tamil. "*Maalai vanakkam. Varavaerpu.*"

"*Periya dorai* De Jurgen does not want to interfere with your cremation rites, nor with the distribution of the sacred ashes. We honour the Hindu custom carried out by eldest son. Mr. De Jurgen—the Boss—is concerned only about *where* you put the sacred ash. He asks only that you place ashes *below* the bathing pool, in another pool, so the ladies may bathe.

"An area will be cleared down there. You may hold a sacred blessing of the new site, and that part of the river will be sacred to Hindus. *Purindhadha?*" Understand?

The head man stepped up, dressed only in a loin cloth like Gandhi, and a turban. He was an older man (though likely only forty), with deep, purple-black weals across his back and shoulders.

"These are honourable words, Meester Geelmor, *sinna dorai.* But can we trust your word?"

"You have our word."

There was rumbling among the workers as the head man explained Jack's offer.

"Then we accept, *sinna dorai.*"

"*Amam! Amam!*" shouted the crowd, cheering.

"What did you say? What are they shouting?" demanded De Jurgen, looking perplexed, disturbed at the sudden jubilance. Henshaw held on tight to his gun.

"I said they can still put their ashes in the river, only further down, sir, well below the bathing pool, and we will honour that. Obvious solution, everyone happy."

"The devil you did!" cried De Jurgen. "Since when are you bloody *periya dorai*? Since when are you the owner of Netherlands and Weyweltalawa, Gilmor?"

Jack trembled with indignation, as if stung.

"Well, if I were the *periya dorai* of these plantations the workers wouldn't be in the bloody state they're in—*sir*."

Suddenly he could not stop. What was the matter with him?

"Bloody disgrace to humanity, that's what. Starved and beaten and tortured—yes!—deprived of medical services and schooling, underpaid, overworked shreds of civilization."

"You—you! You dare to speak like this to your superior? Get out! Get out of Weyweltalawa at once! You're fired! Take twenty-four-hours' notice, you and all your half-caste tribe."

Twenty-four hours was the standard notice time on company estates.

"*Oh, go to hell!*" cried Jack.

Now he was done for. He wheeled about and pushed his way through the crowd, which fell back for him, to reach his car. The workers thronged around his car, crying. "Little boss give hell to Big Boss!"

Drums began thrumming far and wide that night, across the hills, and all the following days. A refrain resounded: "Small boss Gilmor tell Big Boss De Jurgen to go to hell!"

(Oh, that bush telegraph!)

31.

BY THE TIME HE RETURNED, the servants knew everything. They stood huddled in the darkness by the outside kitchen. "Boss get sack."

Jack hastened inside, where Mildred was waiting anxiously in the living room. "Oh, Jack, pet!"

"Well, what's done is done. We're out. And I'm not sorry." This, defiantly. Lovely Weyweltalawa. He had until the next evening muster to pack and get out. There was always that ruthless edge to being sacked in the colonial empire; the British were uppity, ruthless buggers, priding themselves on their toughness. Well, he could be tough, too.

"We can go to Normandy, to Father's, for now," said Mildred quickly. She did not ask how Jack got the sack. Loyal to the core—that was the quality he loved in her right then.

He was trembling. "Whisky!" he called, and sank into the armchair.

Asaf, the little houseboy—what would become of him?—came running with the decanter and a glass balanced expertly on a round tray. A smart little fellow. Oh, well, if he was lucky he'd be passed along to the next manager, along with the servants.

He took a deep gulp.

"Another."

Drums were rumbling in the forests, out there in the menacing half-light. Torches would be lit, the chanting would begin, the head man would be consulted.

"I'll ring Tommy right away. And Van der Berg."

He'd need Tommy to bring a small lorry in the morning to take their things—such as they were—away to Normandy estate, to his father-in-law Titus Delaney's place. They planned to stay there for the time being, until he could get another position. He knew De Jurgen would notify Carson and Cumberbatch. The company might or might not offer him another posting, assuming there were available vacancies, but the usual way of getting another plantation was through the grape-vine, through knowing the right people. He groaned miserably. This was where membership in the best club counted. Damn Henshaw. Damn the bloody English.

He lit a Peacock and smoked furiously, thinking.

"Lally and Fiona can help me pack our clothes and possessions first thing in the morning," said Mildred firmly.

There was the hunting gear, tents, rifles, and guns—all his. His radio set, records, victrola, motorbike, and car. He shook his head. Not a stick of furniture. They had so few possessions after years and years of planting. Nothing. All belonged to the estate.

"What about Rajah, Daddy?" cried Aidan. His first though was of Daddy's great white horse, on which he rode grandly around the estate on dry days. "No Rajah?"

"No Rajah. He belongs to Weyweltalawa," Jack replied with a sigh.

Like so much else, thought Aidan sadly. For the first time, he realized that Daddy did not own Weyweltalawa or anything in it. Besides the personal effects they bought themselves, tea planters used everything at the behest of the owner and tea company.

Scottie gripped his *kutee,* jumping around shouting, "No leave *kutee!*"

"Where are we going to *live*?" wailed Lally. She was a boarder at the convent school, but this was her home.

"Oh, shut up, Lally," said Fiona, who was excited at the

prospect of moving. She was hoping they would live closer to Colombo, to the fine city life of cousin Felix. Now her new life would begin at Kandy Convent in earnest.

Jack rode his bike over to the tea factory and used the telephone in the head office to call Tommy on the long-distance telegraph system that served the island. The task would take at least an hour. "Weyweltalawa one-two-three calling," he said over and over again. Everyone on the party line was listening in, which was practically the whole tea country. After three quarters of an hour of this, he was hoarse, but Tommy was finally on the line: "So you get sack from big boss, Jackie-boy?"

"Yes, yes," Tommy agreed to bring a small lorry round twenty-two hairpin bends.

"Just a small one, Tommy. We don't have much."

Word got around in the upcountry, and by morning all the workers on the estates knew that Jack Gilmor, *sinna dorai* of Weyweltalawa, had been given the sack. Of course they did. And the story would get blown out of all proportion in the telling; all sorts of fantastic versions would emerge: Jack heard that he'd struck De Jurgen in the face, kicked his balls, threatened to drown him in the pool, or that De Jurgen had shot his gun at Jack and missed, and they'd come to blows over the Tamil labourers—well, that part was true.

Finally he reached Mildred's distant "cousin," Emil Van der Berg, on the telephone. No one in the family was ever quite sure what the relationship exactly was between him and Mildred, but he was a big landowner and he had a number of tea, cocoa, and rubber plantations. He was therefore influential, if hated. His great-grandfather and Titus Delaney's great-grandfather had come to Ceylon together seeking their fortunes and had married—Sinhalese style—two sisters. This had led to a confusion of intermingled descendants.

"I know of just the position for you, Jack! It opened up recently," cried Emil. "Not to worry. I know the owner. I'll put in a good word for you. You're a good planter, Jack. You've got a good reputation. There's nothing to fear. The estate is Madeniya, in the low country, if you don't mind that. Kegalle district...."

Low country, in the world of tea, meant lower status.

The confusion. The haste. The order: out in twenty-four hours. The children were frightened. They had to leave their home! They had gone to bed in Weyweltalawa and woken up to the prospect of a new home somewhere else. They were to stay with Granpa Delaney for the time being. Aidan felt tears welling.

"It's not our house. It never was," said Fiona curtly.

The servants clustered in the kitchen, alarmed. They already knew. Everyone did. Ganesh came to the back door, weeping. "*Vanhakkam.*" Then, to Aidan, "*Pudi matthia.*"

Jack gave the servants a gift of rupees out of his own income, a sum that was over and above their wages, and a sari cloth each. He gave Ganesh two white shirts, one of his old hunting knives, and his old pipe.

"*Romba nanri*, master, *ecaman!*" Ganesh bowed and put his hands to his forehead, weeping softly at the sight of master's pipe.

"*Nan poyittu varaenga*, Ganesh. Goodbye."

There was little to pack. The furniture, beds, and the kitchen stove belonged to the bungalow, and would be passed on to the next tea planter who took over the post. The Gilmors would inherit furniture and beds from the next estate they occupied.

Jack knocked back a whisky straight, then poured himself another.

"Pet ... pet, what for all this drinking at this hour?" pleaded Mama.

Tears streamed down Jack's face. The shame he felt about his situation now took hold. Fired. Twenty-four-hours' notice, like a coolie.

"Don't cry, Daddy." Aidan lifted his small hand to his father's face, his heart breaking.

"Go, son. Stay in the bedroom and help Lally."

Jack saw only too clearly the moment, decades back—oh, long ago—when himself was a boy of ten or so, older than Aidan. He'd been so frightened, angry at his father, Owen Gilmor, who'd been given the sack from his position as *sinna dorai* at Gampola. Instant dismissal. The shame. Everyone knowing why, including Mother. She'd taken off the day before with a servant and Jack's sister. (Jack had hidden in the water barrel by the outside kitchen.) Mother, his sister Myra, and his younger brother Grayson went to Auntie Bella and Uncle John's place at Pennylands. The disgrace swept over Jack once again: Jack himself had caught his father having sex with a Sinhalese servant girl—not even an educated one, but a *seevakayaa* from the village. The moment had been distilled in Jack's memory. That afternoon, he'd set out with his new air-gun, a Christmas present from Father, accompanied by one of the kitchen boys, who carried his kit and tiffin for him. Creeping together through the thick foliage of the forest to shoot their prey, parting the leaves softly, carefully, they had come unexpectedly upon a naked Sinhalese girl cavorting and splashing in a deep pool fringed with undulating ferns and long sprays of blossoms—a sylvan scene of such loveliness that it had caught his breath. Except that there was Father, naked, his fine European clothes flung across a rock, his fine underwear abandoned. The girl leaned back against the slab of rock, half in and half out of the water, her mouth open wide....

He and the kitchen-boy, Vijitha, had stood gaping. Vijitha covered his mouth; he had giggled at the *periya dorai* with a servant girl, her breasts long and slinky like golden-brown mangoes. *Periya dorai's* hands were like paws, clutching greedily, his arched body clamped over the girl's, their breaths and bodies coming together. "*Ahm-mah-tah-hu-kahn-nah,* master fucking," he had snorted softly.

Of course, the servants were the first to know. The stable

boy, the *appu*, the cook, and even the *vani varsa* who cleaned out the lavatory holes and drains—they were all sniggering. The mighty sahib caught fucking, *ahm-mah-tah hu-kahn-nah*, like a dog in heat, with a servant.

And then the baby that followed: a girl, Samira. His father's ignominy. He'd been forced to live in the village like a native with that woman and her baby, his marriage over. He was finished as a planter. Owen Gilmor? Too drunk to stand. An alcoholic to the end of his days, like many a planter in those hills.

Jack recalled his father's stupidity. The English planters had all the women they wanted, white or brown, without compunction. But a Eurasian? That was another matter; it meant instant dismissal. Owen Gilmor had got uppity. He had had it coming to him, they said at the club. Thinking he could get away with it. Thinking he was an Englishman.

Jack wept for his father as much as for himself, leaning against the old teak sideboard, above which hung a photograph of Nuwara Eliya—the Englishman's playground, a distant dream. He could certainly say goodbye to membership in the elite Hatton-Eliya Club now. In tea country, nothing could make up for being fired; it was part of the unspoken code.

He poured another whisky, trembling.

"What for tears, man?" laughed Tommy. He'd arrived with the lorry. Big, jocular reliable Tommy Goonesekere. He gave Jackie-boy a giant bear-hug.

The clothes were packed in the old tea chests; the few books they owned had been ravaged by silverfish. They kept the red *Planters' Directory* (the planters' bible), his guns, and a curved ornamental Kandyan dagger that had been passed down for generations on Mildred's side from her royal ancestors. And the family photograph album with aged sepia photos of a by-gone era: old man Gilmor, their white progenitor, back in the 1880s, astride his horse outside a plantation bungalow, with a gun and his hunting dogs. The past. Colonial life.

"Jack, pet, at least you have the offer of this new position in Madeniya, thanks to Emil Van der Berg," urged Mildred. "You have not failed. You are an honourable man, pet. You spoke out for the labourers; there is nothing of shame in that."

At evening muster, at sundown, they drove away, Jack trailing behind the lorry in his Standard 8. Row after row of workers stood to attention and bowed their heads as he passed by. The drums began, a lone mournful thrumming across the estate and jungles and the hills beyond:

"Little boss *sinna dorai* Gilmor speak truth. Give hell to big boss De Jurgen."

And so their lives at Weyweltalawa came to an end, and Aidan mourned with all the grief of a boy who was too young to understand. Beautiful, lush Weyweltalawa, with its cool misty mornings, dew dropping from the deodars, and sunlit paths leading to nowhere, winding through their lives. It was all lost forever: Ganesh and the Garden of Eden, with its subterranean waters and slithering snake, golden-flecked and flicking of tongue amidst the Tree of Knowledge of Good and Evil and the two Angels, the place of a young boy's heart.

32.

THE MADENIYA TEA ESTATE was in the Kegalle district, a dry zone in the low country. The surrounding hills were not nearly as high as the mountains around Weyweltalawa, of course, but the land rose steeply around the estate nonetheless; it was an arduous climb. Mama and Daddy were happy there. Of course, they had to cope with the loss of face before the Sinhalese servants. (That low country Sinhalese were not as pure as upcountry was a commonly held belief.)

"We are not as pure now, Daddy," Aidan cried.

"Pure? Who says so?"

"Lalitha. Low country is not as *pukkah*."

"Nonsense! Who's *pure*? You tell me! Bloody rot."

The long days were hot and dry, twenty degrees warmer than in upcountry. It became humid only during the southwest monsoon; otherwise the wet clothes—which the *dhobi* lay on the rocks down by the river—were dry in an hour. Gone was all that rain and mist, the sudden downpours, the constant damp feeling, the silverfish, and the billowy low clouds that had suffocated Mama with claustrophobia. But gone, also, was the eerie mystery of hills and mountains folding into each other, lost to sky.

There were tall palmyrah palms on the new estate, their bushy heads waving like fans. A beautiful garden and shrubbery was laid out; planted by the previous manager, it was an oasis with flowers violent and vivid of hue, unlike the delicate soft pastels of an English garden so beloved of the English tea planters upcountry. Hibiscus and hydrangea, vivid azaleas, scarlet gold, all flowers that loved the sun, vibrated against a powerful blue sky. There were toddy palms and coconut trees and tall rain trees. No more dour deodars and mountain pines. Around the pond in the lower terrace, spiky cactus trees were in bloom, their luscious flowers trembling at the tips. Dark mynah birds squawked in the treetops; they were like crows, noisy and convivial.

A large pink tamarind tree flowered in the middle of the lawn, the hue of sunrise.

In the evening, at sundown, you could drive a few miles over to Kegalle to see the bats. Clouds of them filled the air, fluttering from the fruit trees where they'd hung nesting by day. They were as large as crows, with great whirring wings and pointed teeth. "Ugh," said Fiona.

Night birds began their whistling and cooing. Aidan lay on his bed listening … the rustling of strange animals out in the darkness, the sensation of miles of black-folding hills stretching away, not a soul within calling distance. An occasional, agonized screech of something caught out there in the night, in the claws of something else, its life gone in an instant.

A gecko clung, motionless in the heat, to the ceiling of the children's bedroom, day and night.

"It'll fall on our faces!" cried Lally.

"No it won't, silly. It just stays there."

The house was large, painted white, with a teak shingled roof. There was a central portico and pandara over the front door for shade, modern windows, and French doors leading out to a descending terrace. There were five large bedrooms, and a private office for Daddy, which adjoined his bedroom and where the estate safe was kept. This was where the wages for the labourers—picked up by Daddy monthly from the tea company in Colombo—were kept locked up. Daddy now had his own telephone. Water was piped in from the lines. Wonderful! But, most of all, the house had electricity; it had its own British Hornsby dynamo in a shed at the back, which was looked after by a technician. No more kerosene lamps (though Aidan missed their golden gentle glow during the evening).

Madeniya was a large estate with over a thousand Tamil labourers. It produced both tea and rubber: close to fifteen hundred acres of tea, and just over six hundred acres of rubber. The rubber section was run by a separate superintendent, John Perera, a Eurasian like Jack, and a fine fellow. They got along at once; as part of the tea planters' network, they had both been students at Holy Innocents School, and so they had memories of schoolmasters, escapades, and schoolboy jokes in common; they could reminisce endlessly about cricket matches won and lost in that distant, innocent time. "Got my first cap there, man," beamed Perera.

Jack was in charge of the tea plantation.

Periya dorai, Big Boss, superintendent, at last. Jack could hardly believe his good fortune, how karma had worked out. His salary had doubled, increasing his prestige, especially within the extended family. "That Jack will always fall on his feet," said his father-in-law, Titus Delaney, at Normandy. "Put him in the Sahara Desert and he'll find water! He could sell sand to the Arabs, our Jack."

He increased his insurance premiums. Peter de Groot drove down from Colombo one steaming hot day, perspiring heavily, his shirt collar damp and soiled with sweat. He climbed the rocky incline to the Gilmors' bungalow. Though "low" country, the terrain was hilly and dry, and it was a steep winding climb up to the bungalow. In parts of the estate tall pampas grass grew ("Watch for snakes!"). The servant brought Mr. de Groot a Lanka lime with a shot of gin (didn't smell the breath), and he and Jack sat in the dining room to get down to business. Mr. de Groot advised a substantial increase in Jack's premiums due to the coming Independence. "Who knows what the future has in store?" he intimated.

Jack raised his eyebrows. "What the hell, man?"

"Well, there is uncertainty in the country whenever there is a transfer of power," said de Groot haltingly. "Best to be insured against every possibility, Jack." Mr. de Groot was sweating already at the uncertainty of life. His daughter Lily was married with two children, living in a moderate, so-so situation in a moderate section of Colombo; the younger girl Esmé was in Kandy Convent as a boarder, he stressed proudly, but fees were expensive. "Fine plantation you've got here, Jack. *Toost!*"

"*Toost!*"

Jack had an assistant superintendent, a *sinna dorai*, working under him: Alister Denbow, another Eurasian. As he got to know him better, Alister confessed laughingly one day that "Denbow" was not his actual name. Not his *real* name. (What was "real" in Ceylon?) Seemed that his old man, Fergus Bowden, who had come to Ceylon from Scotland, had inverted his name from "Bowden" to "Denbow" for his half-Sinhalese children, for obvious reasons: he had a wife back in Edinburgh waiting for him, the bastard. It was same old story. Denbow's ironic laugh rang out amongst the coolies who kept on with their work, tilling the ground with hoes. Jack felt a sharp stab of emotion, but did not speak of his own great-grandfather, Sinclair Gilmor, another rotter.

Jack felt a new kind of ease, even closeness, with his new colleagues. The owner was a Sinhalese, Richard Wickramasingha, a wealthy businessman in Colombo. He was a Keraly man, a Christian, who was acquainted with Mildred's Sinhalese family on her mother's side. When the first Christmas at Madeniya approached, Jack decided he would ask Wikramasingha to provide the workers with a new set of clothes each, as well as new saris for the pluckers, and a five-pound bag of *dhal*. Being Christian, he could hardly refuse.

Tea did not like heat; it liked warm and wet, which is why

it grew so much better in the highlands. Planters in the low country had trouble providing enough water for the sensitive tea seedlings and protecting them from the hot sun. Denbow took Jack around the estate and showed him the network of shallow channels, which they'd dug to bring water from a small dam, and the sluices for carrying water to the tea bushes and nurseries. The channels were sloped gradually for drainage. "Very well done," nodded Jack. There was also a good preponderance of *Gliricidia sepium* bushes among the tea terraces to provide shade for the tea leaves. The usual lopping at the forks took place at intervals throughout the year to prevent too much shade, which could cause blister blight—a sort of rash, like chicken pox—to form under the leaves of the tea bushes. The cut wood was used as mulch and put back into the soil, explained Denbow. Tea loved acidic soil; it would not grow at all in alkaline.

Jack loved his work. He loved being out all morning inspecting the factory, the labourers, and the nurseries with the KP, who was contracted out by the company, a knowledgeable man. He lay the beds, ascertained that the soil was suitable, took and oversaw the branch cutting, and planted inter-nodal cuttings. The nursery *kangeny* was paid two-thirds of the contract rate up front, and the other third after the work was completed. Jack accompanied him, checking on the fracturing of young plants at the regular six-inch height, and observing the delicate process of transplanting the bushes to larger nurseries. He planned to allow some tea bushes to grow into full trees, to provide seeds in the old-fashioned way, as well as to employ the modern technique of taking cuttings. Tea bushes had to be renewed every thirty-five or forty years, and he had some areas with seedlings that were ready.

Hawk-eagles wheeled across an azure sky. He paused his work for a moment and shaded his eyes, looking upwards at the dark shadows. He was too thrilled with his position as big boss to take the usual long breaks, one of the perks of the job.

Traditionally, the *periya dorai* was known to go off hunting for days, indulge in long siestas, and spend an inordinate amount of time at the club drinking with pals, and no one begrudged him for it. He had usually earned the privilege from his early creeper days onward.

Of course, low country tea was not comparable to Nuwara Eliya tea, which had a golden liquid body and was highly prized, nor to the esteemed silver-tipped "tippy" teas favoured by Felix Gilmor, the tea taster. But low country tea was a satisfying brew, nevertheless: full-bodied and strong, though lacking the subtlety of Dikoya, Kandyan, and Ratnapura teas. It brought a good price, and it was drunk all over the world. So Jack was enthused; he was determined to bring Madeniya up to a standard of excellence and to impress the management, Carson and Cumberbatch in Colombo. He wanted the esteem of his labourers, which he sensed he had, for no other reason than his brief sojourn into spiritualism. He owed his new-found spirituality to Mildred's father, Titus, who had tried to get in contact with the spirit of his dead wife, something Jack had hoped to keep secret. Impossible, of course, in an estate bungalow with servants who knew everything. But far from losing status, or arousing the ridicule of the labourers, Jack's dabbling in spiritualism only increased his prestige. Soon everyone on the estate knew that *periya dorai*—Big Boss Gilmor—spoke regularly with spirits. The *sahib* had special rituals: a small wine glass that he turned upside down in the centre of a card table, and cryptic glyphs, magic letters of the English alphabet set in a sacred circle around the glass. This took place in the evening, in the master's living room with the lamp dimmed, reported the awed house servants one and two, who made a habit of peeking through the slats in the out-kitchen partition. Big boss and mistress Mildred then put questions in sacred English to their God, saying in low voices: "Spirit, are you there?" (This was not unlike their communion with their own medicine man, the *wetherala*.) The little glass *moved of its own accord,* swore the servants—*Aiyo-o!*—while his Christian God gave Big Boss Gilmor messages. The labourers had never had a *periya dorai* who was guided by spirits. The tea flourished, the yield increased under his mystical powers, and Carson and Cumberbatch, the big bosses in Colombo, were pleased and raised the coolies' wages by half a rupee.

Trelawney had been Jack's ideal; he was the superintendent of the Aholagalla estate, which was upcountry in the best Hatton district. This was where Jack had started out as a creeper when he was only fifteen, fresh from Holy Innocents. Funds had run out after Father's debacle. Uncle Henry, the manager of Loch Lomond in the low country, had urged him to take up tea planting, to follow in the family tradition. He'd got him into Aholagalla with Jim Trelawney. "No better planter upcountry."

But Jack had admired Jim Trelawney as a man; the planter fulfilled his youthful belief in the good Englishman. He was tall, fair, straightforward in his dealings, and honest in a way that a man plays a game of cricket—"fair play, I say!" What heartened and impressed Jack was Trelawney's relationship with the labourers, exceptional for the 1930s, so different from De Jurgen's at Netherlands. Trelawney established a dispensary on the estate for the medical needs of the men and their families, and he had employed an itinerant Tamil nurse from Colombo to assist in women's medical problems and childbirth. "What? A *nurse?*" Jack recalled the planters at the club laughing, amused. "Their women just drop their bloody bairns on the ground when they're ready; they're used to it." But Trelawney had persisted. He applied for a government primary school to be built not far from the coolie lines, and he got it. Amazingly, Joan Trelawney, his wife, assisted at the school, voluntarily teaching English. She spoke fluent Tamil like Jim. She even started a choir of coolies, teaching the music using old tonic Solfa. They learned opera; they even sang the "Chorus of the Hebrew Slaves," the worn wrinkled labourers and their wives (who pulled shawls over their heads), at a club function. "Hell, it should be the bloody chorus of the Tamil slaves!" the planters jibbed, amused. The wives rolled their eyes. (What would this crazy English woman think up next?) On the estate, Trelawney got his engineer to divert water from the main pipe lines to the coolie lines, to provide them with running water. (There was usually a family of eight or nine to one small room.) Little wonder the labourers admired and respected him. "*Periya dorai* Trelawney good boss man."

That was a long time ago, when Jack had been young and eager and fresh to the work, anxious to prove himself, to rise up in the planters' world—a world of hunting and hard drinking. And now he had.

Mildred was happy for Jack, and she, too, loved the heat and sunshine of Madeniya, the bright flowers, the dryness. But it wasn't much of a life for an intelligent woman, when all was said and done. Tea planting was a man's job. The wife belonged in the home, in the estate bungalow; her role was to be the mistress of the house. Yet, ironically, even the usual duties of the home were now denied her due to the servants. The ennui, the tedium of long sunlit hours alone in a big bungalow trying to keep occupied and "keep up appearances" before the servants caused a certain debilitation of spirit. The extra servants that came with Jack's new position—he now earned twice his old salary—meant that there was even less for her to do. The head servant, Thomas, was in charge of the Sinhalese servants: first house servant, second servant, and a bevy of lesser ones, including the new little houseboy, Sisera, who brought their tea in the morning and saw to Jack's needs: polishing his boots, laying out his clothes, etc. There was a kitchen *appu*, a stable boy, someone to look after the birds in the aviary—it was endless. The stables were at the end of the yard with a small servants' quarters attached. She felt like something was missing at the heart of her life, a feeling that she kept from

Jack. It was as though she had no purpose, as though she was not needed in the wider world, beyond mothering the children.

With the children soon going away to school, Mildred anticipated a dread blankness that would be filled only by Scottie, who was becoming more rambunctious by the day. Fiona had already left for Kandy Convent, excited about her new uniform and displaying a certain arrogance she felt befitted her new status independent of her parents. At that moment, Mildred had felt Fiona growing away from her. She could not bear the thought of losing Aidan as well, and then Scottie, who would join him at boarding school in a few years. Of course, it was essential that Scott have the same opportunity. Scottie was to be groomed for the elite position, perhaps in law or government, that Jack hoped he would hold one day in Ceylon society, especially with Independence coming. All the chief ministers and government leaders in Ceylon went to the English Public Schools: St. Thomas's, St. Peter's, Holy Innocents.... Otherwise what would become of Scottie? He'd be like a village boy.

Jack took Mildred regularly into Colombo to cheer her up. They'd have lunch at the fancy Galle Face Hotel, and then Jack would visit the Pettah, where he enjoyed the usual perambulations of his old friend, Mr. Saeed. Mildred never met the older man, for she liked to visit the cathedral on such occasions. Mr. Saeed said he was intending, as a minority (Muslims made up less than one percent of the population), to vote UNP, United National Party, and hope for the best.

Their neighbour in the next estate over was Mr. Perera, a Buddhist. One day a week, in Buddhist fashion, he would open his coconut estate to the poor and serve a vast free meal of rice and curry, rotis and rice pudding, according to the holy *dharma*. Sometimes he'd invite along the local Buddhist priest, an old, quiet, kindly man, who put a garland of blossoms round Mr. Perera's neck and chanted. Jack took Mildred and the children along to help with the serving (good for their karma). Aidan and Lally loved ladling out bowls of rice and *dhal* and handing out *chapattis*, but Fiona turned up her nose. "Mama, the people smell…" she whispered, turning away. "They have cooties."

"Don't force her, pet," said Daddy.

Lally was sorry for the poor people with sores and ragged clothes from the villages around. "They're *starving*," said Fiona, shocked. She wanted to go home; this was not the role she imagined for herself as a grand English lady, with several sets of cutlery gracing her table. What would the elite girls of Kandy Convent think? Not to mention the girls from the more exclusive English Girls' Mountain School up in Nuwara Eliya? She had to don an ugly, smelly, greasy apron, like a servant, to keep her English dress clean while she ladled. "Disgusting!" A low, alarming chanting arose from these poor villagers, a strange hum from their throats. They were thanking Mr. Perera. "Isn't it beautiful?" cried Lally. "They're blessing Mr. Perera!" But then, Lally was a nitwit.

Jack was relieved and flattered when Mr. Wickramasingha invited him to join the Kegalle Club. They had dinner together in the new bungalow. "Settling in nicely, Jack? Been round to the club, yet?" He meant the Kegalle Club. Jack had intended to drop by, but had been so busy learning the ropes of his new position. And now here was Emil Wickramasingha offering to sponsor membership. He felt an exhilaration; he was being accepted, respected.

The Kegalle Club was already known to Jack, of course, from the many inter-club cricket matches he'd played in over the years. It was a pleasant, old-fashioned, unpretentious place, with tall feathery tamarind, acacia, and almond trees around the oval. There was a simple wooden clubhouse with the usual lounge and bar, and a side room for dining with ceiling-to-floor picture windows overlooking the vista of distant low hills.

"Beer, old chap?"

There was a casual sense of ease and camaraderie at the club. Eurasians, Sinhalese, Ceylon Tamils, and a few white people mingled amiably over a few toddies and beers. Even Mildred found herself unexpectedly welcomed and respected at the perfunctory Sunday family get-togethers, typical of all planters' clubs. The children played outside on the green under the watchful eyes of an *ayah*. Mildred was soon engaged in interesting conversation, feeling at ease with the Sinhalese wives as they sipped their toddies and lime. They were full of talk of the upcoming election in September, and they expected Mildred to have an opinion. It was the first time they would be voting for a Sinhalese Buddhist prime minister. "One of our own, free of the British yoke," cried Mrs. Abeyasinghe. She was a robust woman dressed in full Kandyan sari, with gold studs in her nose and ears and gold bracelets on her arms.

"I imagine we're all UNP here, United National Party," tinkled Mrs. Ratnayake, glancing hintingly at Mildred to declare herself, though it was a foregone conclusion: Don Stephen Senanayake of the UNP would win. He was a *goigama,* part of the land-owning class, and the only possible candidate who could get a sizable majority. Mrs. Amarasuriya agreed. "A fine man, and so distinguished-looking. Oxford-educated, English-speaking, with that impressive, cultivated accent," she gushed.

The Senanayake family was strict Buddhist and kept all the *poya* days, dressing in white when visiting the temple. The Sinhalese peasants were all for him. He was something of a hero to them, for hadn't he been jailed by the hated British in his youth? Here the English planters stiffened. As a youth, he'd been foremost in the insurrection back in 1915, otherwise known as the "anti-Muslim riots" against the Moors, who had been called "Cochins."

"The Moorish businessmen were known for their Shylockian ways, artificially fixing prices on foodstuffs and getting fat and prosperous just like the Jews," insisted Mrs. Abenesekere indignantly. "*And* seducing our Sinhalese girls. One can't blame the Sinhalese. Perhaps things had got out of hand though," she admitted, as they always did in Ceylon. Tempers had flared. Sinhalese goon squads, incited by the Buddhist monks, had attacked Muslim shops and businesses, dragging Muslims out of their dwellings in Colombo and all the small towns they inhabited on the coasts. Terror, murder, rape, torture—until the British had intervened. Martial law had been declared. "Brutal!" cried Mrs. Abenesekere, again. "The British forces were brutal!" Which, of course, made Senanayake all the more heroic for having rebelled against them and been thrown in jail. But being a *goigama* and a graduate of an English public school, he'd been quickly released, unlike the poor Sinhalese dolts who'd languished, naked and tortured in their fetid cells, until they died.

But that was long ago, 1915....

Mrs. Wijeratne was of the opinion that Senanayake—"Don"—would sweep the polls.

"An absolute certainty," agreed Mrs. Wickramasingha. "Wouldn't you say, Mildred?"

"Well, there is universal suffrage now," Mildred replied cautiously. "Jack and I have seldom voted, being so isolated up in the hill country, far from the polling booths," she added apologetically.

Mildred realized, then, that the ladies would, of course, know about her brother Quintus, who was going around the estates stirring up the coolies to vote, urging them to cast their lot in with Thondaman and the Lanka Sama Samaja Party, or the LSSP. Leftist, oh, yes, definitely. Trotskyite. Almost communist.

"I mean ... everyone gets to vote this time, even the Tamil labourers, and there is the Lanka Sama Samaja Party...." Mildred felt her voice trail off. She wasn't certain what she meant to imply.

The ladies frowned. "Lanka Sama Samaja Party?" What nonsense! Mrs. Abeyasinha had never heard of anything so ridiculous. (A man of Senanayake's stature—Oxford educated—was now on equal level to a Tamil Indian coolie running around in a span cloth?)

Mrs. Wijeratne agreed. "Personally I am thinking we can totally discount the coolies in this election. Absolute numskulls."

"They wouldn't be knowing a pen from an *eetie* pick." The ladies laughed merrily.

Mrs. Vaithalingam had sidled over. She was Tamil, though of the same social standing as the Sinhalese wives since she was the wife of Punithavany Vaithalingam, a high-ranking Ceylon Tamil of the *vellala* caste, equal to any Sinhalese *goigama*. Mr. Vaithalingam was the owner of several large tea and rubber plantations in the low country, and a fine upcountry estate. He was also a successful investor in lucrative land deals and business interests in Colombo. Nothing to fear there, thought Mrs. Wijeratne.

Indeed, Mrs. Vaithalingam assured them that of course she and Punithy were voting for "Don." She wore a sari the Tamil way, the midriff covered, the silk draped around her entire body.

Many of the husbands of these Sinhalese ladies were not actual hands-on tea planters themselves; they merely owned the vast estates and hired managers like Jack to run them. They tended to live in their fine houses in Colombo or stay in stately bungalows with the best vistas on their estates, which they visited from time to time. This kept communications open socially in the local clubs, which was very important politically. Their families had made astute investments in the land half a century ago, when the British took over the Sinhalese villagers' holdings and sold them out in parcels. Mildred was not knowledgeable about such affairs, but like most low country and upcountry Kandyan Sinhalese, she had heard of the double dealings that had gone on in British land deals and transactions that had left the poor, rural Sinhalese natives eking out a pittance. They were only a little better off than the Tamil labourers who had nothing. Mrs. Wijeratne,

Mrs. Wickramasingha, Mrs. Amarasuriya, and all the rest of the Sinhalese ladies were unaware of this. They had no more connection to the thoughts and feelings of a lowly Sinhalese villager than to a Tamil labourer. To them, people from the low Sinhalese castes were the servants who cleaned their fine offices in Colombo, served in their restaurants and shops, and worked in their houses as chauffeurs, gardeners, and toilet *varsi vannu*. It happened right under their noses, but they did not get it, mused Mildred, who, of course, kept such thoughts to herself.

She had long ago realized that her father's family, the Delaneys, were neither poor like labourers and servants nor wealthy *goigama*. They floated along in the middle, living on their modest cocoa estate, intellectually proud and independent, saved only by her Sinhalese mother's high Kandyan caste.

The acacia trees beyond the windows of the Kegalle Club waved softly in the breeze, their perfume filling the grounds.

The ladies turned to the social possibilities linked to Independence that was slated for February, when Ceylon would cease to be a colony of Britain. When the great day arrived, they fully expected to be with their husbands in the special compound for tea planters, and to meet Prince Henry of the royal family in person in Colombo. They would certainly have to practise their curtseys under their saris, they tittered.

Across the room their husbands stuck to cricket, the latest test match, the Ceylon team, and such. To them the election was a foregone conclusion: smashing majority for the old boy, Don Senanayake, general franchise be buggered. "Don" was one of them, almost. Like many of his kind who wanted to get on, he'd attended St. Thomas School at Mutwal, which had a motto that all of them could get behind: *Manliness and truth, courage, purity, and all those things that make a man a gentleman.*

"Damn right, too," echoed the planters.

The planters socialized with everyone at the club, stood their round of drinks, told smutty public schoolboy jokes privately among themselves, and played cricket with gallantry. Public school types. Jack soon fit in and happily played midfielder on the team.

A ball rose in an arc through a glittering afternoon.

"Jolly good catch, man!"

"Rather!"

Tea, cricket, the bout of drinking that followed. All was well in the former colony of the British Empire.

The sun shining gloriously, the pleasant crack of ball against bat, the gentle applause of the ladies in the bleachers.... Jack was the new *periya dorai* in the district; what more could he desire?

And yet. And yet.

His rejection by Henshaw at the Hatton-Eliya Club, its members' condescension, and their subtle barring him of full membership continued to rankle. Jack still hankered after acceptance; he still wanted to be one of the elite, to be an Englishman. It was like a dull fire in his gut, simmering.

The position of secretary was open in the Kegalle Club. No one wanted it; took up too much time, the planters complained. Jack got it by default. As a superintendent, he had as much free time as he wished to allot himself, as long as the running of the estate was competent and profits assured. As club secretary, he would be responsible for arranging cricket matches and schedules, correspondence, phone calls, and inter-club cricket matches. It was the latter that beguiled Jack. The coming year, 1948, was Independence year. Independence Day was set by the British for February 3, 1948, which was about six months away. As secretary, he needed to consult with other clubs, including the one at Hatton-Eliya about plans for the full participation of tea planters in the great event. It meant that he had to drive once a month across the hills to the Hatton-Eliya Club to meet with the club officials. He already knew that Prince Henry, the king's brother, was coming to officiate at the ceremony, King George VI being too sick to attend. The English planters at Hatton-Eliya might affect superior indifference—the British were, after all, handing over power—but no one wanted to miss out on the solemnities: balls and dinners in Colombo, and meeting His Royal Highness. Where would Ceylon be without the bloody planters and the income they brought to the bloody economy? Ceylon would never survive without tea. No English planter worth his salt would miss shaking hands with His Royal Highness.

Jack agreed. He had been a few times, by now, to the Hatton-Eliya Club. At first he'd been anxious about crossing Henshaw's path, and certainly nervous about meeting De Jurgen again. De Jurgen had passed him at the bar as if he did not exist, averting his gaze, his face stiff, but Henshaw had been a gentleman. The planters' instinct to stick together extended to their non-white comrades as needed, and Jack's new position as *periya dorai* of Madeniya, with a thousand labourers under him, deserved genuine recognition.

"Congratulations, old chap. You deserve it." Henshaw extended his hand in a firm handshake and offered to get Jack a whisky.

"Same thing, Gilmor, whisky and a touch of Lanka lime?" he asked, smiling wryly.

No one questioned that Gilmor was there to help coordinate Independence celebrations for the district, along with Ratnapura, Hatton-Eliya, Uva, and Kandy. He was perfectly acceptable and accepted (though only to a certain point). Jack still yearned for that moment, which would surely come one day, when he would be invited to be an associate member in the illustrious club with its heavy colonial mahogany woodwork, hushed lounges, and wide staircases. Only men were allowed through the front doors; ladies came through a side entrance by invitation only. Over the hearth were portraits of

His Majesty King George VI and Queen Elizabeth wearing a diamond tiara. A portrait of Winston Churchill hung in an alcove. For God and King! The billiard room was ringed with stags' heads on the walls, with plaques indicating who had shot them. A sign reading *The Rules of the Game of Rangoon Snooker* was nailed to the wall. In another corner stood an elephant's foot, its leg chopped off below the knee. "Jolly good shot!" Nearby on the wall was a large map of the planters' districts of Ceylon and the principal estates. All as it should be. With pride he deliberately let slip, casually (one did not boast, something the English despised), that his daughter was at Kandy Convent and his elder son was about to become a boarder at the Catholic boarding school, Holy Innocents. He knew how much this was taken for granted by the English.

"Yes, my son is in upper fifth there," said Chapman, a youngish, ruddy-looking Catholic Englishman, who had not been in the colony for long. You could tell, from his fierce sunburn, that he had not yet learned how to protect his sensitive English skin. "Damn good school, I'd say. Anderson went there, I hear."

Jack basked in the glow of this new bond with Chapman, a fine Englishman.

Yet he felt a pang of guilt. Aidan did not want to go to public school; he cried constantly with a deep sorrow. Aidan was a sensitive child with a good heart, Jack realized. But all the more reason for him to mix with other boys, toughen him up, like English boys. Aidan was too young to understand the advantage of a public school education at a top Catholic boarding school, Jack told himself; it was a passport to the professions, to the coveted Ceylon civil service, and to tea planting. (Creepers were chosen from senior prefects at St. Thomas's, St. Peter's and Holy Innocents, as everyone knew.)

All the English planters sent their children away to the best public schools. It was a given.

33.

"**D**AMN AWFUL," TITUS DELANEY CRIED. "He only seven."
The Delaneys, especially old Titus, were all opposed to Aidan being sent away to boarding school at such a young age.

"Well, I went to St. Sylvester's Prep at six," Jack pointed out.

Neville, Mildred's oldest brother, who had been educated at Cambridge, suggested sending Aidan to St. Thomas School in Mutwal, where his son Nathaniel boarded. Nathaniel, a brilliant student, came home every weekend. "The two cousins would be together, so boarding wouldn't be such a shock," said Miriam, Neville's wife. She was German-Jewish, tall and lean and analytical.

Jack no longer spoke to her. For one thing, she was an agnostic—no, an outright atheist—and very outspoken for a woman. She'd once contradicted Jack, in front of everyone, saying that the Catholic Church was no saint, and that in the Middle Ages the popes themselves had married and even had concubines and illegitimate children galore. Jack had been incensed. He now thought of Miriam as "that woman of Neville's." She also went around dressed in a sari, for God's sake, and spoke Sinhalese like a native, opening up conversations with village women here and there and everywhere, to Jack's annoyance. (A clear eccentric.)

Everyone in the family, it seemed, had an opinion about Aidan. They'd gathered at the Normandy estate around Grandfather Titus Delaney, the autocrat, with his wispy white

beard, narrow, sensitive face, and piercing eyes. A decent old
chap, really. Jack was fond of him; as a father-in-law he seldom interfered. But he was stubborn (and another atheist). It
was absolutely imperative that Aidan not board with him, as
he wanted. "Aidan can live with me, Jack, and go to school
as a day scholar, as all my boys did. He can go home to you
every weekend."

Aidan's little face had lit up. "Oh, can I, Daddy?"

If only they would understand. Boarding-school education in
an elite public school was essential, the passport to everything.
Of course Aidan would be a boarder.

Tears welled. Aidan burst into deep sobs. Second *appu* had
strapped his trunk, and saluted. It stood in the hallway of the
new estate bungalow at Madeniya, ready for first servant to
put in Daddy's car.

He knew he was to attend Daddy's old boarding school outside Kandy. Fiona was already at Kandy Convent with Lally.
"Fiona didn't cry when she went away," said Daddy.

"Cry, Aidan. Cry! Cry!" laughed Scottie, dancing around
his desolate brother. "Cry! Go on. Cry! Cry! You're going
away to school."

"Rascal!" said Daddy affectionately, tweaking Scott's ear.
"You'll be going one day yourself."

Aidan understood he was to be made into an Englishman.

"Come, now, son. It's not so bad."

"You'll like it once you settle in," said Mama hopefully.
"There'll be boys your own age to play with. You have no one
here, only Scottie. You'll make friends...."

He hadn't missed having friends on the tea estate. He'd had
Fiona and Scottie and Lally. And Ganesh the gardener.

"Oh, forget Ganesh. He was no suitable companion, an old
Tamil servant. That was the old days, anyway, at Weyweltalawa."

They wanted the best for him, he knew. And the best was an

English education. They wanted him to speak English fluently (and get rid of that damn colonial Ceylonese sing-song he'd picked up from the servants). Boarding school was the tradition of the great public schools of England, the custom of English aristocracy, but it was alien to the customs of Ceylon, Granpa Delaney pointed out.

"But I'm only seven, Daddy." Aidan had wanted to cry.

Aidan pulled at his uncomfortable school tie that was choking him, the stiff, scratchy school shirt buttoned to the throat in this heat, the heavy drill shorts and heavy cloth blazer ordered from England, and the tight, scrunchy, hard shoes that pinched his toes—ugly, ugly. He was used to running barefoot like a village boy. Well, all that would have to stop now.

"Fine uniform, *podi mathia*," said the Sinhalese servant with a smile.

The servants bowed to Aidan, putting their hands to their foreheads. Why bow? Servants never had before. Aidan burst into more tears. Oh, he wished he were back at Weyweltalawa going fishing with Ganesh, dressed in his little cotton vest and under drawers.

Sobbing, Aidan gripped his little overnight bag bravely. He tried to understand, but couldn't, that he was being sent away from Daddy and Mama, from his home—alone. Mama hugged him goodbye. He did not understand for how long. Now Scottie would be at home, alone, and he would have Mama and Daddy all to himself.

"...Good for you, son."

"It's a hell of a thing, Jack, man," said Uncle Ted, glancing sympathetically at Aidan, "sending the poor little devil away. And you've cut off his curls." Uncle Ted turned around in the front seat of the Morris and winked at Aidan, and passed him a stick of gum. "Cheer up, old fellow."

Uncle Ted had joined them to keep Daddy company on the lonely journey back. He was Mama's older brother, though

not as old as Uncle Neville. Ted was Daddy's favourite brother-in-law—everyone knew that. Tall, fair (fairer than all the
other Delaney brothers and sisters, that is, who were dark
skinned like Mama), he was always cheerful and laughing.
Ted enjoyed a drink and a joke. "Heard the one about the
priest, the rabbi and the yogi, Jack?" He played the guitar in
the evenings with Granpa Delaney out on the verandah of his
cocoa plantation. He'd written some poems once for the *Ceylon
Times*. The caption had called him "Our Eurasian Poet," with
an accompanying photograph. *I lie in the lull of a tropical day,
longing for I know not what....* He was not a member of any
club; he was too poor. He spent his time wandering about his
father Titus's small coconut plantation, "pretending to work,"
Daddy would tease.

Uncle Ted knew the opposition of the family to Aidan going
to boarding-school and was on Aidan's side. "Wouldn't put
my dog with those priests." (Perhaps he was a socialist, like
Uncle Quintus and Granpa Delaney.)

The socialists in the family were against him going away. So
I'm a socialist, too, then, thought Aidan, feeling the burden.

They reached Kandy in the evening. He saw a row of tall King
palms and kitul trees along the dusty streets; shops with corrugated iron roofs, covered with trailing bougainvillea; and street
vendors cooking over glowing little coals, roasting chestnuts
and rolling little *wadi* balls in their palms. There was the great,
famous Kandy Temple of the Tooth. A row of *bhikkhus* with
shaved heads and folded arms, looking younger than himself,
wended single file along a sandy path by the lake on their way
to evening *puja*. They were dressed in saffron robes. Were the
little boys happy after being sent away from home so young?
The lake glowed violet in the evening calm.

It was a small Sinhalese town with a dusty main street.
Thatched houses on shaded dirt paths peered out, half hidden
among palms. A cow wandered across the road and some pea

hens clucked. The river ran by the school, the great Mahaweli Ganga, slow, insidious, murky-yellow.

The school nestled behind wrought-iron gates. Low brown wooden buildings that had once been used as army barracks by British soldiers during the war were the buildings for the younger boys. There was a low dark chapel and an oval cricket pitch. A statue of the Blessed Virgin Mary stood gazing down; Aidan thought he saw pity in her eyes. There was also a small Buddhist temple off to the side, near a gateway. He heard Pali chanting in the distance, musical and low.

The school motto—*Ad Astra*—was written over the door in Latin. To the stars. Aidan began to sob.

"No, Daddy, please Daddy, no, no, don't leave me here," he cried, tears running down his face again and dripping onto his new shirt. "No, no! I'll be good, Daddy. Please no."

"Aw, this is damn awful, Jack," said Uncle Ted. "What the hell are you doing this to Aidan for, man? He's just a little kid. Look at his tears."

"Well, I went."

"Damn cruel. I'll never ever do this to a son of mine, man," declared Ted, who was a confirmed bachelor. He patted Aidan and wiped his tears.

They were ushered into the headmaster's room. Father Antonius was grave. "Welcome, Mr. Gilmor. Always a pleasure to have the sons of old Holy Innocents boys return to our hallowed halls." Daddy subscribed to *Lux Coeli*, the alumni magazine.

They walked over to the dormitories for the junior boys, called the Sunrise Cottages, where Aidan was to live. "Please Daddy..." But the words would not come. Daddy was so proud that Aidan was going to boarding school, that he was wearing an English uniform like an English schoolboy, and that he would receive an English education. Aidan's eyes brimmed again with tears; there was an overwhelming sadness, a burden that he now felt, to live up to Daddy's hopes and pride in him.

"Goodbye, son."

One last hug. Uncle Ted saying, "Damn shame" again as Aidan sobbed and sobbed. Then they were gone.

34.

"COME ALONG, AIDAN," said Miss Goonetekele, the matron of Sunrise Cottages. She was a stocky, kind Sinhalese woman dressed in a white uniform. "You'll soon get used to things. This is your bed."

The dormitory was a long low wooden room with about twenty narrow beds in two rows. The walls were bare brown wood, which gave the room a sombre effect. There was a row of small windows that let in a pale, greenish light; it was like being underwater. At the far end were lavatories that smelled of urine and dettol, wash-basins, and showers.

There was nowhere to hang his clothes.

"Oh, they go with the other boys' things in that large cupboard."

Miss Goonetekele gave Aidan a small wash-basin, a bar of soap, and a small face towel. These were his, and were to be kept beside his bed on the small bed-stand provided. Each boy had the same stand and wash things, all in a row. She showed him a large open cupboard area where he was to hang his clothes, which had all been labelled by the servant at Madeniya.

He heard a loud bell. It was time for afternoon tea: bread and butter and tea in the long refectory. There was a din—boys' voices, loud and strong, startling him after the quiet solitude of the tea estate. The boys were brown skinned, like himself, some of them likely Burghers, Eurasians, or Muslims. He felt confused, dazed. Tears rose in his eyes, and he tried to bite into the unfamiliar bread, which was fresh and good. You could eat all you wanted. A prefect, a tall, dark-skinned boy, maybe a Tamil, strode down the aisle with a switch. He cracked it over Aidan's hands. His hands stung. He suppressed the cry. What had he done?

"New boy, what name?"

"Aidan Gilmor, s-sir."

"Upcountry?"

"M-Madeniya."

"Huh, low country. Kegalle District."

The college was huge; he would never find his way around. He was taken on a tour of the school by a prefect, who showed him long corridors, large rooms leading to more rooms, the chemistry room, the library, a room for this, a room for that, and finally the long dormitories, including one for seniors which was called the senior wing. (How long would he be staying here? Forever and ever.) There were the priests' quarters: "You don't ever go there. Off limits."

He felt sick when he went to use the lavatory. A stained, foul toilet bowl overflowed with boys' defecations, bubbling up, and crawling with cockroaches. A chain hung mid-air. When you flushed there was a hissing, gurgling noise but no water. The water tank was empty; the whole sewage system was backed up. The smell was foul. He didn't want to put his small buttocks over the bowl; the thought of cockroaches crawling up his bum made him sick, but he had to urinate. He began to cry, huge sobs welling up again. This was so terrible. Daddy surely couldn't know about this. He stood a little distance from the bowl, aimed his penis at the hole, and let his pee fall where it may, then ran.

At lights out a monitor said: "*Pace cum vobis.*"

Under his blanket Aidan could hear distant chanting again. This time it was coming through the open windows from the Buddhist temple far below, beyond the wrought-iron gates; the monks were intoning the Pali scriptures. He whispered his own prayer to himself, gripping his scapula (a relic of St. Anthony, a piece of his hair or maybe a tiny shard of his bone, wrapped in a little cloth pouch that he'd been given at his First Communion.)

"Please, St. Anthony, please let Daddy come and take me away soon. Please, oh please…. Oh please…."

35.

WHAT THE HELL WENT WRONG? Senanayake had failed to get a majority. The figures told the sorry tale. In the new House of Representatives, which was supposed to lead Ceylon into historic Independence, a quarter of the MPs were socialist. They belonged to that damn new LSSP, the Lanka Sama Samaja Party, which the people called the Equal Rights Party.

Worse, Ponnambalam, the Tamil leader of the All Ceylon Tamil Congress party, had culled thirty-three percent of the vote. He, now, unbelievably, held the balance of power!

The English tea planters were consuming extra pints at the club, in shock. "To think that those Trotskyites stole so many votes from Don!" echoed Ethel Henshaw, speaking for the English ladies who sat together in a clique at the exclusive Hatton-Eliya Club.

The Muslim waiters, decked in smart uniforms with bright brass buttons and cheery red fezes, were kept busy.

No one underestimated the significance of the situation. Senanayake now had to rely on Ponnambalam and the All Ceylon Tamil Congress to prop up his government, which, of course, made Ponnambalam the king-maker. He lost no time using his new power to demand protection of Tamil rights. An unbelievable turn of events. But the real hidden power, to the more astute observer, lay with the estate Tamil labourers.

The Sinhalese wives at the Kegalle Club were equally shocked, but also mortified and genuinely confused that their own Tamil workers—coolies!—had had a secret agenda all along. It was outrageous that they had supported a party of their own, the Ceylon Indian Congress—with the stress on "Indian." They had had the temerity to vote against their masters—the ingrates. The estate labourers had actually captured seven seats in the new parliament, thereby boosting the total number of Tamil seats. The ladies could not imagine how the coolies had even *known* how to vote! Someone, perhaps that infuriating Quintus Delaney, must have shown them how to scrawl an *x* on a ballot, which only showed how vulnerable the election process was. To think that a bunch of illiterate coconut-heads who lived in stinking hovels had virtually created a balance of power for the Tamils. (The Sinhalese ladies understood that right away.)

"Well, there are government schools on many estates," murmured Mildred, sipping a Lanka lime. "The labourers are not all illiterate, especially the younger ones."

Mrs. Abeyasinghe and Mrs. Wijeratne bristled. "And much thanks we are getting for it!"

But—coolies!

The figures showed it. The Tamil labourers had not only accrued seven seats in the House of Representatives for the Ceylon Indian Congress, but had also influenced the outcome of twenty other constituencies, preventing the UNP from getting a majority. Astounding.

Infuriating.

Senanayake now had to play his cards carefully to stay in power as first prime minister of an independent Ceylon. The trick was to get Ponnambalam, leader of the All Ceylon Tamil Congress, to come on-side, which proved not to be difficult.

G.G. Ponnambalam, though he liked calling himself a "proud Dravidian," was not so different from Senanayake. Both men belonged to the same elite class, and both had been English-educated: Ponnambalam was Cambridge-educated (Christ College), English-speaking, and very wealthy, a *vellala* caste; and Senanayake was high-caste *goigama*. Both families had investments in rubber plantations, plumbago mines, what have you. They were cut from the same cloth, when it came down to it, scorned the Marxists. Ponnambalam certainly had no more concern for the poor Tamil coolies than Senanayake. It never occurred to either of them—or to the new Sinhalese nation—that a Tamil tea picker, or a lowly urban working-class Sinhalese, could be prime minister, as in Britain. A Clement Atlee (son of a lowly local teacher) or a Lloyd George (nephew of a shoemaker who lived in an outlandish little village in Wales with an unpronounceable name) for prime minister of Ceylon? Never.

So Senanayake offered Ponnambalam a post in the new Cabinet, and Ponnambalam, of course, capitulated, mumbling something about it being best perhaps to be more moderate in his views after all. "*Ootha!*" cried the Left-leaning Tamils. What the fuck!

Well, what else was new in this world? the tea planters wondered. They felt they had seen it all. The carrot had been a plum cabinet post; it was smart move by Senanayake. (He'd learned well from the British.)

So Ponnambalam crossed the floor. It was a sensation.

"*Athiku-ootha!*" Mother-fucker! cried the Tamils, enraged. "*Saklian!*"

But Senanayake, the wily old bugger, also invited a Sinhalese orator, Bandaranaike, to join the cabinet. Young Bandaranaike—SWRD, as he liked to be called—was the leader of the new Lanka Maha Sabha. Oxford-educated, he was a match for Ponnambalam in debating, his skills having been honed at the Oxford Debating Union. The House was spellbound at their performances on the floor, and so was the country. Even the planters took note, those able to get their shortwave radios working, that is.

They represented two nationalisms in a verbal duel: Ponnambalam for the Tamils, Bandaranaike for the Sinhalese. (In a sense, they also represented Cambridge versus Oxford, which appealed to the English planters' sensibilities.) No one seemed to notice that their brilliant nationalistic speeches were delivered in English. "*Aiyo!*" sneered the Buddhist monks. The *Sangha* in the Temple of the Tooth was simmering, as always, in indignation. Why weren't parliamentary sittings conducted in Sinhala? they hissed. The English ladies at Hatton-Eliya recoiled. The monks couldn't possibly mean it. MPs speaking in Sinhala?

Senanayake continued to speak the English language, ignoring the *bhikkhus*. All was well.

The official opposition was now socialist: the Lanka Sama Samaja Party, or the "Equal Rights Party," which was propped up by the Tamil labourers.

"Ridiculous!" cried the planters' wives.

Something would have to be done about it, vowed Senanayake.

36.

A SLIM WAVE OF GOLDEN LIGHT seeped through a gap in the Venetian blinds, which meant it was around five-thirty. Mildred was slumped next to him, buried in the sheet, her curly dark hair pressed against the pillow. Her nightgown had fallen open, revealing full, rounded breasts with long, dark nipples. There was a tentative knock on the door and the new houseboy, Sisera, appeared with the bed-tea. Jack sat up.

"*Sa-bhah u dhaa-sah-nahk, podi.*" Good morneeng, sahib. He parted the mosquito net and placed the tray carefully over Jack's knees, his eyes skirting away from Memsahib Mildred's breasts.

"*Sthoo-thiy,* Sisera."

"You are wanting any more else, *podi*?"

"Hmph."

The boy saluted and quietly closed the door.

The day slowly dawned with the scent of eucalyptus, the shriek of peacocks and mynah birds from the aviary, and various clunking noises: banging of pans from the outside kitchen, water being sprayed. The drift of heat was already rising, violet and sweet, over the distant hills. It was a moment he loved: pre-dawn—that soft pearly light seeping over the mountains; the sky the hue of a tamarind tree before the gentle buds open; the freshness of a new dawn, a new earth, before life stepped in.

Today was the day that Senanayake, whom Jack liked and admired but did not entirely trust, and Ponnambalam, the leader of the Ceylon Tamils whom he definitely did *not* entirely trust, were to hack out the future of the bloody country. Unlike the Sinhalese, the Tamils had not been pleased with the new constitution proposed by Senanayake, based on the old British Soulbury Commission.

As Jack understood it, what Ponnambalam wanted was "equal-equal" power, fifty-fifty in the state council—half Tamil, half Sinhalese. The Ceylon Tamils had always been in government service under the British. They spoke excellent, fluent English and were loyal to the British Crown. Consequently they had always been favoured and given high positions in the coveted Ceylon civil service and the professional classes. They had served the British well.

Now the Tamils feared a backlash from the Sinhalese majority, once the British handed over power in February. Ponnambalam had warned that that there was no provision to prevent *administrative* discrimination against them. *Oothi*!

But the British in Westminster knew that a fifty-fifty distribution of seats would infuriate the Sinhalese. The Muslims were also against it. (Where would a fifty-fifty split leave *them*?) Besides, the British had their commercial and industrial interests to consider. In the end, scorned Quintus, only British interests would be protected.

Jack listened, aghast, as Senanayake enunciated his famous words to the Tamils, which were later taken up and echoed profusely in the *Island* and the *Times of Ceylon*: "I would not refuse bread because it's not cake!"

"Bloody hell!"

Independence day was definitely set for February 4, 1948.

The Tamils seethed. The labourers on the estates were restive. There were clandestine meetings by torchlight after dark, down by the river, in their homemade *kovil*.

"Where the hell *was* Ponnambalam, their leader, at this moment of crisis?" they cried. He was across the ocean, in Whitehall, desperately trying to make a last-ditch effort to persuade the British to give the Tamils fifty-fifty representation and equal language rights. Of course, the wily British were going to do no such thing. They cited the "noble intentions" of Senanayake. After all, Don was an old boy from St. Thomas College. Its motto: *Manliness and Truth*.

37.

ALL WEEK JACK HAD FLOWN the new Ceylon flag emblazoned with the lion and scimitar from the roof of the tea factory. The gold, triumphant Sinhala lion, now in power. Overnight he felt he was in a different country, that he had suddenly become another person. For the first time, he was aware of the Sinhalese half of himself, and he felt a certain unfamiliar pride. (He did not ask himself why he was spending thousands of rupees trying to make his son a little Englishman at Holy Innocents.)

"The British are granting us our freedom," he cried, swept away by an unfamiliar emotion.

"Well, they took it away from us in the first place, man," said Quintus.

Quintus had a bush of wiry black hair and piercing black eyes, like his father, Titus, Jack's father-in-law. He was short and swarthy, with a heavyset face that showed his ancient Kandyan lineage from his mother's side. He barely remembered her.

The few English planters at the Kegalle Club had gone to Colombo to watch the Independence Day ceremonies from the planters' compound. The planters had been important to the British economy; tea always held pride of place. Jack and Mildred, like most of the modest planters, had stayed behind. It was seeding and transplanting time in the nurseries, though Jack gave his workers the day off to celebrate independence. But the Tamil workers had retreated to their coolie lines;

the women were making special foods over open fires and the drummers were thumping their drums ominously. Jack understood why the coolies were not overly jubilant. "What would independence bring us, with the Sinhalese in power?" an old *kelavar* had appealed to Jack. They looked in dubious silence at the new Ceylon flag flying over their heads, above the factory. Gone was the Union Jack they'd revered.

All day Jack had been twiddling with his shortwave radio to hear on-the-spot commentary from Vernon Correa, Ceylon's "golden voice of radio." Bursts of cheers and the loud, truncated blare of percussion bands, Scottish bagpipes whining in the background, could be heard from the parade ground at Independence Square in Colombo. This was followed by the cold nasal twang of the true English accent of His Excellency, accompanied by sudden high whines, whistles, and rapid Morse-code-like pips emanating from the radio. "God bless Ceylon, G-G-God bless our c-c-country." Vernon's mellifluous voice spluttered across the radio waves and up the mountains, and Jack's eyes filled with tears; he felt the stirrings of deep emotion.

"Come now, pet, no need of tears on this day." He was experiencing, once again, an unexpected flood of national love for his new Sinhalese country, for that Sinhalese part of himself, so long buried. Mildred had a more cautious, balanced view, typical of her reserved nature, which had been one of the reasons he'd fallen in love with her. "Yes, it is good the country is free of British rule, pet. No one likes to be under the power of someone else."

Titus Delaney, Quintus, and Ted had driven to Madeniya to join Jack and Mildred. They were to watch the day's ceremony at the Kegalle clubhouse. A projector and screen had been rigged up in the lounge by "Tiny" Amesekere. The planters and their families were to watch the day's events on the *British Pathé News* after sundown.

Hard drinking was already underway. The celebration was

tempered somewhat by the presence of the Sinhalese members and their wives, swathed in saris—it was a sobering thought that they were now the ones in power in their saris and sarongs. They were the new rulers.

The older English planters knocked back some serious whisky.

Jack and Mildred, along with Titus, Ted, and Quintus sat in the darkness of the club lounge with the other planters and their wives. They stared, hypnotized, at the independence festivities playing out before them on the large makeshift screen. Their faces were uplifted with sardonic but amazed expressions as they watched the regimental march-past on Independence Square, accompanied by the swish of Sinhalese soldiers' kilts. A Sinhalese children's choir sang the new anthem. "History in the making," intoned the commentator.

The first Ceylonese prime minister of Ceylon, Don Senanayake, decked in English black coat and tails and top hat, Prince Henry, Duke of Gloucester, in a morning suit, and the Duchess in a tailored English suit, carved hat, and pearls, received the Salute. Prince Henry was greeted by the new governor general of Ceylon, Sir Henry Monck-Mason Moore. Another salute. The Sinhalese dignitaries bowed low to their Highnesses.

"Bloody rot," muttered Titus in the gloom. "Sh-sh-shush!" from the audience.

They watched as Mrs. Mollie Dunuwila Senanayake, Senanayake's wife, dressed in full sari, curtsied low before Prince Henry. "How long did she practise *that*?" quipped Quintus. More *sh-sh-shs* from the spectators in the dark. But the Delaneys and Gilmors were in fact as awed and silent as anyone else, overtaken by the event whirring before their eyes. The old Kandyan throne of their great-grandparents' era had been resurrected from somewhere and buffed up for the event, blessed by the *Sangha*, who sat in pride of place on the dais. (A faint anxious shudder rippled through the Catholic Church, no doubt.) The throne was symbolic; it represented the return of the Sinhalese to power for the first time since their defeat by the British in 1815, an event that had been foretold by the astrologers and soothsayers.

"It's the end of an era," said Titus.

The Sinhalese wives, the only ones who knew the words, joined in singing the anthem of new independent Ceylon loudly, the words echoing round the club: "Namo maaa-thaa Lanka..."

Namo nama Matha
Sundara siri barini...
Surandi athi...
"*Mother Sri Lanka, oh Mother Lanka, we salute thee...*"

The new lion flag flew bravely on top of the Kegalle clubhouse.

Meanwhile, up at the elite whites-only Hatton-Eliya Club, feelings ran equally high. "I can't believe it! February 4, 1948, Independence Day," said Ethel Henshaw to Nettie Matthews. She felt dazed, as if someone had hit her on the head with a mallet.

"A Ceylonese government," echoed Nettie, equally astonished. The worst fears of the English planters had been fulfilled.

The jubilant sound of Sinhalese tom-toms had been ringing all over the island, night and day. Tamil drums were more dour.

The Sinhalese servant put down the silver tray on the low rattan table between the ladies; it was replete with a silver teapot, a spare pot of hot water for seconds, and comforting English bone china, cups, and saucers imported from Worcestershire decades ago. There were still servants, thank God, though ignored, of course, by the English ladies. Essential to "keep up face." The servants seemed sullen, resentful. They had the power now; they were not going to smile and be pleasant for the English anymore, observed Nettie Matthews. "*Comme ci, comme ça.*"

It was unreal. The country was no longer His Majesty's Crown colony. Mrs. Henshaw's hand trembled as she lifted the teapot to pour, struggling to absorb what had happened. A brown-skinned prime minister—call him Sinhalese or what you will—was now in charge. Senanayake was already en-sconced in Government House (the King's House!). He also had a family house in Cinnamon Gardens, the enclave of the rich and powerful, where nary a British planter would ever have the money to find himself.

"Don Stephen Senanayake," repeated Nettie Matthews, as one citing a foreign dictator new on the world scene. At least he had good English Christian names, for all his Buddhism. Ostensibly a "simple villager," as he'd presented himself for the stupid rural voter, he'd been born in the Sinhalese suburb of Botale, Negombo, in what was already being referred to as "*former* British Ceylon." His family kept Buddhist *poya* days. (Gone, the power of the Christian Church in one fell blow.)

Ethel Henshaw's lips tightened in a firm line. She would not be one to desert the fold at this hour, she said. (However, she'd sent her two girls and son back "home" in the care of the Foresters, who had booked a berth on any P&O liner available at the first breath of independence.) The Foresters had feared the inevitable collapse of the tea industry without the British at the helm. Nettie Matthews had it that the new constitution, fashioned by Lord Soulbury, was British. A British constitution. Well, that changed prospects considerably. Whoever heard of a Sinhalese constitution?

The men had a more optimistic view. They'd been knocking back more than a few whiskies—straight. Ceylon was still in the British Commonwealth, a new Dominion, which was a relatively recent concept devised by Westminster. This would keep them in the fold. That was important.

"Damn right too," was the general consensus. "Where would Ceylon be without British administrative know-how, British engineers, British culture, language, and education?" cried Dawlish, *periya dorai* of Killarney.

"I'd damn well say so!" echoed his fellow tea planter, Riordan.

They knocked back a few more whiskies and several toddies.

As in the Kegalle Club, a projector and screen had been rigged up in the lounge of the Hatton-Eliya Club for the planters and their families to watch the day's events on the British Pathé News.

They watched in silence as His Royal Highness Prince Henry; Lord Soulbury, the former governor of Ceylon; Sir Henry Monck-Mason Moore, the new governor general; and Prime Minister D.S. Senanayake executed the transition of power from imperial Britain to the new, independent former colony of Ceylon. A wall of coconuts and pineapples had been strung up on a great *pandal* in Colombo to greet Their Royal Highnesses: "Welcome to Ceylon, Your Royal Highnesses." A large placard was also strung over the road, on which Their Highnesses' photographs had been affixed.

"Coconuts and pineapples?" cried Ethel Henshaw. "Well!"

Prince Henry, the king's younger brother and the duchess sat on a royal dais. The prince, a balding, round-faced, middle-aged man dressed in a naval uniform with enough medals on his lapels to sink a ship, looked bored. He wore the sash of the Order of the Royal Garter across his chest. The duchess was in white, with a tiara on her head. The planters especially admired the duke's majesterial stance. With his straight spine and stiff upper lip, he appeared to be the epitome of Englishness as he saluted at the flag-raising ceremony in Independence Square. There were military bands and a march-past. It was gratifying at least that Senanayake and the Sinhalese had to swear fealty to His Majesty King George VI, who was represented by the new governor general, Sir Henry Monck-Mason Moore, who now was symbolically the "king of Ceylon."

"Damn right, too!" cried Dawlish.

The signing of the declaration followed. In attendance, droned the voice of the commentator, were His Royal Highness Prince Henry, His Excellency Sir Henry Monck-Mason Moore, Prime Minister D.S. Senanayake, C.H. Mulhall, Sir Oliver Goonetilleke, and Sir Arthur Ranasinghe. A children's choir sang the new national anthem, "*Namo mah-thaa lanka*," again in Sinhalese.

The English planters and their wives didn't understand a word. Then the British national anthem was played for the last time. To a man, the planters rose, standing stiffly at attention, drinks in hand: "God save our gracious King!"

"I give you the King!"

"The King, I say!"

"The King!"

As the old Union Jack was lowered, there was a low *Ah-h* from the audience. "Damn shame," echoed the older planters. "A lot of British boys died for that." The new Sinhalese flag of Ceylon—with the single gold lion holding a curved Kastane sword in its right paw, symbol of authority—was raised, followed by a sombre silence from the audience.

"Bugger the Ceylon flag!" cried young Horton, suddenly; he was *sinna dorai* of Carlisle. He dashed outside onto the verandah, unfurled the Union Jack, and hoisted it defiantly to the top mast of the Hatton-Eliya clubhouse flagpole.

"And that's where it's damn well going to stay!"

38.

AIDAN HAD LITTLE IDEA of the great changes transforming his country. He quietly mourned the disappearance of Mama and Daddy in his life, and prayed on his knees nightly for their return, still wearing his little hairy scapula over his chest under his vest, as penance. He hardly understood Father St. Sebastian when, after morning mass in chapel, he reminded the students of the special Independence Day holiday.

Great-Aunt Agnes, the mother of his second cousin Colin, appeared mysteriously in the visitors' room at Sunrise Cottage. Auntie wore a gracious English linen frock with rows of pearls at her throat, like Queen Elizabeth, and a large, woven sunhat; she also carried a parasol. In honour of Independence Day, she was taking Aidan and her son Colin out to the English cake shop in Kandy and then for lunch at Queen's Hotel. The boys should know that the rule of the British was over.

After English cakes, doughy and sickly-sweet, they visited the zoo. They observed caged birds and animals, and watched the elephants being bathed in their compound. They saw a tiger and a lion. A small cheetah paced back and forth in its cage, its red fiery eyes wild and desperate. Longing for freedom, thought Aidan piteously. He longed to undo the bolt.

"Fine specimen," said the Sinhalese keeper.

They had lunch, sitting nicely in Queen's Hotel, the boys keeping their elbows in. White-coated Sinhalese waiters served them dainty cucumber sandwiches, so English, and mango ice cream with kitul treacle sauce. How Aidan loved Auntie.

The new Ceylon flag now hung in the corner next to a photograph of D.S. Senanayake and the King and Queen of England, who were far away in Buckingham Palace.

"That is the lion of our ancient Kandyan kings, from whom you are descended on your mother's side," said Auntie Agnes. She had never mentioned this fact before, that the Sinhalese people were descended from a lion.

"Now we're bloody royalty descended from lions," muttered Granpa Titus Delaney when Aidan informed him and Uncle Quintus later of this during the holidays.

"*Half* royal," Uncle Quintus was to quip, laughing mysteriously.

Auntie Gracie smiled and wiped her lips discreetly with a linen napkin. Queen's Hotel was gracious, colonial at its best: white-coated waiters, white linen on the tables, and decorous flowers, frangipani and orchids. The waiters clicked their heels and bowed when you asked for more water please, with lime. "You will remember this day, boys. Today marks the passing of an empire."

Aidan understood that perhaps he might no longer be an English boy. Yet he could not imagine being Sinhalese. He did not want to be bare-chested; he did not want to wear a sarong and go to temple with a shorn head. He already *was* a little Englishman.

Colin was one of the smartest boys in Holy Innocents; he had gotten all As on his report card. Did the priests know they were cousins? Colin was a fine orator, and the priests held him in high esteem. He was also a cottage prefect now that he was fourteen. He understood "Independence."

"Mama, do we still stand for the King at the end of the film at the Regal Theatre?"

Auntie considered. She had a silver dish of ice cream, which she tackled daintily with a long silver spoon.

"We-ell, I'm sure they will be playing the British national

anthem *and* the Sinhalese anthem (which had not yet been finally approved), so you can stand for both."

"Is Senanayake King of Ceylon now?"

"No. Sir Henry Monck-Mason Moore is our new Governor General. He is living in King's House—now Government House—in Colombo. He also can stay at the King's Pavilion here in Kandy whenever he is choosing, and also can be taking a break if needed at King's Cottage, Nuwara Eliya." She pronounced it as one word, "Nareliya."

"He will be representing King George VI at the opening of parliament and at military parades."

Auntie paused. "His Excellency Sir Henry Monck-Mason Moore is King of Ceylon."

Say what you will about the transition on February 4, 1948, it had been peaceful. There was none of the bloody slaughter that went with Indian Idependence and the Partition, observed the planters. Smooth sailing all the way, the said, not a machete raised.

But it was over, the great British Empire in Ceylon. Now that new Sinhalese fellow Bandaranaike was on the rise. Senanayake should watch it. He was a snake in the grass, that Bandaranaike, the leader of the so-called Maha Sama Sabha, Great Sinhala Association or some such thing. He actually wanted the education system—all the schools—to be conducted in the Sinhalese language. "Imagine, Shakespeare—*Romeo and Juliet*—acted in Sinhalese!" cried Nettie Matthews. Absolutely dangerous fellow, agreed the planters. Called himself "SWRD"—Solomon West Ridgeway Dias, or "Solly" to his friends. "I ask you," said Nettie Matthews.

Tall, lean, urbane, and Oxford-educated, young Bandaranaike smoked a pipe like an Englishman. He was an intellectual, another Sinhalese nationalist nutcase.

The planters agreed something should be done about that crackpot.

Quintus and the leftists were claiming that Ceylon Independence had been "a fraud," damnably so. Take the post of Governor General, for instance, cried Quintus loudly at the club. Damn insult. *King of Ceylon!* Laughable. Same old trickery.

The Sinhalese were now the ones in power, holding the reins. But the British still held the whip.

Dawlish knocked back another whisky at the club. He was the top planter in the district and well-known to Jack and other planters. But all that was over; he'd be off on the *Stratheden* before the monsoon now that Independence had come. He would try his luck in Australia with the Aussies. They had the colour bar, but he was on the right side of it. He had no intention of living under bloody Sinhalese rule, he growled to the planters standing at the bar. He'd had enough of watching the so-called celebrations of Independence on the bloody screen, What was there to celebrate?

Many an English and European planter was single. They either had English wives who were back home in England, or they took "country" wives (like Jack's own grandfather, that old bastard Gilmor) or, like Dawlish and Renforth, they simply sampled the beautiful little Tamil girls who were all around them on the plantations, Jack reflected. And he knew all about that. Planters like Dawlish had the *kangeny* pluck a girl from the terraces. When he tired of her, she was dumped at the edge of a field or back in the coolie lines. She was not good for much once she'd been used; no Tamil would touch her. She became the slave of the *kangeny*.

Mrs. Henshaw and Mrs. Matthews stuck close to their husbands. But those native gals were used to it, they told themselves; their morals were quite different from those of English girls.

Jack was aware—indeed, it was common knowledge—that Dawlish and his mate Renforth frequented the brothels of Colombo when they made the monthly journey into the city to pick up the labourers' wages. They made it a regular weekend of debauchery with plump, luscious, Tamil tarts—"little fucking sluts" Dawlish called them. (Jack would recoil when they boasted about picking up Sinhalese or Eurasian women in the back streets of Colombo, and their nights in cheap hotels. He had not known white men to speak like this about women. What happened to *manliness, truth, and gentility?*)

Jack was certainly not sorry to see the back of those two in Ceylon. Nor the other planters like them that were part of the exodus from Ceylon at Independence.

39.

THERE WAS MRS. GUNESEKERE, assistant matron, a few male staff, and Father Sebastian. The long white dormitory stretched away from Aidan, its rows of beds neatly arranged. They had green coverlets and pillows—one pillow per bed. The cots were of cast iron, with iron bedposts and railings.

At the head of each boy's bed was a small wooden stand on which was placed a basin, a small folded towel, a bar of soap, and a toothbrush.

On rising, at the gong, each boy took his basin, which contained his toiletries, and carried it to the bathroom area. There was a trough with round taps and running water. You collected your water to wash your face and clean your teeth. "Hurry along, now."

Aidan was invariably slow and sleepy-eyed, always careful, always anxious to do the right thing. He was frightened of the priest on duty that day, a tall, heavy man in a flowing white robe, with a brown leather belt around his waist. A long wooden crucifix dangled around his neck, reaching his waist.

Aidan balanced his bowl carefully in his two hands, padding slowly down the centre aisle. Suddenly, *Whack!* "Faster, you oaf!" A bamboo cane had smacked his buttocks, stinging. Screaming, he dropped the bowl, and the soap and toothpaste skidded across the floor. He couldn't stop himself—he shit his pants in fright.

Tears filled his eyes and streamed down his face as he stood trembling in shame before Father St. Sebastian. He felt the shit slide down his legs to his feet under his nightshirt. Father St. Sebastian grimaced, amused, a wry twist of a smile. The other boys watched, round-eyed, terrified.

"Oh, get along with you, Gilmor. Clean yourself up."

Weeping, Aidan scrabbled on the floor to pick up the fallen things, gathered up his bowl and soap and toothbrush and hobbled to the lavatory—a hole in the ground, crawling with the cockroaches that terrified him. He wiped himself as best he could with his little hand towel and dropped the soiled shirt into a laundry basket. Naked and shamed, he padded back to his bed and got dressed.

At the end of term, on the last day, Daddy came to pick him up and take him home. At last! He stood with his box in the front hall under the school motto: *Ad Astra*. To the Stars. Daddy greeted school officials and priests. He was dressed in a fine white linen suit and Stetsun hat. Father St. Sebastian made a point of coming over to greet Daddy. Then he brought up the time when Aidan had soiled his nightshirt in terror, referring to it as a joke, getting his side of the story in first, of course. Light-hearted. Aidan cringed with shame and pain. "And your son actually shit his pants he was so scared, Mr. Gilmor. Ha! Ha!"

Now Daddy would tell him off, bursting with indignation at his son's suffering. Aidan waited, closing his eyes. Then opened them. Daddy gave a faint, forced smile, affecting amusement. "Yes, Aidan is a slow-poke in the morning, Father. It's the same at home." But it wasn't like that! Aidan wanted to cry. He beat me! But the words would not come. He felt that sad helplessness of a little child who cannot make an adult understand, forever at fault. If Granpa Delaney had been there he would have given it to the priest, Aidan was sure; he might even have hit him (Uncle Quintus would have!). What could he say to Daddy on the long journey home? A boy shitting his pants in fear—it was an after-dinner anecdote to be passed down, over

time, in the priests' dining room.... "Remember that time when
that Gilmor kid shit his pants in terror? Ha ha."

He bungled his handwriting over and over. The teacher kept
putting the pen in his right hand. "You must use your *right*
hand, Gilmor, not the left. *Right*, Gilmor, I said. *Right, you
duffer!* Trying to be different, eh?"

The bamboo cane came down heavily on the back of his
hand, leaving a deep, red weal. He whimpered. "You said
something?" Another whack. How can I write, if my hand is
broken? he thought pitifully to himself.

The only success he had was in the curly Sinhalese script-writ-
ing that was like embroidery across the page, all curves and
dots and quivering tails. Carefully he copied the exercise from
Kumarodaya's Sinhalese primer, doing his best to replicate
the ancient Sinhalese script of his mystifying past, inimitable.
Mr. Sundranayake either did not notice he was left-handed or
did not care. He allowed him to have the pen in his left hand.
Aidan was shocked and amazed at the difference, at how easy
it was to work and concentrate, though he had to be careful
not to smudge the ink as his elbow and hand moved in the
wrong direction across the page.

But in other classes his brain clouded over, confused, as it
struggled to make the squiggles with his right hand. It seemed
to be the wrong way around to him. His brain could not seem
to think straight; it was as if it were backwards. "A backward
child," the priest wrote on his report card. "Not suited to
academics."

He struggled on. It did not occur to him that it was unfair,
unjust. The right hand was the correct one: the priest and everyone said so. He had to fit in to the world, not the world to
him, not be a misfit, frowned Father St. Sebastian. He tried to
hide his left-handedness. Only at home, on the estate, could he
hold his boat and kite and eating utensils with his left hand;
he could hold his fishing line in his glorious left hand, and no

one noticed, only Thomas the gardener. He was surprised how strong and light-hearted he felt using his left hand, surging with confidence. "An ungainly, bumbling boy," said the priest. Yet how lithe, how fleet on his feet he had been, running through the bamboos down to the turquoise pool in the jungly scrub.

He failed. Failed even math, his good subject. His columns and numbers were nothing but a scrawl, covered with blots as though they had been written backwards. He felt sadness when he thought about how much hope Daddy had had in him, the money he had spent on him, how much he had wanted his son to do well and live up to his ideals. The school was gathered together in the great hall for report card reading. Each boy's standing was read out. "Farouk (top boy), Edwards, Geeragamasinghe, Ravat...." The Muslims were always in the top five; they, along with the Tamils, were all brilliant in maths. Near the bottom: "Gilmor." His shame was complete.

There was a hush. Boys craned their necks to watch as Aidan and the other "dunces" made their way up the aisle to the stage. Tears were already pressing against his lids; he was sweating and trembling.

"You failed English and grammar *again*, Gilmor."

"Lower your shorts." The headmaster's eyes glittered; he seemed to enjoy Aidan's naked shame. Aidan obeyed.

He unbuckled his shorts and let them drop to his feet, then his little cotton underpants. He bent over, his brown backside exposed in front of all the boys, his scrotum hanging down. He wept. "Oh, no, sir, please.... So ... sorry...."

Whack! Whack! Whack! Whack! "*Now* will you learn your grammar?" He knew he was pissing. A small yellow pool was forming on the stage.

"Next boy, Senaratne...."

He pulled up his shorts and shuffled down from the stage. The rows of quiet boys, rows and rows, were very still. Not jeering, not grinning, but quiet and subdued. They were glad it was not them.

His second cousin, Colin (Auntie Agnes' son), was one of the top students at Holy Innocents. He excelled in everything. Aidan was in awe of Colin inside the school, but outside, when they went out for afternoon treats with Auntie Agnes on half-day holidays, they were friendly and Colin was kind. They did not speak of Aidan's thrashings (that made it normal to be beaten by the priests, nothing to complain about).

Colin was on the debating club, and he always won his debates. He was tall, slim, and handsome, with pale skin, flashing, dark, merry eyes, and a nice face. He also was a good bowler and was on the school team. And he excelled in English. He always walked off with the English prize. The priests looked favourably on him; they considered him a credit to Holy Innocents College, to themselves, and to the Holy Virgin.

He was head prefect in Marlborough House. He boarded, but went home every weekend. That made all the difference, Aidan realized when he was older, old enough to understand these things. A priest was not going to thrash a boy who was going home to his parents every weekend. Auntie Agnes lived close by, in Kandy, in a small house. Colin's father was in insurance and travelled all over the island regularly. Colin did not see much of him. His father would meet up with Daddy for "drinks." Had Colin ever been thrashed and called a "duffer?" Hardly likely.

Aidan joined in singing the old school song, which Daddy had sung before him: *"By Lanka's waves we love our school, Sing to the stars...."* And so on. *"Pledge our troth... through the years.... Holy Innocents forever...."*

On some half-days Auntie Agnes came to the school to visit. She always brought the two boys a carrot each, saying they were good for the eyes. Then they would go for treats and afternoon tea in the English pastry shop. During these visits, Aidan was happy. Auntie Agnes never asked him if he was treated well in school. (Daddy paid very high fees for him to board; for him to be beaten and abused, he longed to say.) And so Aidan understood he was not to speak of the pain and cruelty. (Wasn't it cruel to beat a little seven-year-old boy for nothing, just because he was slow carrying his wash basin? Just because he was left-handed?) So he didn't.

Colin never asked him how he liked Sunrise Cottages, if he was happy there, as if he presumed he was. Colin loved Holy Innocents, and he especially liked Latin prayers and the Latin mass in chapel. *"In patriis filiis...."* Aidan began to understand that he should go along with what happened to him because it obviously was not unusual; it was part of school, puzzling. So he did not speak of the abuse to Colin, either. No one else inquired, not even Mama or Daddy. "You're lucky to be at Holy Innocents," they would say. "It's a great opportunity...."

Aidan remembered that Granpa Delaney had not wanted him to be a boarder, and that he had suggested that Aidan live with him at Normandy. Aidan knew why Daddy and Mama had refused. It was because Granpa was something called an "atheist," like Uncle Quintus. This was a very terrible thing, but Aidan did not care. Granpa Delaney was kind to him; he took him lovingly by the hand during the holidays and talked to him like a grownup. They would walk down the Normandy estate road amidst the aroma of cocoa, hand-in-hand, with Granpa's surveying instruments. Granpa said, "Now you can be a surveyor, Aidan. You are learning the contours of the land and perspective." And though Aidan didn't have a clue what the big words meant, he understood that Granpa was sharing part of his work on surveying the plantation. Granpa had been one of the first to graduate from the Ceylon surveyors course at Perediniya College, on the island. He had a little skimpy beard, and he smelled of cocoa and tobacco. During the evening they would sit out on the verandah with Uncle Quintus and sometimes Uncle Neville when he came over from Gal Oya, and all three of them would play their guitars softly in the melancholy night. *"Sarabande...."*

Then Granpa and Uncle Quintus found out that Aidan was beaten at school for using his left hand. "By God, I'll give him a good thrashing, that Father!" cried Granpa. He came to the school without telling Daddy, simply appeared and demanded to see Father St. Sebastian. There was a to-do, and Titus Delaney threatened God knew what. Aidan felt that thrill of exoneration. He hid out in Sunrise Cottage. An adult, a family member, his grandfather had stuck up for him. He imagined how differently Granpa would have reacted to the incident in the dormitory when he'd pooped himself in terror, and he felt sad, because it had not been Daddy fighting for him. Daddy had not protected him.

Aidan was walking slowly and sadly behind the juniper hedge and the laurels. He was enjoying being alone for once, far away from the noisy calls of boys at cricket. Then the man, the Tamil assistant named Coomaraswamy, came from behind, suddenly, and took hold of him stealthily, so quickly he had no time to cry out. His heart thudded. What was happening? Then he was being pulled quickly back behind the laurels, thick foliage. He heard the crunch of leaves, and saw the adult's hands, big and brown with thick raised veins; he seemed to take it all in, the heavy gasps of breath, the smell of bodies, the hand fumbling at his shorts, pushing them down with an expert tug. (He's done this before.) Aidan's little buttocks exposed, his little bobbing penis; now the hand, the big hand gripping his little dick and a big, fleshy sausage-like thing pushing between his buttocks from behind. "I'm going to throw up," Aidan thought and he did, as the teacher gave a lunge, moving the Thing back and forth. He was bringing up his lunch over his feet. Then it was over. He recognized the Tamil as the assistant who helped the priest with the boys at games. "The devil get you if you tell anyone. You get it, boy?" He shook his head, crying, "Yes, sir, yes, sir...." A slurpy wetness was sliding down his legs from behind. Quickly he fumbled to pull up his underpants and shorts, sobbing, wiping his mouth against the bottom of his shirt.

He would never speak of it. What words could he use? He didn't know what had happened, and at the same time he did. Something very terrible had taken place. He had been singled out, and he must not tell. Not ever. Of course not. Shame engulfed him. Now he knew he was weak. *I'm a little boy, I'm only eight.* He ran across the grass to the priests' lavatories in the priests' private wing, behind the flaming red coralita trees, their brilliant little petals falling over the flagstones like drops of blood.

It was cool in the passageway; there was a cool whiff of disinfectant and a pale greenish light in the lavatory stalls. Jesus and His Bleeding Heart hung in a gilt frame on the wall, holding out his arms like wings, looking piteous. Mildew covered the tiled walls. He threw up again in the lavatory bowl. The priests had flush toilets that worked. The toilet bowls were ceramic, and when you pulled the chain water rushed out of a pipe inside and washed everything away clean. "Your sins are forgiven. Go in peace, my son....."

"Thank you, Father."

His legs were smeared with horrid gunk from the man. He took a cloth initialed with the school's initials—HIC for Holy Innocents College—and tried to wipe his trembling legs so no one would tell. So no one would know his shame.

"What are you doing here?"

It was Father Cuthbert, the old priest. He was bent over; the boys called him "hunchback." He peered at Aidan.

"I ... I was sick, sir, I threw up outside. I kept throwing up. I'm sorry, Father, forgive me." He began to cry. There was his rumpled smeared shirt, his smeared legs, his swollen mouth and eyes.

"You're from Sunrise Cottages?"

"Yes, Father."

"Don't cry, son. You've done nothing wrong. Go to matron and ask for a clean shirt and shorts. Say Father Cuthbert sent you." Father patted his head.

"Oh, thank you, Father. Thank you."

"I know it's hard for you. I've seen you cry often, my son. Try to enjoy your time here with us. Be happy. God is with you."

He longed then to crawl into kind Father Cuthbert's lap, lay his head on his chest, and tell him everything, everything.

The Man again. Mr. Coomaraswamy a deep shadow across the grass. Aidan was in King Edward Cottages now that he was older, in middle school, and the toilets had improved. There were soiled wooden seats and a chain to pull, but there were still cockroaches—how they ran!

He tensed. The boys were returning from games after tea. (They'd been served mounds of lovely thick slices of bread and butter and jam—all you wanted in the refectory. The school at least fed them well.) There was Coomaraswamy sitting on the grass as if nothing had ever happened between them. He was with a group of younger boys. He was one of the cricket coaches, of course. The boys were horsing around. As Aidan passed by he saw Coomaraswamy slip rupees to one of the boys, and then to another. They put them in their shorts pockets and ran off, grinning. One of them was a pretty boy, fairer skinned, part Sinhalese like Aidan himself (a Eurasian). Aidan hesitated. He did not yet understand that he was a pretty boy himself, with his soft curls, thick long eyelashes, and pouty lips. He was slender, with a certain gentleness. He wondered about the other boy, feeling helpless and angry. There were shadows across the chapel wall from a leaning feathery tree in the bright, bright sunlight that hurt his eyes. The shadow was cool and violet.

Inside, the chapel was dark and secret.

How proud Daddy was a few years later when Aidan was

made an acolyte. He began serving Father Cuthbert at the altar, dressed in a white surplice. He would hand Father the silver dish of wafers, and bow. Then Father Cuthbert would lift the "host," the body of Jesus—what was left of it. "*Lavabo inter innocents manus meas....*" I will wash my hands among the innocents.

During the mass that followed the Speech Day ceremony, Daddy and Mama had to kneel before Father Cuthbert and Aidan and bow their heads, while Aidan rang the little communion bell three times during mass. "Our son, the acolyte...."

Jack let drop casually at the club that his older son, Aidan, was now an acolyte at Holy Innocents. "You know how it is," he said modestly.

"Jolly good for him, old chap."

One day, open lorries went rolling by the wrought-iron gates. They were full of painfully thin men dressed only in spancloths with rags round their heads, weeping women in saris, and wide-eyed children. A voice said, "They're Tamils being deported," and then, "under the new laws." Aidan didn't think of Ganesh. The bell rang for prep far off. He turned and hurried across the cricket pitch.

40.

THE FIRST ACT OF THE new government had been to expel the Afghans. No one had been sorry to see *them* go. They'd been the money-lenders who'd charged a hundred percent interest. (You borrow a hundred rupees, you give two hundred back.)

"Good riddance," everyone breathed with a sigh of relief, and bucked up.

Senanayake had then turned to more serious business: what to do about the Tamil labourers on the estates. (Get rid of them.) He had quickly passed the Ceylon Citizenship Act that year, 1948. It was to change the history of the people of Ceylon forever.

The point of the act had been obvious to everyone: to deprive the estate Tamils of citizenship and the right to vote. It had stipulated that "non-Sinhalese" people—the "Indian" Tamils—had to provide documents showing that their paternal forefathers had been born in Ceylon, going back several generations. They were to take their documents to a designated registration office. Ridiculous! What poor, illiterate Tamil labourer could do that? They'd been locked away in virtual apartheid on the estates for half a century, they cried helplessly.

Outrage. The legislation sparked protests from Tamils across the island, especially the estate coolies who had the most to lose.

"What for having to prove our birth? We never had to before!"

"That was then; this is now," retorted the Sinhalese officials.

Jack had been shocked. He'd discovered that under the act he, too, was not considered to be a citizen in his own country. A very painful truth now resurfaced. Old grandfather Gilmor, the original British ancestor from back in the nineteenth century—the bastard—had not married Granny (old Burmese "Granga," beloved of all the children). Not married, that is, in the English Christian sense of the word. She'd been merely a "country" wife. She'd given birth to ten children, all of whom were now designated illegitimate, including his own father, Owen Gilmor. She had been a country wife, but she had had no marriage certificate, no birth certificates for the children, and no signed papers before the law. There was *no proof,* Jack reflected bitterly. He didn't have the vital deeds that were so necessary for the UNP officials who were administering this new Ceylon Citizenship Act. What for papers, in the past? There was no need for a marriage deed in the Sinhalese tradition; the nuptial day had been chosen in keeping with the auspicious date, the phase of the moon, and the configuration of the planets (Mars, Venus, and Jupiter). It was set by the astrologer. The union was then blessed by the Buddhist priest after he drew up the horoscopes.

All of this meant that Jack was as disenfranchised, as stateless, as his lowliest coolie.

"More whisky!" he called harshly to house servant number two from where he lay slumped on the *charpoy* out on the verandah. "And soda."

The Tamil labourers turned desperately to Ponnambalam, head of the All-Ceylon Tamil Congress. Surely Ponnambalam, who was highly educated and now the Minister of Agriculture in Senanayake's cabinet, would oppose the Act.

But Ponnambalam's hands were tied, as Quintus and the leftists had predicted. He was too indebted to Senanayake to oppose him. And did he really care all that much about the plight of low-caste Tamils, tillers of the soil? Ponnambalam might call himself a "proud Dravidian," but he'd never sat in a thatched hut eating out of a coconut shell, or had to shit in the fields. What had he to do with Tamil labourers on tea estates? The labourers, Ponnambalam reminded himself, had voted Marxist against the upper class, against Ponnambalam and Senanayake and the UNP. They were dangerous, Senanayake had pointed out softly. So Ponnambalam had signed; he'd given tacit consent to the Ceylon Citizenship Act on behalf of the Tamils.

"*Okka oatha!*" What the fuck! cried the labourers, betrayed.

"*Thevidiya paiyaa!*" Son of a whore! "*Saklian!*"

Without citizenship, the Tamil labourers lost the right to vote, which meant the number of Tamil MPs in parliament plummeted from thirty-three percent to twenty percent. They had lost the balance of power. Too late, Ponnambalam saw the trap.

"*Turoki!*" Traitor!

Absolute uproar in the House.

But there was no going back. The Ceylon Citizenship Act was a *fait accompli*, Ponnambalam be buggered. Ponnambalam was *dhoosi* (dust).

Thai oli!

Jack had been drinking more than a few whiskies. "Pet, pet, Jack," objected Mildred, distressed, "What for this drinking?" The Tamils were rebelling, threatening to revolt. He spent more time now at the clubs during working hours; he even made the long trip up to Hatton through winding mountain roads to visit the Hatton-Eliya Club. He'd wanted to hear from the English planters there; he wanted to be reassured by their air of invincibility that he and his family were safe.

"What, goons attack us up here, forty-seven hundred feet in the air?" They'd been bemused. "They'll first have to manoeuvre twenty-seven hairpin bends!"

"And make sure they don't fall over the precipices with their jeeps and guns." They'd roared with laughter.

There were sixty kilometres of hairpin bends between Pera-deniya and Nuwara Eliya.

Besides, the government would never allow it. Tamil rebels attack planters? Tea was the core of the Ceylon economy, boasted the planters. The British in Britain drank one hundred and seventy-five million cups of tea per day. Ceylon couldn't do without the planters and their know-how.

But that June news began seeping through from British Malaya. A white British rubber planter was murdered on his estate one night in the lonely mountains, not far from Sungei Siput. He'd been alone, working late in his office. He was killed at point blank range by young Chinese communist guerrillas, who'd then slipped off into the jungle. Then two more planters were killed, a manager and his young assistant. The British planters were marching to Kuala Lumpur demanding protection from the British Governor. They were finally granted guards, Sten guns, and ammunition. They were concerned, isolated from each other in those lonely mountains. (The planters upcountry in Ceylon could certainly relate to that.)

One wife had apparently mounted a machine gun on her verandah—Good God!—to protect her children while her husband was off fighting. It shouldn't be happening, but it was. The British governor had called a state of emergency. "Damn right," muttered the planters.

Ethel Henshaw, rather bravely, thought Jack, refused to be sent back "home" in the event of an uprising. She said she'd rather die at Eric's side if it came down to it. "Rubbish, Ethel," said Henshaw. "Nothing's going to happen here. We're perfectly safe." All the same, he bought extra guard dogs for the bungalow—Alsatians were favoured. De Jurgen and other planters followed suit.

An "alien" was now a person who was not a "British subject," whatever that was exactly. Jack swayed in confusion. The English planters now found themselves, for the first time, outsiders looking in; they were no longer in control of parliament, the judiciary, the civil service, or the education system. They were British. That still carried weight, of course, pride of place. In the old days, the issue of citizenship had never arisen. It was enough to be English. Now they, too, were not Ceylon citizens, unless they relinquished their British passports. "Like hell we will!" they cried.

41.

THE CEYLON CITIZENSHIP ACT had become law on November 15, 1948, two hundred and eighty-five days after Independence.

All the leftists voted "opposed."

The Ceylon Indian Tamil Congress: "opposed."

Nevertheless, it was a done deal. As a result, 850,000 Tamil estate workers were excluded from citizenship. Only 145,000 had qualified; the rest would be deported. That left over half a million Tamil labourers in limbo, even though most of them had been born in Ceylon. The Tamil workers had always feared the Sinhalese would expel them, and now it was happening. Where were the British? Lord Soulbury had guaranteed them suffrage, protection against discrimination, they protested.

But the British were no longer calling the shots.

Jack's world had shifted; it was as if the ground beneath him had suddenly given way. He thought anxiously of poor old Mr. Saeed. He must now be designated a "Sonnahar" under the Act; but perhaps not.

"Another whisky!" he called to house servant number two.

"Send them back!" the Sinhalese wives cried harshly at the Kegalle Club. "They don't belong here! The Tamil labourers were *never* citizens."

"Idiots," muttered the planters, over their beers. Where the hell would they get labourers for the estates, if the Tamils disappeared? Were Mrs. Goonetilleke, Mrs. Wickramasingha, Mrs. Gooneratne, and the other Sinhalese wives going to go out in the hot sun and bloody well pluck tea from dawn to dusk?

Besides, India did not want them back! Mr. Nehru knew only full well it would create a precedent. If he took in the "Indian" Tamil labourers of Ceylon, he'd be inundated with millions of coolies from all over the globe demanding the "right of return" from wherever the bloody British had taken them, which was everywhere.

The Tamils said they were British citizens. "We've always been under British protection!" The Tamil women wept down in the coolie lines.

The planters were concerned. Ethel Henshaw, at Hatton-Eliya, said to Nettie Matthews, "What are they doing to our coolies?"

Senator S. Nadesan, brilliant, respected Tamil civil rights lawyer rose in the House during the debate in the Senate Session, to object. His was the small voice of reason. He questioned the meaning of the statement that Ceylon had the right, as any other country, to "determine the composition of its population."

"*Sari! Sari!*" Hear! Hear! rose from the Tamil side. They beat their desks in approval.

"What about Hitler?" asked Mr. Nadesan. (Shuffles and exclamations of indignation from the Sinhalese side.) When Hitler had started to "de-citizenize" the Jews in Germany, pursued Mr. Nadesan, every civilized country in the world had condemned him. Hitler had said he had "absolute power to determine the composition of the population of Germany," stressed Mr. Nadesan. "And he did. He decided that to his own satisfaction," added Nadesan quietly.

"I ask you: are we doing the right thing, the fair thing, the honourable thing, here?" he continued in a deadly accusatory tone.

"*Sari! Sari!*" The Tamils thumped their desks again.

Pandemonium broke out.

"Order! Order! I am asking for order in this House!"

"*Oothi!*"

"*Aiyo...!*"

Felix appeared. He'd driven down from Colombo in the midday heat; it was safer that way since everyone took an afternoon break in the city.

"What the hell's going on, man?" he cried. Being so dark-skinned and part Tamil—anyone could tell—he'd feared being waylaid by goons, pulled out of his car and roughed up. Anything could happen to anyone, nowadays, he mourned.

"Tamils hacking Sinhalese to death? Sinhalese attacking Tamils? What happened to *ahimsa*, Buddha's non-violence?" he asked sardonically.

"*Ahimsa* be buggered," said Jack gloomily. He offered Felix a Peacock, and then lit one himself.

"Whisky, Felix? It'll calm your nerves."

"Not for me, thanks, old boy. I'll take gin, with a little lime. Better for the stomach."

"Gin!" he called to the servant. "And a dash of Lanka lime."

"We've always got along in the past, man. In the small towns and villages, anyway," Felix persisted, as if wounded. He drew nervously on his cigarette. "We shared festivals, family celebrations—Sinhalese and Tamil together, real camaraderie." He meant the educated upper-class Ceylon Tamils. "Some even intermarried. People were kind to each other." Good God, look at his own family, he protested. His father's mother was full Tamil, and Aunt Cicely was married to a Tamil doctor, bloody hell.

Felix looked immaculate, as usual, dressed in a light linen suit for the city, fine silk shirt, gold cuff links, and white Italian leather loafers. He was the man about town, thought Jack. But Felix did not have a beautiful Eurasian or Tamil girlfriend on his arm this time.

"Bloody country going to the dogs," Jack agreed.

"And the Buddhist priests putting their irons in the fire, stoking up hatred and attacks against the Tamils. That's what Quintus says."

"He'd better be careful or he'll end up in Welikada with the others."

Welikada was the old British prison in Colombo. Senanayake had just released some political prisoners who'd been detained for over a year under the so-called Ceylon Securities Act of 1947. "He wouldn't want to end up there." Both men looked startled.

"Well, he's a hot-head like your father-in-law, Titus. He supports that crazy Tamil labour leader, Thondaman." But Felix had a sneaking admiration for Thondaman, being part Tamil himself.

"It's the fault of the British colonialists, say what you will," cried Jack. "Before they came, who thought of these racial divisions? Who cared what part of the country you lived in? Them and their damn censuses." The census defined your ancestors, culling information about where they lived, their occupations, income, and religion. There had been one in his grandfather's time in 1891 and again in 1946. "Damn racist rot, nothing else but!"

"I'm afraid the British knew even when we took a shit and how many times."

The men burst out laughing.

"You can't blame the British for everything. The Sinhalese and Tamils can be the most bloody caste-conscious racists themselves, going back a millennium. But they're our people."

Mr. Saeed's shop was locked, the windows boarded up. Mr. Saeed was at the back with his little grandson, in a hot, little room, huddled over a tall glass *samovar* of percolating tea. Mr. Rasheed stood by, inspecting a carpet from Afghanistan. Business was bad, said Mr. Saeed softly. He was too afraid to open up shop. Gangs of Sinhalese youths, goons, were constantly on the loose in the neighbourhood attacking Tamil and Muslim businesses, shops, and homes. The police did nothing. "What to do?" Mr. Saeed's eyes filled with tears.

He did understand who he was under the new act. He'd been born in the Punjab, now "West Pakistan," and he'd come to Ceylon as a child with his parents. That must be it. The Muslims did not know where they stood; meanwhile, they were being beaten up along with the Tamils.

"Maybe things will improve," said Jack, with a hope he did not feel.

"*Inshallah.*"

After leaving Mr. Saeed, Jack walked cautiously through the Pettah towards Old Fort. He planned to make his usual stop at Cargills for whisky. Then he would go to the Carson and Cumberbatch offices and pick up the labourers' wages. The Tamil guard who now accompanied him on his journey for protection would be waiting there. They would drive directly back to Kegalla over the hilly terrain. The guard had a Sten gun, and Jack carried a gun and rifle. They would stop for no one.

The Pettah seemed to be as busy as usual, despite the outbreaks and skirmishes. The bazaar was packed with shoppers, pedestrians, beggars, and people getting into rickshaws and taxis. There was the usual insane commotion of traffic, screaming sirens, horns, bellows of men with bullock carts, mangy dogs scrounging in the garbage piles, goats, congestion. There was also the usual stench of rotted fish and hunks of meat hanging on skewers with their acrid odours; stinky rambutans. Some of the small shops were boarded up, like poor Mr. Saeed's.

Jack glanced anxiously around while simultaneously keeping his face averted. Appearance was everything in a sudden riot. It mattered more than essence. He looked like an Englishman, in his khaki drill outfit and English sun-helmet. A regular fair-skinned *pukkah sahib* tea planter, looking neither left nor right, mouth a firm line, eyes like bullets, like the English.

As he approached the corner of two cross streets, York and Chatham, he suddenly saw her: Lily de Groot. *Lily*. Standing at the kerb, with two blond little boys dressed in blue-and-white sailor suits and brimmed hats, so obviously Dutch with their broad, fair features. He saw her slim breasts against the fine cotton of her dress, breasts he had never so much as laid a finger on, he'd been so respectful and innocent at twenty. Her fair hair was drawn back in a loose chignon beneath her sunhat. Then she was blocked by a lorry. Gone. He felt a sharp pang of something, a sense of the past that could never return; it was as though his heart would burst. He leant against a column, trembling, and lit a cigarette. He would likely never see her again.

But, of course, he did.

The next week in Colombo he called around to see Peter de Groot. He was in his office, a small suffocatingly hot room—the ceiling fan wasn't working properly. It was in a poorer district on Madawana Street. Jack asked casually about Lily—Lily! He said he'd glimpsed her, recently, in the Pettah. How was she? (After all these years—twenty years.)

Lily gave piano lessons in the area at the school of music, said Mr. de Groot affably. She passed through the Pettah often to do some shopping, or to take the boys for ice cream. The younger one was looked after by their *ooomah*, his mother. Mr. de Groot was also concerned about business, with these gangs of goons wandering the streets looking for trouble.

"Do you want to cash in your policy, Jack?"

Jack looked startled. "No, why would I?" Not yet.

"I saw you, Lily, on the corner of York Street last week, in the afternoon."

"And I saw you."

They glanced at each other with sudden knowledge. They were sitting in Fenmore's English Cake Shop, taking afternoon tea together. The little shop was in one of those old, colonial back streets. Jack had instructed his guard to wait at Carson's.

Her eyes were a deep, calm blue, like the *nitali* lily, after which perhaps she'd been named. The flower was beloved of the Sinhalese, and the name meant "colour of a sleeping woman's eyes," or something like that. Nitali blue.

The moment swelled.

He struggled to get a hold of himself. "I asked your father about you, how to get a hold of you. I—I wanted to see you again, after all these years." His voice trailed off lamely. She wore a pale-yellow dress, ruched over the bodice, pushing out her breasts. He longed to take her in his arms, a ridiculous and deceitful thought.

"You've done well over the years, Jack."

She appraised him calmly. He'd dressed up that day, just for her: fine linen suit, stetson hat, silk shirt—so English, a proper *sahib*. He'd always been a dresser, she remarked. He grimaced. "You deserted me." She smiled subtly, challenging him at once.

"I was just a youth of twenty, a creeper at Poonagalla. I didn't understand. I'm sorry."

"I know. But..."

"And you've married, had children." He smiled.

"It was a good proposition, arranged by *vader* (father). Young women without means have to take what they can get, compromise."

"You're happy?"

She smiled back. "Henryk is a good, solid man, a kind man. That matters. And he loves me."

He gave a quiet smile. Her answer was so Dutch, so practical. And in the end, she was in not so different a situation to his own, perhaps.

"And you?"

"We have a good life, yes. I love Mildred and the children, yes. We have two boys and a girl." He felt a lurch inside. Solid, dusky, loyal Mildred. He felt panic: what was he doing here with Lily de Groot, toying with the past? What was he up to? Mildred, the children—Aidan, his first-born, Scottie, his beloved. His life, the last twenty years, floated by. But it was good to see Lily again. Awkwardly, he fumbled for her hand, wanting to make something up to her.

"Yes, well, our lives went on different paths, Jack. What was that poem in senior school English class we had to learn? "Two paths beckoned ... and I took the one less travelled by...." It was as if she had read his heart.

"'The Road Not Taken.' Robert Frost." he smiled.

"...And that has made all the difference."

The sound of his name—*Jack*—like that on her tongue, in her high, clear voice, like a temple bell. Another lurch. He trembled. He told himself it was curiosity—and it was—but there was also a deeper urge to see himself, how he was when he was twenty, reflected in her. He longed to re-live something irretrievably lost. It was foolish, impossible, but he yearned for it anyway, for the self he had lost before he'd even been aware of himself. (His own pale complexion and hers, so pale and creamy against the moving dark background of colonial Ceylon, yes. Her name LILY tattooed on his chest, over his heart, hidden under his fine shirt.)

She knew about his children; she'd heard about them through Esmé, she said. Her little sister, he recalled.

"Not so little now. She's seventeen. At Kandy Convent, boarding," she added proudly. Fiona never talked about Esmé de Groot, he thought vaguely. Perhaps they were in different dormitories. Fiona was like that, somewhat on the arrogant side, like himself.

He looked directly at Lily's face, which was shadowed beneath her old-fashioned Dutch bonnet; the hat had a large brim, in the old style. He struggled to recall feelings of long past, feelings that perhaps she felt too, but she was being careful, distant, wary he supposed, and somewhat sad. He felt it, a certain *ennui*.

Lily had to pick up the boys from school; she had no extra servants. Nothing had been declared between them. Time had seemed to hang suspended—what did that mean?

"Whisky," he called to the young waiter, who was dressed in white livery with a wide black cummerbund and a fez. Son of a *sammankorar*, so defined by the new Act, no doubt.

"What for all this drinking, pet?" Mildred was troubled.

"I saw Lily de Groot in the Pettah, today...."

"Oh? And how is she? She's married isn't she? With two boys I hear."

Of course. The bush telegraph, always. He smiled. "She's well. Life goes on. It's a bit of a shock, though, seeing someone like that twenty years later. She's still the same."

"I'm sure she's not. I'm sure she's quite different from when she was a seventeen-year-old. As for all of us, Jack, pet."

He burned with fever at the memory of her, the soft, yellow dress, the ruching over her breast, the long, plump arms, very white underneath. Her eyes and lips, a torture.

"Let it be." He spoke harshly, then felt abject. Mildred's steady perturbed eyes, deep Kandyan eyes, direct, penetrating and intelligent. She had very dark, dusky, solid Kandyan features that he'd always prized, always valued as a gift. With Mildred he could be himself, be understood; she recognized the dark Sinhalese aspect of himself under his deceptive fair skin, his Englishness. Mildred knew and accepted that Sinhalese temperament, his boastful camaraderie, his love of showiness at times, his volatile depth; she knew and gave allowance.

He took her awkwardly in his arms. He knew he was not a good lover. Of course he knew; he was embarrassed, fumbling, always the adolescent, some part of him atrophied. And Mildred understood that, too. "It's all right, pet," she would murmur afterwards, after the intense rush of sex. And it was.

They always knelt at their bedside at night, side by side, for prayers. "...*Blessed be the fruit of thy womb, Jesus.... Pray for us sinners now and at the hour of our death."*

But now he burned with desire for Lily, and shame, his forehead a weight, as if he were panting through the days, longing for the week's end and his return to Colombo. Keeping to his work schedule, overseeing the labourers who moved like stick figures through the fields and nurseries, like ghosts through the pollarded trees, the heavy dry heat, the brilliant, cloudless sky.

An anhinga balanced on the edge of the tank where the sluices were cut out of the soil. It ruffled its feathers, pressing its beak into its rump. Then dove swiftly and struck.

"I wasn't good enough."

He'd told his guard again to wait at Carson's for his return. He and Lily went to the Victoria Gardens, a place they had visited together as young people in love, a safe refuge at midday. It was deserted, silent; the foliage was still under the high, hot sun, the zenith of the day it was called. The city silent and still, the mountains, the sea, everywhere sleeping in the midday heat, life suspended during the drowsy siesta. Parts of the gardens had tall bamboo and other thick bushes ablaze with furry soft down, nestling thickly—a secret place. The path was shady; the trees cast long violet shadows. They reached a pond, cool and still and stately. Through feathery trees, stood tall king palms, their luxurious top-knots like powerful plumes, trunks very straight and erect; they looked like Englishmen.

There was an old arbor in the gardens that was shrouded with thick, trailing sprays of bougainvillea—red, purple, violet, like paper flowers, profuse. You could bury yourself in them forever.

They could see the Indian Ocean in the distance beyond the laurels, dazzling silver and gold with little fishing boats skimming the surface, their sails billowing, like tiny toys.

The still heat, the swathe of sunlight across hot flagstones, coralita and hibiscus, and rhododendron brilliant scarlet, hot and drooping in the fiery sun. But he felt energy, energy for her.

"Your family rejected me. *You* rejected me."

"It was the times, yes, Lily. Stupid. Stupid and cruel. I admit."

"It was because I was Dutch Burgher. And Protestant."

"Yes. Yes, if you want to put it that way."

"I knew it."

"I loved you, Jack. But what do you know at seventeen? You are really still a child. First love." First blossom, then the inevitable fading.

Her lips formed a firm line. She looked objective, calm. He felt helpless, confused against her Dutch strength. She still attended the *kerk*, she said, with her sons.

He felt rage, a deep, violent disgust against society, against Ceylon and the Sinhalese and the British and the Tamils, too, come to that, with their racial spites and differences. Their prejudices and cruel hatreds were like little snakes that slithered and writhed inside you, and caught you as a child in your innocence. And you never escaped; no one did, say what you may.

He was clenching his fists, thinking of the Citizenship Act, of the latest Sinhalese diatribe against the Tamils: "That was then, this is now." He felt a new understanding of, and respect for, Quintus.

"And today?"

He thought again of the Sinhalese, smug, taunting now that they had the upper hand. That was how it was; no nation was exempt.

He turned towards her on the bench where they sat, side by side, the arbor drenched with perfume of flowers, heady. He kissed her on the mouth, hard, greedy for the past denied. There are kisses that are long and deep like the swell of the ocean, and you are lost. Suddenly she wrenched herself away, petals broke off the sprays of frangipani, white petals crushed underfoot.

"*Nee. Mijn Gott!* We are a proud race, the Dutch. D'you think you British are the only ones to feel glory? We were masters, once, and don't forget it, *mijn hier vladerland!*"

She spoke passionately, a Lily he had not known. (Had he ever known her?) Her eyes stared, hard and blue, trembling near tears as if she were going to cry.

He saw then how deep the hurt had been. He'd rejected her; yes, he had. He hadn't fought for her, hadn't opposed his family's condemnation of her, their cruelty. You could only blame the prejudices of the time so much, she seemed to imply. Only so much. He hadn't fought back; he hadn't defied Granga. And he'd gone on to be happy.

He touched her hand, lifted it, and kissed it, and this kiss was pure, kinder, a kiss of compassion, of sorrow, of reconciliation. "I'm sorry Lily. I hurt you...."

"Poor Jack," she quivered, softly now. "Always trying to be an Englishman..."

He flinched. He felt something crumple inside, as he was laid bare suddenly by her.

Yes, he was an Englishman—but what the bloody hell was an Englishman when it came down to it? And he had married Mildred, who was full Sinhalese; he had committed his identity to his Sinhalese side, to a Goonesekere. He was brown, not white. Lily's lip quivered; she was about to cry again—tears were starting to form in her eyes. (He'd been a young *sahib* at twenty, lording it over her, making the decision, yes or no, she the subservient Dutch, if you will. Is that how it had seemed to her?)

"But you're not, really," she said softly. "You're not real English, not fully, as I am Dutch. I'm pure Dutch at least. It may be old Dutch, but I go back...."

The old words of the old anthem rose between them. She sang now under her breath, defiantly: "*Het lieve vaderland...*" Long live the fatherland. "*Edel en hooggeboren / Van keizerlijke stam...*" I nobly born, descended from an imperial stock.

He flushed. He was taken aback at the racism in the words, Lily's attempt at defiance, self-respect, quivering between them. She had been the victim of the times, but time could shift with the wind, and it had—that was the irony. They were both outsiders now, outside the Act, aliens, or so it seemed.

"*You will not conquer me now....*" The tears were trickling down her cheeks now.

"Lily, you don't understand...."

"Oh, but I do."

They were trapped by the history of Ceylon, she cried. "We are getting out. Henryk is booking a passage to Holland for us and the boys. While we have the chance. The offer won't last forever."

The Netherlands had offered free citizenship to all its ex-colonials who wanted to leave Ceylon.

Jack was shocked. Lily gone from his life, from the island of Ceylon.

"When do you leave?"

"Hopefully this October."

"What about Esmé?"

"We can't afford to take her with us. She'll stay with Papa and her *ooma* to finish her schooling, until we can send for her one day. Besides," she struggled for words, "she's so English now. That's what her fancy Catholic Kandy-convent-education has done for her, made her a little Englishwoman!" she said bitterly.

"I wish to God we'd never been the conquerors!" he cried.

"*Gefelicit eerd!*" Best wishes!

During morning ablutions he stared at his bare chest in the mirror. At her name, LILY. It had been tattooed forever across his heart, like a mantra—the insanity of youth! Love was a form of madness. Now it was the insanity of middle years. He was in his prime, nearly forty. Was that it, the approaching male mid-life crisis?

What had he been thinking? Or feeling? Yet he was safe. He felt relieved; the surging had stilled. Nothing had happened, he reminded himself. One sudden kiss. Was one kiss of any consequence? It was something he would have confessed to Father Balderelli in the old days that already seemed a century ago, up at Weyweltalawa. Something quietly sealed his heart.

42.

"WHAT ABOUT US?" cried the Muslims. Where did they stand in all this?

"They'll soon bloody find out," muttered Quintus. The Citizenship Act dealt with the Moors, too.

Quintus and his father, Titus Delaney, had come to stay at Madeniya, as they often did to keep Mildred company. The life of a tea planter's wife was a lonely one, as they well knew. They played their guitars in the long evenings, melancholy songs by South American composers, and listened to the BBC overseas service.

The Muslims, now referred to as "Pakistanis," found themselves in limbo; they did not belong in Ceylon or Pakistan. Jack thought anxiously about poor Mr. Saeed.

Were Moors to have special consideration, like the Ceylon Tamils?

The following year, 1949, Senanayake passed the Indian and Pakistani Residents Act. It claimed to enable "Pakistanis" to gain citizenship in Ceylon, but in reality did anything but.

The passing of the Act led to confusion and disarray among the Muslims. They soon joined forces with the Tamils, even though each resented the other. Who was a citizen? Who was not? And what did it *mean?* Senanayake's real objective also soon became clear when the Act was swiftly followed by an amendment. The Amendment Act No. 48 decided who could, and could not, vote, once and for all. The estate "Indian" Tamils, for instance, were stripped of their suffrage. They were deliberately left off the voting registers and lost their seven seats in parliament.

"Bloody hell!" cried Jack. He marched outside and indignantly pulled down the Ceylon flag. The proud Sinhalese lion fluttered down from the roof of the factory. Defiantly, he hoisted up the old Union Jack.

"It'll take more than that, man," said Quintus.

"My boots! Sinha!" Jack would ride that morning down to the lower slopes and tea terraces. They bordered the Sinhalese village land, vestige of another era. The villagers had been there since old Grandfather Gilmor's era when the British had brought out the Waste Lands Ordinance Act. This marked the beginning of the British takeover of Sinhalese land, which had been helped along by the Tamil *chetties*. They cunningly wrangled with the Sinhalese over non-existent deeds and documents. "What for deeds?" the Sinhalese villagers had cried innocently. But the *chetties* had served their British masters well, cleverly depriving the villagers of their land and their precious chena rights to cut jungle scrub.

Jack drew to a halt at the edge of a village and patted Galahad's mane. The pony neighed and blew air from his nostrils. Horses had been in Ceylon since the time of the Arabs, who had brought them to the island.

He could see the villagers dotting their paddy fields, treading the tender rice shoots, following the bullocks in the hot sun. Their little thatched huts were half hidden in the cool shade of palm trees and thick trees. There were fires burning; the villagers controlled the fires to cut back vegetation and scrub. The entire plantation of Madeniya had once been theirs, before the British and Dutch investors had taken over so easily. The British and Dutch had had "book and deed," mourned the villagers; the colonial masters had defined the new plantations that brought only poverty and malnutrition, cholera and dysentery to the villagers. Jack had seen it as a child, and later as a creeper.

Yes, he thought, the Sinhalese had their history of injustices and miseries, too.

More insanity. More uproar in the legislature. Fierce battles of wit and will between Sinhalese and Tamil. Unbelievable!

The Tamils threatened to appeal to His Excellency, the British Governor General—the "King of Ceylon"—who no longer gave a damn. They claimed they *all* had a right to citizenship, from "time immemorial."

The Sinhalese said, "No time immemorial! We were here first!" They had definite proof: the great *Mahavansa* (an aged, tattered, faded document going back to the fifth century AD, written by a monk, a *bhikkhu,* now kept under lock and key, and guarded by the military.)

"*Ootha!*" Fuck the *Mahavansa!*

"We are the 'chosen people,'" the Sinhalese insisted, "deemed by Buddha himself."

"Well, don't be forgetting Buddha was an *Indian*," the Tamils retaliated. Hah!

"The dynasty of Kandyan kings goes back twenty-three hundred years," boasted the Sinhalese.

"But the kings sent to South India for their brides, all the same," taunted the Tamils. "More beautiful than Sinhalese woman, more luscious breasts."

Besides, the last king of Ceylon *was a Tamil,* Sri Vikrama Rajasinha. Hah!

And so on, and so on. *Dhoosi.*

All was *dhoosi.* Dust.

People who had a British parent could now apply to be British subjects, announced Britain, the Motherland.

"They're standing by us," many older ones cried—people

like Felix's parents Auntie Bella and Uncle John at Pennylands, and Auntie Agnes, Auntie Jessie, and old Titus Delaney. Auntie Jessie talked about leaving the damn country and going to Australia as soon as she got her British passport. (Many of the English planters had already left for Melbourne or Sydney.)

"Leave Pennylands?" cried Uncle John. Unthinkable. They'd been there forever. Felix had been born there.

"Sign of the times," said Auntie Jessie grimly. She was not going to be a second-class citizen in Ceylon under the Sinhalese. Granpa Delaney and Auntie Agnes said they would stay with Auntie Bella and Uncle John; they were too old to go gadding off to the other end of the earth where the stars were upside down. Besides, Auntie Agnes, Colin's mother suddenly appeared in a sari and said she was Sinhalese now—one half of her, at least, she grimaced.

So Jack was an alien in his own country, on his own plantation, among his own labourers, he thought bitterly. Together they were aliens. Strange. But now he knew.

"Here come the aliens," teased the English planters at the Kegalle Club, lifting their pints of beer.

"Bugger the Act."

The Sinhalese were now on equal footing with the British planters—before the law, at least.

Whisky, beer, and *arrack* flowed. Jack ordered double whiskies—straight—all night.

Then King George VI died on February 4, 1952. "In his sleep at Sandringham," said the palace bulletin nicely. As if the coolies, sprawled on cold cement floors of the coolie lines in the colonies, knew or cared what Sandringham even was, said Quintus.

All day, intermittently, Radio Ceylon and the BBC overseas service played the "Dead March." It echoed through the bungalow at Madeniya, a slow, somber dirge. It was raining in London, a grey day with mist wafting up the Thames. In

Madeniya it was gloriously hot and dry. Bulbuls chattered over the paddy fields, and ruby-throated hummingbirds swooped, their long bills quivering; insect-eating plants slowly opened their enticing tendrils. *"In life and death, oh Lord...."*

The planters in the clubs lowered their flags half-mast. "The King is dead!" To a man, they bowed their heads and sang His Majesty's favourite hymn, "Abide With Me," among the acacias and flowering rhododendrons.

Jack proudly lowered the flag on the estate. He stood at the foot of the flagpole with Denbow; the KP, Kumaraswamy; and the tea factory manager. They saluted, feeling somewhat foolish since none of them were army people, but it seemed like the right thing to do.

"I thought we were done with all that," said Quintus.

"We have a new queen."

"*We...?*"

Crowds had gathered in London; the footage played on the *British Pathé News* in the cinemas in Colombo and Kandy. British women sobbed, working men doffed their hats: the British in mourning. The King's cortège went down Whitehall, past Marble Arch; little erect figures passed on tiny horses, their helmets flashing, following the draped gun-carriage. The three queens—three living queens—were clustered together with black mourning veils over their faces: old Queen Mary, Elizabeth the "Queen Mother," and the new, young Queen Elizabeth by the Divine Right of Kings.

"Damn rot," said Titus Delaney.

At twenty-five years of age, Elizabeth Regina was now the Defender of the Faith, Queen "by the Grace of God" of Great Britain, Ireland, and the British Dominions beyond the seas; head of the Commonwealth; Queen of Nigeria, Jamaica, Barbados, the Bahamas, Grenada, Papua, New Guinea, the Solomon Islands, Tuvalu, and so on, and so forth.

Now Ceylon ministers had to express fealty to a woman, take the oath of loyalty. "A lot of bunkum," said Quintus, who was definitely a leftist like his father, a supporter of the Equal Rights Party, the LSSP.

The Tamil coolies, like the Muslims, believed themselves to be highly in favour with the new Queen. She was on their side; the British promise

But a month later, Senanayake fell off his horse galloping across Galle Face Green and was killed. Jack knew then that trouble was coming. *The Times* and the *Islander* were full of it.

On March 15, 1953, the astrologers' omen was fulfilled.

Aiyo!

43.

A T KANDY CONVENT, Fiona had nothing to do with Esmé de Groot. Of course not! (Thank goodness they didn't share the same dormitory.) Fiona was in St. Euphrasia's dorm, while Esmé was in St. Bridget's. Fiona was careful to avoid Esmé when she first arrived at Kandy Convent, averting her face after Prep. But it was free hour when she heard. "Fiona!" Esmé had come up to her eagerly that first day. "It's Esmé, Esmé de Groot. Remember me?"

Fiona had flushed. The wealthy Eurasian girls, some of them very fair and English-looking, whom she really wanted to get in with, were looking curiously her way, though Esmé was of no importance to them. The Eurasian girls and the Dutch Burghers tended to keep to their own cliques (the Muslims girls stayed with the Muslims, and the Hindu and Catholic Tamils stuck together as well, chattering away in Tamil). "Esmé...? Oh, yes, I think I do remember." And she'd turned away. The next time Esmé approached her, she carefully looked into the distance or switched direction and passed on, leaving a pained Esmé looking after her.

But Fiona soon found herself painfully excluded from the wealthy Colombo Eurasian set she so desperately wanted to be part of. It was made clear to her, when she boasted of her Scottish blood, that she was not "English" and certainly not Scottish. "What, a native like you? With those Burmese eyes?"

said Irene Wijeratne, a tall Eurasian girl with large greenish eyes and fair skin—as fair as Esmé's, who was a Dutch Burgher on her father's side, pure descent.

The word stung. The word "native" was reserved in Fiona's mind for servants at Weyweltalawa and Madeniya. She realized that she was not "English" after all, but something in between; she was not even full Sinhalese, and the "real" Sinhalese girls also scorned the Sinhalese half of her. "Monkey nuts," they would say, giggling, referring to her glittering almond-shaped eyes. Fiona would feel incensed. She was Eurasian! British!

On Sunday afternoons the girls were allowed to wear their own clothes from home. She decided to step out like a Scottish girl, in a tartan plaid—the Gilmor tartan Daddy had ordered from Scotland for her—with a Celtic brooch pinned to her scarf. Her appearance drew gasps of amusement. Simply ridiculous. "And where d'you get that name, Gilmor, from?" sniggered Kavisha Weerasinghere. "Cat's alley?"

"Oh, now then, that's not kind," said Pradeep softly. But her look of pity was far more galling and aggravating than Kavisha's outright taunt.

Fiona took herself off, sneaking up the back stairs to the deserted dormitory. She locked herself in the lavatory cubicle and wept bitterly. She stared in the washroom mirror at her olive skin and curved eyes and thick, black hair, black, black.

No one must know of her shame and humiliation, not Mama or Daddy, and certainly not Lally. She would hide her pain under a façade of gaiety and defiance—"Don't care! Nothing can touch or hurt me again." Not ever.

Of course Fiona did not receive the invitations she had hoped for at vacation time. She was not invited to the Colombo girls' homes in Cinnamon Gardens, or to join their families at exclusive Nuwara Eliya for the races and the endless rounds of social teas. Certainly not to the exclusive Hatton-Eliya Club. There were no English girls at the convent. They attended

Mountain School in Nuwara Eliya, the school for the British residents' children. It had an English headmistress from the "old country" who sported a tweed suit and brogues, English teachers, a strict curriculum, and good old English discipline: "Chin-up, *rah-rah*, cold showers. Rather!"

She longed to belong there. But now she knew, finally, that she would never fit in. But it did not stop her wanting to, to be her English half, to be English like them. After all, it was what she was! But now she belonged to the Eurasian set and she hated it. She was not even a full Sinhalese *govigama*. She understood, now, that her Scottish name, Gilmor, together with her Burmese eyes and olive brown skin, was like a message, a racial signal, a source of gossip, a way of placing her.

Meanwhile Lally, in senior school, with her dark skin, long, tangly, black hair, and black eyes was taken for Sinhalese, and she did not care, did not even bother to contradict the assumption. Well I *am* Sinhalese, on Amma's side, she thought, and then felt sad, for she hardly remembered her mother. She chatted away happily in Sinhalese to the girls, and even exchanged a few words with the Tamil girls; she'd picked up some of the language from Jack on the estate. The Muslim girls, the "righteous" ones, faced east in the courtyard when they said their prayers, and silly Lally loved watching them. "Really Lally!" frowned Fiona. "They're *Mohameddans*."

"But it's so beautiful, in its way," cried Lally, and she really meant it, the nitwit. But that was Lally. She had only months to go; she was leaving the convent at eighteen. Fiona struggled to be top dog

"Well, my father *is* Scottish!" she cried, with her tartan and Celtic pin. The girls laughed, amused. Fiona Gilmor was too much! But she was not unliked.

Esmé de Groot was of pure Dutch descent (whatever *that* meant), on Peter de Groot's side, but she was poor, poor, poor. Her father had struggled to send her here. She was only in a Catholic convent because the de Groots could not afford the fees for the more elite Protestant schools. Sometimes Fiona saw Esmé sitting with other Burgher girls, on the stone steps in the sunshine, the same Esmé de Groot who had worn Fiona's hand-me-downs at Weyweltalawa, and no shoes. The convent uniform was supposed to mask each girl's identity and social status, but Fiona saw how it really was, where she stood. No, Fiona Gilmor would have nothing to do with a de Groot.

The dormitory was full of long, cold, neat rows of identical beds, crucifixes hanging on the wall, and piteous pictures of St. Veronica. (Really, another white woman, Fiona thought. To be white was to be sacred.)

Kandy Convent was on hilly terrain, on Mount Leo, which overlooked the surrounding town of Kandy. The life Daddy and Mama had chosen for her was that of an upper class "British" colonial girl of Ceylon. And they paid big fees for it.

"Fifty Hail Mary's, Fiona Gilmor, for wearing your skirt above your knees."

One evening, during prep, Isanka Weerasinghe passed by Fiona's desk ("Please Sister may I sharpen my pencil?") and hissed, "Burgher girl!"

Fiona darkened and jumped up, toppling her chair with a crash. "I'm *not* a Burgher, you bitch. I'm not, I'm not. I'm—I'm half British!"

Too late, she realized her ridiculous mistake. "Oh, only *half*? We're *half* British, are we? What happened to the other half, dearie?"

The girls ran off laughing. They'd got to Fiona Gilmor.

Then came another soft, dusky evening at the convent before bread and milk was served in the cool refectory. But Fiona felt heavy rage. She wouldn't give herself away again, she vowed. She tried to recall the prayer Daddy always said, the Prayer of Saint Michael—what was it? "*...And do thou O Prince of the Heavenly Host cast into hell Satan and all the evil spirits who prowl throughout the world seeking the ruin of souls....*"

She wrote her weekly letter to Mama and Daddy during Sunday quiet hour, boasting about her new friends, including a Sinhalese girl, Sumatha Sunandarikra, whose father was in something called the "Cabinet" of the new government. "We're special friends. She's invited me to Cinnamon Gardens."

"Fiona is making good friends," said Mama, pleased that Fiona was learning to get along with all sorts of girls. "That is very important in life, Fiona," she wrote back.

Like an English girl, she began to make fun of the Sinhalese and Tamil matrimonial advertisements at the back of the illustrated magazines in the library, tittering over phrases like: *Sinhalese parents seek professional honest kind partner for their daughter thirty-two, slim, very fair, pretty. Prefer engineer or doctor. Send horoscope.*

"Oh, just listen to this!" she cried. "Respectable Buddhist parents looking for groom for daughter, twenty-seven. Very fair. She is having *kuja dosha* in her horoscope. Please send that kind of horoscope only...."

For some reason, the Dutch Burgher girls found this hysterically funny, so Fiona found it ridiculous, too.

"You'll never get a husband, Karitha," she mocked the Sinhalese girl. "You don't have *kuja dosha* in your horoscope, with that brown monkey-face of yours." *Kuja dosha, kuja dosha, kuja dosha....*

"Monkey-face yourself, Chink-eyes," Karitha Sumarasinhe retaliated, and at once Fiona felt that helpless rage bursting inside her chest again; she was ashamed of her hated Burmese eyes from her hated Burmese great-grandmother, and she was terrified that girls would find out that great-*aahch-chee* had only been a "country wife." Fiona was unaware of her own fragile beauty; her long, almond eyes were seductive and alluring.

Fiona still imagined that she would meet a fine young English planter at the club, the way the English girls did; matrimonial ads were for native girls.

"Your father will have to mortgage his plantation to get a dowry to pay someone to marry you, Fiona Gilmor," the girls bantered. "And it won't be Clark Gable."

Fiona had been only vaguely aware of the upcoming general election and the possibility that SWRD Bandaranaike would become the new prime minister, overthrowing John Kotelawala who had succeeded Senanayake after his death. Bandaranaike was going to restore Buddhism to the island. Buddhism was as alien a religion to Fiona as it was to a real English girl at Mountain School, and always would be.

But the Sinhalese girls had a new swagger to their walk. Bandaranaike had won the election in a big landslide, they boasted. He had promised to pass a new language act: Sinhala only. All the Sinhalese girls were talking about it after prep, deliberately conversing with each other in Sinhala, even in front of Sister St. Maria.

"English, English!" cried Sister St. Maria, one of the older sisters; she had a taut face with wiry eyes.

"The language of our country is Sinhala, sister!" they chorused impudently. "We can speak it now as much as we please. *Namonamo matha sundara siri barini....*"

Poor Sister St. Maria and the other nuns were nonplussed. Fiona tossed her head, "I'll not speak that servant language."

Many of the English girls had left Mountain School, it was reported. They'd been sent "back home." That meant England. "Well, good riddance," cried Fiona, but inwardly she felt dismay, as if the bottom had fallen out of her world. Now she was left behind in the convent, in this country of Ceylon, undeniably part of the Sinhalese cohort who rejected her and flaunted themselves. She no longer had Lally to confide in, either. Lally had landed a job as a dormitory assistant in Mountain School itself. It was a great opportunity for Lally, everyone said.

"Well, I wouldn't work as a domestic for the English," pretended Fiona. "How can you, Lally?"

"You are smarter than Lally," said Mama quietly, "so do not judge her. Lally is doing the best with what she has. And she has a chance to meet important people at the club up there, through Daddy, and make a good match."

44.

THINGS WERE COMING TO A CRISIS point. Sir John Kotela-wala, who had succeeded his uncle, Senanayake, as Prime Minister ("Uncle-Nephew Party," quipped the *Ceylon Times*) had angered the *Sangha* of monks. Sir John had decided to call a general election in the middle of *parinibbana*, the sacred commemoration of the birth, enlightenment and death of the Buddha, a major event in the world of Buddhism, akin to the anointing of the Archbishop of Canterbury in England. The *Sangha* had planned a huge festival and a procession through the streets of Colombo and Kandy. The Buddha's holy tooth was to be displayed to the people. There were to be Kandyan devil dancers and musicians (to ward off evil spirits), not to mention the blessing of the tooth itself: all of which Kotelawala sublimely ignored.

The ignominy, raged the Buddhist monks. Old humiliations under the British were revived. They demanded that Kotela-wala declare Buddhism the state religion, build fine Buddhist schools all over the island, and put an end to Catholic funding. *Aiyo!* (Jack thought sadly of poor Father Balderelli in his worn cassock and broken sandals, teaching in his mission school.)

But Sir John refused. Cancel the election? By God, no.

The Chief Monk Buddharakkitha vowed to enact revenge. He'd formed his own military party of monks, the Eksath Bhikku Peramuna. "Well, I ask you!" cried Nettie Matthews to Ethel Henshaw over tea at the club. "A Buddhist army? What next?"

The monks turned to the dark horse in the running, young studious Bandaranaike and his Sinhala Maha Sabha, or "Great Sinhalese Association." The planters in the clubs were at once on the alert. A wily devil, SWRD Bandaranaike understood the poor, devout, ignorant Sinhalese villagers with their homemade shrines. He'd appeared at his rallies in a flowing white sarong and white *baniyama*, wafting among the adoring crowds. He was a slim, attractive person, and he wore spectacles. He was quite fair—obviously of Aryan descent—and much favoured by the women. The Sinhalese villagers and rural classes thronged to his speeches: "Ceylon for the Sinhalese—and damn the British!"

Of course, Bandaranaike had made a point of hastily switching to Buddhism on his return from Oxford. He'd thrown away his silly Western pinstriped suit, a political gesture that had appealed to the natives who fell for it hook, line, and sinker. A leading politician flaunting a long white sarong was a novelty in the new Ceylon. Ethel Henshaw controlled herself in front of the servants over afternoon tea, pouring graciously, but her lips were set in a firm line.

The planters imbibed extra amounts of whisky, beer, and *arrack*, with growing alarm. There was no doubt the young Bandaranaike had put out a clarion call as he cleverly appropriated the Buddhists' grievances into his new political party, the Sri Lanka Freedom Party.

"Let us take everything from the British and treat them like shit !"

"Well, I don't like the sound of *that*," said Ethel Henshaw.

"Bandaranaike's crackpot theories were just too much," cried Nettie Matthews. The English wives certainly didn't have much understanding of the meaning of the *parinibbana* and Sinhalese Buddhist pride in the Buddha's tooth relic.

"Well, it *is* the 2,500th commemoration of the Buddha's

death," Mildred explained calmly. "You can understand how the monks feel about Kotelawala ignoring it." She sipped her tea, the finest Oya blend. Sunlight quivered over the polished floors of the club. Jack had persuaded her to accompany him this one time up to the Hatton-Eliya Club, with the promise of visiting dear old Father Balderelli, but, as a non-white, she felt very out of place among these *memsahibs*. She sensed they resented her presence.

"How do they *know* how old the Buddha's tooth is? Was someone keeping count?" cried Ethel Henshaw, with passion. "Did they even have calendars then?"

"Likely the sun and moon and a few planets."

Nettie Matthews remonstrated that British archeologists had deemed the so-called "sacred tooth" of the Buddha to be nothing more than that of a crocodile. It was three inches long, for goodness sake.

"I ask you!"

And that fellow Bandaranaike had exploited it for all it was worth. He'd been positively fawning over the *Sangha*, and the monks had been all over him, too, wanting him to win the election. (There were rumours that the venerable chief monk of the wealthy Kelaniya Temple, Buddharakkitha, had been behind Bandaranaike's surge in the polls. He had been well compensated in return, receiving a private shipping deal for his investments, as well as the promise of a high post for his reputed mistress. He was also to be appointed Minister of Health. It was the talk of the Colombo bars, and of course hot topic of gossip in the planters' clubs.)

"So much for Buddhist vows of purity and poverty," sniffed Ethel Henshaw, who was in agreement with Sir John about not canceling the election. "Imagine! The nerve of those monks."

There was reputedly a large Western-style double bed in Buddharakkita's personal room for his mistress in the *vihara*, reported Nettie Matthews. "Quite shocking, that, and a little sordid."

"Quite."

No one gave a thought to the half million Tamil labourers still lingering miserably in the mindless limbo of the Ceylon Citizenship Act. They were awaiting deportation, like others before them.

The sun was lowering over the western hills, which were lit up in that pale rose hue slowly deepening to crimson streaks, a holy time. It was six o'clock. Suddenly darkness set in as the curtain of the East descended.

Beyond the club, the faint calls to muster from the estates....

45.

SWRD BANDARANAIKE HAD TAKEN the election by a land-slide. (He'd appeared at his inauguration dressed in that long sarong and a flowing white scarf round his neck. Now what the hell did *that* mean?) He was now ensconced in the Prime Mnister's official residence at Temple Trees, out on the Galle Road in Kollupitiya.

The English planters stared gloomily over the rims of their whiskies after a day in the fields. A socialist government! There was already talk of nationalizing the tea estates. "Good God!"

The Ceylon Tamils, educated at the best private schools, were enraged. They realized for the first time that they *were* a minority, not much better off than the Muslims who made up merely six percent of the population. In no time Bandaranaike passed the promised Official Language Act, known on the ground as "Sinhala Only." The island exploded.

Sinhala now replaced English as the official language of the country. Popular opinion swung all the more fervently in Bandaranaike's favour, even though he could not actually speak a word of Sinhalese himself. (It seemed he'd been hastily taking lessons ever since his return from Oxford.)

The nationalist cry "Sinhala Only!" was on every villager's lips. At last, the Sinhalese peasants and workers had something they understood.

"What for commotion?" cried the Sinhalese wives at the Kegalle Club, raising their arms. Their gold bangles and bracelets tinkled. "No one objected when it was 'English Only' under the British. Now it is 'Sinhala Only,' and they can be liking it or lumping."

Funding for Catholic schools ceased. Holy Innocents College and St. Thomas's Anglican Schools were left floundering. "Let them raise funding as the Buddhists have had to do this long time." Father Balderelli was deeply shocked. Many former English residents and planters lay buried in the cemetery, *in aeterna,* at Nuwara Eliya. (A thing of the past; their gravestones were toppling.) "We have only God to rely on."

Chaos seemed to spread quickly across the island. Jack reeled, sickened. Tamil women were beaten and raped, hacked to death by curved Kandyan knives; then Sinhalese girls were hacked to death by Tamils in reprisal. Tamil against Sinhalese, Sinhalese against Tamil; God against God, devil against devil. Tamils in Colombo began sending their wives and daughters to Jaffna in the north, for safety. The Tamils and Muslims owned many shops and businesses in the Pettah and downtown Colombo. The goons moved in on the rampage. Shops were ransacked or burned outright, the occupants emerging in flames. Again the police looked the other way.

"Where is it all going to end?" cried Ethel Henshaw to her friend Nettie. It was difficult to imagine, especially when one had to rely on a Governor General with a name like Sir Oliver Goonetilleke. Oh, say what you like about the old British administrators, but they would soon have put a clamp down on these ruffians, cried Nettie Matthews. A third set of iron bolts was installed in the Henshaws' and the Matthews' bungalows.

They had been talking about the riots: a Tamil woman had been caught by goons, soaked in kerosene, and—

It didn't bear thinking of.

"I say, Gilmor, care to join the club? As a full member I mean.

Fairfax and Stratton could sponsor you." Cunningham, an old Englishman of superior stock, cocked his pipe at Jack, condescending bugger. "Numbers are down now. They've been dropping for a while, I'm afraid."

It was the moment Jack had longed for: the offer of membership in Hatton-Eliya Tea Planters Club, a "whites only" club, one of Ceylon's most prestigious.

But the words ricocheted as if he'd been shot, wrenching his gut. They only wanted him because membership was down—the old boys had been deserting the fold after Independence; the English were going back home or taking off for other climes, South Africa and Australia.

Now they needed Eurasians like himself to pad the membership; they wanted his money. Now they were willing to allow in the mixed, dark races. Incensed, he wheeled about, fists clenched. It was an insult, a humiliation, by God! He heard his own voice, rasping, cold: "You can stick your bloody membership up your arse, Cunningham! *Go to hell.*"

He drove recklessly back down the mountains, careering round every hairpin bend, not giving a damn. The sun beat mercilessly through his reversible roof, the words reverberating like little hammers on his brain, over and over: *Numbers are down ... numbers are down....*

He was free. At last. That was all it took, after all. He laughed bitterly. His stupid little lie seemed to fall away, toppling down decades of his life. Something had passed, forever. Something new and bright surged in its place.

Meanwhile, fear mounted on the estates. Richardson of Fairhaven was found murdered on the way to Colombo, shot through the head and left by the roadside; the wages he was carrying stolen. Some planters took to having armed guards with them when they made the monthly trip to Colombo to pick up the sacks of rupees from the company headquarters, for it was a long lonely journey at best; sometimes it even went through jungle. The only reason Jack felt he was not attacked was because of Quintus, whom the Tamils knew and respected as a fighter for their right to form unions.

One day, Emir Van de Burg was dragged off a bus in broad daylight, in downtown Kandy. He was hacked to death, apparently over some nefarious land dealings that he had conducted half a century ago with Sinhalese villagers over chena rights. "Settling old scores," was the general opinion at the clubs. These Sinhalese had memories like elephants. Still, the planters were shaken.

Then De Jurgen went missing from Netherlands. He was found murdered at dawn. He'd been skewered alive on the last hairpin bend on the road to the estate, his pitiful tortured body still pulsing. The planters tried to shield the ladies, but of course it got out. The news spread like wildfire through tea country. It was the talk of the bars in Colombo. Some whispered that it was "retribution;" he got what was coming to him, what with all those "crucifixions" he had committed. Still, he was a white man. The planters drew together indignantly, deeply shocked. Everyone took to bolting their bungalows with triple locks like the Henshaws, hiring extra guards, and ordering sandbags as bulwarks.

Jack found himself sobbing uncontrollably, sinking to his knees. Not just for De Jurgen, and certainly not for himself, but for a lost ideal he'd cherished. He'd had an idea of the labourers, a sense of respect and camaraderie that he now felt had been betrayed by whoever had committed such a heinous act; cast out like fiery angels from the Garden of Eden.

"It is a terrible thing, but you are not to blame, pet...."

He knelt for a long time at his nightly prayers: "*Oh thou, Prince of the Heavenly Host, cast into hell Satan and all the evil spirits who prowl throughout the world seeking the ruin of souls....*" But to no avail. Something was broken.

46.

THE RIOTS, THE VIOLENCE.... Jack wanted to get away, emigrate, escape Ceylon. The timing was ironic: he was touted to be the next VA, Visiting Agent, the height of his aspirations in his planting career. But no more.

He wanted to get away forever, to leave the country of his birth. Anywhere would do: Indonesia, Malaya, Australia, England ("home"). Anywhere but here.

He would never fit into the new Ceylon. English speaking, English-educated, a Catholic, manager for the old British imperialist regime, and unable to speak fluent Sinhalese, Jack Gilmor suddenly found himself on the wrong side of history. But he saw that his children would adapt eventually. Of course they would. That was the pain. Aidan, Fiona, and Scottie would become Buddhist, speak Sinhala, marry Sinhalese spouses. That, most of all. ("My God!!" he could imagine the ladies at the club.)

"This is foolish thinking, pet," said Mildred sensibly. But, she, too, was anxious. Burghers and Eurasians—their class of people—were leaving in droves. Passages were fully booked on the P&O line. They had found ways. It was then that Jack realized that the Gilmors could not leave: they had no bloody documents, no deeds, no passports. He knew what he had to do.

Everything depended on Mildred now. Quiet unassuming Mildred Goonesekere Delaney. The "Goonesekere" name on her mother's side was what counted now with officials. The tables had been turned. Jack as *pukkah sahib*, *periya dorai*, master, no longer counted for much. It was Mildred who was in favour with the new government, with the "Sinhala Only" Act, with the new laws. Being a Goonesekere brought privileges. It paid to be Buddhist, Sinhalese, Sinhala-speaking. And Mildred was all of that.

Mildred could speak Sinhalese fluently, a fact that was suddenly important. She'd been Buddhist as a little girl; she had gone to temple to take *sill* with her mother, Aidan's granny, before converting to Catholicism. Her mother, Una Goonesekere, had been a full Kandyan Sinhalese descended from Kandyan royalty, something Mildred had never publicized under the British, but which suddenly afforded her status, security. Mildred was suddenly in favour, even though Aidan and his brother and sister had not been given a Buddhist education, and had attended English-funded Catholic schools, speaking "English only" (and would not be marrying Sinhalese). "Damn well right!" snarled Jack, knocking back another scotch.

It was his Sinhalese relative who saved them. Tommy Wickramasinha wangled the necessary documents written in Pali by the Buddhist priest at the temple, "proof" that his Sinhalese forebears had been born in Ceylon. This afforded Jack residency under the new act. Now Jack could file for passports to emigrate to the Dominion of Canada. The time had come.

Suddenly the island seemed to sink into turmoil. White people were being displaced by Sinhalese; some said it was about time they got their come-uppance. Britain offered warily to take in a certain number of ex-patriates and Eurasians as British citizens; after all, they were part of the British Commonwealth. The Netherlands, old Holland, came up trumps. Anyone, it seemed, with Dutch blood could claim the "right of return" to the Netherlands, Dutch citizenship guaranteed. Except that Peter de Groot and his wife, Annemieke, could not avail themselves of the offer. Peter explained quietly to Jack that they were too poor.

They were sitting together in Mr. de Groot's office. Jack twirled his sunhat nervously. He needed to cash in his life insurance policy. Peter de Groot agreed, sadly. He and his wife had only a small policy, hardly enough for them to survive on in Ceylon, let alone Holland, which was much more expensive. A great deal of money was needed for a passage on the P&O line, and they would need even more to establish themselves in Amsterdam. Their nineteenth-century Dutch was likely old-fashioned, too, maybe laughable, said Peter de Groot softly.

"It's a bad business," Jack agreed. "I'm only too grateful, Peter, for your advice about increasing my policy when I did."

Mr. de Groot smiled wryly. "The company will go bust if any more clients cash in their policies to get out of the country."

He hesitated and leaned forward. Mr. de Groot had aged, Jack noticed. He had deep blue circles under his eyes, sagging jowls, desperate sort of hair. He was certainly not prosperous. What would become of him and his sickly wife, of them all, in the new Ceylon?

Mr. de Groot was thinking of Esmé, his youngest daughter. He wanted—hoped—Jack would take her with him when he left in September, he pleaded awkwardly. "Lily will be okay; she has a good husband, but there's little future for Esmé here, Jack. I know it's asking a lot. Please. I ask from the bottom of my heart. She'll be safe in Canada with you."

Tears filled Mr. de Groot's eyes. "She's seventeen now."

"For old time's sake." For the love of Lily. *Lily!* Emblazoned over his heart. Jack felt a deep wrench. It was a bitter moment, for he could not take Esmé de Groot. He could not take one more person, he explained, due to the quota.

Canada had a quota of fifty persons allocated to Asians. Jack had been granted only five family members. By special dispensation immigration officials had allowed him to add his wife's younger sister, Lally. "We can't leave Lally behind, Peter

... you understand? I'm so sorry, old chap. There's nothing I can do."

"Moving to Canada? Don't do it, man!" cried the planters.

"Canada? They live in igloos over there. Freeze your balls off."

"They've got mosquitos with bites like hypodermic needles, not like the little midges over here; they'll eat you alive."

"Better the devil you know...."

Even Neville was concerned. He and Miriam wouldn't leave Ceylon. He'd decided to identify with the Sinhalese side of himself, for he spoke fluent Sinhala. But he still wore Western clothes. He and Miriam felt safe in Gal Oya; the dam was well under way, far from Colombo and its troubles. Bandaranaike needed the dam to build a successful economy. Even so, they were concerned about Jack's future; they were worried about him venturing to an new country at age forty.

"You won't have the salary in Canada that you earn here, Jack."

Not by half. No more big income. Still, Jack was determined to go. Though who knew what lay in store for him in Toronto? Mildred agreed.

Neville remained doubtful. Jack had no job waiting for him there, no prospects. The Gilmors were sailing to London first—the heart of the world, of the great British Empire. Neville had first-hand experience with the English at Cambridge, years before. "They're not that nice to you, the English," he warned. "It's not the 'home' you think it is, believe me, Jack old chap."

"And you won't have servants," said Miriam horrified. "Mildred can't even boil an egg. And as for vacuuming and doing her own laundry, scrubbing floors...." Miriam trailed off, looking aghast.

Of course, some Eurasians were sensibly marrying into Sinhalese families, the better ones. But not the Gilmors.

No one spoke now of old Sinclair Gilmor. He no longer mattered. A snapshot of him, taken in 1905 outside the tea factory, showed a fine figure of an Englishman wearing jodhpurs and a topee, rifle over his shoulder, hunting dogs bounding around. He sat astride his horse, gazing into the past....

And so the Gilmors sailed safely away, taking Lally with them, that October day in 1956—so long ago, long before the riot of 1958—leaving behind Felix and Colin and Neville and Titus and all the rest of them. Lally shrieked when the funnel blew, and everyone went *"Oh, Lally!"* The *Stratheden* pulled slowly away from the pier. "Anchors aweigh!" cried the crew—away from Ceylon, from Colombo, from tea country. Weyweltalawa ... Madeniya... Poonagalla... Nuwara Eliya ... everything they had known and loved. It was the time of the full moon, *poya* day, when Buddhists wore white and took sprays of frangipani to the temple.

They happily crossed the Indian Ocean—so deep, so blue, the deepest ocean in the world, and the most mysterious— congratulating themselves on leaving Ceylon. They had saved themselves. They did not look back as the island of Ceylon got smaller and smaller and eventually dimmed to a speck on the far horizon. Then it was gone, melting into the mists that swathed the island, the violet sun. At such a moment, Jack Gilmor could not know what was to pass in Colombo in a few years.

Lily de Groot Saram, shopping late in the Pettah with her younger sister Esmé and the boys, would be caught up in an ambush in the riot of '58.... Roving lawless goons, out to get the Tamil and Muslim merchants before the evening call of the *muezzin* across the rooftops and the glittering fiery sea, would set fire to the stalls, burn down shops in the cross-streets and back alleys, and drag out the terrified occupants; old Mr. Saeed and his grandson begging for mercy.... The heat, the intensity of the hatred, the howl of death, rivulets of blood ... poor Mr. Saeed's final scream as they pull down his grandson's pants, the knife whizzing. "Oh not that! Not that! Merciful Allah!"

It is too terrible, the things that happen in this world; what would happen to his little grandson....

Jack, gaping through the mist as the *Stratheden* turned westward, could only sense this prophetic destiny, like a dream— was it for real?—the wave of flame spreading over Colombo and the Pettah, the final conflagration. Two angels appeared hovering over the city, hanging upside down. He'd turned to look at the last moment—of course he had—and beheld them, surely the Angels of Death glistening in their effulgence with glowing wings ... what did it mean?

Slowly they reversed and rose through the air over the city— fiery swords in hand, hair streaming, eyes lidless—ascending at last from the Garden of Eden and the Tree of the Knowledge of Good and Evil, the paradise that was.

ACKNOWLEDGEMENTS

I am deeply indebted to Angus Orchard for his invaluable recall of his Ceylon childhood under British colonialism, and recollections of the social, cultural milieu of the tea planters; my late father-in-law, tea planter Thomas Orchard, *peria dorai* of Madeniya Tea Estate, Kegalle, and other tea estates under British rule in Ceylon (now Sri Lanka), for his many colourful reminiscences, and to my late mother-in-law, Helen Orchard, for her many personal recollections of life under British colonial rule first on a coconut plantation and then as a wife on a lonely tea estate; and other members of the Orchard and Delay family for their memories and anecdotes over the years: Dawn Orchard Sauer, Ian Orchard, Jack Crabbe, whose reminisces as a tea-taster in Colombo was most useful; Edith Delay Dylong, David Forbes, Michael Delay, William and Marlene Delay.

Special thanks also to my daughter Mandy for ongoing help and support and encouraging enthusiasm, Lorna Wheatley, and Don Heald for his patience untangling computer chaos. Special thanks to Inanna Publications "readers" for their insights and recommendations, and to my volunteer "readers" of the manuscript in its various stages. I am deeply indebted to: Karen Ferguson, Jane McCaig and her critique that turned the book around, Joan Sutcliffe, Linda Symsyk who covered the manuscript with red scrawls, and Susan Taylor.

Special thanks and gratitude to Joycely Alfred, who immigrated from the Northern Province of Sri Lanka, for his kind help with my Tamil, and to Sinhalese Buddhist monk, Dr. Bhante Saranapola, my meditation teacher at the Sinhalese West End Buddhist Temple and Meditation Centre, Mississauga, Ontario, Canada, for his kind help with my Sinhalese and insights into Buddhism.

In Sri Lanka, thanks and appreciation for much kindness shown: Rohan Pethiyagoda, Chairman, Sri Lanka Tea Board for kind advice and information; Ananda Fernando, Director Maskeliya Plantations, for his kindness in arranging a visit to a contemporary tea estate. I'm also deeply indebted to the kindness of the Delay family in Sri Lanka, especially Hansi who provided much practical help and advice, Sisera Delay and his wife Daya Ariyawansa who invited me into their home, Wasantha Delay and family for their kind support; and also Dr. Senath Walter Perera, Professor Neloufer de Mel, Shiroma Benaragama, and Vijitha Yapa.

Last but not least, my deepest gratitude to dear Luciana Ricciutelli, Editor-in-Chief, Inanna Publications & Education Inc. who saw value in this book. My heartfelt thanks.

For readers interested in further studies, my research included:

A History of Sri Lanka, K.M. De Silva (Oxford University Press, 1981).

The Early History of Ceylon, G.C. Mendis (YMCA Publishing House, Calcutta, 1932).

The Growing Years: 150 Years of the Planters' Association of Ceylon, 1854-2004, by Royston Ellis (B.P. Options Ltd., Colombo, Sri Lanka, 2004).

Christ in Kashmir, by Aziz Kashmiri (Roshni Publications, Srinagar, India, 1973).

The Man-Eater of Punanai: A Journey of Discovery to the Jungles of Old Ceylon by Christopher Ondaatje (Harper-Collins Publishers Ltd., New York, 1992).

Insight Guides Explore Sri Lanka (APA Publications, London, 2014).

Tamil Dictionary, ed. Clement J. Victor (Hippocrene Books, Inc., New York, 2004).

Sinhala Phrasebook and Dictionary (Lonely Planet, Melbourne, 2008).

Photo: Mandy Orchard

Granddaughter of a Welsh coal-miner, Thelma Wheatley immigrated to Canada in her twenties to teach, and obtained her Master's degree in English at York University. She married a Sri Lankan in the 1960s when "mixed" marriages were frowned upon. Wheatley bonded closely with her Eurasian Sri Lankan in-laws in Toronto, who were part of the British colonial empire in Ceylon (later, Sri Lanka). She is the author of award-winning *"And Neither Have I Wings To Fly": Labelled and Locked Up in Canada's Oldest Institution* (2013), which was short-listed for the 2014 Wales Book of the Year Award among other awards. Her first book was about her autistic son, *My Sad Is All Gone: A Family's Triumph Over Violent Autism* (2004). *Tamarind Sky* is her debut novel.